ENCORE

A Contemporary Love Story of Hypnotic Abduction

TANTRA BENSKO

IB
Insubordinate Books

Cover art is a section of a photo by Carlos Caetano

Sign up for the newsletter at
www.insubordinatebooks.com

To people who review this book on Amazon: THANK YOU, Luvs!

Book III of The Agents of the Nevermind

IB
Insubordinate Books
Berkeley, CA 2016

ISBN: 069212747X
ISBN-13: 978-0692127476

Dedicated to
Pablo Schwartz

“One of the year’s best thrillers. Tantra Bensko’s *Encore* is one of the most sophisticated romantic suspense novels in recent memory. Like Diana Gabaldon’s *Outlander* series, Bensko's story is told over a rich bedrock of history, real-world myths and legend. The novel is a perfect entry point to the work of one of today’s most distinctive voices.”

— BestThrillers.com & LISTED AS ONE OF TOP THRILLERS OF 2018

“For all the mind bending implications of Bensko’s ideas around identity, the passionate heart of this novel is a gothic romance about a young woman trapped in a castle under the spell of an abusive powerful man. As is traditional with gothic, the true struggle is an inner one to reconcile opposing desires as Miriam tries to understand her feelings for the men in her life and distinguish fantasy and reality.”

— Harvey Thomlinson, Make-Do Publishing

“Novelist Bensko weaves elements of history, myth, political intrigue, psychology, magic, cultism, religion, and romance into a tight tapestry of contemporary Gothic storytelling that has the reader as entranced as the novel’s protagonist. From the description of Miriam’s post-abduction ride to her captivity in the castle, one is reminded of such Gothic treasures as *Rebecca* and *Wuthering Heights*. As Dune’s deception continues, and the reader is given a deeper glimpse into his psyche, it isn’t hard to imagine Charles Boyer creeping around in *Gaslight* as he tries to untether Ingrid Bergman’s grip on reality. But this novel is no knockoff.

It is a unique and exceptional example of what Gothic literature should offer the reader: the elevated heartbeat, the sharp inhale of breath, the chill up the spine. These are what all fans of the genre seek. Bensko’s talent to deliver these thrills oozes down every dark and dreary hallway she leads the reader.”

— Kat Kennedy, The US Review of Books RECOMMENDED

"This story is downright nifty. I was drawn to the potential social ramifications and how easy it is to get taken in by a good narrative (both figuratively and literally). It's good entertainment and might make for an interesting book club read."

— Gabrielle Sally, The Romance Reviews 5 STARS ROMANCE REVIEWS TOP PICK

"It is the kind of book that is impossible to put down, and when I had to I longed for it! I wanted to be reunited with the story I had grown to love and the characters I had become invested in."

— RedheadedBookLover 5 STARS

"In this immersive and gorgeously written story, Tantra Bensko has crafted a modern tale with Gothic overtones that satisfies both our childlike imaginations and our adult passions. This rich, complex world is worth exploring, and wherever they went these characters begged me to follow."

-- Alex Dolan, author of *The Empress of Tempera*, www.alex-dolan.com/

"It is a masterwork of storytelling with a very sharp edge and a keen wit to boot. It peels back the intricate subderma overlaying each major character's persona, revealing our all-too-human vulnerabilities to mass suggestion. And it once again points up the critical need to be ever vigilant in guarding our very thoughts in an increasingly invasive society."

-- Publishers Daily Reviews

"An intriguing, and romantic tale, Bensko writes with a wonderful flourish and deals with themes of how easy it is for us to be swayed by suggestions. *Encore* is an entertaining read with plenty of adventure and magic."

— A. H. Wang, *The Imperial Alchemist,* www.ahwangauthor.com

"I believe it clearly captures the paranormal and suspense genres to an exceptionally high standard. I was hooked right from the opening chapters and was left overwhelmed and intrigued when I put the book down."

-- Literary Titan 5 STARS GOLD AWARD WINNER

"Many wonderful considerations are brought to light such as governmental control of people, the use of occult intelligence agents and the misappropriation of cultural legends to create artificial alliances."

-- Readers Favorite

"Bensko has delivered something dark, baroque and hauntingly disturbing with lush prose and imagery sure to delight any discerning lover of the written word. With all the hallmarks of a classic, *Encore* is a Gothic Fiction fans dream and is definitely deserving of your time to read. It is recommended without reservation!"

-- Book Viral

It is so rare to find a writer who can combine abuse, mind control, corporations bent on destroying the environment, and government conspiracies with cocky humor and a sci-fi overtones.

— Grady Harp, *San Francisco Review of Books*

CHAPTER 1
GOOD TIMES WITH COLIN

A cardboard rectangle blew against the gym window with a bang. A poorly drawn green stone dominated the sign, with the words spray-painted below it: "FREE THE MOLDAVITE!" It stuck in front of my face before sliding along the glass. Stragglers ran along the street, struggling to hold onto billowing signs with slogans like, "REGULATE GEM SALES." A spidery tree branch flew through the blustery air. Though I saw the limb and braced myself for the bang, I still jumped and grabbed my stomach when the wood struck the glass. My friend Colin and the others operating the exercise machines let out their breath in sync after the branch slid to the ground; the glass remained intact.

Colin put a comforting arm around my shoulders. That very first time that I experienced his touch produced a startling buzzing throughout my body, coinciding with the biggest lightning strike I'd ever seen. I spun toward him, and he hugged me tight. With my eyes closed, the thunder made me envision the golden shape of the branching electrical bolt in front of me -- in Colin's body, extending into my own.

Exercisers yelled in surprise, then snickered, setting off an uneasy boisterousness I took too far. Weather wasn't the only thing on my mind.

"Did you feel that?" whispered Colin into my ear, his breath exciting me.

"Absolutely." But did he mean what I hoped he meant? The charge between us. Intensity of light force flowing through us.

I stared at Colin while we worked out with a pull-down weight machine before my last non-performance of my troupe's season. Trying not to let my obsession with a married hypnotist blind me to the charms of the single fellow right in front of me, I willfully opened myself up to ask a question. Is there more to this friendship than I realized? I watched his sculpted pectoral muscles under his tee shirt: at thirty-five years old, he kept himself in good shape. Thirty-five and a half to be exact; *exact* was how he liked it. Precise movements. He did the proper number of repetitions on the machine each time.

"Oh, come on," I teased. "Live a little." As he counted his reps, I said the wrong numbers out loud to throw him off. He needed *some* kind of adventure, even if it was playing with numbers.

"Miriam! You rascal!" Colin's silver watch glinted as he flicked my bum.

Next to him, I revised my exercise in the gym to include a spontaneous mime routine, rambunctiously chasing my errant eyebrows around with my facial muscles while the eyebrows avoided capture. I even knew how to wiggle my nose. When I was a two-year-old girlie, Papa taught me the artistic skills of a mime so that I could entertain at art gallery openings. Even at age thirty-four, I had the knack of pretending someone else.

Using that skill to bond with Colin distracted me so I didn't cannibalize my fingernails, worrying about the performance that evening: I had to look my best at the theater, down to the tiniest detail. Long fingernails, taut face and body, curled hair. Our show dramatized the history of that green stone that played such a significant role in conflicting utopian legends. Seats cost double that night.

Colin's face twisted, trying to look serious. He broke out laughing.

Ha, I won. I can keep from laughing longer than you can.

"Miming, huh. Clever way your father had to keep you quiet around the house. I should have thought of that." He elbowed me.

"He made me be Charlie Chaplin," I said, imitating the silent film comedic actor.

Colin mimed being sad.

"I fancied being Marcel Marceau, but Papa said he was dumb because he was French. So, I worked up a Cubist Marceau mime routine to get back at him." I acted out an aggressively Cubist painting at Colin, angling my elbows, threatening with their edges as I bent my knees, ready to strike.

We hopped on the exercise bikes, staring, eyes bugged out, tongues curled, eyes wider, pointed tongues toward our chins. We rode the exercise bikes faster, with exaggerated weaving, bobbling our heads. Colin and I were made to goof around together. I'd known that since meeting him at the gym.

He was definitely not an actor. He was in his element when working at the publishing company, and the flamboyant lifestyle of a thespian was not for him. But he knew how to play!

Someone waiting by a weight bench chortled; two people dropped weights and breathed out giggles. I loved making their days better.

The TV high on the other side of the building blasted the weekly episode about Atlantis. Most riders in the row of stationary bikes paid rapt attention to the earnest narrator going on about that mythical land. Chumps. The popularity of that prime time show kept interest in theories about ancient civilizations, so our theatrical performances dramatizing them sold out.

Squelched snorts at each other's facial exercises made bikers strain forward to hear the TV. The narrator was on about royal British ancestors hailed from Atlantis. I swear, I can't believe people really take Atlantis seriously. But I suppose it's partly shows like ours that encourage them to be that daft. And naturally, the British have always said ("always" meaning -- as long as it was politically useful) that Atlanteans who stayed proud and nationalistic, and stayed around in spite of vast and horrific flooding, were fine, upstanding citizens compared to those scared weaklings who migrated to Shambhala instead, back in the day.

But I had to give that news station credit for being more egalitarian, for not downgrading Shambhala to being evil in comparison to Atlantis's lofty perfect. (They could leave the demonization of Shambhala job to our troupe.) She said, "Here, we see Shambhala, the kingdom of happiness according to Tibetan Buddhist prophecies beginning in the tenth century." The hokey CGI rendition played behind the newscaster, in pastel colors, with ageless benevolent giants directing smiling people working on some kind of super advanced technology.

The newscaster said, "The Asian legend was that — one day, attackers would endanger Shambhala's devotees. In response, the Tibetan King of the World would leave the secret realm of Shambhala to show up out of the blue with his army of freedom fighters and win. Tibetan Buddhism would take over the world, guided by spiritual light of the green Stone from Heaven, Moldavite."

Well, good, that's a start. But acknowledging that Atlantis was also a legend would be a pretty reasonable next step if you ask me. No, saying such a thing these days would get newscasters fired. Because they had to do what the Agents of the Nevermind told them to, of course. They had to follow the agenda perfectly unless they wanted to get assassinated in front of their children. They had to imply that the descendants of the fancy-dancy Atlanteans were the British royals. And the royals have always therefore had the right to colonize and command whoever they wished. *Sure, this story has been around for centuries, but come on. Give it a rest!*

Colin and I poked fun at the news anchor. Thirty years after the establishment of the Nevermind intelligence agency and their Occult Revival still held sway over reporters as much as ever: not one rebellious newscaster in all that time. Thunder and a lightning strike made us cringe and shut up. Then, we peeked at each other with shy sparks.

Huld, the seven-and-a-half-foot-tall actor in the Bennu performance troupe, in which I was a standby, hopped on the bike on the other side of me. When I peered in his direction, I noticed bikers staring up at him. Huld grunted louder and lower than anyone else, his huge jaw jutting forward. He was the only giant I knew personally.

Huld liked to get pumped right before an evening's appearance just like I did. Difference was, he actually got to perform on stage in front of a real audience every time. A major role, playing one of the Atlantean giant ancestors of the queen. He didn't even have a standby, as there just wasn't anyone available resembling his unique features well enough to take over in case of illness. So, he got paid extra to be 100 percent reliable. He didn't get points for bragging to the actors.

Huld glared at us as we executed our facial exercises, his mouth a hatchet, his pupils tiny, his forehead shelf overhanging them. To be fair, he wasn't the only one frowning because of our guffaws. We turned our faces toward the bikers, sticking our necks forward like chickens.

Normally, I'd never bother anyone. That day, I had to lift my mood, or I'd explode from anxiety over the upcoming production. My pressure valve released in laughs. Most people outside the expressive theater crowd didn't know what to make of me, especially down south.

The man beside Huld sighed, got off his bike, and lumbered to the booth where the manager worked. He pointed at us. He wasn't chuffed. I saw where he was coming from, but Jeez. Live a little.

Colin said, pointing to the complaining man: "Our dissenter has dirty toilet paper stuck to his shoe." Our sense of humor was in sync.

I didn't move my mouth while I threw my voice, pointing at him, and making a squishing sound of poo, in sync with his footsteps.

Bikers looked at the man's shoe. We'd thrashed their team. No way they'd win *that* battle. Throwing your voice is impressive enough to get serious points.

I wondered how many young people recognized the Agents had been pushing that topic down our throats ever since they got their man, Planda, into the U.S. presidential seat in the early 90s. He would have lost the election due to being afflicted with the endocrine disorder, gigantism, if they hadn't used the pervasive belief in ancient giants of Atlantis pedigree. When deliberately throwing off hormone levels to create gigantism in people like Huld became a trend, life got a little weirder.

And the whole King Arthur nonsense would have stayed hidden in the higher echelons of secret societies and intelligence agencies. But no, since American dimwits voted for the tall President Planda, now people had to bicker about that pseudo-history on social media, breaking up marriages and families. "Are you a King Arthur believer or not?" "Are you into Shambhala or Atlantis?" "Do you believe giants were supernatural?"

The news anchor said, "While a few years ago few people thought much about Moldavite, it has recently become a heated topic of debate. Because of this second year of extreme and mysterious Moldavite scarcity, we've seen growing clashes between people rooting for Shambhala and people rooting for Atlantis as the rightful owners of any remaining pieces of that green gemstone."

Video screened behind her, showing people holding signs:

"REGULATE GEM SALES." "TIME FOR A DATABASE." "BUDDHISTS RIGHTS." "MAKE IT FAIR."

Pointing to the TV I said, "Hey, I recognize a couple of those protestors. I've seen them in the audience at our show. They enjoyed themselves."

Huld glared like I'd said something terrible.

The newswoman continued with video of a handsome doctor bent over a pregnant woman by the side of the road, with her hair stuck to her face from sweat. "Today, a heroic doctor trying to get to work delivered a baby in stalled traffic. The proud mother, a hard-working public-school teacher, could have lost her child because of the protestors."

"Last night, in a debate at a local university, a pro-Shambhala student stated the popular opinion that the descendants of impure Aryans in Atlantis became black magicians hell bent on imperialism, migrating to Egypt before their evil ways sank the continent.

"Here's a clip of his speech. 'They created rituals out of their worship of Osiris, the core of the ancient mysterious Bennu Society we still have today. In fact, they created that Society. A pure, good-hearted branch of Atlantean Aryans migrated to Shambhala in Tibet, a land of peace and harmony that will bring a revolution as it sends out beams of consciousness-raising energy through the rarest of gems. The magical stone, Moldavite, will evolve the rest of humanity to be more like them.' Most of these protestors in the Free the Moldavite Movement are Republicans calling for an end to the monarchy."

The camera shifted to show his opponent. "A student in charge of the pro-Atlantis club said just the reverse had occurred. 'Shambhala is the home of the violent path of evil destruction. Atlantean giants are supermen who have reincarnated in bodies made worthy of them today through Giant Jack Human Growth Hormone. Atlanteans have a right to own Moldavite.' The two young men came to blows in the debate hall, causing a fight to break out. Two students are dead, and one is in critical condition in hospital."

Lightning stuck a nearby tree. A worker at the gym ran to turn off the TV, so it didn't fry.

We had a couple minutes to work out: time for preparations at the theater. I was looking forward to the shower to warm me up before I dipped into the hypnotic trance backstage with other standbys: I'd use the hair dryer and curling iron to get my hair perfect.

Huld's pale, tight lips sliced straight across like a gash. He caught the eye of the manager and made a violent slicing gesture with his hand across his throat.

The manager walked up to us and said, "We've had noise complaints. I'm sorry, but I have to ask you to leave."

I looked over at the giant while doing the most mischievous revenge facial exercise I knew as we got off the bikes.

Colin sniffed and said, "So, no shower for you before I drive you to the theater. Well, none for me, either; I've got that late meeting at work."

"I guess we should stand out in the rain for a while," I offered, shrugging.

We grabbed our bags from the restrooms and headed toward his car. I'd see ol' *Huld* back at the theater soon enough.

❄

Just what I needed when the entire existence of my acting career depended on that performance. Gah!

"Yeah, too bad about your hair. But I have a jug of water, soap, and washcloths in the trunk."

"Why am I not surprised?" Always prepared, that man. A wholesome boy scout. He seized the freshening supplies, and I huddled in the passenger seat so no one would notice us wash up and change clothes. He folded his sweat pants before inserting them in a firm plastic bag with a nice neat zipper. I had to admit I was sorry to smell his pheromones go. Mmm.

Turned out he wore good-boy boxer shorts. No surprise there. But he sported some snazzy legs. A little pale. He changed into business trousers.

Nothing to do about my sweaty hair. Lifting my sticky bangs, I washed my face. He helped me remove my shirt, though I left on my moist bra. The way his fingers moved across my skin as he gathered and lifted my tee-shirt got my attention. Something suggested he'd wanted that a long time. He luxuriated in the moment. My body responded to his touch in a way that surprised me, and with nothing covering my bra, there was no hiding it.

He put on that gel that made him look far too civilized for my taste. If only he'd go with me to wild places I went in my mind -- like intense roles I played in the Bennu troupe. If only he'd go with me to the exotic pagan erotic wonderland my mentor Dune and his wife Susan must explore together. . . Could we have a chance at something more than flirty friendship?

Arms akimbo in his tiny car, washing my back proved awkward. Suavely, Colin said, “Here, let me do it for you,” taking over, pushing my hand out of the way with a gently commanding force I didn’t expect. Mmmm.

What should I do? Chance ruining a great new friendship with hanky-panky?

The lukewarm water trickled better against my skin when he did it with the right pressure to send pleasure shivers along my fascia, vibrating it against my bones. When I faced him, my lips relaxed forward as if seeking his. Colin slid his fingers across a nipple, almost as if by mistake.

I moaned. This put him in a different light.

I thought I spied something out of the corner of my eye. I looked up. Huld stood *right there*. Bent, looking at me.

Abdominals tightened. I covered myself with clothes and scrambled to a normal sitting position, then rethought it and curled back. Huld's lantern stiff jaw. When our eyes met, he narrowed his heavy-set eyes into slits and nodded extremely slowly. Gah! His hair dripped onto the side of the car. Drip. Drip. Drip. Then, he turned his whole body, his neck too thick to move normally. And without looking back, he strode across the soggy grass to the gym.

Freak. Should he be in our troupe, or was he too dangerous? But he and the troupe's hypnotist, Dune, were close and I was too nervous to complain. If I wasn't let go that night, maybe I'd move into a position with enough power I could angle for Huld to tone down his creep factor or get out. Not fair that giant could shower before the show.

I wished I wasn't calling a cab after the show.

❄

Even when a speeding hearse tried to cut us off, forcing us to swerve onto the curb, splashing water on a passerby, Colin, handled it like a pro. He didn't even curse. Such a competent driver. I never worried he'd do anything impulsive to endanger my life. So, when he took me to the theater that Friday evening, I didn't judge the distance between cars or push on an imaginary brake. I didn't remind him about hydroplaning.

Instead, I still stared ahead, preparing to give the great non-performance of my life.

My legs were warmed up, my thigh muscles firm against the seat. "I'll buy that lavender dress I want next season, should I get the chance to prove myself worthy tonight."

"I can tell you're ready to act *most* passionately, my friend."

"Ready to wait in the wings with the best of them." I was ready for my muscles quivering for dance, wanting to be free on stage. I was prepared to instead sit in a chair for two hours while Susan got to play in front of the adoring audience.

In my mind, while I sat on the chair backstage, I'd be moving along with Susan's every swoop and lunge under the stage lights, and ride into the air lifted by invisible strings. "Yeah, I'm primed to listen from the greenroom to the applause for the actors on stage. Endless bravos. Encore. Bravos."

I'd go home to my drab house that night after waiting out the performance. I didn't even bother decorating until I became a somebody, married to someone revered and spectacular. I persuaded myself to settle for a normal, boring relationship. But then, I'd have another dream. The usual, in which I'd be saving the world with a magical Twin Flame husband, and I'd remember: I knew I was destined for something great.

Colin said, "I know It's your last chance. Your verrry last." He raised a thick eyebrow. His exercises were serving his flexibility well.

What were the chances of finding another star who resembled me enough I could be a convincing standby? The nights I'd taken over for Susan hadn't gone so well . . . *Stop thinking about it, Miriam!* My stomach rose against my heart; I tried not to remember it.

"You'll probably have to pay that loan back to the mayor if you don't get to prove yourself tonight. He would be at least proud of you for trying? Maybe not charge you interest?"

"Papa accept me? No, that's hopeless. I'd have to turn into the prime minister for Papa to give a hoot. Be better at her than she is."

"Did your mama teach you to love yourself?"

"She did OK."

"If you want therapy, I know someone good. It might help how you relate to people and make life decisions. I mean, growing up that way --"

"At a hundred and fourteen quid an hour?"

"Well, yeah. But if I can snag the next best seller, I'll get a big enough commission that I'll spring for a session or two. Miriam?"

"What, you're saying I've lost the plot? We can't hang out unless I get right in the head?"

Colin rested his hand on my thigh and I breathed slowly. I petted delicate tufts of hair on the backs of his fingers. He wasn't particularly interested in theater. It was super of him to drop me off, before he went to his meeting, so I could transform into a replica of Dune's wife. Move like Susan. Radiate into the audience like Susan. Not much payoff for mimicking her. Didn't even get Dune.

Ah, Dune. The troupe's resident hypnotist. Most impressive man I'd ever seen in my entire life. By far. Gorgeous black hair. Cheekbones to die for. Women sure get stupid around men like that. Well, *I* sure as hell do. Start that awful longing for being the person he loves most. Go figure.

I dug in my purse to offer to pay Colin a few dollars in gas money for the times he chauffeured me to shows and rehearsals. Nice guys like Colin couldn't prove themselves to women they liked, because unavailable bad boys like Dune distracted women.

"Don't worry. The autobiography I just picked up for Be Yourself Publications is going make me a hefty commission. I know an acquisition editor isn't as famous as the Bennu troupe, but --"

"Our troupe is not exactly paparazzi-bait."

"But you're the equivalent in the artistic world. I mean, not *you*, just yet, but. . ." He stumbled over words. It was best for him to leave it alone.

Colin winked at me with those long sandy lashes. The luxuriousness of his wink made my breath came harder for a while. I played with his hair. The gel made it stiff to my fingers.

Hair loosened from the hold of the gel as I'd planned. Curving strands fell across his forehead at a rakish angle. He turned his head to traffic behind us, and the movement of his hair across his face made my heart pound. The bangs were wild and sexy, flattering his deep-set eyes and concave cheeks. "Mmm. That makes me want to kiss you. Is that bad?" I leaned over, and he looked at me, swerving and nearly scraping the car next to him.

"Miriam, I have a perfect driving record, and I'm keeping it." His lips were shapely, and I stared at how they curved up on the ends. Our playful time at the gym made me want him. Passion of that moment overcame the times when he was too tame to stir my wild soul. The world of sensuality was alive besides playing a role behind the curtain.

He pushed his hair back into place, for his asexual business style, taming my impulsiveness. He straightened his tie: he was going back to the publisher's office for the special meeting soon after. I flipped his hair forward and kissed his neck. Desire surged through my body again. He was so fit.

"Sorry, Miriam," he said, pushing his hair back into robotic position again and gripping the wheel in the rain.

My throbbing and surging stopped. Damn.

After we sat in silence, he offered, "With Susan's cancer, all it would take for her to have to step down and let you substitute for the evening would be an uncontrollable coughing spell."

I sighed. "The narcotics she takes must be powerful. She shifts her coughs on stage into feral animal-noises."

"Clever."

When Susan was dancing the role of the ancient Egyptian flamingo deity, Bennu, she turned them into the sounds of hedonistic fire, her arms outstretched, her head back, spinning around, the feathers swooshing around her. Her sick sounds became a signature of the troupe.

I must have looked mopey when I looked across his car, contemplating his boring navy-blue suit: perfect for a cog in the system. In the back of his car were books in that awful brown box color with flayed masking tape, with the novels, creative nonfiction, all riffing off the lives of real people. Be Yourself biographies. What a nauseating motto, at the top of every book on the back cover in sickening Pepto Bismol pink: "Just be yourself!" God, I'd rather *die*.

My eyes drooped. Hard to raise the eyebrows fascination with Colin's world. Whenever we went for walks, when trying to match his clipped, polite stride, I felt as if I were inside, still. In a cage. I wanted to pace. To pounce. Fly into a glorious realm.

That was likely my last night ever wearing fuchsia sparkles and paint and a flamingo mask before giving up all hope and going back to waitressing. Vinyl floors with dirt in the corners. Formica counters with gum stuck underneath. Flat shoes making that squish, squish sound. Customers eating alone while watching reality TV on their phones.

Clocking in and clocking out. Bringing people junk to fatten them. No excitement to give me the energy to keep smiling at every customer like they were wonderful when none of them were. Great actors and dancers, musicians and artists didn't eat at the kinds of restaurants where I'd get a job.

Florescent lights. Adding up change. Pennies for tips. No time to practice dancing, leaping and twirling in the air, gauze flying behind me. Nope: Tupperware. No longer dramatizing esoteric, history. Flies. Flies buzzing. Fly in the soup sent back, being punished. Getting older day by day without a chance to be with a powerful ceremonial magickian like Dune, the charismatic-as-lightning hypnotist making me his. I would no longer have a transcendent dancer to inspire me to breathe twice as fast. I would miss artists painting my portrait as if I were made of translucent veils.

Just me -- not being in the same playing field as Merce Cunningham, Maya Deren, Pablo Picasso, Mary Shelley, or the Bronte Sisters. Horrors. Called "honey" by men with gray prickles on their triple pale chins and told I was doing a great job. Great? What did that even mean to a waitress? That was me. That was the real me -- *ordinary*. Unless the night took a turn, and I showed the world what I do: be Susan.

And all it would take to make me forget about the horror of my possible future would have been Colin letting his hair be sexy for me for a few minutes. I could get lost in the thrill. That's all it would take! I wanted to wring out the gel.

So, he reminded me, as if it were necessary, of, "Susan's last show ever. Big night." Yes, she'd stretched her career before she went off to die of smoking. The question: was she stretching it a day too long? Would she collapse that night? Hell, it would be her fault if she did. Little Miss Puff Puff.

Colin bent to the side, brown eyes dark and deep, pupils dilated, looking into mine. It seemed there were no space between us, only energy, compassion, love connecting us as one. He straightened his head up to bring me with him into cheeriness, as his optimistic smile crinkled his temples. He kept looking at me, his smile angelic, as we sat idling at the light.

I smiled back to be polite. But my cells were like a furnace, burning like I was wasting my time second by second. Like I didn't have time to relax, and I got more done by frowning. I needed to get back to worrying and heart palpitations, to obsess over and over the nuances of my acting moves in case I was called to perform while believing myself to be Susan.

I fancied the stop light changing so we both looked ahead again. To the future.

My last time ever becoming Susan inside and out, I'd listen backstage to her acting out the roles like Bennu the resurrection deity. I'd be King Arthur's wife. An Atlantean High Priestess. Hundreds of people swept away, inspired to achieve gracefulness.

The performers radiated their auras radiated into the crowd. Dune had trained us well to do that, making sure our auras connected with the audience. They'd love us more than they loved any other, without knowing why. Cleverest trick I'd ever heard of. Dune was a genius. Susan's standing ovations were out of this world.

I blurted out, "I still don't understand something Susan keeps hidden from me. What it is, I have no idea."

I'd never been able to get the hang of becoming exactly like her when Dune hypnotized me to believe I was Susan. He'd trained me well on how to breathe in her extra auric energy, even without being required to see auras, but just feeling her soul-substance, and sucking it like an energy vampire. Well, not "like" an energy vampire, technically. I *was* one, for hire. That way, I could fool the crowd on an intuitive level: I "was" Susan, and their favorite star. Our shows weren't cheap. But I wasn't confident I was successfully taking on enough of her thoughts and amorphous memories inherent in her aura.

Colin said, "Well, that's normal. I mean, it would be kind of weird if you could be just like her, right?" He smiled, moving his freckles up his wholesome cheeks. If he got more sun, he'd look kind of like a farm boy. He was making up for suggesting I might need counseling. Right. Good try. "Don't you have Susan down pat?"

"No. But I've got to do it. I need to have some use for all that esoteric Bennu-Osiris crap I've studied. Otherwise, I'd have to become a mediocre overqualified waitress. Giving nothing great to the world to justify my existence? Just taking, taking, taking from the earth? Kill me now."

"You give to Earth just by being you."

"Oh, come on. You treat me like I'm important as Susan."

"Well?"

"I'm nothing." Darkness, not the true light. A reflection. Moon Miriam.

I rested my head against his arm. His muscles moved under my head as he drove, bouncing my voice as I said, "I'll become something, though. More than reflecting someone else's light." I smoothed my hand along his arm.

"You're silly is what you are. You're a bright light."

"The standbys only shine for each other."

And for Dune. Colin didn't know what Dune did for us. No outsider could watch us rehearse because the unique reason for our troupe's success might leak. How did Colin stand to live in a pale world devoid of the Dune's hypnotic charms? If only he met him.

I lived for the intensity of the moments when Dune had his way with our psyches. Ordinary consciousness was nothing compared to the trances he put me into. The trances that merged me with his wife. His lucky, lucky wife. To live a life with that master. Tall, straight, dark, smoldering eyes in a face more achingly beautiful than should be allowed. How can anyone make proper life decisions with Dune in the world?

Colin said, "We should get together tomorrow and toast the end of your season. Maybe take in a movie? We just passed by a marquee advertising a documentary about biking the Lake District."

Ah, Colin, he had to make do with a mundane world of ordinary pleasures and reasonable states of mind. He lived alone in his own aura, cut off from everyone else. Cut off from me. I merged only with Susan. And I longed for more.

Shows created a delicious dreaminess no words could explain. The projections displayed across our bodies on stage beamed over the audience. Immersive experience. With the actors radiating their auras across the crowd, like invisible laser shows, we experienced interconnectedness, like love, like being in the womb, like mystical sex, like being God. If God were real.

"If something happens to Susan, *God forbid*, tonight," I said, as I danced around in the seat to imply the rest of my sentence.

"I believe in you, little Pinnochia," he teased. "Standbys can become real people, too. All it takes is a little magic. You never know when it might come your way." He winked. "I'm pulling for you. With me on your side. . ."

"Bennu troupe *has* magic," I snapped.

Dune's hypnosis sessions with each of the standbys meant we

merged with the actors we substituted for. So much, we believed we were them. When I was in trance, I *was* Susan, star of the Bennu troupe. I played the archetypal roles, leaping into the air, wearing fuchsia feathers, flowing, lit by red light. Projected over me the whole time: cinematic fire, smoke, clouds, mist, Osiris Slain, and Osiris Risen.

On stage, I would quiver with the molten lava of being Dune's wife, bringing her brilliance to the characters I was playing, until the wrenching second when the curtain hit the floor for the last time and the post-hypnotic commands wore off.

I would rend in two. I'd give Susan back the extra effluence of life force I had drawn from her, at the moment the bottom of the curtain brushed against the scuffed wooden floorboards. I was shocked each time to become just me. Miriam. For a second it was the recurring dream: looking around, wondering how you got on stage before people waiting for you to do something you were clueless about.

"Sorry. Must have hit a nerve?" Colin grinned as he swerved through the mud-water traffic. We needed to find a gym closer to the theater if I got hired on again the next season. If I didn't get to take the starring role, to step into the shoes of the actress-dancer I admired so much, a gym location wouldn't matter; I'd be too depressed to feel like working out, anyway.

I smoothed down a wrinkle on my costume that ended up being a stain. I should have taken it to the dry cleaners too, with Colin's jacket. I caught myself frowning and rubbed the wrinkle. "I wish stains would go away on their own."

"Honey, I know your troupe's amazing. I'm no expert on acting, but as well as I can remember, I haven't seen anyone else project video of the actors in sync with the show. Avant-Garde deliciousness at its finest." Colin pretended to tip a hat with a flourish.

Yes. A standby playing her role, while the star's image projects on the standby, would create cognitive distance for the audience.

Even with reasonable physical matches between the standbys and the actors, the audience would feel the differences in the auras — thus, the hypnotic merging.

Under hypnosis, I replicated Susan's mannerisms. My actions were further informed by the merging of our auras. Or, was I just kidding myself and was just playing out my idea of Susan? That question would drive me crazy if I puzzled about it too much. I just had to trust the troupe's shining mentor that it was all happening as Dune said it was. That was the way to true greatness.

I closed my eyes hard and sighed. When Colin raised an eyebrow, I shook my head, indicating, "It's nothing."

I tried to give Colin poetic, smoldering looks like I'd practiced in the mirror all year; still, he refused to notice. As we drove on, I skulked. He'd killed my buzzing passion by being staid.

I hoped to shake the wish-fulfillment dream I'd awoken from that morning. I was married to Dune; I'd reached out to touch Dune's high, rounded cheek bones, his shiny black hair. His red lips showed exquisite pain and pleasure with the tiniest movements of pointed corners. In the dream, he dressed like Lord Byron. We lived wild in the gorse, swam in stars together, became wind whipping up wildfire turning heather to passion. We were a lightning storm. We were eternal.

But instead, in my waking life, I was riding in the car with my friend in the familiar city neighborhood, with his heavy dry-cleaning bags clanging against a bar above the back seat. And where were we going? I saw no mysterious caves to explore ahead, no wilderness to dance in, shamanic shadows becoming one, costumes with nine-foot tree headdresses made of lucid dreams. Didn't see us going toward any flying. I mean, sure, I liked Colin. His eyes were lit up. He was always on time. His laugh made everything OK. But losing Colin wasn't like falling into the darkest abyss forever.

I *needed* to feel that. Wild, intense, out of this world reciprocal love with *someone*. After rehearsing the theatrical role in which I elevated into the glorious ethers through transformative, mystical love, I determined to make it real. Because the right transcendent love can free us. The motto engraved on the Bennu's Grail prop Bennu said: *Transcendent love changes the world. Be each other.* What did I want to change? Everything.

CHAPTER 2
BENNU TROUPE AT THE THEATER

I wanted matters to go smoothly (though not so much for Miss Susan) at our season finale, with our biggest press coverage ever. The Free the Moldavite protestors had a different idea. We passed the front of the theater and spied protesters. They forced our audience members, who were properly lined up in a queue outside the entrance, to shuffle past them, heads averted. The protestors even stared at people's eyes.

"How impolite," said Colin. "UnBritish."

Protestors got more attention from reporters than we did. The attendees were multicultural but the protestors even more noticeably so: German, Russian, Mongolian, Tibetan, Japanese, Indian, American. Two carried signs with the image of the Dalai Lama, head of Vajrayana Tibetan Tantric Buddhism. Protestors spoke to anyone listening.

A reporter asked, "Should the government regulate the sale of Moldavite and other rare gems?"

Another reporter asked a protestor on the other end of the line, "You're representing the diverse population who want access to precious metals, crystals, and gems rather than them being bought up first by people empowered to do so by the current state of the market?"

Colin added his version: "Want to get up in everybody's business and make a mess of it?"

I agreed. The protestors wanted Draconian government regulation with endless complexity. But I still wanted to see the protestors treated with respect when airing their views. I sighed in relief when Colin drove me around the side of the building toward the back to our entrance. Yet, a group of activists held signs, chanting there, too. I nodded at the protestors to show I recognized fellow humans with valid opinions, however random. Mostly they called out one or two-word statements. But a few of them articulated their viewpoints more in-depth.

Susan's face appeared on their cardboard weapons. To them, she was the face of Caucasian privilege's anti-Shambhala racism. Seeing that, Colin put his arm around me. "Don't take it personally, honey."

Their signs targeted the Bennu troupe for promoting Atlantis and not representing the Shambhala angle in our history of Moldavite. What a weird, obscure interest these people pursued. *I mean, who actually cares that much about Moldavite? It's just a rock.* Of course, no one had cared much about diamonds until the PR firms had created the associations for them that made everyone need one.

Mongolians repeated, "No bias for Atlantis! Shambhala is the highest."

Oh, come on. To be fair, if we enacted the role of Moldavite in Shambhala, in Tibet or Mongolia, which was believed to be in Shambhala in the Gobi Desert, we'd have to represent all expeditions to that island in between empires. Alliance with Tibet, so close to British India, was coveted because it was a buffer between the British and Russian empires.

So, we'd have to act out popular legends of the King of the World wielding Moldavite as he brought enlightenment to humanity, creating the New Dawn. Japanese expeditions looking for Shambhala, claiming it was actually Japan, so Outer Mongolia and Siberia were theirs by right; appropriating Tibetan Buddhist legends of the King of the World was their game plan.

We'd have to act out Stalin's Soviet expedition. Our show would go on and on. Our audience didn't want to sit through ten hours for the sake of historical thoroughness. They wanted a fun date night with rousing music and pretty dancers.

The Russian occultist Madame Blavatsky said, when Lemuria sank, some survivors migrated to Atlantis and others to Shambhala in the Gobi Desert.

Some people historically presented Shambhala as utopia, the spiritual light of the world. The other camp described Shambhala as evil.

Colin asked, "Do you think your troupe will change the script for next season to accommodate their demands for equal time?"

And oh God, we'd have to act out the Nazi expeditions to Tibet too if we faithfully represent diversity. "No, we can't possibly. The show is just good times, with a little British feel-good-about-ourselves thrown in, right? I mean, no one here is chiming in about Germany, but they were just as important in the race to find Shambhala."

Colin quieted, his eyes searching the air and then countered, "I thought Germany's Thule Society promoted the superiority of the Aryan race, and the giant superman in Thule, which was Atlantis. So, the Shambhala-heads wouldn't even like it if you included that part of history, too, would they? Because it favors the Atlantean superiority meme."

The Atlantean supermen had supposedly bred with a lowly race, bringing on their own destruction. "Sort of, though before the continent sank, theoretically some Atlantean super beings escaped to Shambhala in Tibet. So, there you have it. Before WWII, Germans explored the East searching for the magical place where the Atlanteans had taken their super-duper advanced technology. The Germans wanted to exploit the fancy dance Vril force. I mean, who wouldn't, right? And Moldavite supposedly first came from the planet of the original kingdom of Atlantis, so owning a piece meant you had a connection with vital Atlantean magic that could make you powerful as hell."

The Thule Society's most coveted possession was the Holy Grail for which King Arthur's knights grandly quested. As did Hitler and another Thulist, SS leader Himmler. Not particularly scintillating entertainment. We weren't trying to medicate or audience's insomnia with details of historical accuracy, after all. *We're just trying to get their imaginations leaping around in the glorious playground of Atlantis.*

Back in the day, Britain took little interest in protecting Tibet from Chinese annexation. The Shambhala-heads never forgot.

Huld, pushing past the protestors said, *"Our* Moldavite lineage descends from superior ancestors. They were *giants*!"

The protestors and reporters gasped at how he outright stated his non-PC arrogance. I turned to Colin and mimicked Huld's hatchet face with his eyes bugging out maniacally. I so loved to make Colin laugh.

A Tibetan woman said, "Well, *our ancestors* were invisible they were so pure!" That made no one gasp. It was OK. She wasn't Caucasian.

An actor yelled, "Shambhala-head hippies, go home. Get a job!"

I didn't want to leave Colin's car, not just because of the fray, but because I wanted nothing more than to kiss him. I wasn't used to that. With Dune's mesmerizing perfection, I'd barely entertained momentary fantasies and even a few dreams of kissing Colin, until that day. But, the desire grew more urgent second by second. Idling in his car a few more minutes wouldn't hurt. I leaned toward him just a little.

When he looked confused, I acted like I was preparing to fix his collar, so he'd look good for his meeting at the publishing house. My fingers grazed his neck. I traced upward toward his mouth. It was masculine, well-defined, boy next door. And I wanted it. I edged closer. His lips softened, his eyes landing on my lips. If his quickening breathing was any indication, I was having a powerful effect.

Just as we started to kiss, we were interrupted by banging on my door. Someone hit the side mirror, turning it to the wrong angle. I rolled down the window to reset it. A clamoring of activist voices and hands reached toward me, clawing. "Susan?" "Are they going to give you the Moldavite Grail, Susan? Or is that just a nasty rumor? Do you think you deserve it?"

I felt vile. I shrunk with unworthiness. I tugged at my costume.

Colin grabbed my hands, saying, "Stop, you'll rip it."

He was right as always. I shouldn't take the humiliation personally.

Did I want to be with someone who made rational decisions and made sense all the time? Or someone who breathed irrational passion across the ethers, like Dune, who made me feel like a floating goddess of all the way good and all that was spectacular? Dune was such a bastard. He'd made it impossible for the last two years to even think about having a love life.

A heckler yelled, "You don't deserve the Grail! You stand for Atlanteans and their evil technology! You stand for white supremacy!"

My lips tightened. I tried to whisper to Colin, but couldn't, since we were on public display. We couldn't kiss. I had to maintain the appearance of being Susan, and if she kissed someone other than Dune in public: scandal!

Red words on a sign scrawled, "Atlantis sucks." The woman carrying the sign spun it and on the other side a portrait of a smiling wise Tibetan monk, covered with the words, "Shambhala rules!"

"Free the Moldavite!" signs spun everywhere.

What are we supposed to do -- change the laws about who can buy gems ourselves? It isn't our fault the museum was robbed and Moldavite was snapped up in a buying frenzy. You surely could have bought it just like anyone else if you'd had the foresight.

They roared, "Hey Hey, Ho Ho, Shambhala racism's got to go." A few sported Free Tibet insignia embroidered on their clothes. A short, slender group had uncombed hair, nose rings and torn jeans. Others wore purple nylon, pink lipstick and blue eyeshadow. Hippies wore tie-dyed tee shirts with Guatemalan vests.

One sign featured an impressive painting including the long-dead Russian Theosophist, Madame Blavatsky, who stood stolidly pointing up to the hidden Himalayan utopia of enlightened adepts, the Brotherhood of the Light, in Shambhala.

When he flipped the sign, I had to laugh at the cartoonish image of a frowning Blavatsky pointed down to Atlantis. Her image condemned the silhouettes of wicked Aryan magicians. They represented the Brotherhood of the Shadows, using a huge pink crystal as a power tool. The scenario further popularized by the sleeping prophet Edgar Cayce. It was the old story, told by people like Madam Blavatsky when protesting British imperialism: the naughty Atlanteans polluted their souls, enslaved humanity, and sank part of their continent by using too advanced machinery for their weak ethics to handle.

Secret societies *always* take sides with either Atlantis or Shambhala. Those in the West claim Atlantean heritage. Many people even said the British Isles were the remains of Atlantis. The New Age and subsequent Occult Revival that President Planda instigated led regular people to roll their eyes back and speak in improper accents, reporting platitudes beginning with, "Dear ones . . ." thinking they're channeling the floating adepts that Blavatsky and her successor Alice Bailey were on about.

One sign condemned China, which had taken over Tibet, for being brutal towards dissenters for small infractions. That superimposed on a picture of Shambhala, an idealized pastel version of pristine Tibet becoming misty in the mountains, the King of the World radiating Moldavite, the rarest of all gems.

A few counter-protestors argued with them. The picture on one counter-protestor's sign showed a graph of the large percent of "Serfs oppressed by lamas," pointing out how Tibet's oppressiveness had been at least as ruthless as China's.

Colin reached over and casually held my hand under a towel on the seat between us, making it look to the outside world as if we were not doing anything suspicious. Clever man. My cheeks warmed up and my face felt like a chipmunk's as my muscles tried not to smile with too obvious mischief.

A reporter, with the name tag Mortimer, bent into the car to ask me a question, assuming I was Susan. Because, who asks standbys and understudies anything? *Oh dear, the towel thing must look weird.* "The protestors are offended by the history of British intelligence agencies working with secret societies against Eurasia. Would you say your shows promote a British imperialist bias regarding people expressing their discomfort over being marginalized?"

I started to move my hand out from under the towel, but that would have only brought attention to our indiscretion. "Our goal isn't to dismiss anyone. It's just dancing. You know, entertainment. Fun."

Mr. Mortimer posited, "Don't you think it's time to rethink the message?"

"Well, sure, why not? But I don't think they should make such a big deal of it before a show. We're trying to be innovative here." What if I said the wrong thing? My cold fingers tingled and got clammy against Colin's warm ones.

I was bullshitting. Everyone educated about military history knew Shambhala represented the forces bent on destroying British imperialism in Asia. Of *course,* a British production wouldn't give them air play. *That's how the world works! Get used to it.*

Theosophists twisted Asian myths, so they'd fit into the Communist belief system. Their intention was to gain military allies through mystical propaganda. But it wasn't like the Atlantis legends used by the Brits were any better. *It's all bollocks. Who cares? Just enjoy the show. It's not like people get all bent out of shape about Santa Claus or the Easter Bunny. Get over it, already.*

Mortimer ruthlessly continued. "One *major* historical character who should be in your show is the Theosophist Nicholas Roerich. Why isn't he? Would you call this insensitivity to people of Eastern descent? The people he empowered?"

A reporter bent down next to Mortimer, squeezing in so much her breasts looked like she was wearing a push-up bra. She said, "According to Theosophists, Roerich's mission was to return the Chintamani Moldavite to Shambhala. But you don't mention that at all. And you dare to call your show historical?"

Mortimer added, "Constantine and Genghis Khan even got messages from Shambhala. Seriously, how can you leave that out?"

When I was a little girl dreaming of being an actress, no one prepared me for that question. I stretched my toes against the floor of Colin's car, ready to leap and twirl in the air on stage. I readied to do anything but feel the muscles contracting with being expected to answer hard questions. I didn't relish confrontation with bullies making me feel I shouldn't exist, should never have existed. I wanted to rest my head against Colin's shoulder and cry and have him put his arm around me, pat my head and give me a gold star.

One actor tapped the reporter, asking, "Look, lady. So, what about all the people who perceive Shambhala as destructive? Should we act those out too? You wouldn't like that, would you? Why don't you put on your own show and leave us alone, bitch?"

She momentarily raised her hand as if to slap him. The crowd roared. Cameras flashed. This would not look good in the news. *Why can't people just stop worrying about stuff like that and learn to sit back and enjoy a goddamn show? Get a life, guys! Chill out.*

A third reporter bent down to Colin's window while circling his finger around. When Colin rolled down the window, the reporter leaned over him as if he weren't there. Colin flattened against the seat. The reporter spewed spittle over Colin as he asked me, "Theosophists like Bailey and Roerich called Shambhala the seat of Cosmic Fire. So, wouldn't that fit your Bennu idea? Why not include that in your show? What *not!*" He gestured into the car, the back of his hand striking Colin's chest, and he acted as if he didn't even notice he'd done so.

Colin was being good natured about it all, but his eyes started darting about wildly as if looking for an escape route. Or maybe someplace to hide.

Johnny, the most erudite actor standing behind him, answered before I had a chance to do so myself. The lanky reporter bumped his head when turning around to look at him when the actor explained, "Those Theosophists saw Shambhala as a Luciferian force for sacrificial purification through fire. Bailey and Steiner connected Shambhala with the Anti-Christ, like that was a good thing. You think that's a *good* thing? You're into Lucifer. Is that what you're telling me? If so, you can go fuck yourself."

I followed up with, "Yeah, we have to represent Satanists, now? Come on, give me a break." The Shambhala force, Bailey said, was destructive and dark.

The female reporter regained her composure and said, "It would be lovely if Kevin Frank played Roerich. An excellent actor, able to portray the flamboyance . . ."

"Some would say megalomania . . ." interjected a passing actress.

Johnny added, "Look at the bigger picture. Nicholas Roerich wanted to rule a Buddhist theocracy. He got the Bolsheviks to help him out with legends of Shambhala. It was a way to win over Buddhist countries before England did."

A Mongolian woman protestor wearing a vivid red pantsuit

countered, "Yeah, well, England twisted legends, too! They were attempting to win the Eastern countries over with appropriation."

I said, "Our show illustrates that side of it."

The Mongolian protestor smirked. "Exactly. It shows one side."

"Isn't that how it always goes?"

She asked, "Should it? Does that perpetuate the lie?"

Whatever.

Another protestor put her arm around the red-jacketed Mongolian and added, "And what about how Atlantis' civilization destroyed itself? You know why? Because of 'mating with an inferior ethnicity.' Isn't that just special."

I stated, "Listen, I get it. I really do. That's shit. But I didn't come up with those things, OK? I'm just an actress living in 2018, making a living by doing my fucking job. Back off. Please."

Colin shushed me. He sank into the seat, as if he didn't want to be associated with me anymore. "They're right, you know," he whispered.

No! I wanted Dune. I wanted him to put his arms around me and tell me everything was OK. I needed him to reassure me that he'd worked out all these questions and there were reasonable answers for them. I hungered for him to slip me the cheat sheet, so I'd be able to keep my head high and know that everything these people said must be misguided. We were actually good people, forward-thinking innovating artists adding infinite greatness to the world that they were too niggling to see.

The Mongolian protestor in red, carrying a photo of Blavatsky and Bailey together, turned to the biggest bunch of reporters. She said, "The second head of the Theosophical Society, Alice Bailey, said Shambhala was the vital core of planetary awareness." She waited for reporters to finish taking notes and continued, stressing every syllable: "She said Shambhala will illuminate the West. Why are you leading the resistance to that progress? Why are you siding with the men who colonized and exploited our countries? Who has gotten into your head?"

Well, hm. Much as I didn't want to admit it, that conversation suddenly put occult history into perspective for me. It was about competing appropriation of cultural myths for the sake of forming military alliances. That made a lot of sense and flipped everything I'd been acting out for the past two years. Each person who wrote about the legends morphed them for a political agenda. When political needs rearranged themselves, stories changed. That was the point of all those expeditions to Tibet. After that revelation, I felt weak in the knees, discombobulated, fuzzy. I needed Dune more than ever.

Protestors pushed us as we tried to make it into the performer's door. Two actors pulled actresses through behind them. While I watched, mesmerized, the actresses backed through the crowds, their arms not showing. When they both caught my eyes, I glanced between them as they melted into the theater crowd.

I appreciated the momentary lull in the rain. Standing on the sidewalk so long outside the canopy would have ruined me for the show otherwise. Normally it was a few quick steps when a taxi or Colin dropped me off, so it was easy to stay dry. The moonlight glinted off Colin's shiny car.

He elbowed me mischievously. "My finger-crossing is ruthless," he said, whispering into my ear as I got out of his car. "Expect a miracle."

"Like Susan having a fantastic coughing fit."

"Exactly."

That made me feel a better. I wanted his finger-crossing to have an effect. I willed it to work.

Saying goodbye was hard since I had to hide my growing attraction to him from the crowd. He had to look like a chauffeur. In reply he made the tiniest, most subtle movement, like a homeopathic kiss. Brilliant.

I slunk toward the door like some rubber cartoon kid's toy. My chest caved in, barely breathing, the pit of my stomach knotting. A protester shoved me out from under the overhang into the drizzle. I leaned against the protestors arms linked to keep me out. I bent to enter underneath their arms, moved the butts in front of me aside by wiggling my head, raised and disappeared into the crowd. I made it inside the door.

❄

When I entered the room where actors applied makeup and chatted, all my senses tingled. My skin was an antenna. If I had the chance, I'd be the best faux-Susan the world could desire. If I became a star the next season, so what, if I had only Colin to celebrate with? He liked everything I did. Too easy.

But if I did a fine job capturing Susan's inner nature better than I'd ever managed in front of reporters, *Dune* would be proud of me. Dark, dangerous, delectable Dune Thornley. The sparks between our eyes were enough for me. Almost.

I didn't spy Dune yet, but the dressing room scintillated with anticipation of the last evening. After-party truffles tempted on silver platters in the corner, and someone snuck a drink from a bottle of ginger liqueur waiting under the lamp. The bottle passed around, hidden under costumes, to the sound of whispers. Flamingo-fuchsia color on the walls vibrated with the extra depth and poignancy of Susan Thornley's finale.

The future licked my skin and make it shiver. Susan, the effervescent actor Kevin Frank, another standby and I gave each other knowing looks when an interviewer asked, "What makes the Bennu troupe so beloved? The stars top the charts of actors and actresses searched for indie performances in England." We held our chins high. Our secret, Dune's hypnotic/auric technique --

that was something to be proud of. Besides, they were good actors; I had to give them that.

The interviewer followed up with the usual question. "So, what's the secret of your play's effect on audiences? No one can explain why they leave and remain so attached to this show. I mean, really, it's a drama about a *rock* and cobwebby old legends. Still, everyone falls in love with it?"

We remained silent. A few winks. He'd never guess the actors emanated auras through the room.

The interviewer asked another question. "In your words, tell our audience the relationship between the Egyptian Bennu and the Greek Phoenix."

"They're the same thing," said Johnny, walking up behind the reporter. "Both birds represent immortality and resurrection. Simple. A symbol of initiates being born again as members of secret societies."

One standby passed around silly astrological fortunes on little slips of paper. We got them every day we got together. No one told who wrote the two or three sentences, according to exactitudes of birth.

"What are those?" asked the reporter.

I answered, "We were supposed to spend all day figuring out these obtuse messages and get gleeful when we do. Yeah, right."

Susan showed me hers. "Let yourself be water, drink deeply of the well today, and you will change the world permanently."

My fortune was not as interesting but would be fun to show Colin later: "Reality is overrated." We collected platitudes and failed predictions we stuck at wacky angles around the edges of his bathroom mirror. The fortunes weren't as fun in my apartment.

I hoped Norma got a good fortune this time. She was a talented actress, though mousy with poor posture. I walked over to her and hugged her to prepare her if the fortune was bad, since she believed them.

Norma squealed. She leaned over to her friend and showed it to her, then looked around at the crowd. She hesitated for a while and then stepped out of the room. The friend told another actress, who told another, and it got to my ears. The message said, "Look out the closest window to see your future husband." The closest window was down the hall. Curious, I joined the gaggle of onlookers.

Norma stood at the window, a disgusted look smashing her face. She covered her eyes and backed away screaming.

Reed, or Reedsy, as she called him, the man she had been telling us she loved, held a sign as he stood in on the theater grounds outside the window. I couldn't make it out.

Another actress ran toward her, asking what was wrong.

"The tree! The tree in the yard. It's writhing! It's got a hideous face! And it's waving a sign at me that says MARRY ME! Oh God, oh God!"

Ah, one of Dune's Substitute Hallucination pranks. Brilliant. Those were always hilarious. Just like tricks hypnotists play on TV.

Huld entered the building, after a nice shower, and smirked at what her post-hypnotic suggestion made her see.

Dune had not yet pranked me with the suggestion/fortune combo. Maybe he thought I was too serious to bother with. Dune came in, a huge grin on his face.

I should laugh more often to show him my lighter side. I earned a fortune-hypnosis prank too!

Dune said the words that released Norma from her Substitute Hallucination.

She gasped. "Reedsy! I can't believe it. Yes, I'll marry you!" She waved and nodded.

Reed, hair ruffled, put down the sign and ran around toward the back entrance. So did she.

I strolled back to the dressing room with everyone else. I gave Norma a congratulatory hug. "You deserve it, sweetie," I said. "You're a special one. I hope you bring pictures of the wedding."

"What do you mean? You're invited."

"Aww, thank you. I'd love to go."

I *knew* those fortunes were fakery. Rascals.

I spotted a new art piece on the wall. A flamingo on fire. Underneath it, a golden scroll proclaimed: BENNU. A bit on-the-nose.

Underneath it the placard stated: "When the bird's death approaches, it builds a nest for its own rebirth. It sets fire while sitting inside. From the ashes, it rises again, young once more, and more potent. Making an egg from ashes, it delivers it to the sun god."

The Kev, with a gleam in his eyes, rambunctiously pretended to be that reborn flamingo. He got me laughing, as he jumped on top of a crate, pretending it was the BenBen cube that Bennu mounted. Campy Kev balanced on one foot, elongating his neck. He shot off jogging around the room, hissing and fluttering his arms, as if they were wings on fire. When he concluded, we applauded. Kev played a more animated and adorable Bennu than Susan or I ever was. I'd miss those fun and games. A tear came to my eye.

A Latino stranger, who must have done well in the auditions as Susan's replacement, wandered around the edges of the room. *I might as well go home to bed.* For the director to invite her backstage before casting her -- that seemed ominous. She looked nothing like me. I'd never be her standby. And, she looked more exotic and sexually available than me, so the judges might give her more votes. But she wasn't allowed to be in that room long, as she'd catch us doing our secret techniques. The time drew near.

Susan and I applied matching theatrical make-up, looking at each other while leaning toward the mirror lit with lights. I, who resembled her so closely naturally, become even more of a replica brush stroke by stroke, powder grain by powder grain, deception by deception. I sat close to her in front of the mirror, the skin on my arm prickling with the impingement of her aura on mine.

Susan's pointy chin lifted, as she arched elegant eyebrows, plucking the stray hairs, her skin, grayed, gaunt from cancer. I used the sable brush for hollow cheeks and narrow temples and I plucked tiny stubble to keep my brows raised. My younger face molded itself into Susan's, my blonde hair dyed to match her slightly different shade. I used more concealer to cover up the tiny scars where I'd had my rebellious moles removed, even the ones no one would see through my outfit, a duplicate.

Daily, I'd prepared for the show, practicing emulating Susan's mannerisms, and ready to be her doppelgänger in case she fell down stairs, left due to an emergency, or got an attack of wheezing.

The more aura I breathed in regularly, the more it seemed I remembered about her life. Advanced, freaky occult stuff. I'd read about those things or heard them in the indie-news about the elite. I wondered how Susan felt about all that, but she never answered when I asked. Neither did Dune. That made me think they swore to secrecy and were truly connected to the Nevermind.

Huld liked to hint around that he was an Agent of the Nevermind, and he'd talk about esoteric history, to show off. He'd never have made it into the Agency, considering he left school young, if he hadn't taken the HGH. Gigantism gave people huge advantages ever since President Planda was elected back when the cult first started in the United States.

I fell out of character by squinting my eyes with glee more than Susan would.

I calmed down to Susan's tonality by damping down my heart. But it fluttered, as Dune was in the dressing room, tending to the other standbys. And he came my way. The way he walked was all it ever took to make breath come quick. Every way he'd move his head was a revelation of beauty.

I hid that my eyes followed him in the mirror, admiring his commanding posture as I darkened my lashes. When I looked back at my face, I realized I'd smeared it on one side, and grunting, wiped it off to start again. I wanted to let my chest go free instead of binding it to mimic Susan's smaller bosom. My breasts wanted to show Dune their full capacity, to incite a fire in his own chest.

I imagined taking off the chest binding in a forest, my fullness lit by moonlight. Instead of her old-fashioned straight posture, I'd angle my torso to exaggerate curves. I'd unpin and shake out hair fuller than Susan's. Alternately, I pulled in my impetuous lips, widened my irreverent eyes, and pulled in my assertive chin to approximate Susan's strict domestication.

When Dune came up behind, edges of my skin tingled and imperceptibly reached toward him, as if it could lift away from my flesh. He put his hands on my shoulders, looking in the mirror with me. Susan looked over and stopped moving. I met Dune's gaze, both of us unmoving. His full lips quivered only once, in that way that drew the sharp corners down. It got to me. He looked hungry for me, like he wanted to steal me away and ravish me. Like he would do anything to get me alone.

I was fortunate I got to be near to my idol day after day. My mentor. I was glad I was his type, looking like Susan and her twin sister, whom he'd dated before switching to Susan, from what gossipers told me. The looks we gave each other when we held each other's gaze, his pupils dilating, told me he cared. Electricity when brushed up against each other. And we often held any touch longer than necessary. *It's not my imagination. Too bad I have such respect for monogamy.*

I focused on shadowing my nose to appear narrow as hers. I wished I flared nostrils like Susan. Blushing hot, I was glad the major cast would go onstage soon.

Susan was pale. I asked, "Are you faint?"

"Dizzy. It happens."

"Breathe deep, if you can. I know it hurts. Water, dear?" asked Dune. He brought her a glass, and when returning, said, "I placed the drops in it already."

She began a ragged coughing fit. She wouldn't be long for this world. Studying how Susan drank the water with the special elixir reserved for her, I moved my throat the same way, forcing a dry swallowing. I held in my cheeks and kept my mouth heart-shaped, my chin long.

My chest crushed inward when I thought of surviving without his face. His suave mannerisms, velvety, poised voice. Months before I'd see him. *If* my contract renewed. But otherwise, it could be forever! Horrors.

No. I *needed* mystical intensity making life burn bright. I wasn't ready for a life of being complacent and thrilled about kitchen appliances. Ordinary people drained the Earth. Extraordinary was what it took. Susan, to be exact. Otherwise, I believed I should sacrifice to make room for the plants and animals and for amazing people.

I used more shadow under my cheekbones to match Susan's dying ones. Dune bent to kiss and bite Susan behind her neck, tugging hair at the nape. She spread her legs slightly across her seat. She seemed chuffed to bits by her man's sensuality.

I fantasized about Colin being my hero and making her magically go away for the evening. What difference would it make to her? She'd had a full career.

"Are you about ready?" Dune asked his wife, gesturing with his arm, his full sleeve gracefully.

Susan feathered the last bit of make-up and stood to snog him so intensely she nearly knocked him over. Well, so much for her make-up.

"Let's go," he whispered. "You're warmed up, yes?"

"Hot, more like it." She stood and sidled up to him, pressing herself against his pelvis.

Muscles in the center of my chest contracted and stayed tight, my eyebrow tightening as if my eyes tried to hug each other. My longing palpably connected my heart with Dune's.

"Wait, Susan, I'll induce the standbys early this time, so we can take time to ourselves." When he called us, we gathered to start the process in case he needed to do the full-on hypnotic aura-merge later if we performed during the live show. "Frankenstein time." Yep, exactly. Like being that scientist's monster constructed of more than one person.

Dune reminded us to breathe in a little of our actors' extra auric energy softly, getting the process going in case we needed to suck in their auras more if replacing them on stage.

That skill had taken long hypnosis sessions. After I did it, sometimes I would have a sense of "my" past. I'd checked out if I was getting her memories right; sometimes I did and sometimes I didn't. I read about her in the press.

He was brilliant. Dune was rumored to learn hypnotic methods from the perception management branch of intelligence which began in the 1980s, networking the United States and Britain: that strange organization of ceremonial magick and mind control, theater and lies. I believed the rumor that the Nevermind Agency linked with the Bennu Society at the higher echelons. It only made sense they would be, because Bennu symbolized the return of "people from Atlantis," by way of Egypt. And that was his topic.

"All right. Everyone, keep breathing. We'll be back in a few." He winked.

Kevin Frank, standing by the door, jutted his pelvis to the side. He did his, "Mmmm, baby," thing that always made me smile.

Dune took Susan's hand; they rushed to leave the dressing room, hips touching, and swaying. He didn't even turn around to give me our special look. His hand glided on her butt as she walked with a sway I hadn't seen often. I knew what they would do, what delicious pleasures they would enjoy in the shadows.

She suppressed her cough, hand over her mouth, obviously

trying to turn that gesture sexy. Aww, she deserved happiness, poor woman. I tuned in to her aura even more for a vicarious sensation of their pleasure after they left.

The Kev bowed his body, while sticking out his chest like a Bantam rooster, and showed me his astrology slip, his swarthy pocked face miming awe. His goatee nearly poked my eye. I scanned the fortune through his wiry chestnut hairs. He sang his. "Smoke on the water, fired in the eye."

He popped the slip of paper into his mouth. He ate it, chewing it fast like a bunny. He paused, chewing again, that goof. He looked thick as two short planks. So funny.

I raised my glass of water fast to his mouth, and made him take a sip, grandly, as if fulfilling a prophecy. He swallowed it in a way to make his Adam's apple jump around in front of my face, before wiggling his nose. I loved The Kev. He made work fun.

Then, he got a look I recognized from victims of Dune's post-hypnotic pranks. Kind of zombified for a minute, eyes glazed over the transition. I was impressed he had that expression in his repertoire.

He faded into the crowd. I didn't see him after that. Ah, what a dear. His theatricality was *the* way to be. Superior to dull repression. I loved to imitate his style when we hung out. How didn't Colin join in when we vamped it up at the party after a show when Susan was sick? How'd Colin manage to stand there, stiff and straight, and not suddenly get uber-glamorous with us? I loved *being* Kevin. Sure, I felt awful I'd faltered that night on stage, but my self-confidence came back as I talked more grandly like The Kev, gesturing flamboyantly, like I was a drag queen. I contemplated inviting The Kev for dinner sometime.

The standbys grew quieter, withdrawn, as it grew closer to time for the show. Breathing in our target actors' and actresses' auras for Stage One Readiness, we breathed out own auras to make room to be inhabited by theirs. A mild case of possession.

I made my plan: find Dune over the summer. Even if Dune

and I never touched, it would be the romance of the century. And what other kind of romance was worth having?

I didn't like being Miriam, always the standby, never the star. Living in a tiny apartment, spending a year rehearsing, invisible to an audience. That's why I lost myself in novels and movies, like my favorites, *Rebecca*, and *My Cousin Rachael*.

There would be serious press for Susan's last night. If got to take over, they'd say I was Susan, but later, surely make a grand statement it had been me. Me! And I'd be better than Susan. More people than ever would try come to watch us the next season, and the troupe charged higher rates. More celebrities and politicians than ever would go to the shows; I'd get to meet them, instead of hiding behind a curtain, made up like Susan and watching them drink champagne.

Sitting next to the other standbys, not moving much for a good while, I breathed in Susan's extra auric energy. It infused my body and enveloped me. I saw no colors in the auras often but saw light -- eyes either open or closed. The brightness coming in had her familiar signature frequency.

If I breathed in Susan's life force enough to receive memories, it sapped her. Her performances got listless. I had to be careful and walk a fine line. She already was listless from cancer. I sure hoped she wasn't getting tired because I drained her. I mean, I was her personal trained Psychic Vampire, after all.

I tried to be optimistic about Colin's finger crossing skills.

The standbys' eyes went blanker as they breathed in their actors. Some foreheads got tighter, with furrows to match their type-A actors. Others' lines smoothed out as they matched type-B. Time slowed down. I watched them all grow brighter from their actor's auras seeping into them.

I was an empty hand-puppet about to land into the trash bin. A puppet in the dump, missing its ventriloquist, longing to speak.

I fought the image of tripping Susan walking past me; she would assume it was an accident but get a mild, temporary sprain.

I lifted, and bent into lunges, while inhaling Susan. I got an extra good hit of her. Her aura flooded in full force. I "remembered" being Sylvia's standby, waiting behind the scenes. I "remembered" her making love to Dune. Vague arcane secrets about alchemical life extension. Some ritual. A tiara?

I was high from such a strong hit of aura. Nothing prevented energy from being pulled into my body. I hoped she wasn't depleted from how much of her I took. I didn't want to make her pass out. Or did I? Hmm. There was a thought. I naughtily ramped up the influx of her brightness a tad.

Though invisible to the audience, to my trained eyes, the energy was crystalline, sparkling as it rushed into my body and around it, while creating a subtle costume.

Then, the flow stopped short. Gone darkly dreaming. Fallen into an abyss. That was when I felt the cold, the cracking.

Had I done something awful? Or had Colin? Oh, God, no. I had to get ahold of myself. Everything was all right.

❄

Wandering through the green room later, dodging the costumes with flailing extensions, I spotted Dune talking near the doorway, with a standby with an upturned nose revealing nostrils, her thin lips chattering. The standby stooped, tying her shoe laces, smiling up at him with a mouth on sideways. He breathed heavily, face ruddy, hair and suit disheveled - of course, after a quickie with his wife.

Veins in his forehead bulged. He garbled my heartbeat. I'd never seen him bothered like that.

Susan and I had synced menstrual cycles, like other actresses and their standbys. But I was just a wannabe. Waitress-with-the-Most-Knowledge-of-Esoteric-Lore-in-the-Restaurant. My body crumpled; I breathed harder, tightening my diaphragm to milk the air for courage. I'd soon take French fry orders. No more flamingo deity with long feathers, rising from ashes, with a fog machine and lasers.

I wonder if Dune and Susan vacation in France. Could I bump into them? Cafes where everyone talks with lips pooched out oh so sensual and full. Go to poetry readings, art museums, street dances. Swing on a swing set in the full moon, wearing gauze.

I envisioned doing something hedonistic together. Smoke hash -- well, no, her lungs couldn't handle that. Mushrooms. Ha. An inside joke. She was known for going bat shit crazy at parties when she did psychedelics. Taking off her clothes at inappropriate times and going on about living forever. Or was that her twin? Susan had been slowing her pace. She might not do the street dances in France long; she'd been dragging her feet across the stage sometimes, doing modified leaps lower to the floor each play.

How well Dune treated her had been heartwarming. Bringing a chair to her to sit in whenever she waited backstage. Herbal tea to help her breathe. Rubbing eucalyptus essential oil on her chest. Hand caressing cheek.

I'll comfort him after she dies. I'm already used to wearing make-up like hers to hide freckles. I can style my mane her tame way. I'll offer him a hug. Give him that music DVD by the pagan couple who sing about making love in the woods. Bring raspberries and figs. Who knows, date someday? If he's an Agent, could I handle that? They're corrupt. No, who am I kidding? My body would capitulate, swoon into his arms, be his bliss, his light, excusing anything he did. I might be part of the Nevermind and go to meetings with him, to suggest changes. I mean, if we get married.

The Bennu performers ended conversations, separating into the two groups. The main actors gathered near the entrance to the stage, while doppelgangers remained on call in the green-room, whispering over muffled laughter.

"Where's Susan?" the director called. "She should be in line and ready to go. "Someone check the loo. Look outside. Susan!"

Norma said, "I was in the loo. She wasn't there."

"No one's outside, madam."

Dune walked into the room. His eyes were so leading man. "I haven't noticed her for a while. We left for a private conversation. You know how it is." He ran fingers through his thick hair, looking proud of being a sensual animal, white teeth gleaming down on us.

Jerking his chin upward at someone in the hallway beyond my vision, Dune took a wide stance. "The Kev passed by us in the hallway because he was going out for a smoke. He was taking a fag out of its pack. That was enough to trigger Susan to smoke too. I wish people would stop *doing* that! It's rubbish. Can't you wait until getting outside to take the ciggies out? I mean, you have to walk yards away from the building to smoke, holding it in your hand, anyway. Why be in such a hurry to *hold* the darn thing?"

Actors and actresses talked at once.

Dune overpowered them when he continued his proclamation: "I couldn't stop her. She tagged along with Kevin Frank. Out in the wind, too."

"Has anyone seen Kevin?" inquired one actress. "Maybe he knows where Susan went after their smoke."

People whispered to each other more loudly.

Dune rubbed his head and his wavy movie-star hair lifted. I reached to adjust it without telling him why first, and he pulled back. I had to learn how to stop being so impulsive. "Listen, I'm worried. Moon Miriam, Charles, prepare in case you need to go on stage."

The director said, "Maybe Susan fainted or something and Kevin took her to hospital? What a cock up. Anthony, call the hospital. Kevin's not answering."

An actress said, "She's been pushing too hard to finish out the season. She could have wandered off among the trees in a funk. Even gotten disoriented. Or, she talked to a stranger in a passing car and he'd abducted her!"

Norma suggested calling the police.

"Shouldn't we search for her before doing something so drastic?" asked one of the other actors. "I mean, has anyone, you know, looked around?"

"Right. It doesn't have to be one of us looking. Anyone got a friend in the audience they can ask to search?"

I trembled. I wanted Susan to be all right. I wanted her to walk in, feeling fine -- too late to perform.

No, don't look for them yet! They probably asked someone in the parking lot for ciggies or something, and got carried away with a smoky conversation, went off with them to the store to pick up a new pack, and got stuck behind someone in traffic. But it's their fault they can't be here on time.

Dune spoke loudly, looking around the room when he spoke to me. "Well, Miriam, we'll give Susan a couple minutes, right?" He caught the eye of the director who nodded yes. "But you might want Colin in the audience."

I asked, "Should I get him to look for Susan and Kevin when he gets here?"

"Yes, that would be excellent. He should check out the grounds after the show if Susan still hasn't shown up. But we don't want him to miss your shining hour. It will make him treat you better."

Actresses were whispering to each other, glancing at me.

"My brother is here," said an actress. "I can ask him to poke around."

Dune agreed. "Somewhere inside the theater."

Dune went on about Colin. He knew about my friend, even though Colin didn't know who Dune was. "And Colin will want to take you someplace special after the show, no doubt. Got any place in mind? The Fancy, perhaps?" He made a grand gesture to stress the enormity of what he'd said. The Fancy was the best. "I mean, assuming you two are on good terms now." He gave me a meaningful glance.

I couldn't puzzle too long about how weird that implication

was. I was about to get my big chance! Dune was setting me up for a hop and a squeal. I gulped and worked on concerned expressions. What a lovely image, Colin taking me for drinks later at the most expensive place in the city. This was too good.

A standby bent to me and said, "Funny, that, considering rumors about Susan wanting a divorce. He ain't got room to talk."

Norma said, in her skirt-below-the-knees and hair-in-a-bun way, "You don't ignore a Missing Persons situation and go about your business like nothing's happened. We should look everywhere. What if someone's abducted them? What if they've fallen into a ... I don't know..."

"An abyss?" snarked an actress, while fluffing her hair.

But. . .

Other actors were coming up, agitating for postponing the show. Even Charles, the standby for Kevin, joined into the conversation. *You hypocrite. I don't trust you for a second, Charles. You want this chance. Damn you. OK, I guess I'd better go along with the concern. I mean, it's possible they're in trouble. That would be horrible!*

"We can't go on as usual, even if the police are on their way," I said, making myself nauseous by doing so.

"Really?" asked Dune.

Oh God. He was considering it. Had I convinced him? *No, no, no, no, no! Susan and Kevin be damned! The audience has paid, and they expect it to start on time.*

"I mean, shouldn't all of us be out looking for them?" I opened my eyes wide and pulled my chin back, sincere.

Please say no.

The director said, "We have to call up the standbys now. No time to wait. Miriam, Charles, you're on."

A dream come true. But what if someone had abducted her? She'd never mentioned any enemies. No one had a reason to keep her from performing. Other than Colin. *But, surely, he wouldn't. Would he?*

The other times I'd taken Susan's place had been sudden. I

shook, and my nervousness made me screw it up. This time: smooth.

I ran to the other side of the hall and called Colin using the elaborate antique red pay phone. I enjoyed the rule about checking in our cell phones at the entrance. It made the experience at the theater special. Colin was such a dear, leaving show nights open on his schedule in case I was called. “You did it, Colin. Susan’s not performing. Thanks a million for the finger cross.”

I bustled, breathing, reddening, and ran around as if there were something I needed to do, but there wasn’t. All I had to do was go into the full hypnotic induction with Dune, so I became Susan.

I looked forward to being flipped back to me at the last curtain, and rushing to Dune -- no, I mean to Colin, to give him a hug. He’d be proud.

Rehearsal time would pay off again, only my fourth time taking over for Susan. Before, Susan’s illness in her aura had affected my performance on stage too much. That’s why I hadn’t done my best.

That was the drawback of Dune’s method; we had to get the perfect mix of our own aura’s strength and the actor’s auras. I reached out to steady myself. I couldn’t breathe. I had to forget the notion coming over me like a wave.

Within a few minutes, Colin ran in at top speed, rushing backstage. He must have been close when I called.

He embraced me with force and warmth, eyes lit, yet with decorum. “I didn’t have time to get you fresh flowers, but I keep silk roses in the trunk of the car, in case.” He gave them to me, brushing my cheek with soft petals.

He’d missed a spot shaving; the whisker tuft caught the light. “You’re a darling.”

“That’s me. I’ll put them in your spot in the dressing room, don’t worry.” How adorable. He’d been hiding them all this time.

Colin didn't leave. I didn't move, either. We stood in silence, searching each other's faces for answers.

I blushed when one actress passing by us teased, "Oh, ho ho ho, what have we here?" In fact, I reached out and swatted her on the buttocks too as *she* sashayed past.

"Wait a minute. You've got that important meeting."

He reassured me. "I called the president, who said I can miss it. It's no problem."

What a guy.

Onto my goal of being a better Susan than Susan.

After Colin took a seat in the audience, Dune pulled me to the special quiet spot backstage. He turned me around with his hands pressing against my body. Dune did his usual hypnotic induction technique; as he touched me each place, he named a different place than he was touching me, along with a number. So, while touching my shoulder, he said, "Leg. Five."

With eyes closed, he said, "How many fingers am I touching you with? Four." He was touching me with three fingers. The traditional technique of overwhelming stimulus worked every time to take us into trance. He was taking his time with it, not doing the hypnosis as quickly as usual.

I never remembered the final inductions. I dreamed. I always woke after the show, per the post-hypnotic command, upon the trigger. The trigger was the curtain closing the last time at the end, after the encore. I would partially remember what happened. I'd be in front of a curtain, next to a row of performers, when the trance flipped off. Susan's aura had drained away from me, and I'd be me again. Miriam.

Ah, but I loved being under Dune's sway. He was so strong, stood straight at six foot tall. I loved the command he had over me, to make me whoever he wanted me to be, however long he wanted. And what he wanted was for me to be Susan until after the encore, when the curtain landed. So be it.

"Remember," he whispered, looking away. "Nothing is ever enough."

"What do you mean? Um. That I should never be satisfied? That I should envy other people having it? I don't get it."

"Shhhhh. You will."

He placed a hand on my shoulder and completed the hypnotic induction. After that, I switched from being Miriam and believed 100 percent that I was, in fact, Susan.

As Susan, I walked to the stage for my last show ever. I was grateful to time with the Bennu troupe, and I'd give it everything one last time.

CHAPTER 3
RED VELVET CURTAIN

My life wasn't enough: I envied Miriam. I'd seen my husband looking at her in the dressing room. A little younger, a little prettier, and not dying. *What if she takes over for me next season after I die? Yes, she deserves to take on the leading role. She's good. But what if Dune dates her then?* He gave me a look before I walked on stage; he felt sorry for me. I missed the smoldering passion we used to have. Was he going to go backstage during the show and flirt with Miriam? Ugh. Awful. Too close for comfort.

I had to set aside distractions to get into my first character of the show. *I can do it. Once done with this project, I'll be able to relax at home. I've earned the hell out of retirement.*

As the audience settled into velvet seats, I took my station on stage in the dark. Time for *The Flaming Bright History of Moldavite*. As the warm red lights lit us, I startled, noticing the standby Charles had taken Kevin Frank's place, playing his role as Lancelot. I wondered what had happened to Kevin to make him miss the show.

I faced "Hermes' Emerald Tablet" on the other side of the theater which I did not care for: too ostentatious for my taste.

Scholars claim that famous ancient text describes the creation of Moldavite from the descent of the meteorite to Earth fifteen million years ago. Some say the original tablet was Moldavite. Whenever I remained there waiting for the program to commence, I wanted to take it down, sell it, and donate the proceeds to the poor. The bloke who came up with constructing a humongous theater decoration out of real ground up Moldavite was bonkers. How much money did they have to pay for guards beside it to protect it, day after day, since the price of Moldavite had shot through the roof? So weird that a random rock most people other than jewelers and New Agers had never given a second thought to until it started disappearing off the market.

They say a piece of Moldavite nestled in the hilt of Excalibur, the sword only King Arthur could pull from the rock. Moldavite was the Philosopher's Stone, the Stone of Heaven, or the Holy Grail referred to in the traditions of King Arthur. It was a tool to manifest one's intention. It alchemically turned base metals into gold, and conferred immortality, thus making an adept powerful enough to rule the realm.

Surrounding the rectangular tablet was the over-the-top mural featuring gold leaf designs illustrating the Round Table Knight Parzival, pursuing the Grail, which was hailed the Stone that Fell from Heaven: Moldavite, the meteoric stone. Such a big deal about a piece of browny-green glass. And, not all that pretty. Why King Arthur's Knights quested for it was beyond me. It looked all right when you held it in front of a lamp. But otherwise, it was blah, kind of old mold-colored. Still, the beliefs about the enhanced abilities it engenders in its devotees persist.

Something else caught my eye. Why did Huld have those little yellow flower petals attached to his shoes? Why were they wet? I remembered those yellow flowers at the well house. The one Kevin and I liked to sneak off to so we could smoke inside when the weather was cold, windy or wet. Had Huld taken up smoking? I hoped not. Nasty habit. Bad for the heart. People rarely survived gigantism as long as he had. Their hearts usually gave out long before his age, which was mid-thirties.

We acted out the god Poseidon and denizens living large on the ancient continent of Atlantis, claimed by British pseudo-historians to be the British Isles, naturally. Huld represented an important Aryan giant from Atlantis, a grand role for which he was ideal. Enochian alphabet projected on top of us because it was supposedly the lost language of Atlantis. Who knows if people watching the shows got the concept, but it's not like it mattered. We were leaping about, with beautiful bodies and costumes, fantastically lit, with great set designs and musical score. *What more could anyone want? Who goes to shows to learn history, really, anyway, but losers?*

We danced around dim, transparently ethereal scenes. Projections covered the curls of film dangling from the clouds. The projections entertained with frenetic collages of bent legs, lifted fingers, heads thrown back, hair streaming. The Bennu troupe wove dance and smoke, reflections and masks, whips, ropes, and dark. Sturdy curls of gigantic film surrounded the theater. The auditorium was decorated like an old-fashioned camera.

We ran through our myriad costume and set changes. We acted out how Moldavite came from the planet where the "First Atlantis" was established. We showed how the Moldavite resulted from of an explosion caused by dramatic mad alien scientist experiments that charged their rock with special esoteric properties, maintaining the signature of that prototype of the Atlantis on Earth. When the continent partially sank, some folk escaped to Egypt and some stayed in England where the natives inherited the Atlanteans' right to lord it over everyone. They spoke with authority about occult nonsense, while kings and queens claimed Moldavite as their own.

My long, white lace dress flared wide, covered with tiny mirrors reflecting on the mirrored surfaces of the planet balls. Fire lights flickered in the dim room and a dozen actors danced past me. Dressed in white bodysuits, with bald heads, they flitted in the dark, the muscle-cuts reflecting fine lines of light.

A bright flash lit the crowd. Bald men and women leaped off the stage and danced among the seats, strobe light going. They wore thick, metal complexities as their clothing: abstracted shapes with matte gears, the colors, rich and deeply saturated, the lighting warm, the background painterly.

The resonance hummed, buzzing with diva energy. Flow, slide, glide, smooth along beyond boundaries, beyond claiming to be only one identity, bonded to one body only, a body made of chance. My unexplained melancholy made my performance poignant, so it was maybe my best one ever. I'd done this same play on stage so many times to thrilled audiences. But this time, I felt different. I improvised movements with my arms brushing against my cheeks to wipe away tears.

We acted out a Cabalistic tale of alchemy about that biblical patriarch Enoch. His vibrations raised so high he rose into the fire of the Heavens, unleashing a slew of angels -- the ones supposedly contacted by those famous Elizabethan occultists, John Dee and Edward Kelley. The angels theoretically gave them the language with which to call them. Ceremonial magick made angels carry out their wishes -- such as producing a kinder, gentler Apocalypse.

Obviously, the language "to call the angels" was a spy code Dee used to implement his imperialist schemes that led to the slave trade and colonizing countries. But it made for a gorgeous show, with the innovative combination of projections with the live action. Flights of angels, strung up with camouflaged pulleys, caught the projections just right. They became invisible. Mirrors flashed against the chaotic reflections in the light.

As always, after the first costume change, I played the Egyptian flamingo god. Bennu, the Pheonix, arose out of the ashes of Osiris Slain in a paroxysm of spiritual rebirth.

Our play's interwoven stories included one about King Arthur.

Merlin was Arthur's hypnotist, and I pictured him looking like my husband. *Too bad he's acted by someone inferior to our own resident hypnotist, if I say so, myself.* Our skit portrayed Merlin disguising Arthur's father, Uther Pendragon, as his enemy, Gorlois. Clever chap, that, for coming up with such a scheme. This legend was told by John Dee's favorite lying historian, Geoffrey Monmouth. And people believed it; that's the worst of it. *Humanity is made of gullibility.*

Men in armor with Arthurian emblems stood around the four magickal Watchtower directions, each with an open, wooden chest full of "gold bars" inside, with dry ice steaming. The whole thing disappeared into golden light in the mist, glowing and flowing into black.

Arthur's father, Uther, pretending to be Gorlois, made passionate love with Gorlois' wife, Igerna, at Tintagel. The old narrative everyone knows and acts like it's so romantic. Pretty darn rapey. But our actors and actresses did a great job with it, and so did the costume designers. Rich fabrics shimmered.

They conceived Arthur, the unbeatable British warrior who supposedly expanded the empire into vast countries throughout the world. Arthur's imperialism in the fifth century guaranteed the right of later kings and queen to rule the territories he took. John Dee whispered those rights to Queen Elizabeth I, and thus the battles of competing claims of that occult ancestry began. The old Atlantis VS Shambhala that raged again, enhanced by the Agents' enthusiasm for the Occult Revival.

My memories were hazy; forgetfulness was for the best. I'd have no distractions. Therefore, I could put my movement, my ligaments, my twirls and leaps, into playing the part of Igerna one last time. From my womb flamed Arthur. Musicians in front of the stage played my favorite music of all time. It was glorious.

I was chuffed to be the wife of the hypnotist who made our troupe famous, celebrating my life as a star. Once the show ended, and the applause called us out once again to bow, and to sing the final song together, I did my final encore before I left the troupe to die at home with Dune.

I could rest, to give into the darkness coming for me. My aching muscles could stop pretending to enjoy the pain of daily dancing. I could curl inside Dune's embrace and let his breath take me away into the quiet dark finality. I could become one with the dirt in the cemetery, under the stone with the image engraved: a sword pulled by a fist in a cloud.

Hecklers called out rough sentences that I intensely tried to ignore, so that I didn't lose a beat. They came through to my awareness. "If you're telling the history of Moldavite, why leave out Roerich?"

I wanted to say, "Sorry" to everyone in the audience, but then I'd apologize for breaking out of my role.

I knew what the heckler was talking about. Nicholas Roerich and his wife led an expedition in the '20s, taking advantage of the Shambhala myth. It was all the rage due to the prevalence of the Theosophy Society's "spiritual" political propaganda. Wisdom was supposedly channeled from Shambhala, the Great White Brotherhood and all that rot.

An academic looking Mongolian teenage boy, wearing huge glasses with black rims, and a round cap over his bowl haircut stood up and shouted, "What about the history of Mongol lamas and the Bolshevik cryptographer? Oh yeah, and the Soviet Union Secret Police operative. Their quest would make an instructive dance, don't you think? Dramatic."

I knew about their trek in the '20s to find Shambhala. They wanted to tie the local Tantric legends together with communism and create the Russian version of the Nazi's Supermen. The secret police set up a hidden mad scientist's lair. The Soviet Foreign Commissariat emissaries led an expedition to Tibet at the same time. Britain won out over the Russians; thus, Atlantis became the predominant sanctioned mythology. Under Stalin, the Soviet

Union was persecuting Buddhism, specifically the *Tibetan form as practiced among the Mongols* within its borders.

The director strode on stage and ignored the hecklers. He stood with me, holding my hands. Both of us twisted to face the audience, as he made a speech that moved me and stirred something. "The Bennu bird represents what seems like the end is only the beginning of immortality. To paraphrase the Perlesvaus Grail legend: 'By the power of Moldavite, the Bennu burns to ashes. Ashes renew her. Thus, does Bennu molt into light? When the stone is charged with hearty ritual, immortality prevails. The stone is called the Grail.'"

"Thank you," I said, palm on my heart, bowing and curtseying at the same time.

"My dear, your performances will live on always!" The director presented me with a bouquet of roses, a purple banner attached to it that announced: *Encore, Susan! Be New*.

He thrilled me when he gave me the Moldavite Grail cup with the phrase engraved upon it: *Transcendent love transforms the world. Be each other.*

The director stood tall and explained our reverence for that iconic object as he flexed his muscles to hold up the large, green stone cup. "Moldavite is a spiritual relic. King Arthur fancied the Holy Grail because it caught the blood of Christ when he was dying on the cross. Knights and Ladies at Arthur's Round Table drank from it because it rejuvenated them. Many believe the cup was carved from Moldavite, though others say it was the stone itself that *was* the Grail, because of its holy properties."

"Moldavite, this meteoric glass from the Moldau Valley of the Czech Republic, is called the Grail Stone -- the Philosopher's Stone."

"Stone from Heaven!" yelled a heckler. Yes, that was the term people invested in the Eastern legends used for Moldavite. When that terminology is useful for forming an alliance with Britain, that can be an enticing thing to promote, but it's not the specific angle our performances took. It's all so complicated we can only do justice to one part of the story of that rock and how it fit into English history.

By this time, the audience loosened up, laughing at the dynamics with earnest protestors sitting beside them. The ushers were too polite to ask the protestors to leave. Everyone was sweating into convulsions of embarrassment.

The director continued. "Moldavite was used by the Elizabethan alchemist Edward Kelley as a catalyst to create gold in front of the royal court at Prague. As you must know, this is the rarest gem on Earth. It is now increasingly precious because of its sudden extreme rarity. Occultists claim the gem imparts consciousness enhancing gifts to trained people -- some say, even immortality. Moldavite is associated with the phoenix, the Greek version, and the Egyptian." He held out his arm to the audience to get them to join in saying completing the sentence together: "Bennu."

The audience clapped, and he continued. "The Moldavite Grail is the symbol of our troupe. Our Bennu performances have energized this cup for three years. We now give this to our beloved star on her last day. Let's hear it for Susan!"

The crowd cheered, standing up during Bravos. It was spectacular. Camera flashes went off left and right along the back where reporters stood.

Holding it made me go weak. Our Grail was rumored to be *the* Grail, but I wasn't sure many people believed that. I hoped no one. Even absurdity has its limits.

"And now it's time for our Susan to go off on a nice long vacation with her husband. So, everyone, say goodbye!"

People stood up and clapped, calling out "Goodbye, Susan. We love you!"

Before the last lowering of the curtain, my husband gestured to me from the sidelines to slip out toward him. "Let's go, Susan!" he whispered, with enticing charisma. It was our secret getaway of delight. My husband held out his hand, his jacket sleeve curving like Fin de siècle. What a surprise! No one noticed us ditching. I giggled like a naughty little girl.

We would miss the reception afterward, so I'd have to be extra nice to the cast members later.

He pulled me off into an obscure hallway for an unobserved exit, and off we went!

CHAPTER 4
ABDUCTION

My husband and I ran out through the side door unnoticed. We got in his sleek black stick-shift and drove away from the spires and lights of the city.

Well, *someone* noticed us. A car wove around traffic, gaining on us fast. The driver waved his swarthy, hairy arm out the window, and shouted. Kevin Frank. Poor Kevin.

Dune ignored him.

"Kevin wants you to stop. Let's see what he wants."

"Well, looks like he's fine, doesn't it? Jerk just missed performing in the most important show of the season. There's no excuse for that. I've got nothing to say."

"His standby took over. He did a bang-up job, eh?"

Dune tightened his lips when he peered in the rearview mirror. He shook his head in the most succinct way.

"But what if he's got something important? Pull over, honey. There's a spot right there."

I blew an exaggerated kiss to Kevin. How would I make it up to him for Dune's rudeness? I'd invite him to dinner. No, dinner was too normal. He'd never be able to act out his animated playfulness at something so predictable. I imagined the party we would throw that would be worthy of his time. There'd be boas. There'd be prancing. There'd be yellow and mauve. And my dying eyes would match the mauve, and contrast with the yellow. I'd pull off the end of my life with panache, and Kevin would bring the punch.

I tried to come up with a brilliant sarcastic comment to tease Kevin about how mad he looked when I next saw him. Something to make him hoot. We'd laugh one day at whatever the hell Dune was doing by ignoring him on the road. Dune would wander off, looking nobler than us. We'd make fun of my husband once he was out of earshot and everything would be fine. Kevin and I would throw ourselves into a dance and make it *outrageous. Hold on.* I wasn't myself.

I wasn't sure whom I'd invite to the party who wouldn't bring us down. Call him up and take it round. Or, would I? I was out of place. I wondered if the mini-crab cakes before the show had gone off. I checked my forehead. *No fever. It must be from Miriam breathing in my aura so much. Maybe it's backwash. Because I feel a lot like Miriam right about now.*

Huld's car eased up beside Kevin's. Huld must have been upset with Kevin for not playing his role on such an important day for our press coverage. Huld rolled his window and shouted something at him. They kept screaming back and forth and Kevin looked even angrier. Kevin probably thought he was justified for missing the show, but defensiveness never is flattering to anyone.

Kevin quieted, slowed his car and swung off onto a street. Huld followed him, and that was that. Well, Kevin would always have next season to redeem himself, as long as he apologized to the director. His special charm would pull him through.

Well, I'd order them both special cakes. I'd get them adorned with a cartoon: Huld chasing Kevin chasing us.

"Dune, he's turned around. You missed your chance to communicate with him. Huld was right there, too. We could have said goodbye."

Dune settled back and turned on the audio book of *The Monk*. I didn't bother speaking over it.

❄

"Trust me," he said, after I kidded him about being so engrossed in the dramatic book that he got lost. "This trip will be even better than our honeymoon. Sure, it's not the Moldau Valley, but, it's as exotic as the Czech Republic. You'll cherish it."

Dune and I remained quiet as we drove on through a changing landscape. He laid his hand on my knee as he drove, intense sexual energy emanating from it. Had it always been so electric? How did I not recall? My head fogged. The cancer was collecting my memory fast. Perhaps it was the relief of letting go of choreography. Ahhh. To ease into just being. I settled back against the seat and sighed, allowing hormones to do their pleasant job.

Dune would take care of me as I embraced the fade. The less I remembered about my life, the easier it would be to let it go. I closed my eyes. Perhaps this was Buddhist meditation, being only in the present moment, forgetting past and future, ego, being nothing. Lit behind my eyes from his touch that sent visions of golden light pulsing through me, though everything, through nothingness eternal.

He said, "Susan, you glowed tonight," he said. "Your most enticing show yet. It felt different, didn't it, being the last show of your life?" His eyes searched mine, his mouth waiting as if ready to take on any expression.

I tried to formulate the words. "Yes, *very* different. More . . . complex. I guess the flashing projections got to me. And projecting our auras over the crowd must have been what made me feel strange this time."

"Stringing yourselves in and out through that big roll of film as it's sliding, yes, I think that can get discombobulating to anyone."

"Especially disorienting to someone in my condition." I patted my chest.

"The cancer confuses you, darling. Perfectly understandable. Let me do all your thinking for you from now on."

I laid my head against his arm as he drove, not minding the bounces when he turned the wheel, steering through the lowland heath. The bracken and tiny flowers of the heather shown brilliant in the moonlight.

"You're already looking better. I suspect what you need is rest in the countryside and recreation with a devoted husband. It's time to celebrate the finale of a fabulous career of the most popular performance artist in the city."

I couldn't fathom why I felt as satisfactory as I did. I breathed without the whistle-wheeze. Excess energy galore.

"Everyone expects you to go off to shrivel up and cough yourself up." Aren't people more delicate about how they say that? "It's up to you. We can travel home instead, if you prefer. But if this sounds good to you -- we'll go off into Paradise. To the castle. The deal is, you let go of what holds you back. Alchemical love transforms."

Dune looked at me, his eyes narrowing while my muscles twitched. He drove slowly, barely looking at the road.

"Castle? That sounds vaguely familiar."

"Ol' Luke has been trying to get us to vacation in his family's old castle all this time, yes? He always leaves in the Spring. He has a new alchemy assistant, and he's taken him with him."

"Are you taking the mick?"

He shook his head. Passing headlights showed off his movie-star features.

"Somehow, I don't remember Luke having a castle." I didn't want to admit I didn't know who Luke was.

"Luke gave me a key to use whenever we want. The castle is too damp and cold for his taste. He likes his friends to live in it, maintain the garden, dust, and keep a look out for suspicious people. He sells elixirs he produces in the laboratory there. It's a complex modern process that he labels alchemy."

I guffawed. Sure, I knew from our shows about Hermetism, transmuting mental forces, the Philosopher's Stone's legendary ability to allow ascension into the golden realms. But still, who took that seriously anymore? It made for colorful entertainment and great costumes, but . . .

"You'd be surprised."

"Stone sucks the heat out of you. Isn't it too drafty to be fun?"

Lifting an eyebrow, he said, "You can't tell me you're turning down a free extended holiday in a mystical castle. You can forget your worries and live in the present."

When he took my hand in his, I did what any woman would do if Dune touched her. I swooned inside, doing my best to appear respectable.

He continued. "Drink his mead if you fancy it. It will be marvelous."

Didn't I have something pressing to do at home? I shook my head.

"I appreciate it. You must have put time into packing everything and making all the arrangements. But let's go back. I like to be warm and I'm not excited by kooky things like alchemy; you know that."

Turning onto a fascinating side road, he pulled off onto the shoulder. We stared into the night. "Not too many days until the equinox," he mentioned. "Perfect for moon goddess Jana, the symbol of eternal youth, to look both directions with both faces."

I listened to the sound of the crickets in the calming landscape while I gazed at a thatched shack covered in moss. My head on his shoulder, I said, "The equinox will be nice at our house, too. It's so comfy there. It's handy having our things."

"Luke is fond of the Bennu Society; he's happy to offer indefinite sanctuary to the woman who portrays his favorite deity. Even after he and his assistant return from their vacation in a few months, it will be splendid for us to spend restorative time there. He keeps everything like it was in the past: no TV, no phone, no cancer-causing EMFs anywhere. No Wi-Fi coursing through your veins. That's hard to find."

"But, luv. You want to take a woman dying of cancer away from everyone? I need to keep up visits to the doctor and I'll need hospice. Are you in denial because you don't want to let me go?" I breathed in deeply and waited for pain and tightness. Oddly, nothing.

"Do you want to go back to a toxic life that sickened you? Do you fancy a fag about now?"

"No. I must've kicked the smoking habit without even trying. I guess it was the stress of performing that made me need it?"

"Are you ready for miracle-life to begin?"

"I mean, I fancy a nice lie down about now. Besides, my fave TV program is on tonight and I looked forward to this episode all week. I bought salmon to defrost for lunch tomorrow."

"Is that what you want? A dull, predictable life?"

I'm boring? "Well, no, not dull, exactly."

"Think of the joys of uncertainty. New wonders."

Tearing up, I said, "You're talking to a dying woman here." Going home to die, tick tock, every day worse than the last, while knowing how it would end. Or running to a drafty old castle and going along with Dune arranging my life and death. *Gut feelings are overrated. I guess I should humor him. He doesn't care for it when he doesn't get what he wants.*

Miriam would never turn down something so exciting. She'd kidded me about being a fuddy-duddy. She was such a go-getter, chasing her dreams with all her might, taking whatever adventure came her way. And she admired Dune. The way we shared auras when Miriam waited backstage as my standby made me take on her habits.

"Let's do it." I hugged him while he drove off between the

boulders alongside the narrowing road, under the stars growing clearer as we left the lights of civilization far behind.

"Let's not contact anyone for a while. Make it about you and me. A second honeymoon."

"And then perhaps a death-moon. Realistically."

"Trust the process. I think you might be surprised what sunshine, a chance to do nothing but loving, and fresh meals from the garden will do."

"A break from the news and having to entertain guests."

"Always fancied you as a skiver."

"My pleasure."

"Believe in the message of our show: renewal. You'll be a new woman."

"I do feel healthier. But in other ways, ghastly. I wish I knew medicine for this strange condition. It's like a fugue."

"The lights and the mirrors on stage got to you. Going barmy, are we?" He wiggled his head and lifted his eyes.

I tried to laugh. My stomach knotted up instead. "Dune, this weird thing happened before the show."

"Enjoy your life, Susan. Don't faff around worrying about your dreams. You nodded off before the show. You haven't been sleeping well, have you? Relax. Three. Two. One." He tapped my neck.

No idea what else he said. I trusted him to program my subconscious with something useful, so I cooperated with his hypnosis. When he brought me out of the trance, there was the typical sensation of a mysterious post-hypnotic suggestion. I had an intriguing future ahead of me.

I settled back against the seat. We drove on far across the vivid colors of the heath toward the distant high moors. "I'm a lucky woman." He reached out to touch my breast, as if moving a finger over a flame. I snuggled up to him in the car, the veridian vinyl squeaking.

We drove through higher granite hills, and tufts of trees. I said, "I don't know, I felt . . . lost before the show."

"And now you're found, my love."

"The hecklers were naughty tonight, weren't they? Going on about how they envied us for using so much Moldavite in our shows. And the protest out front was out of hand, worst shilling for Shambhala I've seen so far. That was a great idea to leave out the back to escape them."

"You're welcome."

I added, "The hecklers might have a point, though. The show as propaganda for the Agents of the Nevermind."

"They went too far when they held signs up inside the building. Kept paying audience members from seeing the show they had a right to enjoy."

"Still, they're protesting how the Nevermind got the public to accept proxy wars and coups. You have to admit that the United States Nevermind branch of the Agency destroyed some sweet countries."

He tightened his face so much I got scared he'd fall out of love with me. "We do what we have to do. Being an Agent is grueling, and we risk our lives for the common citizen's welfare. If people don't appreciate what we do to keep our countries running, they can move someplace else."

Neither of us spoke after that. The rolling hills were so enchanting, I let it go for the time being. There it was, in my face. I'd convince him to rethink the Nevermind's ruthlessness one day, but I understood the need for intelligence. The world wasn't rainbows and unicorns. Meanwhile, I drank in the scenery, with pink, purple, rose, green and yellow coloring the moors beneath the full moon. Full shadowy clouds whisked by, the storm gone.

Such empty distances made me lonely. I'd miss Kevin and Miriam, Huld, Norma and the rest. I hadn't had time for friends outside the troupe. Had I? My stomach twitched. "I should have brought books with me. I only had one more chapter in *The Castle of Otranto.*"

"Ah, yes, the book that started the genre of doom. I didn't realize you'd been reading that."

I hit him with the little neck pillow, laughing. He knew, the silly. He'd slipped it in my cubical in the dressing room not long before, and signed it, "With love, from the future." But was it my name he'd inscribed? Odd. Or was it Miriam? I wasn't sure. My brain turned to cotton. "Oh, wait. I'm not. I think Miriam must have mentioned it to me that she was reading it. Er. . . No, that's not it."

"Don't strain yourself."

"I'm gutted. I could have picked up a copy of *Jane Eyre* or *The Fall of the House of Usher* if I'd realized." I hated to admit my fear of being without a character to immerse myself in, even if it was a doomed one. *Dorian Grey* would have been handy. No movies, no TV, to stave off being just me, of living only my life. My hands shook.

"Don't worry. Luke has an excessive library of overwrought literature there. Even *Frankenstein*." He gestured expansively, with his hands off the wheel, speaking with a ghoulish accent. We were far away from traffic on that empty road. "Buahaha."

I refrained from tickling him. That book scared me. I would immerse myself in the story of heroines, and I'd hardly notice dying. That would be all required of me, and that was about all I was ready to handle, anyway: gardening and walking the moors.

"Does he have *Jane Eyre?*"

"His wife read that kind of thing, and he kept her books. I don't remember seeing it around when I visited, but most likely."

How sad, a man alone with so much space. I hoped he'd find someone new before too long. I was knackered: it was hard to keep my eyes open after putting everything I had into my finale. "The families are so far apart," I said, "don't people out here rely on the internet for their social life?"

"No doubt they will soon. It's spotty here and some places have nothing. But they're a solitary lot."

"I hope they get newspaper deliveries every day. Unless they stop paying any attention to the world at large."

"And why not forget? What good does it do them to know what's happening in London?" We passed sheep, white under the moon. Damn. I'd only have books to take me away into the realm of possibilities, into imagination. I'd try to merge into the obscure landscape away from everything, and just not *care*. Just bloody not care.

❄

Rising in elevation, we passed a memorable tor, one of the oddest outcroppings of rocks I'd seen. There were clumps of trees out that way; up ahead was a small forest. Bleary eyes made everything dreamy. My senses heightened when the heath ahead came into focus around an imposing thick shape with rounded edges. The steepest hill around, with rugged, exposed granite on the top, and a large tor in the silhouette of an angel — an Enochian angel, no doubt, hardly able to be patient until that End of the World of which those creatures were so fond. This was as poetic as any to survive some ridiculous Apocalypse.

Dune opened out his right arm in a grand sweeping gesture, presenting me the spectacular view: our destination. . . our destiny. The rough, rude castle looming on the distant horizon could be called, alternatively, "ruins." The palisades, the fence of pales fortifying the castle wore down, replaced centuries ago by the crenellated curtain wall. But otherwise, the castle was intact. The battlement, the rampart topping the castle with regular gaps for firing arrows defined the sky filled with heavy dark clouds, their crests lit up with moonbeams. The crenels and merlons alternated like gap-teeth along the towers.

"Luke's castle is grand. In a decrepit way."

"Fortunately, stone can only decay so much."

We turned into the driveway which was so long could have been called "a road," and halted. We poised between that tor and another one near it, with a puzzling natural pile of rocks eroded into that smoothness. Someone had built a couple cairns and then poured something over them to translate them into sculptures stuck to the ground, impervious to chance. Solid, one big art creation of time and the elements. I wanted to go over to them and rub their smooth surfaces. They'd chill my palm that time of night out there where the wind wept free.

Dune said, "Ready to cross the Threshold?"

"I'm ready. No more stress. Ahhh." An exotic romance with my fit man, to end my days. I'd pretend to be a feudal Lady trapped in her luxurious private bower with a ghost. I'd be an eerie vampire living forever in the mist, or a madwoman in the turret calling out whatever wacky stuff I wanted to echo through the passageways. Castles had the best love scenes. Mystical and urgent, with ambiguous magic opening life to possibilities and forbidden pleasures. Just the artistic tone appropriate for fading into death. My face would grow pale, eyes circled, voice quivering. A true heroine's end of life.

Pointing excitedly, he said, "See the arrow slits? Narrow vertical windows along the walls? The bastions on the corners have such solid masonry it's impossible for anything to get past, ever; the towers' leave no blind spots."

"Well, I guess. It's magnificent architecture. Lighting is amazing, now the moon's out."

"If you pass the initiation, we might move here for the rest of your life. Wouldn't that be lovely?"

I doubted I'd feel like traveling home once my cancer progressed; hopefully Dune would arrange for someone to take care of me.

Wait, initiation? Why ask? I knew by how he said it I'd have to fight the answer out of him. He loved his pranks. Did it involve the equinox? That was a hazing tradition in secret groups like the elusive Bennu Society. Supposedly, members of that occult organization, which conspiracy theorists claimed inhabited the upper echelon of the Nevermind, sometimes came to shows. But no one in the know pointed out members in the audience because their identity must remain anonymous. Whenever Huld smirked about recognizing who they were, I wanted to slap that rascal.

I didn't care for that annoying squint my husband got when he wanted to mystify me, either. There was no getting past it. The dark clouds raced through the sky. Moon beams flashed between them, dappling time.

"If you're not ready to take on your new role out here, the castle will spit you out. Are you ready to go beyond the limits you've always believed yourself to have?"

What the hell did that mean? I wanted to assume he was just getting melodramatic and had been reading some New Age type healer's one-sentence-fits-all arrogant claims about the meaning of illness. So, I said, "Yes. I accept your mighty challenge, your Lordship!" I bent low in the seat in an exaggerated bow.

He held my gaze a long time, without softening his furrowed brows. I maintained my grin. He drove up the driveway far from the road, toward the blustery forest, up the craggy tor and the patched stone walls.

We parked in a huge enclosed lot far from the gray walls with phallic turrets charging toward the moon. Dune explained, "No car park allowed nearby. Luke said it keeps the 'pristine sense of timelessness.'"

"He's quite the poet, isn't he?"

"How can an alchemist living in the most breathtaking countryside on earth not be?"

As we walked, legs covered in spiny plant stickers, we looked like brambles. I got used to the prickles, and I stopped bending to brush them off. I held up my costume. Once my muscular thighs showed, he stopped walking and caressed them, sliding his hand along the smoothness of skin, flaking the stickers off.

"See how some walls slope outward at the bottom? Those are taluses."

"Why slope? Because that's the most important part to make thick, so the enemy couldn't break through?"

"Exactly. Logistics of attack equipment trying to get high enough to reach the windows doesn't work. But the best part is that the people defending the castle can drop rocks from those brettices up there; see, things that look like loos? But don't worry, there's no shit falling through those. So, what would happen when the rocks drop from them, or thrown over the walls?"

"Seems like a bad idea. The rocks would never reach the attackers. I don't get it."

He laughed, more animated than I'd ever seen him. "Because of the slant of the wall, the rock breaks when it hits the talus! Into a million pieces of shrapnel flying out at them. Ha *Ha!*"

That was funny? Here I was, considering castles romantic, and what he was into was how to murder people and poopie. A man thing.

"Wait, you're saying if I walk around the castle, there will be piles of poop?"

"There will. Best not to walk under the latrines. Shit falls into the pits underneath. Luke doesn't put that in the gardens, no worries. He covers it over."

"Well, that's a relief." *Um, not all that relieved, luv.*

The few windows were high up, cramped, heavy glass, with iron bars across the lower ones; only the ones at the top had no glass, the overhangs slanting over them to keep out even rainstorms. The shapes formed by the iron in between the tiny sections were unusual enough I memorized them as we walked toward them. "Do the window designs mean something?"

"Yes. Good question, Susan. Everything in the entire building means something to a scholar. The code is based on the philosophy of numerology."

I'd learned quite a few arcane facts from analyzing the background of our performances, so this could be more fun than working crossword puzzles. "Like when Freemasons carried over the pagan traditions driven underground? When they . . . encoded the ancient beliefs using numerology into the ratios of height and width of Catholic cathedrals?" It was such a weird concept that I had trouble expressing it in words. I moved my hands around in the shapes of squares and circles, trying to get a point across that way. Speaking: so frustrating!

"And the Masons say sacred geometry construction has existed since people escaped from Atlantis when it flooded and they went to Egypt. They encoded the secrets of the dead culture into the Pyramid and the Sphinx."

I chortled. "Yeah, right. Quite some 'facts,' there. Like all those failed predictions that doofus Edgar Cayce made?" I swayed my hip out to bump it into Dune, pushing him while I winked. "That he was wrong doesn't matter, s'all tickety-boo anyway, right?" I used to think Cayce was just a simple Christian country doctor who got his answers from the air during trances until I discovered he'd read all that stuff when studying Theosophy. But teasing didn't seem like the *impressed* mood for which Dune was angling.

Silent, his lips tightened. But if he didn't want a fact-based, irreverent woman unafraid to speak her mind, he shouldn't have married one. Why did he marry me, anyway? Hell, when did he marry me? I didn't even remember our wedding. I gazed off into the distance, trying to place what church we went to, who we invited, what I was wearing. I knew he'd been in a relationship with my twin sister, Sylvia, before me, when I was her standby. Until she died before going on stage.

My memory of her death came in flashes of newspaper articles. While I was wracking my brain, I stopped bothering to pay attention to whatever rot he was spouting off. I decided it wasn't worth getting worked up over, and I bent and picked a lavender flower. I stared into the mandala of its center, breathing its smiling perfume.

The key Dune took out of his pocket caught my eye. I delighted at the inventive shape. I would have loved playing with it as a girl. "It's an alchemical sigil," he said, "and it doesn't work in the way a normal key does. It uses a complex set of directions. As he opened the thick door, reinforced with iron and unpleasant looking spikes darkened with ancient blood, he cautioned, "The rule is that this door has to remain locked from the inside, and I protect the key in a place you must never mess with. You understand, darling?"

"What do you mean? I come and go as I please."

"No, you don't. That's not how this castle works. We're guests here. We go by the rules."

"I'm not a go-by-the-rules woman."

"You are now." He flipped the keys high in the air and caught them with flair.

As suave as that glint in his eyes was, it made me determined. It was his fantasy to spend the rest of my days there. It became my fantasy to leave one day. And not in a hearse.

CHAPTER 5
MYSTERIOUS REFLECTIONS

Once inside the long, curved overhang of the door, he said, "Luke left the portcullis up so we could enter."

I didn't care.

He ignored my scowl and said, "You're in for a treat. Wait here while I activate an ingenious design. But get no closer to the doorway. Wait here; I'm off to the guardroom."

Grunting from the exertion, he pulled and yanked on ropes connected to a winch. The architecture was fantastic, kept as it had been when built centuries in the past by Luke's ancestors as a small family fortress. The sparse furniture was antique, nothing fancy and delicate, spiky or detailed. Everything was blunt, thick, and utilitarian, the only things of unusual value being paintings I spied in the hallway.

I covered my ears against a high-pitched sound above the door, metal on metal, and a row of spikes appeared from above the doorway sliding fast. The spikes attached to a grid that prevented enemies from entering. A second portcullis ten meters from where the first grid fell.

"Brilliant, isn't it? This way, you trap the invader. The arrow slits along the sides of the walls. Archers attacked them while they were trapped in there. And from up there, people threw burning wood from the fireplace." It went so fast, I didn't pay enough attention to satisfy him. "I'll show you later, luv." He looked disappointed that I wasn't excited by the means of killing. His voice lost some of its boyish animation.

As if I were a child, he tried to engage my interest. "Here's a quiz. Do you know why the spiral staircases go clockwise?"

"That I know. Because most people are right-handed. So, if they're holding a sword and trying to run up the stairs, it's going to be awkward. If someone is coming down the stairs with a sword, he'll have the advantage."

"Ah, I love you, Susan. That's my girl." He patted me; his eyes lit up again.

I did so fancy times when we got along. He charmed me. We walked upstairs and passed through the solar (the bedroom), the great chamber, and the granary without comment. Wattle and daub interior walls seemed warmer than the stone. I pushed open an extension of the solar suite, the wardrobe. But I closed it, not wanting to snoop through Luke's clothing.

Fine fabric draped over his arm, he said, "The dresses belonged to his wife, Martha. She died a long time ago, so they're not in fashion. But, they're timeless. Elegant, yes?"

"We have the same build." I started to try one on, but Dune hesitantly reached out to take it. "I'm not sure if it's OK. He's attached to them."

"I won't get it dirty. I want to wear it around the halls. It seems so . . . castley."

His face screwed up. He paced the hallway but came in and relented. "Let me show you your room."

"My bower?"

"Exactly, my Lady." He carried the dress and pushed open a door leading off the solar. Tickled by the garment chests, old benches, and the thick bed with a pink blanket, I tried on the dress.

“Luke can’t stand mirrors,” he said. “I’ll be your reflection.”

When I modeled it for him, turning this way and that, he said, “It was made for you.”

I was thrilled by having my space, even if I might never withdraw into it.

“He kept her paperbacks. You may enjoy the Mary Stewarts.”

"Nice to know he admires a famous female author."

"It's not just that. After White’s *The Once and Future King* made Arthurian legends popular, she pushed that British-ego narrative. Stewart’s *Merlin Chronicles* riffed off Geoffrey of Monmouth’s *History of the Kings of Britain.*”

I chortled. “History, you say! Like Monmouth’s *Historia Brittonum*, the handy genealogy for Welsh princes?”

He reprimanded me. “You’ve made a living the last couple years because of the tales of Camelot. Dancing those utopian fantasies has been euphoric: you said so yourself. So, why so cynical? Lighten up and enjoy the folly.”

Damp, heavy, smelled of wet mossy stone. Echoes, too complex, went on too long.

We opened heavy doors and windows for freshness, so the mustiness tickled noses less. The cold remained, as if in an underground cave. With no electricity or running water, we lit large hanging candles along the rough wall with the matches provided, though it took many tries because of the damp.

With a mischievous look, he asked, “Want to see some murder holes?”

“Do I?” I *supposed* that was my idea of fun.

He took me to a barbican and said, “In most Medieval passageways, they left holes. Now, visualize the olden days, when the opposition is approaching. You can send missiles out through these openings. Or rocks. Hot sand, boiling water.” He looked so damn delighted! “Even carcasses. Shit. Boiling water or tar. Ha *ha!* Brilliant, eh? And they didn’t just put holes in the barbicans, but also in . . .” Who knows what he was blathering on about?

To enjoy a place made of gruesome ways to kill each other, I had to embrace its gory past. When I saw the old dark blood staining the stone, I hoped the gore stayed nicely in the past where it belonged. Britain had become a civilized place with reasonable laws, admirable human rights, and progressive social reform. *Everything will be fine.*

❄

As we explored down the hall, we passed a polished display: a suit of armor on a mannequin on a stand. As I brushed against it, I thought I heard a drop of water landing on the metal. I glanced up but saw no leak. Spooky old castle. Made me want to settle in, dress in flannel pajamas, sip hot chocolate and tell ghost stories around the fireplace.

Then, I shuddered, dizzy. *I don't like hot chocolate, though, do I? Where did that thought come from?*

As we approached the end of the passageway, we came upon a cracked, off-kilter painting of Roger Bacon, the thirteenth century Franciscan friar. He was in the amusing act of using alchemy to convert people to Catholicism. His method? Mirrors and elixirs. Above him in the composition an uncomfortable piece of Heaven broke off and fell to Earth as a meteorite.

I felt uneasy, because I eerily seemed to remember *Miriam* reading about Bacon. Sitting at her table. As if I were sitting there. The disconnection made me nauseous.

"And this one is a Golden Dawn rendition of an Egyptian priest." A gold sculpture of the familiar flamingo god rising from its ashes.

How interesting that Luke also liked Bennu. I wouldn't have predicted a random friend would be into that obscure deity when living so far out in that part of the country, one of the last areas without internet reception. But reception was expected soon.

People out there would transform. Dress like celebrities. They'd forget their rules. Plastic all the way.

When I fondled the elaborate frame, exclaiming over the modernized paint job, Dune indicated his distaste of its garish design. In the earth-toned oils, the priest's eyes closed in meditation as he worked, his mouth open chanting Egyptian words stylized above him. He leered.

Remembering a fun fact I'd read in a newspaper, I said, "Flamingos are kinky. They can only have sex during orgies." Or was it *Miriam* who had read it? I wanted to bang my head against the wall.

"We might manage that," he declared. He leaned in close and kissed me hard.

Paint on the symbols above Bacon had flaked off. It had landed ingloriously on Bacon's eye, sticking out from the canvas, as if applying false eyelashes.

"Is Luke worried about the neighbors stealing the canvases, I wonder?"

"The art pieces are registered to this location."

"What, how?"

"There's a database of important historical original paintings. And besides, even if they considered stealing them to sell on the black market, the famous 'Curse of the Pendergast Castle' would give them something to think about."

"Guess it's not like paintings of historical occult figures are on the radar of folks out here, anyway."

"Right. They're figuring how to keep the trees from getting the blight. They're sleeping out with the sheep to prevent wolves from eating them. What's worth taking here is Moldavite, which is why he made up the ghost curse." I didn't like his laugh, his angular face, his mouth turned down and casting shadows. "Chumps."

"There are some lovely pieces here?"

Searching my face as we wandered, he added, "After our little caper." He winked conspiratorially.

Do I feel slinky or ragamuffin? I liked it when he congratulated me, and I enjoyed being in on little mischievous secrets together. I grinned and winked back. I'd think hard on it and relive what he was on about. Sometimes memories came back when I lay in bed, concentrating.

With only 275 tons of Moldavite in the world, its value is astronomical, and with no more available, I wondered if I should hide the Grail. "A friend has a Moldavite necklace. I think she got it out of a gum machine."

"Bah!" He started to spit. "Listen, Susan, seventy-five percent of the Moldavite you see out there is fake. Green glass. Easy to prove. It's *worthless*."

Something soft against my ankle pummeled my foot. I yelled and jumped back. Two rambunctious rats turned my shoe into a carnival. Dune stomped the main attraction. Their blood squirted and oozed as the show ended. I gave the shivers a run for their money.

I did my best to hide my shaking while Dune grandly showed me everything between the entryway and the bedroom. After such a long drive, I dragged. It was an old brute of a castle, with thick, primitive walls, not like the fairy tale kind. When I sneezed, he put his arms around me for warmth, guiding me through the gloom that the candle he carried only taunted.

A crow flew toward us cawing along the hallway. Dune left me to open the door for it. It cawed at us, over and over. He closed and bolted the door in exasperation.

"Can't you leave it ajar for the poor creature?"

"I'm not taking any chances on anyone coming in." Dune could be such a downer.

"What? There's no one. How could there be?" I opened my eyes wide, but nothin' doing.

The way he watched me with unwavering hard eyes, I felt silly for trying to dissuade him. "This is our fortress, and it will stay so. No church people trying to save us, no letters, no unexpected guests, no stalking fans, no meddling friends. We don't even have mail delivered or trash picked up. I'll go into so-called-town for that. If you hear anyone knock I'll dispense with the bother, you understand?"

"I haven't invited anyone." And I wouldn't, without phones or service, or any kind of internet reception. One of the few wild places left, something to cherish. Still, I wanted to write Kevin a letter to apologize for Dune's rudeness. "So, there's no phone book? I want an address."

"No."

"I'll look up the addy at the post office, I guess."

"Even better, I'll do it when I take it, gentleman that I am. You can just enjoy yourself here. I aim to accommodate: you love to be alone."

Did I? I must have forgotten.

The doors had symbols carved onto them, convoluted shapes I didn't understand. Paint peeled off, moss growing on centuries of grime eroded rock.

In one painting, the author known as "Shakespeare," while holding the alchemical Philosopher's Stone, stood proudly with that con artist extraordinaire, Edward Kelley. The world wouldn't be as interesting if Kelley hadn't made up those Enochian angels, that's for sure.

But if I didn't want Dune to get peeved, I had to pretend to believe Kelley was on the up and up when he stared into the scrying stone and saw angels. I had to act like it was perfectly believable that they taught him a language to communicate with them, so they could bring on a nicer, gentler Apocalypse. It was core to the Bennu troupe's performances. So, what the hell?

Edward Kelley's deformation was obvious in the detailed painting; he'd had his ears chopped off by Emperor Rudolf for failing to come through on one of the alchemical proofs that

Rudolf financed him to produce. They locked up Kelley in the castle in Prague, both his legs severed when he attempted escape. According to folks like Vincent Bridges, he'd supposedly succeed a few times in making gold for reliable witnesses, though the stories didn't convince me.

Dune offered, "That time when Kelley gave it a go, I'll bet the alchemical stone had been touched along the way to the court. That renders it ineffective for producing gold."

"Or," I said, chuckling, "Kelley used gold plating to make it appear he made gold."

"But if it wasn't for him and John Dee and their students, we wouldn't have Rosicrucianism, now, would we?"

Memories of a documentary flashed through my head, dizzying me with images of gold vapor in meteoric glass of Templars, Kelley's red powder.

"On our trip to the Moldavite Museum, you hadn't expected the anti-climactic size of the stones. Until you realized how heavy they were."

I didn't remember, but I was glad I'd gotten to go. That must have been a pleasantly educational outing.

I was used to going along with whatever Dune said. I pretended to believe in an afterlife, in ghosts and angels, and all sorts of illogical things. Themes of our performances centered on people like Kelley's henchman, the Welshman John Dee, Queen Elizabeth's mathematician, geographer, navigator, magician, philosopher, and spy. I humored Dee and Kelley's adorable mysticism, because Dune idolized them.

Yet, as I stood there, I pondered. Why had I believed Bennu performances were Avant-Garde whimsy? We apparently performed public rituals within secret society traditions to impart encoded mysteries to initiates with open eyes.

I suspected that it functioned as the alchemical Sun and Miriam the Moon. Merged through our auras during the shows, we held together the power of the rites. Like the positive and negatively charged magnetic pole of the spinal column through which the universal forces flashed: I was the head. She was the butt. My arm muscles tightened.

"Here's the Chintamani Stone," he said, pointing to a painting in need of restoration.

"The Buddhist equivalent of the Philosopher's Stone?"

He cocked his head, watching my face for signs of recognition, I assumed, to see if I had dementia. He explained things that he and I had spoken of throughout our marriage, when we attended conferences: "King Solomon, Genghis Khan, and Akbar the Great had the Moldavite, and a part of it was at the League of Nations."

I hadn't realized that. "Why is it such a big deal?"

"Freemasons said aliens from the Blazing Star Sirius's White Lodge sent the Stone from Heaven here."

I snorted at that and then looked faux-serious.

"The aliens brought it to Earth to facilitate a globalist One World Order."

"Oh, *did* they, now?" Sometimes my husband just took things way too far.

"One world, ruled by those who have mastered the alchemical powers. Once the transformation is complete, the world will see us for who we are." His chin rose too high. I wondered if he'd been sleeping enough.

Us? Did he mean the Agents? The Bennu troupe? Him and me? The UK? Whatever it was, I hoped he'd get off it soon. Speak of a high horse. He was flyin' and neighin'!

I turned at the next hallway, holding his hand and pulling him behind me but it too led us to a dead end. He treated me like a child when he took my arm and directed me back the way we came.

"Can you show me where Luke does his alchemy stuff? And the Moldavite?"

"I'll show you on the equinox. The oratory is where Luke and his assistant Tommy make the monoatomic gold and iridium powders and such. Do not, I repeat, do not go there alone. Moldavite, after it's charged with the proper spiritual ritual, *is* the Grail. It's our Grail Room. You're not allowed in there, at least not yet."

"Creepy. You mean like the Wewelsburg Castle that had a room in it for King Arthur's Holy Grail because the Nazis believed that utopian Thule was Atlantis? And they wanted to ask the giant super-humans from Atlantis to help them win the war."

"You'll learn what most people other than a few experts have figured out about how Moldavite alchemy produced gold in the past."

"Otherwise, how could the alchemists have earned their royal funding?" I was half-sarcastic.

"Exactly. And why would they have continued if it never worked? Without that guarded secret, it didn't succeed, so it attracted con artists of the worst ilk.

"They invented science, didn't they?"

"See, they weren't all bad. Luke trained with the Cathars and the Knights Templar, which nearly killed him."

"That's intense."

"It's dangerous to do the lunar extraction wrong; toxins can kill a person if space and time are rent. He's lucky to be alive."

"Oh my." I restrained a snicker.

"Lunar extraction extracts the monoatom's spirits."

"Does it, now?"

"Yes, by polarizing the moon to create the solvent and coagulate the auric ethers of the universe."

I drew him to me to stop him speaking.

But after a kiss he continued. "That's why Moon Miriam had to be prepared."

How was she prepared? Gah! A mystery, as usual. I drew my lips back, and I'm sure they became less pleasing.

I've read that we are always attracted to people most like us. But it was more than that. I could see inside her soul. And I didn't even believe in souls. Her soul stormed wild and untamed. How could I blame Dune for noticing her?

Hunger made me cranky, wanting to lash out against his blind belief in the bloody arrogant mysticism that justified intervening in countries to steal their resources. The foundation of our troupe's plays.

Dune said, "The elixir, prepared from Moldavite and administered with the right invocations allowed adepts to see the past and the future, to become immortal, therefore, at least in consciousness, if not in body."

"Sure thing."

"See, here, the aura of the stone is immense: that's where its true power is, not in the physical manifestation of the chemical elements."

"Well, immortality is nice in a novel." But come on. I'd just about had it. Could we go on vacation to a tropical island?

A huge gilded portrait dominated the solar of the Elizabethan spymaster: Sir Francis Walsingham, who set up an international network of secret agents, including occultists. I remembered the history in some detail, considering it was the subject of our skits dramatizing the supremacy of British royalty.

Next to the painting of Walsingham, William Cecil calmly ignored the Enochian angels flying around his head. Dune said, "You're familiar with Enochian history. But did you know that the spymaster Walsingham had brought in Dr. John Dee to the service of his country because Dee told William Cecil that, while he was traveling, he'd found a book by Abbot Trimethus? The book laid out the method of writing esoteric ciphers."

"Esoteric ciphers, oh boy! Just what every spymaster needs most."

"William Cecil asked him to turn them into a spy code. When Dee adapted the cryptography, he passed it to Walsingham, who gave the codes to the secret agents."

Ah yes, those predecessors of the Agents of the Nevermind. It all came down to manipulating people's minds for the sake of gaining power and resources. Dee created legends to claim Queen Elizabeth's right to rule over whoever she wanted. He used his role as Queen Elizabeth's court astrologer to pass along intelligence from Europe. Dee created all sorts of fakery, including that Tudor lineage reached to the Trojan myth of Brutus.

I had a hard time pretending to admire Dee in interviews. Then, the reporters would just leave that part out of the interview anyway, so they had space to focus on my upswept hairstyle.

Dee also said, "Sure, no records of King Arthur going to North America exist, but who cares?"

Dee made up a Welsh prince named Madoc since Dee wanted to get not only the English but the Welsh to support colonization. He claimed Arthur and his mate Madoc had discovered America! So that meant they owned America. TaDa!

Another painting was the pseudo-historian, Geoffrey of Monmouth from the twelfth century who went on about how British Tudors came from Wales and Troy. He held up his book, with light emanating from his eyes. The ghost of King Arthur stood behind him beaming like an old grandfather.

Dune said, "According to Dee, their royalty brought back the Trojan golden age."

Destiny! And Elizabeth, since her ancestor was King Arthur, had the right to *everything*. Handy. Dune kept standing there waiting for me to praise that crook. Um, no.

Instead, I noted, "So, no picture of the Desmond Geraldine family on the wall, hmm?" I mean, I didn't care. I liked the royal family fine, and I was proud of England. I loved it deeply. One rival family pretending to descend from King Arthur was about as stupid as any other. A lad didn't see eye to eye with the favored historian, Monmouth, so he wrote his own pseudo-history book indicating the Irish Geraldine family was in line for the throne -- according to the magician, Merlin, naturally. "But, waddaya gonna do?"

He scowled, flipping his dark hair, his face especially angular. "Your American accent could use some work. Oh, wait a minute. Your accent would sound like this," and he switched to a loutish Irish accent, "if Elizabeth I hadn't won the Desmond Wars against the Irish Catholic family. Rituals, Rosicrucianism, astrology, myth, scrying, alchemy, and cabala put her on the throne. And Luke's ancestors helped."

King Arthur enhanced our show's athletic dance moves. But the way his legend had been used to lord it over other people was a different matter. "Yes, the epitome of Mystical Imperialism, based on nonsense. Fooling people to assume it's true."

"You have a problem with wealthy secret societies waging an occult war?" He looked around us, guiding my eyes to follow his. We surveyed our surroundings made possible by secret society occult wars.

"A war against the Desmond Geraldine family over the right to rule? Because they were Tudors, so naturally descendants of King Arthur?"

"That tactic worked, didn't it?"

"Maybe people should rule a country based on merit and promise. Not legend."

"It's hard to picture you as a Republican, Susan. I know you enjoy the spectacle of a waving queen."

"Oh, sorry, sorry." I didn't want to confuse him by being inconsistent. When a man marries you, he expects you to keep to your principles. Still.

Dune carried water in a pewter pitcher, with the angle of his torso as he poured it worthy of a painting. He then left, with a gallant air in his yellow suit, to the car to fetch suitcases. Touchingly, he'd remembered many of my things on the trip. Hair ties, facial scrub. The perfume was rubbish. I'd pour it out where he wouldn't notice.

I half expected the bed to be dour stone, but it was inviting, an unfamiliar substance.

"Are there any tours? This place is a museum. You'd make a brilliant tour guide if you ever want to retire here."

Dune said, "The curse keeps snoops away. People get the feeling castles are public domain. Like it's their right to intrude on private property. They'd never dream of knocking on their neighbors' door, right?"

"Too bad. So much land around for teaching the different micro-climates. What's the curse?"

"Wouldn't you like to know?" he said, reminiscent of a high school girl.

I picked up novels on the shelf by the bed. I flipped through *The Strange Case of Dr. Jekyll* and *Mr. Hyde.* The curvilinear ink illustrations intrigued me more than investing my concentration in the past's stilted prose and dramatic emotions at that late hour. I prepared to immerse myself in the history of occult propaganda and mystical secrets. I needed answers. What the hell was going on?

❄

A Lady, I held my dress as I roamed on violet, yellow, maroon. I drew water from the well, my arms pumping away their goosebumps as I surveyed curved concentric stone walls along overgrown terraces. Tears won the battle against my eyes. A swooping peregrine falcon startled me. I couldn't help shrieking. I prompted a wolf howl nearby.

In the well house, I discovered a candle and lit it with a match from a wrought iron box. I paused some distance from the well to wash off my pancake make-up, pouring cold water from the ladle into my hands. The water had a blood-rusty tinge of iron oxide, with a scent to match.

I stared into the depths. An owl hooted above me, making me start nearly out of my skin.

Overlaying my reflection, a ghostly image: a translucent

female body disappearing, the moon's roundness obscuring her visage.

I jumped with a gasp, and hugged myself, shivering harder than ever.

I was letting my imagination run away with me. Had cancer progressed to dementia so soon?

I dashed home. I wanted a moat around my overactive mind. I'd throw myself into it and get muddy and splash like a wild pig.

❄

That night, Dune seemed like a distant species. I lay, eyes open, unable to sleep. He tried to embrace me, but his smell assaulted my senses. His hairiness inexplicably astonished me, yet his chest fascinated me with its maleness. I imagined him overtaking me. His fur pressing against me. Mentally, I rehearsed being close.

Something felt wrong. When Dune approached me, his passion brushing up against my thigh, I turned away. The wind moaned, and the walls moaned back, shadows in the dark. A draft made me shiver. A tree hit the wall below us over and over, scraping, and banging. The woods beside the castle on the gray tor above the moors creaked. Branches fell, cracking. The sound of a broken limb banging against a tree trunk wouldn't let me sleep.

Lying there any longer was impossible. I craved the secrets of that exotic location. There was nothing but the surroundings to relieve the astringency in my bones, the acid in my blood, the angst in my muscles.

CHAPTER 6
DIFFERENT

While Dune slept, I wandered the halls, carrying the candle toward the forbidden oratory.

The poor crow flying around has to be what's making the noises I can't place.

That castle would be rough to grow up in. Poor Luke never got to be normal. The nearest neighbor was probably a crabby, stinky old man. I understood how Luke grew so attached to his wife that he saved her clothes. How he'd grow keen on keeping the family history alive when that was all he had. That was more poignant than the online dating of today when people swipe on a myriad of potential dates a day. If one doesn't work out, countless others have posted fetching half dressed photos.

I didn't miss electricity but rather welcomed the chance return to a romantic era. So, why did the castle disturb me? Superstitions meant nothing. Sure, the existence of auras, telepathy, precognitive dreams, remote viewing, miraculous healing, scrying vision and clairvoyance made life rich.

An afterlife didn't convince me. But apparently some amount of the auric substance stayed behind after death. I struggled not to contemplate dying because of the loss of my twin Sylvia's life.

My week in the castle made me wonder if she'd become a ghost. I heard her tinkling laugh and glimpsed her silvery hair flashing in the moonlight as I woke once.

Breathing in Sylvia's aura before Bennu shows as her standby made us so close I hardly recalled her as a separate being. The newspapers made it out to be a scandal that when she collapsed and died right before going on, I didn't skip a beat to take over, so the audience enjoyed the evening. That's what being a responsible standby is. Playing the Bennu reborn. I gave them brilliant entertainment. Sharing auras was profound. I massaged muscles around my mouth. Enjoying my vacation took focus.

Because Dune saw auras well, he described what our auras did, how bits stuck to chairs after we stood, how they pulled back from people we suspected, and drifted toward individuals who appealed to us. A person vampirized someone else's energy accidentally. Part of an aura shot over to someone else we cared for and chose to help or warn. He'd seen bits of auric substance linger after the death of folk with which we worked, hanging around their belongings for months if we didn't clear the space with sage and make it dissipate.

The hallway labyrinthine, I peeked into rooms, looking for the old chapel, or oratory as it was called in a castle. Memorizing my way took time. Would Dune come for me?

When I opened the door to a different room I was assaulted by complex odors thickening the air. I paused in the doorway, parsing out the pungent, sweet, peppery, and then aromatic alcohol scents, one after another. Yes, for major rituals. Frankincense was burning on charcoal, something Dune must have lit before retiring to bed. So, this was his private study when he wasn't deigning to grace me with his presence.

Some animal lived there. I had no idea Luke was a pet kind of bloke. I pictured him maybe with a peregrine falcon, but not fluffy kittens. I speculated about what inhabited it; there was a water bowl, a leash, smelly rags, soft dirty wool bedding pile, and sealed packets of food. The rations were substantial enough that it had to be a large creature. That explained the sounds I'd heard! I'd love to visit and pet whatever it was. I needed something to keep me company.

Something underneath the ground silently signaled to me. I had no idea how to answer it back. How does one speak to silence? Its presence washed over me, and I felt as if had become a negative of a photograph. I became nothing but the pale nightgown I wore trailing through indeterminate mist.

I perused details of the oratory. Too much to take in at once. I started with one corner. I studied furniture, grounding myself in the ancient cloths, the circular drawings on the floor filled in with golden images of Enochian angels, and sigils. On the wall was Camelot and the sword Excalibur being pulled from the stone, with the large piece of Moldavite dull in its handle, signifying the return of Atlantis had begun. And Stonehenge with druids did ceremonies, with that favorite British esoteric quirk, ley lines, painted in, crossing the landscape, emanating into the air.

The library was fascinating. Lots of books on magick. A book on English aristocracy like the Astors who were pro-Germany during WWII. They shared the Nazis' occult interests, such as Shambhala. I picked it up and smelled. That wonderful musty scent, so different from an e-book, that's for sure.

A tome on the esoteric secrets the secret society Golden Dawn had encoded in Enochian chess. A book on the methods of creating golems, tulpas, fake ghosts, and egregores by getting multiple people together to focus their attention on the auric substance making up the invisible ethers of the universe. The people would then imprint their strong belief in a being coming into existence. That seemed a nice way to create imaginary friends and make them so *su*bstantial that they'd sing to you and play with you.

Crowley's *Moonchild* looked intriguing. I slowed myself, so words stopped jumping on the page of his novel based on real life magickians' sex magick. I saw a stack of handmade paper and a quill. I made notes on the book. I didn't want Dune to find the page, so I searched for a hiding place. When I found a pack of old papers covered in enough dust, I was sure no one bothered with that corner; I stuck it inside.

I noticed a strange switchback staircase that zig zagged seven times. Those stairs for miniature people had no railings, no reasons for the turns.

I hesitantly climbed the bizarre steps, as I only had to raise my foot a couple inches to the next one where I fit the ball of my foot. I slowed and took step by step, holding my breath while regaining my patience. I remembered that the castle was the embodiment of initiation. Perhaps this was a Jacob's ladder ritual.

I memorized the numbers of steps going up to the platform, forming an Aztec sacrifice flat-top, then descended. I anticipated that coming in handy someday. The castle was living sacred geometry initiation.

As I walked toward the stairs, balancing, my footsteps echoed more with each step. The pause before each echo grew longer. Echoes came out-of-step.

I stopped; the echoes of my footsteps didn't.

Spinning around, I clumsily knocked over a suit of armor on the stand, sending it clattering. I hadn't even noticed it was there. How could I explain to Dune if it had gotten dented? Still, if armor couldn't stand a fall, what was the point of wearing it?

Sounds somewhere, maybe the crow, scared me so much that I fled. My heart beat and I couldn't stand being alone around whatever was happening. I stumbled, landing hard on the ground. This was appalling. How did that explain the reason for the fallen armor? Dune would have to guess I'd invaded the forbidden zone. I hoped he didn't go in often. He'd think it caught draft, or a ghost tumbled it.

I crept into the solar and eased myself under the bedding. Dune woke only enough to turn over and lay his arm over me. *I'll tell him the crow must have flown in. No, how would a crow get in? Hm. The armor has a faulty stand; it falls over. So, when Dune comes across it, he won't think anything. How would I know that?* No, I had to return, tie a rope to the armor and leverage, setting it back into place before Dune found it.

I persuaded myself the sounds were imagination due to sleep deprivation. I couldn't tell Dune. Dune's fault for fussing with the armor display. I kept my eyes closed against the castle drafts. I uncurled, stopped hugging myself, kicked off hot covers, leaving only the raw wool sheet and lay flat, slipping into unconsciousness.

I fought the sheet in a fitful dream of performing on stage while being thrown shockingly white roses. The flowers shrank as they flew towards me instead of the expected optical perspective of growing larger. When they reached me, the pricks of the thorns jabbed my forehead. They pierced the quantum foam, the minuscule wormholes at the center of each bubble-like bit of the universe.

Through the wormhole came another reality. Lucid, off and on, flashing in and out, I became immersed in a crow pie. I writhed in red mushroom and black crow filling, as it roiled below bumpy uneven crust rising with the heat, popping with little boil bubbles in the oven. With each pop, the air leaving the pie liberated into the ethers.

I threw the roses back and as they soared through the air, they became blackest black. Sylvia said, "Try it. You'll like it. You'll never have to be alone."

❄

"... The Philosopher's Stone. Moldavite." Dune's droning voice swelled louder as I broke through the fog into waking. "How do you like your necklace?" He was talking, next to me. It was dawn. Dune continued: "A very rare quality of Moldavite. Nice mushroom shape, isn't it?"

Rubbing my eyes, I exclaimed, "Oh! How charming. Thank you!" I became someone else in my dreams. I traced the amanita sculpted from Moldavite, the edges of it sharp under my fingers as I caressed bumps on its surface. Who had I been?

Dune smiled, cocking his head elegantly. "I'm here to fulfill your desires."

"I'll take it."

"Getting what you want isn't always what it's cracked up to be." Outside the solar door, a loud, sudden whack, then a dull thud against the floor. Dune jumped up and raced to the hallway. "The trapped crow," he said. I wanted to throw the bird a funeral. Luke would have. But Dune added, "You should cook the damn thing into a pie."

After so little sleep, I shook. A different persona than expected. I wished I remembered more. I slapped my cheeks to bring blood to redden them. I massaged under my chin to drain the fluids. I hoped to look appealing enough that Dune wrapped his robust arms around me and made me safe. I was a shy virgin before, easing into being with him in a new place.

But that morning, I was ready. What had altered? My dreams, going in and out of Sylvia. Surely a common phenomenon for identical twins, after time in the womb. Splitting from one being.

I remembered a dream. Before I woke, I'd been in a car, half naked, being touched in a way that heightened my senses everywhere. The slow drip of water on my body took me into the moment and my anxiety of wishing to move forward, learn answers, be great . . . It all dissolved into enjoying my skin, my nails, the delicious water down my breast and onto my nipple. Someone blew on my nipple as the water dripped, the coolness fantastic. When he lifted his face, under his sandy hair I saw no face, only Sylvia's hand over it, concealing his identity.

I wanted to freshen up. Dowdiness wasn't the best ploy to

attain that extravagant love. I wasn't sure Medieval life was for me. Cold, damp, drafty, and just plain spooky. Unable to find mirrors anywhere, I searched for a reflective surface. Proud of my resourcefulness, I decided I'd use a pewter tray.

Dune spotted me polishing it with a sleeve. After he asked what I was doing, I regretted informing him. Raising his voice, he grabbed it away from me, rubbing skin off my knuckles. He ignored when I exclaimed and rubbed them.

"No mirrors here!" he shouted. "What's wrong with you, woman? Come into a magical world and disturb the way it's always been. No mirrors, no electricity, no . . ."

"Who said I wanted electricity? Have I complained about it once?" He closed his mouth. I smelled him more. I advised him, "You could do with tidying up, yourself, you know. Your hair's sticking up and you stink." I wasn't used to being so brash, and I sought to laugh it off, but he closed in on me.

He spanked me once on the buttocks. He agreed. "Fine. If I put make-up on you before you look in the mirror." He'd never done that. After he finished, he reluctantly held the tray up for me to fix my hair. He held a candle, so I piled it on my head in a way appropriate for such a quaint abode. He refused to hold the candle close enough to be of much use, and I barely recognized myself in the broken collage of dull hammered metal.

I enjoyed the crystal toiletries Dune laid out. I didn't want to inquire if he'd bought them new as a present. I didn't want to be rude and unappreciative if he had. My jewelry looked exciting. I breathed in the scents and closed my eyes, beaming. I opened them to see his face close as he caressed my hair.

I danced barefoot along open spaces, leaping into cobwebs, twirling, focusing on objects to keep from getting dizzy. A wooden broom-handle. A huge pounded copper bowl glinted from the flames. An iron poker on a rack by a fireplace reminded me of home. I wasn't about to lose all those years of daily training and let muscles atrophy altogether, so I worked myself into a sweat. The floor was cold, hard, some places rough, others slippery. I slid with zest. I threw myself against the hallway, in between each warmly lit painting, the colors rich and layered, cracking but dusted now, favoring deep dark red, down the row.

I flipped between each painting, my body slapping against the wall in between them. John Dee, me. The cool hard surface of the frame growing dustier beneath my fingers than we arrived the night before. Aleister Crowley, me. I bugged my eyes out at his portrait when I rolled past it, sticking my jaw at that crazy secret agent. Vincent Bridges, the alchemy historian who maintained the Moldavite from heavens was the catalyst that explain Edward Kelley's alchemical success. Me.

I reveled in the chance to do whatever I chose, with no responsibilities and not even Dune to bother with. He invested a lot of time doing whatever out of sight. Perfect. I'd return to the oratory and set the armor display upright before Dune discovered I'd been poking around.

I sneaked through the hallways, barefoot, toward the oratory, carrying a rope. Life was fun! When I approached the room, I heard noises. I wasn't sure if it was coming from the oratory or near to it, but Dune was obviously close. I took off running back to where I'd been dancing. I started dancing again as if I'd never missed a beat in case Dune was coming. That was a close call. Well, time to enjoy luxuriating in the glories of Medieval architecture.

When Dune came in later and I was flitting about, he laughed and kissed me by a painting of Sir Francis Bacon, John Dee's partner in crime. The rich shade of scarlet that inspired me. That hue of the voluminous incandescent scarf, as Dune spun me and urged me against the wall, was me, was the heat of my passion.

I understood why Dune found the paintings compelling, with the powerful men's airs of hidden knowledge. Their hair was amazing, collars Bohemian, lips sometimes sensual with their inclination to survive forever. Some men had lips drawn inward toward their teeth: I guessed that was from years confronting the unknowable. They withered from pretending to know more than they did: *that* was the big secret shared between them across the hallway.

Pointed toes raised high, I challenged myself not to blow out any candles along the walls as I swished and swerved. The torches blazing on the end toward the stairs made paintings announce a hedonistic hell. The candles lit the men's arch eyebrow ridges.

I did interpretive improvs in front of each painting while I returned down the hallway. Acting out Roger Bacon, King Arthur, Edward Kelley, even Luke's assistant, Tommy. Portraying imperialistic urges, desires to beyond the limits, to make a mark throughout history, to change everything.

On one wall was Pope Nicholas the fifth, above a wide book shelf. This was appropriate, as he'd hired authors to write a library full of spurious history books, pure disinformation. The writers spit in the eye of Spain, which was vying with England to govern America.

I danced the allure of being under the sway of someone else telling me what to feel. The shadowy, intense appeal wound its way through my body. I breathed harder and sweated from listening to my breath intensely alive. I missed Miriam. She cut through the crap. If she thought esoteric history was bollocks, she said so. Even if I rarely let on in public, I agreed with her skepticism. I had to keep up my proper appearance of being into arcane nonsense.

She'd give you a chocolate at the same time as railing about the nonsense, to make her teasing go down easier. She'd give you a foot rub if she thought you were going through a crisis of faith. I saw her cradle Huld's goaty foot in her hands when discussing whether ancient giants had special powers. She put his foot on her lap and poked with both thumbs. He slowed his speech and put his head back, staring at the ceiling. She did it for me, bending over my favorite red velvet footstool in the lounge.

Just because the season was over didn't mean she had to fade out of our lives. I should visit her; no need to have Dune in the room. Dune obviously hungering for a ménage à trois with her had made me uneasy when we were working together every day. Why wouldn't Dune fancy her, considering how much we looked alike? But prettier enough she took away my sense of feminine power when entering a room? With that vibrant skin. Those lips with no wrinkles in them. With such a marked Cupid's bow. Those irises with contrasting edges, vivid and abrupt. He'd pledged to be true.

I wanted her to myself. To push palms into pointy breasts, to pull her long waist to mine, and her breath on my lips. I realized how she felt when breathing my aura before shows. She'd probably kiss me if Dune joined in. I remembered a dream that morning: we three had shared a bed. We hunted together when I pulled a bow. We gardened when I pulled back the leaves of a cabbage and found a striped caterpillar.

I wanted to explore her, the first cries of wonder, the penetration into crevices, the tweak the nipples, to pull the hair at the nape. My reflection made me long for her. I imagined her nude. No, with a flimsy gown, standing before one of the high windows. There were no low windows other than the ones with bars in the sooty kitchen with sunlight shining through, showing her form.

No, a sunny day was too boring for my fantasy. Instead, weather polarized the sky with beams and weighted clouds, rain and rainbows simultaneously; wind blew in, drenching her dress. Then sun shone as the cloud fled. Miriam pulled her clinging gown away from her body. Light revealed her curves, the wetness highlighting breasts pushing against cloth. I detected my natural sex perfume, but I had no complaints, and neither did Dune.

Something in the corner of the reflection. It looked like a suit of armor for a split second. I spun to see behind me and Dune moved just at that moment, blocking my view. I thought a knight moved in the doorway.

Dune counted from three to one.

I asked, "Is someone here?"

"No one is here, darling. It will be nice when Luke and Tommy come home, won't it? Until then, you're free to behave as you wish. Enjoy yourself. Dance like no one's watching."

"I guess I'm just tired."

"You should rest. Naps let a body heal. Cancer can make you hallucinate, you know."

"It can?" I wasn't sure I trusted his claim. But then, I was shaken by eerie old sounds.

Dune said, "Tommy grinds the powders and that might help you recover. He's got a background in compounding poisons and such, so knows the technique. He does Enochian chants while doing it. That's what makes it work. Luke isn't good at it, but Tommy trained since childhood. It brings John Dee's Enochian angels to get countries aligned the right way."

I'd earned restoration. The lung pain had left. Over-filled with life after Miriam fantasy, I was bursting with the need to pleasure myself.

Dune said, "I didn't tell anyone we were coming. Not even Luke. He said come any time, so I know it's fine. But let's keep it special. Make it our wild and windy secret. No neighbors to bother us. I won't even pick up any newspapers in town. It will be Heaven, darling."

Why was he going over this again? I didn't ponder it long.

❄

The second he retired into the study, I headed to the solar. I flung myself under covers to think about Miriam. I hallucinated her taste, her hands inside me everywhere, her cheeks upon mine, as if we merged.

I experienced Miriam from the inside out, flashes of light around my torso. It had to be her aura. A backwash from her taking on my aura. When she sucked my aura before the plays that left a vacuum. A portion of hers flooded mine.

I remembered that friend she'd mentioned. He would do anything to help her succeed. Not matter what. He would keep her safe. I wondered if Dune and I would bed her. Why did I never think of that solution? Why did I blame him for his lust?

When Dune walked in through the heavy, simple door frame, I hid my breathlessness and sweat, pretending to have a fitful dream. I yawned and stretched.

He sat on the bed with me, and we cuddled, then, read dusty old illustrated books from the shelves built into the walls. While he read a biography of a previous chief of the Nevermind, I scanned William Beckford's *Vathek*.

I determined to forget Miriam. A good wife should not let her fantasies stray from her husband. *I made my vow and I should stick to it.*

Dune talked about monoatomic gold drops that I'd taken daily. My body throbbed, wanting deeper, souls meeting, dolphins turning to liquid light as they sang.

Dune quoted from Luke's alchemical grimoire about the physics of ingesting monoatomic Moldavite. The books and pamphlets spread around claimed working magickally with Moldavite made worthy practitioners levitate. People bought Luke's potions on repeat orders, so they must have been convincing placebos.

Dune lay back and smiled, eyes closed. He leaned in and kissed me. I loved his lips on mine. He was my man; I was his woman. The world vibrated strangely.

Enochian angels flew in the canvas above the bed, giving John Dee the famous scrying stone. He stared at the stone, trying to induce visions. They weren't nice angels to invite into one's bedroom, without giving them a schedule for leaving.

It was disconcerting for the Enochians and Elizabethan gentlemen to face us while Dune teased my dress off. Well, John

Dee was all right looking. I didn't mind him taking a gander from behind the frame. He had a jaunty beard and a twinkle. Considering Enochian language was a spy code, I had to wonder how much Dee, himself, believed in the alchemy and angels Edward Kelley went on about. Was he giving the benefit of the doubt, humoring his esoteric notions?

As Dune spoke, he pushed and stretched my body: a bed-dance for two. "You underestimate how necessary you are to the system. You're not a regular woman. Our devotion is transcendent alchemy." He fondled my face affectionately. "The Bennu Society helps people. They test human limits. You'll understand while you're here. I hope it suits you."

Being flattered seemed improper. My naughty parts opened and throbbed when he said I had a secret mission. Life didn't bore with Dune. Geniuses often got unconventional ideas.

We pressed against each other's arms, then our legs. We sat back to back on the bed, pushing our spines into each other, moaning, bucking from the pleasure of the electrical charge.

"Breathe in from the ground," he instructed me. "Imagine you're sucking up light through your spine. Widen it. So wide, the energy merges with mine. I'm doing it too. Can you sense it? Spiritual lightning through us? Sharing the same awareness. We're changing into one being universal."

"Yes. Yes." It was magnificent. I needed to learn more about mystical sensuality.

"Tighten your sex muscles; you're sipping through them and packing universal energy into your body. Tighten, relax, tighten, relax. Keep the buzz in your sexual parts."

"No problem, there."

"Don't let it go away when you draw the power it's generating up your body. Direct your eyes to picture the soul force moving up your skeleton. Turn your eyes up, looking above you."

"I'll bet I look ghastly. A dead person in a horror movie or something."

"No, close your eyelids. Column of light ascending from your sex to your skull."

Spirit moved my body. A snake made of bliss. I moaned.

"Breathe in deeper, and deposit the prana in your body, pushing up and in with your diaphragm muscle, like you're forcing it inside, not letting its energy escape. Add to the bright."

"The high I used to get hyperventilating with friends in the bathroom at school when I was a kid."

"Now, squeeze those sex muscles, and push up with your diaphragm. Turn your eyes back even more so you're looking up higher above your head. Draw consciousness up with your eyes. Push, so your aura light fountains up above your brain. Go."

"Dune! This is the most incredible thing in the world!" My body snaked and so did his. We moved in sync, our shared energy rising.

Twisting me to face him, he continued: "And even better, making love, while utilizing the elixir, makes our energies shine. We'll do a ritual in the oratory. Power built up in your bodies will release into the universe at that moment."

Did he say, "bodies?" How many of me were there?

"Playing the Bennu role on stage wasn't entertainment but it built up to the equinox initiation. You're fire of renewal." He cupped my public mound, a finger going inside me at the same time. I bucked with pleasure. He pulled his finger out and placed it on the spot that affected me the most.

He lifted his hands above my skin.

His auric energy extending from his fingers, stroking me, turning me on.

Dune put drops in my mouth of the elixir with Moldavite, gold, and mummy dust.

It was the love of the century like the characters I'd played on stage. A force for good. Dune was my High Priest. I was his High Priestess. My life wasn't ending. It was beginning. It would never end. I spread out through the universe.

"Sure, you used to be a conventional person." I wasn't so sure about that statement. "But now you're the chosen one, not just an ordinary mortal."

He squeezed his moving mouth against my most special parts, vibrating my tender flesh with his words, his genius, asserting, "Transcendent love can change the world."

My husband was a beast of love, embodied passion, and I was the Grail cup that scorched him with passion-fire. Moist. Steaming. Hot. He pulled my clothes off, lay on top of me and enlisted the precise rhythms of friction that delivered me euphoria. The pauses drove me wild. The syncopation made the thrusts music. Each thrust pushed life force further into my core, and into my spine, and up and out through me, fountaining above my head.

I was me, I was other women, I was timeless, was Renewal incarnate. Here on Earth for some reason. I could incarnate that purpose better when he made me scream with delight.

In my mind, Miriam breathed on my ear and I heard her voice whispering, "Can you feel me rushing through your bones? Your nervous system? We are one." But did she use words? No. Her message was light, branching into dendrites. My spinal cord thrilled, electricity flowing through it that I saw behind eyelids as light. I bucked, my body lithe and animal, licked by an imaginary tongue, when Dune was busy elsewhere.

Dune embraced me tight against his strong chest. I cried out with him when we came together, howling wolves, wilderness, ancient times enfolded into present, future, everything, everything, everything.

My destiny to transformative the world with love. I'd played Bennu two years. I'd played complementary roles: the marriage of strange chemicals in shocking combinations, unheard-of juxtapositions, and transgressive patterns of magnetic charges.

The Hermetic doctrine on the Emerald Tablet, said to be carved on Moldavite: As above, so below. When we create on high frequencies, auras manifest. I had to study Luke's books hard to change the world. Crowley's magickal secrets would be in the oratory. No more wasting time. Because, so often when I asked Dune a question, he deflected. He turned away, and my eyes searched his distant features for some way to bring him close again. Or, he turned toward me, and I pulled in his speculator self, savoring the exciting moments before they were withheld.

I knew better than to expect the answers. Luke was a master of distraction. My role was the female passive reception, the hollow of the Grail, waiting for the wine at the Round Table. How had I earned that honor? If I insisted on an active role, that would lead to the love. In whatever form, in or out of the Penderghast castle.

On a table, next to a coral colored candle, was featured a beautifully illustrated open first edition of *The Chymical Wedding*: an alchemist's allegory about Christian Rosenkreuz, the hero of the esoteric secret society, the Rosicrucians. The book divided a journey into seven days in which Rosenkreuz, was invited, using John Dee's hieroglyphic ciphers, to a castle where strange miracles occurred. The high point was the symbolic royal wedding.

The chemicals were said to enjoy their sacred alchemical marriage in which they produced something more than the original elements joined together mutating through the fiery process. They created the wonders of life, Bennu, rising from its own ashes, new, transformed, biological. The moment by moment turnover of our cells, drying, new ones replacing them. He said, "This book is about you."

"Is that a good thing?"

"There's a manual somewhere on mystical sensuality; I might show it to you, sometime. The practice you did breathing in Sylvia's aura when you were her standby trained you for drawing in my aura and circulating it through your body and into mine."

"Absolutely."

"That's my girl."

Wait, what about bringing my aura back into my body? Do you get to keep it?

I sighed and choked. "What's this pallet for? Do we need it here? It's disintegrating. It's hard to breathe."

If we suck someone's aura into us and never let go of it, does that keep part of them inside forever?

He startled me out of my reverie when he answered my question. "It's where the Lord's servant slept, to keep him safe. No one uses it. Luke's keeping the castle the way it has always been -- it's how he shows it love."

Gruff farmers, used to paying the Lord taxes for the use of the land, maybe still did for all I knew. And what tales of the strange events must have passed through families of servants. I patted the pallet, coughing, dust flying in the air. "Ugh. I need fresh air." I threw it into the corner closet.

"Your wish is my command. Here, you get what you have wanted since we met." He made a grand gesture, the lines of his body so artistic, so compelling. The way he flicked his fingers as he moved them into the air, the noble tilt of his head, striding on high arches -- it drew me to him, wanting to be him, merge with him, be seen by him and still loved.

No, I wanted to show him my prepared, perfected persona, my hair brushed, my ligaments lengthened, my nails filed, my eyebrows plucked. To cleave our bodies yearning to become one, no, to become two so we could see each other, but anguished to be separate.

I danced around the room, sprightly for Dune, until he left. I inhaled as if I had never smoked. The last few days had created a miracle. I was morphing into a mage.

At twilight, we ventured into the fragrance of the heath, with the carpet of flowers lush below our feet. We gathered bilberries and raspberries from the fence around the garden, and prickly squash. I petted the ash tree, nuzzling its bark. I whistled with skylarks. My songs riffing off theirs were in a minor key. I adored the desolation.

I crossed my arms, shivering, craving for Dune's to warm me.

Subtle arms hugged me. I couldn't allow myself to believe it was happening. That way madness lay.

CHAPTER 7
VISITORS

When we woke, we hiked curving windswept hills. As we surveyed the cloud shadows mottling the blossoms, he put his arms around me and kissed. Smells of the heath combined with his skin intoxicated me like my favorite mead poured all over me, the sun shining through me, as I imagined flinging my gold-wet hair, drops flying this way and that, landing on my tongue, my mouth open.

Why so fresh, as if we had only just consummated our vows, I couldn't say, but I wanted him over and over, with my moistest depths, my pleasure-cave of many miracles. I'd start again; time was no master.

"Please be naked in the sunshine." He removed the sheer Black Widow over-garment and slipped his fingers along my neck as I unbuttoned my virginal dress. When I was nude, he dressed me only in the transparent black covering. I danced for him among tiny flowers, barefoot among the roughness, savoring the scratching, the tickling prickles against my feet. Soles shedding callouses from dance slippers.

After he removed his shirt, the tiny mesh of thin fabric between us amplified the sensations as I slithered against him. He instructed me in mystical sensuality. "Breathe life force energy up your body from the ground. I'm manipulating it too. See, it's easier than it sounds, isn't it? Just by visualizing it, you're making it happen. I see your aura; it's working. Direct the energy up, up more, there. That's right."

My warm heart was larger than my body.

"Now, put your palm against the center of my sternum. Send love through it. Yes, that. Now, open to receive."

It was divine. My legs buckled underneath me, my spine spasming pleasure, moving my body into rhythm. His synced up with it, as we stood, exchanging something we were both part of, something eternal: life itself. That was true immortality.

"Walk with me. Don't bother putting on your dress. I'll carry it."

I was liberated, exposed to the elements, across the blooming heather, up the hills.

Dune's smile was incessant. Once home, he said, "I'm going to the buttery and bottlery."

"The buttery and botttlery! It's a nursery rhyme! And something I should know about."

"They're between the great hall and the kitchen. Up against the curtain wall. You'll find it, soon. I'm off for mead, be back." I waited on large woolen pillows. He carried in three glasses of the honey wine and set one in front of a pillow. "I apologize for fetching too many."

He leaned back against his seat, with his arms outstretched on either side, smug as the master of a harem. We twirled, looking out through a gap in the forest over moorland in the distance, as we spun. He lifted me, and I kicked my feet in the air.

How long could I continue feeling wonderful? "I should go to the doctor soon for tests."

"Let's let wonders work. No need for mundane pokes and prods. Live the miracle. What doctors understand such amazements?"

"What about amnesia? I might have had a stroke."

"You'll be fine."

"Then hypnotize me so I can remember."

"No need."

He carried me to the bed, throwing me on it and writhing against me, clutching my hair at the nape of the neck and yanking down. I moaned huskily, took hold of his shirt and pulled it against him. I yearned for time to hasten so he was inside me immediately. He cupped my hip bone, licked the edges of its shadow on my concave tummy, tracing the fine line of tiny hairs below my navel. I panted, purred. He made love exquisitely, slowly touching skin, fervently, then delicately, then fervently again, cycling.

I called out the overwhelming pleasure was too much. How long did orgasm last before absurdity set in? I climbed on top of him, grasping his legs behind me, blond locks sweeping his chest fur. I arched back, thrusting, freeing my thorax to universal love as the world brought me the gift of joy.

He stood and lifted me to stand and pressed me against the wall, holding up my wrists high, ordering them against the rugged stone. Invisible fingers touched me along my collar bone, sliding along my tapering rib cage. I puzzled, as my head curved back, my mouth opening. Warmth along my flank. A ménage à trois. Someone else was there. I'd assume a ghost, or the Buddhist sky walker, but I didn't believe.

Heightened awareness of my skin. Was Dune thinking of Miriam? Was that why I felt her around me? Some kind of telepathic resonance? Dune wanted me to be Miriam, younger, freer, with a stronger sense of humor. Unencumbered with the status of an agent's wife. I was gargoyle with extra arms. I pretended Miriam. That made pleasure divine. All three of us there.

Dune cried out and his eyes shone. He called me Miriam, and modified it to Susan, his voice garbled with pleasure. I understood the appeal of merging with her. What spouse has not called the incorrect name? Lucky I didn't call *him* Miriam.

After we finished and lay there, I grew parched. He said, "I'll go to the well house."

I snarled. When he arrived in the bedroom with a pewter pitcher, I was brushing my passion-matted mane. I twisted and bit him in the face. I did that? Impulse from a submerged part of myself. Some fierceness that knew something was awry. I struggled but found apologizing impossible.

He covered his face. When he withdrew his hands, he laughed tenderly at me, his poor noble visage was so breathtaking my ribs caved, aching to be one with him.

I lost my domesticity when I wandered in the forest. I was losing my tameness in that wild landscape, that fortress of cruel deaths and torments. My aura spread like fog in stretches below the wooded tor, rolling among heather, yellow gorse flowers, reds, purples, golds and greens. I became the heath.

No, I was Dune's wife -- more than Dune's wife. And Dune played a role in the Bennu Society, and the interlocking Nevermind. I longed to be archetypal, fabulous as the characters I played at the theater. I wasn't ready for shouts of "Encore!" to terminate.

But I wanted purity. I didn't fancy being tainted with occult practices applied by the Nevermind. Was that feasible? Weren't there any honest people to assist? Must I go over to the dark side? If I did, I would reorganize the system using my position. I'd persuade Dune to alter the Agency, adjust it to more ethical, less manipulative.

I quaffed a slug of well water, and when I swallowed: flashback. Vivid. Visceral. Liquid. My nightmare haunted me, something horrible happening at the well house. Had I hurt someone? I had the vague, dreamy sensation of exiting the auditorium with Dune, going into the audiovisual closet to make love. Or was that just my fantasy? I'd gone off with Kevin for a chatty smoke in the private little structure, keeping our make-up dry and our hair in place that drizzly night. I disembodied, astral traveling, a frequency wave. A buzz. A beingness.

That was a mysterious time. A break in reality. Part of me had been absorbed into Miriam as she was preparing. Poor Miriam. She must have wished desperately I'd collapse so she'd have her chance. My aura flowed out that night, was absorbed into her while she waited in the green room. And that time, it hurt.

It was troublesome to speak civilly to my beloved at that moment. "Dune, remember before the last show? Did you perform one of your post-hypnotic fortune pranks?"

He winked at me, like, "Wouldn't you like to know?"

A rattle at the gate. Dune put a palm over my mouth. "Shh. Bugger all. No commotion, no spying out a window!"

He ran to the kitchen, then the door, and I overheard him shouting over a young man's melodic voice. They spoke. Dune didn't let him talk much. I figured I had to be mistaken, but it sounded like: ". . . police, I promise you, I'll kill her. So, you'd better promise me. Now. And you'd better keep it. No matter what they do to you."

Yes, I surely interpreted it wrong. I imagined Dune killing a man dangerous to me. But a female who threatened me? If there was a deranged, murderous shrew, he'd have reason to protect me, but I had trouble picturing the scenario. There were indistinguishable threats.

When Dune came back, carrying mead, he drank from the bottle unceremoniously, while offering me none. His shoulders were raised too high. I tried to massage them, so he'd soften but he nudged me away.

"I didn't realize I had a secret admirer."

"You don't."

I hadn't wanted a secret admirer before, considering I had so many fans. I was unwanted. A man willing to track down where we'd run off to. A neighbor. That made sense. I laughed, but Dune didn't join in. How could he guess what I was thinking? I affirmed that the performance art crowd adored me.

I asked, "Is everything . . ."

"Everything's hunky dory. A dangerous mother wolf-hybrid out here escaped from a neighbor, is all. Puppies make them extra protective and unpredictable. People shouldn't raise such creatures."

"Has she killed something? Or someone?"

"I'll protect you, and that's all you need. Don't bother about it. Save your brain for chess, dear. Have a chalice of mead. It's the best year for the bees out here. They're excellent at pollinating, so tomorrow, you shall have Luke's handmade gorse wine." After he put monoatomic gold elixir in, he offered a serving of honey wine.

We played Enochian chess with the little replicas of Osiris, Isis, and Horus. I knew so much about John Dee and Edward Kelley that I was proud of increasing knowledge of the juxtaposition of the occult and intelligence agencies throughout history.

Dune read the instructions to Golden Dawn game which encapsulated esoteric traditions. The occultist British secret agent Aleister Crowley played it, which explained why his portrait gloated over the checkered table. The game was the perfect language to speak between secret societies and intelligence agencies, and Crowley was certainly communicated between both. He did so using deception and turning on friends, organizing gruesome ceremonies and forbidden sex rituals that tore apart all conventional restraints. He employed dubious Tantric rituals, promises of immortality and supernatural strength, overpowering hypnotic charisma, and mixed and matched Eastern and Western legends and occult practices.

It wore out my brain, playing in the near darkness. "Mind if I go to bed early?"

Dune sang a lullaby based on Bennu emerging from the god Osiris Slain, reborn again. "A new Sun arises from the old."

Sleeping fitfully, I burst from that dream to the sound of

something sliding across the lower floor. Or was the sound the end of a dream? I went back to sleep, dreaming of the building growing smaller, choking me to distill my essence into homeopathy, to squeeze me into fluids filling vials of elixirs lined up against walls. I dripped liquid light, light flowing through my body, being the light. I was universal, eternal, spread out into people who opened mouths in communion.

❄

To go forage for food in the forest in the morning, our fourth day, I selected a maroon velvet dress from Martha's wardrobe. Her sensual clothing made me wonder if Luke was a sexy gentleman or simply had riches and status. They had good taste in fabrics, though assessing their style in furnishings was impossible. Luke must have inherited a familial desperation to latch onto the past. He didn't have much else. Neighboring farmers coming round to chat about discoveries regarding capturing moon essence in homeopathic elixirs to aid lucid dreaming? Not hardly.

"Does Luke have siblings?" I inquired, as we launched into the drab day outside, and I scanned the vast expanse. "I hope so."

"Not a one. He mentioned he played war games alone, with miniature knights as a lad. I suspect he still does."

Picking berries was lovely. I felt evil, but we shot unfortunate small creatures on our raid with bow and arrows. Poor beasts, sacrificing their lives for us. It made me cherish them even more.

Trancing while slinking around step by step not requiring thoughts, I luxuriated in a fanciful minute. Summoning drowned memories to well up from my subconscious, I found them inaccessible. I resolved not to fade from my past.

I penetrated deep memory mode, trying my hardest to explain the recurring vague waking nightmare. Had I gone to the well house with Kevin for a smoke? Was that a guilt-dream, instead, because of practically killing myself smoking? Like Bennu, I renewed myself from the cigarette ashes.

Was it a death and rebirth dream, Osiris morphing into Bennu during a secret society initiation? After two years of playing the flamingo rising from ashes, I grasped how that would invade my subconscious. Had Kevin, sporting his watery role while I opened wings and lifted up the stage on pulleys, become archetypal in my psyche?

My husband and I brought leeks and beets from the garden into the castle and prepared a lovely meal. After lunch, someone knocked on the castle door. I fancied that old knocker, constructed like the old pagan Green Man.

Dune disappeared to the guardroom to drag on the ropes and then into the kitchen, emerging with the special key. Dune opened the door, me standing beside him.

I said, "All right?" I saw in front of my eyes not a face but a massive black suit.

I looked skyward. Huld.

"Up to much, *Mrs. Thornley*?" His intonation sounded smarmy, as if in on a joke, and overacting a role when he bowed. "Mrs. Dune Thornley." *Why make a big deal about who I am? He usually calls me Susan.*

The light carved shadows on his face beside his warts. His deep-set eyes were lost in shadow from his overhanging brow. I could get lost in the crevices of the deep creases on either corner of his mouth. He bowed, bending low. Was I expected to bow? Awkward.

This was clearly a secret agent business meeting, their usual insulting friend-banter absent. Everything agents did was too secretive for my ears. But, I elected to learn.

Glad to be wearing the long dress proper for company, I retrieved rose water in pewter goblets from the kitchen. Wishing for a mirror, I hopelessly peered into the soft silvery metal of a pitcher. I had to trust that I looked decent. Our guest had seen me without make-up backstage, so what did it matter?

When I returned to the menfolk, Dune took my goblet, saying, "None for you, yet, dear. Not long enough since taking monoatomic gold."

I reached out to hold it until time to drink.

"Ah, yes," said the giant, nudging my hand away like a greedy child's. "Dodgy ain't it, how homeopathic doses don't work if you eat or drink within half an hour of swallowing them?"

"Mr. Bossypants, are we?"

"Oh, don't throw a strop."

"It's bollocks you showing up before my half-hour wait is up. March right out that door, and we'll start again in ten." I teased him as if escorting him out.

How dare Dune not inform me that he'd scheduled a visitor? Where was the formal tea set?

I tried to be a gracious hostess and give the giant the benefit of the doubt. Huld would have been a normal guy if not raised in a cult. Huld couldn't help his parents being true believers who purchased *Giant Jack* comics and Halloween costumes. Why wouldn't a kid want to be part of the Giant Jack club and be a superhero if all he had to do was take HGH injections and grow so tall he reached higher objects, got to be alpha male, land better jobs?

Voices echoed; sounded like someone else talking down the hallway. The castle held the cold of centuries.

Dune opened a door in the wall, gesturing to head up the winding stairway leading to a turret. We held our hands over our candles; we wore hoods against the breeze.

Dune and Huld lagged behind and talked cryptically. When I swung around, Huld looked at me quizzically, as if he knew a secret and I was darling for not knowing it. They spoke, trailing me, about some ritual essential to the Agency. Something to do with re-genesis and making hidden wealth to fund psychological operations. Something in the context of the Occult Revival that had perpetuated New Age crap. And something to do with British Agent Aleister Crowley.

Did Huld expect me to I cook him a meal? There was a limited supply of vegetables from the garden. I wanted to dance free, barefoot, through the hallways, singing. Not cook for a lumbering man and a half.

A soft rhythmic shuffling behind. But no pets in the castle. Hmm. The guys dragged nothing along. . . I didn't want to stare offensively or ask, "What *was* that sound?" *Just the pipes. Wait, no plumbing in the castle . . .*

Distracted by struggling to remember friends who attended dinners or parties, played tennis, rode horses, or boated with us. Was I as lonely a person as Luke, no friends visiting? I stumbled on the stair.

And then, that noise again behind them like a child walking in sync with an adult's steps, pretending to spy.

I noticed a painting below, on the round turret wall, of the usual armor display. I watched Dune's expression. Nothing changed. So, he hadn't come across my act of naughtiness in the oratory. I still had time to set it upright when Dune left. I'd send him to town to mail a letter inviting Kevin Frank to dinner. If Dune invited Huld, I should be able to invite Kevin.

I realized the armor display may not have represented a person but a set of historical armor meaningful to the Penderghasts. I hadn't noticed the picture. The rich oil sat back into a niche in the wall. Dune had outdone himself this time. I interrupted them, but I was the extraneous person who didn't matter, obviously. Not being any kind of agent made me irrelevant.

When reaching the top of the stairs, Dune showed me the view through the glassless window high above the countryside. No buildings except one I could make out in the far, far distance. I enjoyed the jagged hill with granite showing through and crimson flowers glorious. Stone and wood, obscured by boulders and ridges. Crops planted near it and goats leaping about on a tor. Between us lay an impenetrable cliff into an abyss of a valley.

I turned to the massive table in the middle of the chamber with the rounded wall. Behind the bench imposed yet another picture of Luke. This time, he sat as if an invited guest pointing right at me. I didn't want to square off against that picture, so I sat beside it.

Huld announced, "The flick about Shambhala is comes out in two weeks."

Yes, the land Hinton called Shangri-La in an absurd film that didn't do too badly at the box office.

Dune lifted a bushy black eyebrow. "That soon?"

Huld continued, banging his huge fist on the table: "We have to go all out to counter the movie's effects. We don't want no one getting soft on Eurasia. We need *support* to stand up to them bastards."

I asked, "Why does that matter so much about a movie coming out?"

Huld's voice grew higher when he said, "Last thing we need is hordes of people going on about how the giants of Atlantis was actually the selfish baddies. And the Shambhala people was the nice guys." I could certainly see how he'd take it personally.

I asked, "Because of the hecklers at the shows being so disruptive? Are you concerned about fewer people attending the show next season?"

Dune shook his head as if what I'd just said was stupid and said, "It's high time for the Nevermind to put out another Atlantis movie to counter the Shambhala buzz."

Myths had surely been thrown into higher competition than ever because of the stink with the protests at our last show over which mythological heritage had the right to lay claim to Moldavite. It was already heated. I'd recently lost friends I cared a lot about because of that polarization, because they aligned with one heritage or the other, bickering on social media, trying like mad to find some DNA proof they came from a kingdom that didn't even exist, trying to go back and fudge history. I just shook my head. If my friends were that hysterical, then I didn't want to hang out with them, anyway.

The turmoil generated lots of click bait and ads romanticizing one myth or the other as being the best heritage, and articles the best line about Atlantis to pick up birds. Movies and TV shows about Shambhala and Atlantis, King Arthur and John Dee were all the rage. The most famous actors accepted the roles, certainly a boon for actors with gigantism.

Huld said, "I can't believe no Agent didn't kill the Shambhala producer. He's super anti-Atlantis. Brotherhood of the Shadows my ass." This statement seemed practiced, the way he glanced sideways at me as if to check my responses. The conversation between the two men was too on-the-nose, as if they said it for my benefit while pretending to ignore me. Whatever game they were playing drove me crazy.

But I did feel for Huld, growing up with his ego wrapped up in being superior because he was the "reincarnation of a giant from Atlantis." He did a good job in public pretending like he believed it. But seeing through the lies one layer at a time had to feel lonely. "I can see how that would get old," I said, putting a hand on the giant's, patting it with sympathy. "Lumped with bad magicians."

Huld looked disgusted. I stared down at the huge veins marring his hand.

I asked Huld again why exactly it mattered so much.

"Well, little *missy*, caring about the world, now, are we? Hmm?" said Huld. "Well, let me give you a beginning history lesson. The Russian mystic called Nicholas Roerich said he carried the Chintamani Stone, (the Moldavite, to you, missy) to the Far East. You want to know why?"

"No, I don't." In fact, what I wanted was to kick him across the room. Why wasn't Dune coming to my defense? Missy, indeed.

"To reunite it with its mother stone in another die-mention." He gestured to act out the scene of the Moldavite floating over the land in the higher frequency realm. "The viberation of Shambhala, Land of the Immortals. And now, everyone wants a piece of that, printo, so they can be immortal too."

I wasn't stupid. "You seriously think I don't know that? Back in the day, Roerich said every Tibetan Buddhists he happened to meet conveniently went on about how, 'It's the time of Shambhala!' Just piping up out of nowhere. Yeah, right."

Seemingly without irony, Dune added, his face long and slack, "Roerich said the monks out there were keen on the King of the World hanging out in the King's Tower holding the hunk of Moldavite to illuminate the world."

"And then the King's army is prophesied to come down and destroy evil with a rock," I added. "So, *that's* bizarre." Were we really having this conversation?

Huld nodded in agreement. "Reality ain't the point." Some layer underneath the surface was crying. How long ago had he figured out his heritage was bunk? Yet, he was able to convincingly hold up his head with that noble look on stage, exemplifying the wonderful Atlanteans of old.

Dune looked at him like he wanted to kill him.

Huld was implacable. "Point is, agents been competing for allegiance *throughout history*."

I clarified, "Appropriating legends of either Atlantis in the West or Shambhala in the East. How un-PC."

"Got it, now, missy?" *Hate him right now.*

"That's whole point of the Bennu troupe's shows," said Dune. "Since some occultists say Shambhala is benevolent and Atlanteans used black magic, we've got to work hard to reverse that perception. Thus, beautiful you star in the show, and everyone loves you and everyone loves Britain."

I hesitated, rubbing my forehead which hurt from furrowing. I was still missing a piece. "I totally understand the reason for the rivalry mattering in the past, but . . ." Something wasn't adding up. There was more to the story: I just knew it. Some secret hid within the walls of the castle; I determined to discover it on my own.

Huld explained, "People like the Russian spy who created Theosophy was all about promoting globalization with whatever lies she needed. She said she went to Tibet, but you *know* she didn't." Thank God someone finally admitted it. "She jabbered on about the Great White Brotherhood of Tibet. Nice name, huh, for an organization in charge of our lives. Cool, eh?"

"Racist, actually." Yes, I played the whitey anti-white privilege race card.

Dune squinted. "Blavatsky said the geniuses who left Atlantis popped off to Shambhala in Central Asia and the ones who stayed were morons."

Well, duh. Where did he think I'd been the last few years? I said, "That's old news. Blavatsky pretended to get messages about Shambhala from Masters proving. . ."

"Pretended to?" interrupted Dune. They were both going in and out of protecting the story and tearing it down. I felt woozy like Alice in Wonderland. I needed a nap.

I stood my ground. "Yes. The giant Atlantean Masters had *ooooo* psychic powers." I waved my arms around. "And while the majority of the race became corrupt, the priest-kings stayed pristine and migrated to Shambhala in the Gobi Desert to instruct the fifth Aryan root-race. And she, of all people in the whole wide world, happened to have an in with them."

Huld said, "Meanwhile, Brits said the scaredy-cats who ran away from Atlantis went to Egypt. And the brave ones stuck around. And Atlantis is now called England."

I queried one more time, "No, seriously, why is it such a big deal for ordinary people right now who the good guys were back then and where they migrated?"

Dune answered, "Britain has to counter the legend that Shambhala was where the Brotherhood of Light lived. And we have to counter the legend that Atlantis (otherwise known as England) is where the Brothers of the Shadow operated. It's the Order of Eurasia VS the Order of Atlantism. We have to make it obvious we're were on the right side if we don't want to look like jerks and be made fun of." He looked down and shuffled his feet. I could see the little boy in him.

Huld stepped in with a sneer. "Britain and Russia was after who would control India and import their opium. Britain won. The U.S. is still in the import business so. . ."

Dune got more honest than I'd seen him when he clarified, "Atlantis is our gang. Rival gangs poach from each other. They convince recruits their gang is the best. That's all it is. All it's ever been. Pride. Go team go, yay! And it's the history of ally and axis in WWI and WWII. History repeats itself." I was proud of him for admitting it.

Huld smiled at him too and added, "Roerich, the Great White blokes and Madam Blavatsky's Theosophical Society all talked about the King of the World in Shambhala. They said he used Moldavite to send out this frequenthy to purify the world, right? Well, what are they purifying out of it, exactly? Us."

I had trouble taking it seriously. "Let me get this straight. The power from the Far East makes everyone Ascend, a big ol' happy Globalist family in the sky. All praying to Moldavite hovering around over the ground in this desolate Shambhala place no one can actually get to, but the Brotherhood thinks is swell. So, adepts hang out up there and beam their light out through this rock gifted by terrestrials to save Earth from us. Sounds legit."

"Sure, why not?"

I said, "Moldavite's kind of boring rock, anyway, if you ask me, but people pretend it's pretty." No one would care much about the gem if the media didn't turn it into such a big panic. People worried they'd be trapped in a lower dimension if they didn't get the rock and chant woo woo over it immediately.

Huld's voice got rougher. "Giants from Atlantis need to win the war. The Bennu troupe shows about Moldavite is ammunition."

I'd read history books, researching political meanings behind the fairy tale quality of our skits. But still, being married to an Agent, no doubt I was savvier than I remembered. I felt like I was in one of those dreams where you're lost and late. You find yourself on a stage supposed to say your lines, but you have no clue what the play is. And everyone is watching and waiting. You do your best to fabricate good lines without sweating so much that saltwater drips down your eyebrow and dangles there. It goes in your eye, and you can't do anything about it. And you're just trying to figure out why your foot is a chicken.

I understood our hecklers. And why Huld and Dune worked against the clock to counter the new Shambhala movie coming out. Shambhala was associated with undercutting British authority; Agents didn't want that legend in the forefront. Movies, games, comic books, novels, songs all had to push the wonder-Brits and super-American angles. Meanwhile, Republicans going on about forgetting ancient legends of royalty got in the way big-time and so did the growing atheism of the younger generations.

Any competing narratives had to be controlled opposition. The Nevermind riled up two sides, arguing with righteous indignation. Divide and conquer worked.

They had to hide the history of the Russian Madam Blavatsky's fight to free India from Britain's rule and the Russian Roerich's attempts at fostering Tibetan independence. Sometimes the machinations of Mystical Imperialism were so obvious, even when entertainment twisted the reality, that it got people researching. Thinking: never safe.

I tried to maintain dignity. I didn't care about the two men who were talking down to me. I kept my lips loose and full, not tightened in embarrassment. Most of the castle was sparse; this room was full. The pretense of not minding Dune and Huld's dismissive treatment twitched my cheek. I stepped up to everything around us as if each object was far more engrossing than my fellow performer. A chart of hieroglyphics, talismans, embossed thick books, an arcane map with charming pictures of dragons, featuring Atlantis, with a sketch of a giant standing square in the center of it.

Through the window, I noticed a huge sundial on a distant hill. I surveyed intriguing shapes in the turret walls, rich colors, rough mosaics. Structures with paganism inherent in the geometry. Echoes of sacrifices. Hedonistic times, bestiality, Tantric sex rites, deathlike trances and rebirths into secret society loyalty.

I remembered that Tantric secrets were supposedly preserved in Shambhala. So, considering the East/West competition, I was surprised to see that the statues at the castle were dakinis. The supernatural ladies who aided Buddhist Tantric initiates danced inside a circle of fire. Dakinis were the souls of murdered human women, close companions of practitioners who sacrificed them in ritual fires. The dakinis then haunted the area where they had been killed, holding skull cups and cleavers.

The next step in Tantra Yoga was to kill the dakini's ghostly form so the adept could absorb her energy into his by drinking an elixir made from her pain. Something about that made me queasy.

Huld cleared his throat so loudly I jumped. He seemed an intruder into our vacation. They didn't include me any further in the conversation about Atlantis and Shambhala. Two teams poaching players from each other. All agents had to do was find irrational ways to claim the most supernatural conqueror heritage for their country and everything was hunky dory.

Myths competed over right of royals to rule Britain and other countries in the past, but was it still relevant enough for all that hubbub? There was King Arthur: always handy to pull out that ancestry. I had trouble taking it seriously, considering Geoffrey of Monmouth's histories were not in the least concerned with fact.

And there were ol' root races. I had to admit my husband was a racist, going on about superior giants in Atlantis with epic ritual battles. Fleeing to Egypt when Atlantis flooded, building the pyramids, and that nonsense. And other Atlanteans fleeing to Shambhala, in the Himalayas.

Ever since the giant President Planda got the whole Occult Revival thing going decades earlier, keeping the New Age trends prominent, people pored over their notes trying to force it all to make sense. Weasel logic.

President Planda had won the election decades before because of popularizing the pervasive belief in ancient giants of Atlantis. The Agents in the media had convinced the population that the giants had taken their historical records and fled a cataclysm to go build the Egyptian pyramids where they encoded records of their civilization.

Planda had revived that popular mythology to garner votes because he had gigantism. He was gangly, with hooded eyes, elongated hands and feet and an overhanging brow. He reminded voters that ancient giants were superior to normal humans and got everyone in a supernatural frenzy. They all joined his cult.

It had always worked that way. The powers that be in England and the U.S. wanted to control other countries. They made it palatable when they created coups and installed puppet dictators. It helped their cause if they claimed their pristine ancestors had once conquered those locations so, they'd been theirs all along! They reclaimed their territory, so they ruled over with the proper supernatural ancestry and fulfilled the prophecy. Their ancestral line would rise again, turning Earth into a utopia.

Agents arranged the occult societies, cults and myths to hook people on spiritual beliefs that made them privileged. They hooked them with practices that blissed them out and made them think illogically, so they became gullible. If they merged the religious tenets, esoteric traditions, and faux histories filled with paranormal beings, they created allegiance in whatever countries they wanted. Just like Theosophy.

I wandered away, rudely turning my back on them and stood by the window. I tuned them out. They droned on about the balance of power between different countries, which ones to take down, which ones to prop up, puppet dictators, proxy wars, coups, working behind the scenes for the United States.

Put off by subtle sounds in the room, I didn't care for being ignored. Bewildered by how little I remembered, I feared dementia. The cancer had taken a turn, and left my lungs alone, but had infected my brain instead.

I stretched in the sunlight coming in the window, and I leaned out. I was enticing in that position. Moving just the right ways to make the men pause in their conversations, distracted by my pulchritude, was fun.

Huld said, "Excellent view, isn't it?"

Cheeky bastard. I did more strengthening exercises in the window, pressing my hands against each side, lifting myself up, pushing myself back. No longer bored, I enjoyed ligaments and nerves, my hair against my skin, and the breeze against my face.

And what motivated my interest in exercising instead of listening to a privileged political discussion between secret agents bent on changing the face of the globe? Because outside the window, I saw a comely man in a rough tan suede jacket. I wondered who he was. Luke home early from vacation? The build looked about right, though it was hard to tell, considering his fondness for formal castle-wear.

It was the man with the musical voice who knocked earlier? Yes, I made myself sexy for Dune from the backside. But I fancied the mysterious stranger. He looked ragged yet graceful.

I still wanted Dune every day, with his flared nostrils, his straight neck and his capable stance, able to find the exact tiny circular movements with his fingers on my sweet spot that drove me wild. Yet my interest was piqued by the man staying outside on the castle grounds. I wondered if it was the same person whom Dune had threatened at the door. I felt a magnetic pull toward him.

I glanced over my shoulder to ensure the men wouldn't notice and I waved out the window at him. He waved back, excited like he knew me. I made a beckoning gesture, swaying with the hedonism of honey wine. I spilled drops down my bosom.

The men continued their discussion and sketched codes on parchment, going on about the effects of some ritual. Gibberish. The effect of being dismissed, objectified and targeted made me go all dreamy. So did the mead. I lived a parallel life. Kissing the man below would be like reading a novel or watching a film. I could always go back to my regular reality as if nothing happened.

The stranger strode toward the castle. How risky. Am I luring him to his doom, positioning him in range for Dune to shoot?

❄

I excused myself and spiraled down. They'd left the entrance door unlocked. Their mistake was my joy.

The stranger in suede was right there, standing straight, eyes lit. I wanted to be the person he thought I was. I wanted him to press his heart against mine long enough that time stopped.

When I walked out, he pulled me away, and ran. I pulled back and wrenched my hand out of his. "What are you doing?"

"Don't you want to leave with me?"

"You walk up to a castle and steal away the Lady for no reason, just like that?"

"You . . . don't. Want to?" The light in his huge brown eyes, surely what people meant when they talked about soul.

"Why would I?"

"I expect nothing. Just let's get you safe to the city."

I wanted to lift my fingers through his hair in my hands, to traipse through a fairy tale together. My life was established; there was no rational reason to leave. "I'm fine here. Why wouldn't I be?"

"I'll wait."

He was my *home* in a parallel world. My heart expanded to include him, to include everything, everywhere, always. We breathed in sync, cheek to cheek.

Huld and Dune called out simultaneously, running up behind me. Dune grabbed me and pulled, covering my mouth with his arm, holding me too tightly against him. The giant ran inside and returned with a bow.

"Something's not right," said the stranger.

Damn straight it isn't.

Dune shouted, "You come on someone else's property and won't leave. You try to steal my wife away. Something's not *right?* Go on, get to your car. Drive away home, you nasty, little man. Don't talk to anyone ever about this. Got it? You'd live to regret it."

When the man in rough suede walked off, invisible taffy pulled between our hearts. Had I heard right when Dune said, "If you do, I'll kill her." If so, this was intense for discussing a wolfdog.

Huld was scheming with him about something, bent down to speak in Dune's ear.

I said, wimpy and demure, "It wasn't my fault. Someone left the door open."

❄

I sulked off to bed, and the men went back upstairs. But I didn't stay there. Instead, I sneakily crept upstairs and along the floor behind the biggest furniture. I got close to the men to spy on them and see what I could learn. I covered my mouth when I giggled.

They conversed for a good while before anything came

through clearly. Huld asked Dune, "How d'you like the product placement on the broadcast last night?"

Product placement?

"It was excellent. Good choice to include the 'MOLDAVITE POWER' and the 'MOLDAVITE FOREVER," and "GEM OF IMMORTALITY' signs. Everyone will pay top dollar for Moldavite now, especially if it's ritually enhanced. Our statistics show they pay more for stones spiritually charged by Shambhala-heads. Sales for stones charged by Atlanteans rose by five percent this month after the latest King Arthur pageant incident."

Holy fuck!

"And having the newscaster interview the activists in front of the poster for our show -- perfect composition."

Huld took a deep bow, his face reddening as it dropped, veins bulging. That bow! With that lantern jaw coming at you, the overhanging brow and too many cells in that body, too many veins and arteries, for the blood to keep up with. He was one of the longest living people who took the medical HGH injections. Many died by twenty. Hearts couldn't fulfill the extra requirements. I was honestly starting to wish he'd been one of those who died.

Dune talked to the giant so softly, I heard something like, "Change of plans."

And then the name "Kevin." It couldn't be Kevin Frank. It had to be Kevin Frank.

What would Kevin do regarding a corpse and double instances of creating a patsy? Was he messed up in drug running? I envisioned him buying drugs to give people. He knew how to have a good time.

Some assets didn't realize they were intelligence agents. That tactic was used well before the Nevermind poached mind-control experts from the CIA, who learned techniques from the Nazis brought to the U.S. with Project Paperclip after WWII. The assets were overpowered, like Manchurian Candidates.

I hid well, folded up on the floor, leaning my back against the wall behind furniture I wasn't familiar with: a wood thing covered with a lilac and lavender cloth that even smelled purple. I listened to whispers impossible to make out. I tried to rest without sleeping, no, to sleep for a moment. Just a moment. Let my brain process this new information.

My eyes opened wide when Dune spoke again. "Place the DNA sample with the forensics expert at the lab."

"Check the dissolving powder in the water did its job of obscuring her appearance enough, but not too much. The water level might have differed from we expected because of the rain. Could be diluted. Carry some if you need more."

"No doubt the bloating will be dreadful enough they can't identify the contrasts. They're playing dumb about discovering the cadaver until next week. Good thing no one goes to that theater during its off season: that'll be one smelly raising of the dead."

That sounded outright deceitful. I wasn't sure I could go on cohabitating with an Agent. Whatever they did wasn't moral. Obscuring the identity of a murder victim? Or a murderer? Or both?

I'd been trusting, being there with my loyal, sympathetic husband. The mysterious rage boiling up underneath turned to shock. Horrible! My hands clammy. I shook. My lips got so dry they chapped second by second.

I had had to squeeze my nose to stop myself from sneezing on the dusty floor. What would I say if they found me, hiding, listening to their conversation?

Dune said, "Sure, this way, the truth will never emerge. Once the police find the body, I think we've got a . . ."

"Watertight case?"

Dune chuckled.

As they stepped about the room, raising and lowering the volume, I only picked up bits and bobs. "What they think doesn't signify. We're immune. Agents can do no wrong. Cheers."

"Cheers. But, I mean, for certain, the Nevermind has your back. But sometimes . . ."

Dune interrupted him. "There's no 'sometimes' involved. This project is sanctioned. The rite will go down in the Bennu cult's history."

I wasn't sure what they chatted about. It seemed complicated and I hadn't swotted up on deception. It was so awful sounding, hearing about the double dealings Agents of the Nevermind no doubt did all the time, it made me nauseous. Oh, yeah, and mead. I'd somehow forgotten all about hangovers.

Huld made me weirder than ever. Like he played some archetypal role in an inauguration into a death cult. Half of me was in the underworld, and half in the upper world.

Dune had informed me, through obtuse hints, about the equinox ritual. I felt like one of Dune's post-hypnotic suggestions took me over. I intuited the ritual on so many levels it was dizzying, as if I'd already started it in some dreamy parts of myself. Nearing the date, part of me rose, another part sank. But for a moment, the two aspects of me would unite for the equinox. Not my usual Sunday afternoon thought.

Part of me left Atlantis and rose to Shambhala. I existed in two mythological ancestries merging into one. A compartment launched on a mission to make the public believe in one legend being supreme because it fit into the prophecy of their people.

It was something about the White Tsar talking up Britain in channeled messages from an Ascended Master from an ancient culture, a Master who claimed to be from the best root race. And he'd remained oh so pristine and pure. Natch. I played both sides against myself in an Enochian chess game ritual. A section of me, down in the ground, waiting to arise, waiting to become the New World. *Damn*, I got freaky!

Dune had given me a love note that day. I pulled it out of my bra, but I'd spilled mead on it, and the ink had run. Damn, my dress and bra stained with blue ink. I peeked inside, pulling the wet dress away as I looked down my collar. My breast was painted too, words against flesh, from where the paper had imprinted against it. Lifted by the sheer material. "TRANSFORMATIVE LOVE." I put the note down on the floor as I lay hidden behind the bronze trunk. I was trolleyed.

But what were they talking about? Placing whose DNA sample in the lab? Could be talking about anyone. *What* truth about a body? Were they framing Kevin? Protecting him?

I scooted out of the room on my butt and then sat in the hallway just outside. I got up and padded off to get a huge pitcher of water to drink throughout the night.

Only later would I remember what I overheard in that room.

CHAPTER 8
BEAUTIFUL DAY INTERRUPTED

I woke with Dune asleep beside me and a psychedelic amanita in my fist. Now, *that* was the dog's! What a thoughtful gift. The phoenix, the Greek variant of Bennu, symbolized of that psychedelic mushroom. So, I devoured it, expecting fun times with the daylight.

I observed a fly crawl over his face a protracted time and I didn't shoo it off. Including when it clambered about in his ear.

Amanita, the origin of the Easter Egg. . .

Mystical sex with Dune would be splendid if I was tripping. Has he ingested an amanita already? I didn't wish to miss out. Adventurous. Anything could develop.

I eased out of bed without disturbing my husband, lit a candle, and sneaked into the oratory. I had to correct the armor goof in Luke's workshop. The library seemed the obvious place.

Wait. Had I woken Dune? No, the scuffling sound was in the room. Maybe rats. The sound came from the floor. I knew Dune couldn't be there, but still, I cringed opening the door. My heart was beating hard. I was a girl stealing a dollar from a mother's purse. Dune preventing me from visiting the oratory seemed preposterous. Creeeek. The armor display was where I'd left it. Yes!

I closed the door and stooped to the armor. I thought I'd remembered the display landing slightly differently. Rats had been worrying it. It was heavier and more awkward than I'd imagined. I was afraid I'd drop it again and break pieces off. But using the rope levered to a hook on the wall, I set the damn thing upright. It stood on its own, balanced. Well-made display.

I took in the surroundings. Some original altar clothes and religious tapestries were still intact. One wall was stacked high with boxes of alchemical homeopathic and gem essences ready to mail.

As I slid past the choir stalls, more of the original oratory furnishings came into view. A painted rood-screen and an altar chest. A burnished church plate, glazed windows, embroidered vestments. I could make out where the chaplain said the Mass and led prayers. And there was the area where the knights performed customs of the Night Vigil when their old selves were crushed, and they were reborn from the ashes into loyal knighthood.

While the castle was minimalist, with nothing fancy, this room was elaborate, with hidden corners, curtains, a cage, a loft, the section where the singers sat when it was a chapel, the podium, the splendid copper piped organ. I admired a painting, of Luke in the usual suit of armor, working with the slender assistant, Tommy, produced in the style of the Old Masters. I hadn't noticed it when I was there before.

Between them was a figure of a woman with a smaller woman inside her, pale and translucent. And inside her was a smaller woman, barely visible. Each woman had a sigil painted on her forehead. I had no notion what the little squiggles signified, but they looked like they held impressive arcane secrets. The women sat on a throne constructed from ground Moldavite. The throne glowed and was levitating, with Enochian angels on the upper edges. A long-haired angel blew a horn, and the other held a British flag. I couldn't help touching it, the texture was so rich. Dry and scratchy. I swept off inches of dust, then realized how noticeable that was. I dusted it with my sleeve, but that was more noticeable. I had to hope dust covered it before Dune entered that room. *He won't go there until the equinox ritual.* It was already the morning of the eighteenth.

I thumbed through the titles hungrily, fascinated by how many branches of intelligence manipulated occult history to persuade the public to embrace war. Agencies employed charismatic visionaries. Then, when alliances changed, agents morphed the legends once again. I picked up more paper and the quill and took notes.

A sound. Stopping moving, I prepared to dive under a table. Nothing. I didn't want Dune to find me snooping around where he had instructed me not to go. I found paper and a quill and made notes. I found a place to hide them.

I discovered a section of books by the Gothic novelist, Lord Edmond Bulwer-Lytton, who inspired Madame Blavatsky to found the Theosophical Society, leading to Nazism. Tibet invited the Nazis to protect it from Chinese Communism. The Nazis gained their belief from Lytton that their supernatural Aryan ancestral utopia, Thule, was Atlantis. And they were determined to learn from Tibet (the homeland of Aryan migrants from Thule) how to use the Vril and breed a pure bloodline in which the power of the Atlanteans could manifest. The subjects Lytton concocted about an underground race using the Vril force was no fantasy out of the blue, but popular legend.

I leafed through his novel, *Vril: The Power of the Coming Race*, which altered the course of history. He detailed initiation rituals into occult secret societies, harkening back to Egypt, which influenced Blavatsky to look to Egyptian initiation rites in her early Theosophical texts. Only after the Theosophical Society moved to India did she switch to the East as the basis for metaphysical knowledge.

The book in the castle library was first edition, with a leather cover. He continued the trend of mystical propaganda. The author believed in a hollow Earth, which the Nazis took seriously. I wouldn't discuss the book with Dune because the plot promoted Shambhala as the best ancestry.

Dripping water on the roof as the storm began made gorgeous circular visuals arising from the depths of the oncoming mushroom trip. My eyes lit up the vibrating pages. I continued on, horrified that Bulwer-Lytton was a darker figure than I'd realized. People actually took his fiction seriously like it was history. I guess people just wanted the narrative to *be* true.

Secret Agent Crowley was one individual who had promoted Bulwer-Lytton's fiction as being fact. An oil painting of him and Aldous Huxley arm in arm stared down from the library wall, lit ominously by the candles. Chins up and eyebrows arched, they reigned over that section as if challenging anyone to dare question any of the nonsense. Crowley was always up to something. He and his cronies created the British intelligence drug ring, the Golden Dawn. Crowley didn't mess around with his mysticism.

I read on, doing my best to follow the words as they fluttered and layered in 3D, studying about the predecessors of the Agents of the Nevermind and the Bennu Society.

Huxley lurked behind the opium war against America, that rat. Huxley left Britain and moved to the U.S. and wrote movie scripts. Meanwhile, he put together an Isis cult, with lots of famous authors in it.

He got multitudes of people into consciousness expanding drugs while he was working with the CIA. Huxley worked with Sandoz, the company that made LSD and psilocybin for MKULTRA: the CIA's mind-control program. The head of the CIA Allen Dulles, and Timothy Leary bought the LSD and enticed the hippies into the scene. Those CIA guys got all those vulnerable kids going to San Francisco to live in the safe houses and join cults and get hooked on the drugs the CIA imported from Vietnam.

They chunked them in jail. Yeah, that threw the anti-war activists off target.

Hell, those 60's and 70's kids couldn't even *find* the target after that. They were the arrow, the bow, the pulsating universe, a dream in the mind of some Eastern deity. I identified with them when the mushroom came on. That's what I'd been missing around the stodgy old castle in the middle of nowhere. Drugs.

Then, I spotted a book on moving sacred energy between sex partners. I read through the first pages, wishing I could take it with me. The pages had incredible mandala illustrations superimposed . . . No, mind hallucinated the vivid colors.

The text of a Western mystical sensuality straightforward, non-denominational method of circulating energy described what Dune, and I had done. It ended with a stern warning never to end a session as he had instructed me. "One must *always* finish by directing your own aura to be comfortable in your own body only and your partner's aura to ease its way into inhabiting her body and only hers. Otherwise, you will do dark magick. You will be a vampire. You will tie your beloved to you, trapped forever unless you sever the ties, even after death.

"This has long been a prevalent part of Vajrayana, Tantrayana Tibetan Buddhism. Lamas traditionally use this approach to vampirize the twelve-year-old girls they get drunk and force into performing ritual roles in their practices. The men then draw feminine essence from them and discard them the next day as worthless to society or they often have killed them and even dismembered them in the burning grounds as meditations."

This answer to my earlier question shook me. I thought of making love with Dune. I thought of drawing in Sylvia's aura. Dune had never trained us to separate them afterwards. I was a vampire. And so was Miriam.

I didn't feel like studying anymore. I stashed my new notes with the others.

Strange sounds. How vividly my mind played tricks. That

comforted me; I'd surely been hallucinating the sounds in the castle all along. The sinuous smoke from the blown-out candle entered my nostrils. It hit my palate. I closed my eyes. I was smoke; I was gray dance. Hallucinated music came from nowhere. Its patterns spread tiny quantum foam dots, magnified to my vision because I was going beyond humanity, beyond mediocre limitations everyone took for granted. I caressed every wall with the center of my palm. I pressed my cheek against the cool smooth stone.

As I slid across the walls, my top button knocked off when it hit a snag. My breast popped out. I reached to the silky skin. I heard tinkly laughter submerged in my psyche. Me, but not me.

My skin savored the rough grout between the stones impacted my womb, like yet another story inside. Other stories inside *it* remained untold, so many of them. These inner stories disappeared into the distance in a paisley design, fading out into the fog. The fog between us all. Soft and protective, our friend.

Bending and reaching as high as I could. I pulled up a chair to stand on and stretched far as my body allowed into the limitless above; my spirit continued upward. Above me were corners, but I didn't believe in corners anymore. They became multi-corners, morphing rounded, impinging on reality and turning colors. I became wisps and overlapping swirls.

I lay in the chair with overlapping visions of Bennu as an alchemical symbol, representing the chemical color changes. My thoughts became red, orange, yellow and then dream. I tunneled back into the dark ethers of something else, becoming someone else, distilled, a daikini, someone not me: Sylvia.

I spun inside a tornado tightening fleshly pleasure rooms opening. As the orgasmic tornado turned. Exquisite light ran through my loins. I was a beast of passion. I was liquid pleasure. I, as Sylvia, spoke aloud, the vibrating voice layering one wave on top of another wave: "Any life is mediocre compared to this liminal life. Do not leave me. Do not let me die."

I roused in the morning, glad I'd made it to bed and hadn't gotten caught in the oratory. I was Susan again. I'd dreamed of my sister, enriching color and touch, possibility and thirst for adventures. *I'm convincing myself not to neglect my sister.* Memories of her as a toddler arose in that fuzzy way infant memories reappear out of the blue.

As Dune slept, I fondled his collar bone, his hair, his eyelids. When he awoke, and we started the day, Dune applied make-up on me. I lined his eyes too, so sexy after that I could hardly contain myself.

Dune took me into the depths of the castle before letting me get dressed. The stairs dusty and cobwebby, I wasn't so sure barefoot was the best idea.

And then, I saw, in the torchlight: the cistern. They were often part of castles on little rocky hills, as the wells couldn't be dug for a steady, reliable reserve source of fluids for a large army defending the castle Lords and Ladies. It was carved out of the rock below, more porous and rough than the stones brought there to form the walls. Sand filtered the rain, supplying it healthy spa minerals.

The torch's reflections were grand. The walls had pigment from ancient dyes, which I hadn't seen elsewhere. Stones were smudged with what looked to be iron oxide, turning it red. Other rocks were tinged with green from a chemical added to the mix. It wasn't precise and fancy, but that's how the castle was. I preferred it far more than shiny modern expensive. The place was an animal to cherish, bestial, thick and simple, mysterious.

When I turned, Dune's shirt was already off. I regretted missing the process. But no, actually, the sudden impact was more dramatic. Shockingly so. His muscles were artistic, not too bulky, but cut. Water reflections dappling that V chest. Dune undressed the rest of the way, his jaw firm, not smiling, but maintaining a seductive look, I did too. We stood naked, facing each other across the cistern. He flicked something hanging beside him: a combination of pipes, bells, springs, and pouring water. Once set in motion, it continued, and the peculiar movements created pleasing sounds.

The cistern was a long narrow rectangle, appropriate for swimming laps in. I held my hand out to him, and he mirrored me. We sauntered into the cistern and drifted onto our backs, luxurious, breathing in sync. I approached Dune and laid my hands against his torso, feeling him along the slender waist. I savored the sensations on my palms as I lifted them and placed them again on his flesh, and I explored territory outward across the vector of his chest. I savored the moment, immersed in more hedonism than I usually allowed myself.

I slid along his arms as I pushed them out and up. I pressed Dune's wrists against the wall. I held both wrists with a hand, and with the other pulled the hair at the nape and nibbled and licked his shoulder. Dune moaned, his head falling against the wall, as he waved his pelvis toward mine. I grabbed hold of his hips and tugged him toward me.

He commanded, "Susan, breathe universal energy from the ground. You know how it's done. Turn your eyes up above you, like you're looking high up, higher, and higher, drawing the energy up with the direction of your eyes. Earn each inch of the height with expansive joy, with the wisdom of your higher self. Perfect."

I loved it. I was a fountain of bliss.

"Now, spread your vision out, way up there; look at the plane you've arrived at. The higher frequency world. I'm doing it too. Let's explore it."

Silent after that, I didn't see much but colors and geometric shapes. I could only hope he was seeing the same thing. It didn't matter. We were explorers, adventurers of other worlds.

The strange music, made from water pouring from one container into another, the pressure hitting chimes, the chimes hitting bells, and so forth delighted me. No wonder he wanted to take me to the castle, just us. I hoped for no more visitors, no more business, nothing but this, this, and this.

Loud, insistent knocking. I'd break apart our auras later.

Dune picked up the sheet, and I threw on underwear as I hopped. I waited outside the kitchen for Dune to get the special key, and we went to the door. I hid behind a corner and peaked. The police cared about my well-being. This was a party.

It was the stranger in suede again, but this time, he wasn't alone. There was a car and two bobbies, flashing their badges.

I bent to grab the sheer fabric draping the chair and wrapped myself in it, stepping forward.

The stranger's tan jacket was becoming more deer-like; he had a sensitive face with high cheekbones, big brown soulful eyes, quiet, poised movements. His eyes lit up when he saw me. His brown skin glowed translucent.

Infinite longing to be his was my sickness.

Dune stood there shirtless, a hypnotic black magician from Atlantis clasping the black sheet around his neck as a cape, unmoving, dominant as ever, both feet planted flat on the ground. He commanded, "Don't say anything. I'll handle it."

The cop came closer.

"This man," Dune said, "seems to have mistaken my wife for her standby. Colin has lost the plot and thinks my wife is the woman who takes her place. He's such a gannet."

That's *Colin*? Miriam mentioned him. A close friend she'd known a month or two. She'd mentioned he was handsome, but that there was someone else that fascinated her so much she couldn't begin to consider him as a lover. Too bad for her. He was a catch!

The stockier one jerked his gun at Dune, silently commanded him to go outside.

In a minute, Dune said, "Look, let me get you Susan's photo ID. It's over here."

"Tell me where it is, and I'll get it. Keep your hands up."

"Yes, that's my wife if you look at the driver's license picture over there. Susan Marie Thornley."

"I see."

"She's fine. We're on vacation. It's not us you need to be concerned with: it's our stalker, here. He tried to abduct my wife from the premises."

I wanted Miriam to be fine. I relived the conversation I'd overheard. Colin should be in the loony before he hurt someone. But, still, nothing was right.

"In fact," added Dune. "Miriam had told me her boyfriend had been vicious. Well, this is her boyfriend. She said she worried he might hurt her. I'd check about to see if she's alive."

I said, "Miriam said nothing about having a boyfriend. She talked about a very nice close male friend."

Dune spoke louder. "I hope Miriam is safe. There have been multiple reports among members of our troupe that Colin was abusing her. Some said they feared for her. Will you make sure?"

I was shocked. I'd had no idea she was suffering through that. I remembered seeing bruises once but assumed she bumped into something.

"Gone off his meds," said a policeman. "Eh, off your meds?"

"I don't take any meds. Look, I'm perfectly sane."

The other one looked at Colin sadly before handcuffing him and putting him inside the car. "You've got to stop harassing these innocent folks, now."

The tallest policeman, an unremarkable looking young man with a shaved head, pulled me aside, whispering, and asked me, "Are you all right? Are you really Dune's wife?"

"Of course, I am." I showed him my wedding ring with the inscription from Dune. I was glad he didn't ask for our address back in the city. Or any details as my head filled with cotton.

I pleaded, "Be nice to the fellow. Colin seems like a kind soul."

"Unless we find reason not to, we'll release him. But listen, you seem impaired. Are you certain the statement is correct?"

"What statement?"

"Did this man accost you on this property?"

"If that's what Dune said."

"I understand, ma'am, but please answer the questions. Did he grab you and coax you to leave?"

I wanted to save him and say no. But, I'm an honest person. And I'd be calling Dune a liar. So, I said, "Yes, that's true."

"Do you want to press charges for attempted rape or attempted kidnapping, trespassing on private property . . ."

I thought about it. If he'd killed Miriam already and had gone insane, he could be dangerous. It could be wise to lock him up.

On the other hand, Colin hadn't hurt me. Yet.

I wanted to see him more. Some mass murderers were attractive. I would have fallen for them. Scary.

I took the risk. "No. He's been a gentleman. He's kind enough."

Dune walked up to the policeman and said, raising his voice with each sentence, "I think you forgot to check something before following up on this ridiculous lead. Do you know what you forgot to check?"

"No. But I have a feeling you're going to tell . . ."

"Hell, yes, I'm going to tell you. I'm a bloody Agent of the bloody Nevermind."

The policeman stuttered for a second before regaining composure, as he walked. He uttered, "I'm sorry, sir. We won't bother you again." He looked back over his shoulder, adding, "Whether you need help or not." That was not a sentence I'd soon forget.

Dune pointed at me as if stabbing me right through my heart, and said, "Get inside."

They spoke outside. Dune asked, "Do you think they'll arrest Colin? Do you think he'll be able to post bail if they do?"

The policeman answered: "His mental issues will make him a

suspect if she's missing. We'll watch if he's a threat to himself or others."

"We're assuming Miriam has jaunted off on a vacation. But if she's murdered, well, if detectives find his DNA samples, fingerprints or shoe prints at the scene of the crime, at that point, yes. The forensics lab in the city is well-connected. Agents compliment it all the time." He scowled at Dune.

The policeman handed Dune a piece of paper to sign, saying, "This statement that this man is trespassing on your property if he ever returns should carry extra weight with your *No Trespassing* sign near the road."

Dune signed it with relish.

When he closed the door, he said, "A good Nevermind wife pretends she never heard secrets of the Agency. Intelligence secrets are matters of national security."

Colin, Huld, and Dune were all dangerous men. And I was there with them isolated from everyone. Police would no longer help.

Dune turned, his sculptural bone structure idealized art. Even as I stood there watching the back of his head as he went to Luke's desk, I wanted to hold onto him, pleading for answers.

I wanted Dune like wildfire. Stupid, *stupid* woman feelings. Stories from my friends and stories online told about women going down some crazy rabbit hole because they fell in love with someone who sucked them in. And here I was doing it, myself. *I'll never laugh at one of them again.*

I wanted to run into the woods. To free myself from how much I wanted him, I'd have to go toward something else I hungered for even more intensely. I fantasized I could find Miriam and Colin and huddle together in *their* world. Like children climbing into a fort, we could be the good guys together. Someone could bring snacks.

I'd even wanted to hitch a ride with the police. I didn't fancy struggling to explain a vague sense of unease to men in uniforms under harsh lights: "I'm having these subtle problems with my husband, nothing I can put my finger on. No, he's being nice. Anyway, can you take me someplace? By the way, the owner's gone and we're here instead." No, not how it's done.

My mind swirled. I tried to follow the angles of what I might have heard. But swirls don't do angles well. The back of my throat got sticky. I could barely swallow. I tried and gagged. Oh God, poor Miriam. I curled over inside, my intestines groveling at my heart.

Sure, she had a crush on my husband and maybe had taken his attentions from me. What woman could resist his charms? She didn't deserve to die.

Colin might be luring me into the abyss with him, to lure me into the deepest, darkest part of the little forest, to do who knows what? I tried not to imagine him slitting Miriam's veins. The image kept coming, making me shudder. I shook my arms and tried to imagine other ways he could have killed her instead. He could have bludgeoned her. Poisoned her. Thrown her in a lake. That seemed most likely. A body, bloated in the water for days. My face scorching and my muscles clenched, I paced around the room to shake them out.

Light from the window through the trees dappled everything for a minute; it was hard to hate my life. I was glad to be alive. Glad. I wouldn't take it for granted ever. No, not one day.

I put on clothes. If she was dead, what a sad loss of a life. She was honest. An earnest woman. She could have gone on to great things. Even living a normal life day by day, frequenting cafes, going for swims, climbing the hills, and skipping on cobblestone: that was stupendous.

I teared up when I remembered her rich golden strands of hair among the other variations of blonde. The flaxen, the brown, the red. Those golden ones lit up like fire when she was out in the sunshine.

I watched Dune writing at Luke's desk, his body turned to the side with the grace of a dancer. I had to push away my feelings for Colin. There was no one left to flee with, running naked, my hair streaming, lifting me, twirling me around over the gorse and the heather. I didn't want to leave with Huld. If I wanted to be human and cuddle, I had to cling to Dune. He was all I had. And I couldn't help it. I was made of passion.

CHAPTER 9
SNEAKING INTO THE WORLD OF SECRETS

The next morning, when Dune took my hand, I accompanied him to Martha's wardrobe where he chose a long, elegantly beige dress for me. Draping it over his arm, he bowed, with perfect posture, neck lengthened, chin torqued at a formal angle as in a historical romance film. "Here, you're shivering." He helped me into the black spider web covering with flared sleeves and a sheen that captured the candle-light, producing patterns on the pale fabric. I wasn't used to dressing that way, but nylon street clothes and tennis shoes were blasphemous at such a romantic location. While buttoning the collar, I saw a mammal outside the window loitering in the trees in the distance. Colin? I bent over and peered into the distance.

Dune must have had good peripheral vision. He bent his elbow, as if for an Elizabethan dance. "Ah," he said, escorting me from the window, "it's an animal rummaging again, isn't it? Come on, let's step out of this draft. Look, Susan, don't get caught up in the little stuff. If you bother about the details. I thought you realized how critical you are, but you're still missing the big picture."

He settled his knuckles against my upper back, pressing into the muscles. Ah, the massage. I braced against the wall, leaned my head backward, and closed my eyes. Had he located the places that needed massage most? "Breathe, while looking here along the top of your skull. When breathing out, squeeze the throat muscles so I detect the air passing through. Tighten the muscles in the diaphragm in and lift up; just be careful. Lift your eyes. Perfect. How much light can you see behind your eyelids? The red looks brighter, yes?"

That was a fantastic meditation technique. I smiled, letting my eyeballs relax beneath closed lids. I was expanding into a plane a few inches above my head. I repeated it, experimenting, rising a few inches higher, looking left and right above my head. I relaxed outward, keeping my eyes at the right focus to imagine spreading out at a higher level of joy. I could abide at that level.

Dune led an expedition to a blissful utopia floating in my aura. Auras could do a lot; they overlapped, spun through each other, killed or healed, left bits and bobs behind, disclosed secrets.

I faced the window. I wanted to lead an expedition to that invisible realm with Colin. Pure. My aura ached for him.

On spiral stairs, Dune supported me over eroded steps. We traversed echoey tunnels to a room, its curved entryway alive with spiders. He destroyed webs before my face. A spider dropped onto my eye. Its feet tapped my eyelashes and tangled up in them. Swatting, I knocked it away. Ugh!

"They aren't poisonous," he said. "Ignore them."

I opened my eyes into cautious slits.

It would be nonsensical to leave a brilliant husband for the crazed ragamuffin stalking us like an animal of prey outside the fortress I had the opportunity to live in, protected, adored, learning esoteric secrets, ravished by a debonair magickian.

I imagined the soundtrack. Vigorous and exhilarating, I'd leap through the air in red lights against burnish orange in the painting behind, my leg out in front in yellow tights. Singing in the air, expressing archetypal powers. I missed the theater.

"Since I'm better, I should return to my career."

"Your career has moved on to a higher level. It's here, around you, now. Don't worry. There is an audience. The Bennu Society meets here. You won't need to dance for them. Unless you want to m'Lady." He bowed.

The way he said the words made me tingle. He chucked under my chin with a winning smile. His slightest movements were exquisite and commanding. I was still breathing light. This was the yoga of auras. Moving my body to expand beyond it.

"I'm getting to the age when I'd struggle with the rigors of dance. But I could act. I'm fortunate that Papa and Mama got me lessons in both from an early age. What would I do if I stopped performing in theaters and only did it for the Bennu Society?" I was chuffed my cancer had obviously gone into remission and possibilities for my life spread before me.

"Raise a child. That's the natural next stage of our marriage, as planned."

A baby sounded delightful. But I wasn't sure about committing to Dune. I imagined him a dominating father. I had to reconsider that choice.

My eyes drew to a lush painting on the wall and he said, "The frame's painted with gold leaf. The paint's infused with monoatomic gold. Luke worked at night, by the windows." It glowed.

"Why?"

"To let the moonlight fall on them."

"What for?"

"To activate transformational properties."

My sinuses clogged when I picked up a heavy book to dust. "I don't think much about such things. Do I?"

"You've forgotten the effects of the vials of the homeopathic powder." He opened a filigreed box and took out a vial. The way he lifted his mouth was just too tempting. "I've had you take them daily since we married."

"Oh?" *Ha, homeopathy.*

"And Sylvia took it before that. You remember how that made her glow, too."

I remembered her from memories captured in photographs stuck on the theater's greenroom walls. The beach, building a sandcastle, wearing pink and orange terrycloth dressy-thingies over bathing suits. Sylvia in the front yard with a robin on her shoulder.

I stopped dusting and stood. "Until she died."

Dune looked at his desk and turned his chair to face me. "Oh, come off it. You don't even remember her dying. Describe her funeral."

I couldn't. A cemetery. Her tombstone. I got nothin'.

When I gasped after an inexplicable noise, I asked Dune, "Am I imagining sounds?"

He looked in the wrong direction, and shook his head, no. "Maybe you're hearing the gauris," he said, "as the Tibetan Book of the Dead calls them. Otherwise known as dakinis or sky walkers. Some, after the right sacrifices, are angelic, bright fairylike. Those appear at the end of the initiation. Others are demonic, horrific. Encountering them happens on the path to Tibetan Tantric enlightenment."

"That sounds ugly. Why traumatize people?"

"The gauris try to induce people in the Bardo who have died to be reborn, trapping them in the Wheel of Life. Alchemy governs them, and Tantrism subjugates them by raping them, skewering them, burning them. . ."

"That's enough ways to kill them, thank you." I didn't believe I heard wails and lures of sky walkers, but it was still gruesome to contemplate how Dune's eyes glittered discussing violence.

"The sky walkers were once living women, you know, put through Tantric fire sacrifices."

"Like burning witches?"

"But more perverse." He smiled delightedly.

"And *why* hear such a thing in this castle, pray tell?"

"The Great Art is a tradition here. Luke's ancestors studied alchemical masters who traveled to the East as soon as possible. The *Klachakra Tantra* is the last scripture of Vajrayana Buddhism, so it's the most modern representation of the practice of Buddhist alchemical Time Tantra sex ritual."

"You said a mouthful. I don't understand why people focus on extracting gold from base substances."

"It's beyond that. Kelley may have been the only person to master that, using the Moldavite catalyst."

I rolled my eyes. "You can't tell me you believe that."

"Why not? But if you look at gold as meaning wealth, Tantric rites manifest riches. Alchemy is more than that. Healing, enlightenment, elixirs for sorcery, the initiation path combining chemical experiments with yoga and Tantric sexual rituals."

"You're talking Asia? What about Europe?"

"They do the same. Egypt founded it and branched to India, China, England. . . Bennu is the symbol. Alchemical texts about chemicals fusions are erotic scenarios." He leered at me, miming pouring liquid from one beaker into another. "Besides, levels of initiation revealing deeper meanings of what 'spiritual gold' means. It refers to the Philosopher's Stone, or Hermetic Elixir. Spiritual gold symbolizes that catalytic stone, Moldavite, transforming the adepts who pursue the path into becoming supermen."

"How did they do that?"

"The alchemical initiate endures successive transmutations as in homeopathy, removing the actual substance through successive percussions to leave only the esoteric essence.

"The adept's personality disperses then recombines, reconfigures, repeats, like Tantric rituals when the practitioner dissolves his ego to reconstruct himself as divine. Coarse matter transmutes through the Tantric alchemical law of inversion."

"Coarse matter? That's basic stuff we see around us? Lead?"

"Yes, and in the rituals, they use everything base -- poo, pee, menstrual blood, cadavers, eye of newt, whores. Women."

"Lovely."

"It's burned, covered in soot. That's the alchemical blackening stage and turned into an elixir in the whitening stage. The divine Buddhist goddess, the Woman in White, the sky walker, who remains, is both the sexual fantasy of the man and also the elixir in a glass vial. The elixir is given to the vajra master during sacrifice. Every European adept and every Tibetan Tantric master seeks this out. Read about it one day if you don't believe."

"Great, I'm ready!"

"Not yet. The grimoire goes into great depth. I'm already breaking the rules." He looked around as if expecting someone to overhear him. A crow, rat or ghost?

"Well, go on, then."

"After the adepts drink the elixir of the ethereal feminine, she disperses into his psyche. He has absorbed and overcome the feminine, taken control over her. He becomes the lord of both genders."

"What happens to the woman? Does she die? Or is she cast off?"

Dune refused to answer.

"The adept parents himself. He marries himself, has the male energies moving up the right side of his body and the female energies moving down the left. He connects the female of the base to the male of the crown, the magnetic polarity of the spine buzzing and growing more intense. This finger is female; this one is male. Can you feel it?" With his index finger, he touched my tailbone. My pelvis thrust forward as if a snake made of fire.

"So, basically, that's what our shows dramatize."

For a moment, I had a stab of memory that wasn't my own. It felt like it was Miriam's memory. What the hell? Her running along a field, chasing an owl at night. I shook my head. I had to stop going crazy.

"They're public rituals of the Bennu Society."

So, they glorify the European branch, but only skim the surface. "Anyone with a ticket can take part."

"Private advanced rituals occur here."

"Sacrifices?"

He only winked. Was he back to his usual obtuseness?

"You feel something profound from drinking the elixir. You never took interest in their recipes."

I made a funny face. He was right, no doubt.

He continued. "Don't try to understand it, not linearly. Everything happens at once. On multiple parallel planes. Endless variations pulsing out of tiny quantum foam wormholes." He strode over, stretched tall and stood above me, his puffy Byronic sleeve brushing my shoulder. He bent over me; his lips in front of me. "And here, we have little need for something so boring as memory."

I cleared my throat and waited, instead of acting on impulse. I asked, "It's dreamy here, isn't it, where contradictory things can happen at once?"

"You couldn't even begin to tell your friends secrets of the universe. We're going further into the mysteries. This is your victory."

"I have a destiny made of love?" *Someone is right if they say we're special. Don't we?*

"The elixir helps you understand how important that is. Take another dose. Accept your divine nature. The role you play in the renewal of the planet out of the ashes of ignorance and despair. Your true nature as the secret to immortality. You are the true Bennu bird of our age."

I *had* forgotten my divine destiny. I couldn't review on my life and lay out what had happened.

He reached into a brilliant red cabinet and lifted a bottle shaped like a serpent wound around a large egg. The egg coloring resembled the early stages of an amanita mushroom when it was egg shaped, with no stem, sitting on the ground. The top of the bottle was the snake's head sticking up above the egg.

Dune flipped the egg back at the jaw hinge, pulled the tongue to open the inner seal, then stuck in the spoon. He pulled out the spoon with powder, and he held it to my nose. I breathed it in hard, and then he gave me two more. I floated bright. *It could be the placebo effect.*

I couldn't tell if he was taking the piss. What he said was ridiculous. But it was tempting to believe. My mind slid through identity and consciousness, anyway.

He kissed me hard. The mouth of that dark wizard was too luscious to be a saint. The mouth of someone resembling me, with a wild destiny wrapped in mystery. Dull metal dragged the floor again, near the door. It moved an inch. The ethereal doppelgangers of Luke and Tommy? Imprints of monks and priests that visited for months at a time, doing just that. Auras could linger, ghosts in both life and after life. I was becoming more sensitive.

"Rats," he said. "Nasty health hazards, aren't they? I hate to poison them though."

"Poor little creatures. It's their castle."

"You don't mind hearing them here and there sometimes, do you?"

As we walked toward the door, something brushed my arm, but when I turned, nothing there. Nothing at all but a shadowy trick. *Must have been a moth.* I hugged myself, pulling my clothes tighter.

❄

That afternoon, in Dune's absence, I explored the forbidden. He sanctioned sections of the castle to show-off and take credit.

I crept to the oratory, past beakers, glass jars, rows of vials filled with solvents, tubes. I picked up paper and quill, and continued walking past preparations of spagyric plants, metals and salts, elixirs of gemstones, monoatomic powders, mineral magic.

I decided which must be the Moldavite Room: the exit in the back of the oratory led straight to it. The inlay of the Grail-shaped green stone provided the clue. But it had a custom-made padlock. I wanted to fortify myself with knowledge; something big was coming.

The numerology in the castle held meaning. These ritual-obsessed people never allowed random numbers in a padlock. I tried combinations of numbers, riffing off the stained-glass windows, the strange stairways. I tried numbers from a scroll in the oratory depicting Crowley's Enochian sex magick ceremony. It worked.

I opened the door: two hundred tons of rock.

Boxes loomed, marked with Moldavite information. Part resembled a museum, ledges and racks of spectacular pieces. Each shelf had plaques with historical tidbits; I skimmed through, taking notes. I'd enacted a minor part of its history. I read familiar legends on the plaques written in matter-of-fact tone. "The Stone of Heaven belonged to the Emperor of Atlantis and then he sent part to King Solomon and the other parts to a Tibetan monastery." How many New Age sorts of folk who collected Moldavite necklaces, pendants, altars, and wands in spiritual practices believed that history?

Is sneaking around an addiction? No, a grand plan.

The pithy summations on the plaques put everything in perspective. "Nicholas Roerich, the Russian explorer who traveled through Asia in the 1920s and 30s, discovered the Magical Chintamani Crystal. He transported the crystal to a Tibetan monastery called Shigatse, the esoteric Land of Immortals. He carried the rock there to reunite it with the motherload to fulfill a prophecy. Russian Madam Blavatsky wrote about, and the British Theosophist Alice Bailey channeled, Shigatse, headquarters of the

Great White Brotherhood, home of Ascended Masters. This mother of the New Age created what she first called the Tibetan Lodge and 'channeled' a Tibetan master about how Shambhala was the seat of purifying Cosmic Fire." Was something in the castle going to be purified by fire?

I believed in channeling when younger. So many fake things in the world.

A scroll showed a woman holding a piece to her third eye and seeing visions, and a man using it to channel healing to a sick child on a blanket. A youthful person held onto it, lying in bed while his astral self hovered. Another held it while drumming beside a fire and his shamanic self ran through woods with cheetah spots. An old man rested with fragments of it on each chakra, and an old woman held it as a key to open the Hall of Akashic Records.

Neolithic talismans and amulets in the shape of fertility goddesses were displayed under glass. A horrific painting on wood showed the gem falling from Lucifer's red forehead, his eyes fierce, flames searing the air around him. An angel waited to catch it. In the next panel, the angel carved the Moldavite into the Grail as Adam waited behind him, in Eden.

A vajra, a tool of Tibetan Vajrayana Buddhism, otherwise known as Tantrism, perched on the top shelf, centering concentric circles of velvet. It represents lightning as a weapon and the penis. Traditionally constructed of gemstones, this featured Moldavite.

"Roerich took a sample to Europe to bolster the League of Nations. When the League of Nations faltered, he took the Moldavite to a monastery in Tibet." So, this mentioned highlights of Moldavite history from the Shambhala side of the story. Just the contrary of what I predicted in a castle where Dune brought me.

Why did the Bennu Society counter popularizing awareness of the Buddhist history? Why fret over the Shambhala movie coming out? Or did they act concerned to fool me? That made sense, considering I listened to top secret exchanges.

"Monks in Tibet and Mongolia announced the King of the World would come from Shambhala with an army to eradicate evil and rule Earth with the power of Moldavite. Asian chronicles say aliens from a planet circling Sirius gifted the stone. Sirians gave Moldavite to the King of the World in Shambhala."

I found it curious that Luke displayed that plaque, considering intelligence agents subverted British colonization with that prophecy. Roerich, Blavatsky, The Tibetan, and Alice Bailey hyped those myths to unify Russia with Central Asia, India, Mongolia, Tibet and China against British imperialism. Buddhist Asia's expectations of the White Tsar rising out of Shambhala with a mission to free them made them amenable to Communism. And Moldavite would shine the light of utopia to create a nice, pastel "Dear Ones" existence.

The English grew comfier when Annie Besant and Charles Leadbeater took over the Theosophical Society: Theosophical alliance reversed from Russian and Asia to Britain.

Someone other than Luke hand-wrote the placards. When I knocked a placard stand onto the floor and picked it up, I noticed the back featured another language. Connection to the only Moldavite museum in the world, the one in the Czech Republic? The museum robbed blind a couple years before?

Had the plaques come from that museum? From the bookstore. Stores nearby. I paid more attention. "According to lamas, citizens of Orion presented Chintamani Stone to Earth to aid our spiritual evolution." Hm.

And, there was a box in the corner labeled, "Mummy dust." *Got to love it.*

I grew confused from time to time by the odd sounds. The room breathed. I shook it off; I'd heard it previously, and nothing transpired. Old castles could be creaky.

"Muhammad took pieces of Moldavite to Mecca."

Why display placards from the museum? Had Agents robbed it? *Right after Dune and I honeymooned. A marvelous thing we visited when we did.*

"Vincent Bridges claimed Edward Kelley used Moldavite to precipitate gold for the emperor in Prague. But he couldn't keep doing successful alchemy and the emperor punished him."

Hold on. Dune had mentioned something about our caper at the museum. Caper had a few definitions. I hadn't considered "robbery." Wait.

I noticed a draft. When I looked toward the door, I startled. The armor display faced me in the hallway. Stunned when I saw the volume of stone, I must have left the door open. Dune placed the armor to make me guilty for trespassing. Embarrassing.

I flew to the door, bracing for Dune to chastise me; he wasn't there. I called into the oratory to no answer. No reason to leave. *If in trouble, it should be worth it.*

I returned to my shocking line of inquiry. The possibility shattered my notion of myself. True, I remembered little of my past. Still, I'd assumed I was a law abiding, honest person. Was I a thief?

I flipped from an alkaline little body to an acidic, cringing in the corner. My muscles hurt as if thrown in ice.

Dune and I raided the museum and stashed loot in Luke's castle. This reminded me of nightmares of burying someone I'd slain.

But even that didn't explain the volume of rock. A major portion of Moldavite in existence.

I searched boxes for papers explaining the situation. *Wait. Is Dune coming? No?*

Moods turned into a carousel. I rehearsed what attitude to hold. I'd stand up to him, yell sarcastic accusations. But why?

I had to *understand* before he returned. I ran to the door. No one. I knelt, opening a box in the back corner; a Brown Recluse spider crawled out. I bolted, throwing the box, striking the edge of a shelf. The stones on the end rocked, rattled, slipped toward the edge. A gorgeous rock fell. I gaped when another fell. I caught it with lightning reflexes, stomped, hunting the spider which rushed toward me until I squashed it.

I opened the box and stood back, waited, tapped the box, plucked the top page by its corner, no spiders. Receipts for the last year. Then, I registered. Each receipt was for Moldavite. The Bennu Society created the Moldavite shortage.

This is where it gets real. They'd bought it from countless people selling online through online stores, personal websites, indie-commerce, small businesses making jewelry. From collectors online and in person. New Age stores and gem shows. Spiritual groups and mediums. They'd even bought the fake stuff.

Why?

Mad alchemists used the largest mass of Moldavite in the entire Earth to contact the souls of Atlantean giants? To contact Huld's reincarnation family?

Many people still trust that magicians in Atlantis used crystal technology too advanced for their ethics, sinking the continent. Was this a repeat? Was the Bennu Society reversing electrical charges of rituals to make Atlantis rise? Luke used a room full of Moldavite to make the elixir?

They hoarded it to prevent Shambhala-heads from performing competing rituals? If so, why display plaques, honoring Eastern-centric mythology?

Taking notes on sales and the theft, detailed numbers, dates, codes, names, locations, everything, I couldn't condone the forced scarcity, even if it was legal. Our theft was legal just because Agents act for the country. No law forbade one organization buying a gem. Not unless the Free the Moldavite activists lobbied enough, the proposed law passed.

I slid past the armor display and locked the padlock, popped into the oratory and stashed my notes, and put the quill in the drawer.

Time to face the consequences of snooping.

❄

I practiced excuses for breaking the rules. I concentrated on my talent for figuring out the numbers to the padlock. *Yes, that's my angle.* And I'd make up for my mistake. I dusted.

I stiffened my stomach as if shielding it from a blow when Dune's footsteps reverberated in the corridor. When he stepped into the solar, I dusted with enthusiasm. I braced for chastisement, but he looked tranquil. I said, "Dust carries parasites that makes people get colds."

"I'm fine. Are you worried you might catch a bug?"

"No, no, just thinking of you. Don't want you to get sick."

"Thank you, darling."

After dusting with increasing speed, I burst out, "I'm not superb at going by rules, am I?"

"Are you using something unconventional to dust? The vinegar works fine."

Hm. He ignored my transgression in the forbidden rooms. Was he gaslighting me to punish me? I tested different tactics. "Museum thieves are naughty." I gave my best "flirty girl needs a spank."

"Oh, you remembered, did you? That's my girl. I'm chuffed you're embracing your past. Yes, you were spectacular at the museum. Top-notch team work."

"You put me up to it."

Laughing, he kissed me.

I said, "So, rituals to get attention of Atlantis giants, eh?" Stupid question. "Finished with this room, on to the next." I scooted out, dusting the paintings in the hallway. The first painting portrayed ancient Atlantis, so I skimped on dusting, hoping that if Dune came out to engage me further, I could distract him from that concept. I untied the red laces across the lace covering my bosom and exposed a shoulder. When he came around the corner, I bent invitingly to dust the spymaster Walsingham.

Dune pressed me against the wall and leaned into me, making me breathe fast and drop the rag. Even though I changed the topic, it still felt odd he avoided the question. Was he covering up the Atlantis ritual?

"Is Luke a closet Buddhist? Does he favor Shambhala?"

Furrowing his brow, Dune retreated. I grew eager to grasp why Luke embraced the Shambhala myth and the importance Moldavite played.

In Luke's castle, other than that room, nothing indicated he was a Buddhist or Hindu. "Is Luke into the Hindu manuscript, the Vishnu Purana?"

"What's that?" He circled my ear with his thumb.

"It includes the original depiction of Shambhala."

"When?" He crowded up against me again and sucked one of my fingers after another.

"In the fourth century. Shambhala birthed an incarnation of the avatar to destroy invaders, contributing to the golden age. Is Luke interested in the Kalchakra?"

Those Buddhist texts referred to the land of Shambhala and the destruction of invaders, ushering in a golden age.

Dune shrugged. Suspicious. Instead of a ritual linking to Atlantis, a ritual to link to Shambhala! Why would the Bennu Society switch allegiance back to the troublesome days when the Russians headed Theosophy?

I wouldn't mention Agents buying up all the Moldavite. He hadn't caught me. *I'll pretend I have no clue how they had so much of it. I began to suspect they obtained it purely for financial reasons, to make it worth more, so they could market it later and fund Nevermind psy-ops.*

Turning away, I hugged myself against the chill. When the goosebumps left, I put my hands in my jacket pockets. I noticed a scrap of paper in one. I started to mention it to Dune. Had he passed me a love note? I read the first sentence. Ink on a torn page of an ancient alchemical book: "Tell no one about this note."

I laughed and glanced over at him, grinning. A rich meta-joke. I almost showed the paper to Dune and praise Luke for his sense of humor until realizing it wasn't Luke's handwriting. I'd seen his writing around enough. It smelled like the paper I'd found in the oratory. I turned it over and discovered unfamiliar tiny writing on the back.

Something isn't right. Does Dune have a multiple personality? Dissociative Identity Disorder commonly occurred among Agents. Often their programming from youth. The whistleblower, N--, had spoken on indie-journalist Brandon's video on the CIA's MKULTRA programming which became a core technique of the Nevermind.

One of Dune's personalities had written me the note and didn't want the alternate personality to know. Multiple personalities each had their own handwriting style.

I excused myself to the loo, the most private place to read the minuscule print as the candle flickered and sizzled out: "Trust your gut, not your eyes. Don't let Dune die until he frees you from the spell. Don't escape unless you're free."

I sympathized with Dune, an isolated part of his psyche writing cryptic things. When had he lost control of his cohesive personality? Trauma too much for a person to handle causes the psyche to split.

The note was part of some game, or a relic from a demented guest in the past. A rat had carried the note and put in my pocket to build a nest.

I'll keep acting like I don't know what's going on. I mean, not that I actually have any clue, anyway...

CHAPTER 10
SUSTAIN

Next day, once I stopped slumping from guilt, I acted like a Lady with her Lord. Only took a week in a castle. I moved with grace and style, dancing among mottled furniture.

A new painting had appeared, an old painting taken. *I can't abandon a sick man. Dune needs help.* But a word about a psychiatrist and he'll throw a wobbler.

Nameless dread welled up under my skin. Chest muscles clenched together. Dune had arranged a healing holiday for me, which created a miracle. Get back to living instead of preparing for death.

My beloved stood by me, mentored me into a theatrical star. He'd made exquisite love, was a patriotic hypnotist. Chewing my cheek, I drew blood.

I danced into the kitchen where Dune drummed on pots and we sang. I built a fire to heat water to wash soaking dishes.

When my hunger grew savage enough to comply, Dune picked up rope from the corner of the kitchen and asked, "Are you ready to gather bracken at the bottom of the cliff? It's not bad. Not too bad."

Rope I'd used to lift the armor. Is Dune taunting? His expression gave nothing away. I longed to go out.

We geared up and headed out. We stayed clear of the peat bog below when he taught using a bow to hunt red deer, fox, and mountain hare.

I shot a hare. Watching life-force fade, and the shocking red made my breath come heavy. I was the blood, life force fading, was forest. I was past, was past time, was beyond space, was the life I took and ate, and I was its death.

"I'm looking forward to reading Luke's ritual grimoire," I said, carrying the hare, blood dripping on my dress and shoes. Wiping with one shoe with the bottom of the other made me trip. Dune took it with a gentlemanly nod. Sharp plants poking up jabbed my ankle. "I want to study the equinox ritual in the oratory library."

"No."

"Why?"

"The Woman in White remains innocent."

"What if I don't want to?"

"You will."

If I robbed a museum in the Czech Republic, I could do anything. Black-hearted bitch.

Then, we paused at the rustle of footsteps among the trees. He pulled me to him, running toward the castle which wasn't far. I craved turning to see if it was Colin, but I was pressed against his coat. I heard Colin calling. It made no sense if the police had him in custody. They let him go!

Why didn't Dune warn me the man outside abused Miriam and people worried for her life?

Dune had his hand over my ear; I couldn't make out what he said.

"What?" I said.

"Shh!" He whispered. "It's nothing. Just a tourist tosser, but I don't want them to ruin the mint magic of our day with chatter about where to get decent scones and how primitive we are out here with no internet reception."

I panted. "Tourists doing a little forest loitering?"

What if it was Colin? Dune put his hand over my mouth as we ran. It was all I could do not to bite.

Dune was so obtuse it put my teeth on edge.

I had to face it. Something was going on with me. Beyond a miraculous healing of cancer and a persistent memory-fail that made me question my thoughts. Why did I hallucinate footsteps? Considering I was probably invited to secret meetings, did I forget? How make everything right?

In heated fantasies of Miriam, we romped through the forest in diaphanous dresses, barefoot, long hair streaming, merging into each other, out of each other, scissoring each other as we floated above trees, moaning ancient songs.

I'll escape to Miriam. Would she take me? She's missing.

Could I walk outside alone, much less trek to a missing woman's house in the city? Even if I found the key, stole the car and drove with no idea how, wrecking, risking being pulled over without a license, well, he was an Agent. He could do no wrong in the eyes of the law. Officials with his project would hunt me down.

Colin would be OK out there. He hunted animals. If he hiked enough, a neighbor would relent and help him out.

Maybe I should do that?

What would I say if I ran up to a neighbor, my lips all dry? "Hi, can you help me run away from my husband?"

"Why?" they'd ask.

"A mysterious note? I heard soft noises?"

"You have rats. It happens." Oh, so reasonable they'd be.

"I saw visions? Smelled odd scents? Forgot everything?"

They'd drive me to the loony.

Legally I can't disclose Agent business. Besides, there's no point: no judge would prosecute Dune for vacationing with his wife, for exhibiting subtle oddities as she healed from terminal cancer.

I took steps in one way, then the other. I had to commit to remaining. Learn dangerous secrets of a gothic ritual. OR I had to commit to becoming a fugitive, accompanying a murder, hiding from an intelligence agent.

I was skint. Our cell phones were at the theater. But I could try to use someone's once I got into range. I didn't remember numbers. My memory of friends and family was an odd haze.

A raven cawed. A deer in the distance. I writhed free, and, bow and arrows on my back, set chase fast, calling to Dune, "I've got this one." I was chuffed Dune didn't insist on coming with me. Pretending to hunt allowed me to disappear in the forest, an excuse to run away. I'd just keep walking.

I should hide daytimes in trees or in a crevice, cliff, a stream, or huddled in the bushes, and wander to a helpful neighbor.

I ducked behind a bush and watched for activity. Stillness. Rich smells of the heath made me breathe them deeply. I said goodbye to the castle. Romantic, that it was, and horror.

Strangely, more than my husband, I'd miss my standby's boyfriend. The hardest part was leaving him to languish sleeping in the branches, dewy in the night chill, with no rental car I saw, no phone reception, no sympathetic neighbors anywhere. Forgetting Colin was challenging, though he had a sweetheart.

Unless he'd killed her and was available. *Ha, just my type.*

The moon lit a balmy night. The flowering ground cover smelled like freedom.

Something stirred and hid behind a tall bush full of huge thorns. Colin, *right there!* He arose, dusted himself off, and looked around, crouching as if flexed to defend himself. His face bled.

I embraced him! Touching his body with mine, I gasped. My vision lightened. Harmony whooshed from him, overtaking the sky. Gray circles of air, not visible but to the auric-sighted, spun in front like a tornado opening at me, enclosing me, stretching me to my outer limits, twisting me beyond them into more oxygen, more glory, more Colin.

I could use him to escape. I pulled back, holding onto his elbows, my eyes wide in front of his. I took a deep breath and then shut my mouth tight. Even if we escaped without capture, think of the dangers.

Withdrawing, I shook my head. Pushed him on the chest, his pectoral muscles delicious under my palms. That wouldn't do. Crazed men assaulted women all the time.

He clutched my shoulders. "What?"

I raised my hands between his arms and pushed outward, freeing myself. With deep set hazel eyes pleading, he kneeled before me. His jacket torn, face sooty, hair tangled, he said, "Let me take care of you."

I turned, so he didn't see my bemused smirk. I headed toward Dune.

Colin called, "Wait! Don't go! Come home with me. This is your chance!" He lunged toward me and grabbed me, bruising my arm, his eyes wild.

I refused to go with a madman. He spun, sprinting, holding onto me, dragging me down. I landed on the corner of a flat rock in front of the door, cutting my knee.

I stifled a scream. I pushed my attacker's hands away, kicked him in the groin, to growls of pain. He almost followed me out of the forest where Dune could have seen. I flung him down.

"Go, then!" he cried.

I bent to catch my breath, glad I'd had the strength to defend myself. What an arrogant, delusional bum. Far too persistent a stalker to flatter me. He didn't want me because I was special or as lovely as Miriam. He wanted me because he was deranged, and that was that.

I ambled toward Dune, calling, "Deer got away."

No one loves me more than Dune. I didn't want to take a chance getting caught for my indiscretion. I ran away from my protector!

Dune was rational. I hugged Dune for comfort. I agreed with him. I'd been naïve, needed to listen to my husband. He knew what he was talking about when he said I shouldn't wander out there alone, for fear of that desperado. And I'd bitten Dune.

I looked around for honey for the bite to prevent infection. I'd planned to help the attacker Dune shielded me from! Smearing the disinfecting goo on the tooth marks, I bandaged his cheek. Whatever he was going through, I'd help him. In two days, I'd learn secrets lifting me to the skies.

CHAPTER 11
PEARLS AND PEWTER

I awoke the next morning to a door creak. I glanced around, envisioning the Bennu Society meeting at the thick tables, drinking mead from ancient tankards. Maybe knights died there, and their ghosts teased me. I wasn't sure about ghosts before. As good a place to start as any.

I was groggy, but when Dune offered exploring the property, I perked up. He handed me a cup of gorse tea.

Mummy dust was portrayed in one painting, prescribed by an apothecary. Beside him, customers levitated from the effects of the monoatomic gold residuals from the tombs of Old Kingdom Egypt. Mummy-duster-ingesters looked hundreds of years old, gray beards reaching across the artwork. I yearned to leave the cobwebbed, crusty old castle turning me into mummy dust.

I leaped about when we emerged into the sunshine. We found sour berries. A squirrel caught in the trap Dune had put out before bed spasmed when we approached. Poor creature. So much fur, and mucus in the corners of the poor thing's eyes, and feet partially gnawed off. No denial possible. No claiming to be civilized while picking up animals with eyes wide and paws gnawed.

My life was easy compared to Colin's. I imagined him eating

weeds, pooping in holes, washing with dew. Who knew where he nested, where he ranged?

Dune put the squirrel in the sack over his back, adjusting the bow he carried. He showed me an empty nest, and where to search for eggs in the spring. I felt strangely like Miriam, who would have felt more compassion for the squirrel than I did. She wouldn't have been able to eat it. In my moment of feeling like Miriam, I was vulnerable, fragile, alone in a vast wilderness of confusion and despair.

I willed myself to fully remember who I was: *Susan*. I must have always presumed, as an Agent of the Nevermind, Dune tortured people, controlling their minds, creating delusions, for a political agenda. The illusions made proxy wars profitable, regime changes bloody, destroyed the reputations of whistleblowers. Just par for the course.

Yet, I knew Agents believed they did the correct thing for global balance of power. They sacrificed relationships, the ability to tell the truth, chances to goof around and follow where their passions lay. They performed responsibility to the government of a country of wonderful culture. And those qualities made Dune stand tall.

Overhead, a sound, and cracking of a branch. Colin fell, his body twisting from the tree, his foot caught in a vine which ripped from the tree with his weight.

Dune gave him the two-fingered salute at the sound of the thud.

Colin struggled to free himself from the vine that held his foot in the air, then rolled away into a run.

Dune drew his bow and arrow and set chase.

I called to him, "Come here! Dune! Stop it!"

What right did Dune have to wound the poor man? Sure, maybe Colin was a deranged murderer. But it still didn't seem right to take the chance of murdering him. With the legal route, Colin would have a trial. Well, men will be men. Sometimes they take protectiveness too far.

It was a puzzle. Why had I married a man with dubious moral standing? Part of me chose a crazy stranger's life over Dune's at that moment. I would have shot Dune to prevent him hurting Colin if I'd had a bow and arrow, myself. I'd only borrowed his that day when he taught me to improve my skills.

I called out to Dune, "What are you doing?" But he kept up the chase.

I ran after him.

I wanted to call Colin, instead. How inappropriate. Yet my chest ached for him. Colin ran towards a car in the distance, which he'd pulled far off the dirt road, to a low area in the shade.

He fumbled with his keys, and Dune, to his credit, didn't shoot the man with the arrows but instead, with perfect aim, which he'd tried to teach me in the past in our back yard at home, shot out all four tires, one. At. A. Time.

They were unique tires for an uncommon small car. There would be no easy replacing of those bad boys.

I pounded him on the back. "So, now he can't leave. What are you thinking, Dune? You wanted him gone. He'll be here permanently. Or, until he dies out there."

He gripped my wrists and held them together, shoving me away from him. "You didn't want me to kill him. I did the next best thing. He won't be abducting you, now."

"Let me go. I'll see if he's all right. I need to take him some water. What do you expect him to do now?"

"You will not! You're not to talk to him, do you follow me?"

"I will if I want to!"

Dune spun around and drew the bow and shot the arrow. Colin made a sound like a creature in the distance. The animal in me was magnetized to the animal in him. We're all wild here. And getting wilder by the minute.

Dune picked me up and carried me into the castle while I battled against him.

He was strong, and he was animal, and we were going mad. All of us, madder, and madder, in the isolation of the wild.

❄

When he set me in the entrance, I pummeled Dune's chest and tore his shirt, sweaty, clinging against his muscular chest. "How could you do that?"

"Protecting my woman from being abducted by insane trespasser. Did you forget he's unstable? You're *welcome*."

"I guess."

"If you don't appreciate the value of my bow and arrow skills, no reason to hunt for you. You do it. If you want meat, get it yourself, woman. If you can. I'll be watching you from the tower. I'll see if you talk to Colin. But he won't approach you, now, will he?"

"No, he probably won't."

"I'm effective."

"I'm famished." Long stretches without food made me dizzy. Berries would not be enough. I needed to hunt. If Colin tried to attack me, I'd shoot him with an arrow.

As I chased a hare, arrow ready, my stomach turned. I was inclined to pet it, and feed it snacks.

I pulled it ligament from bone from muscle from organ, from lymph and vein. From sweat and fur. From feather or tooth. Life was gore. Life was death.

The hills were stupendous. Bird songs kept me company until I returned home, bloody, and triumphant.

No rental or borrowed vehicle anywhere. *Probably hitched a ride.* A series of rides was possible in two days, with excellent luck, and money to pay off drivers.

If Colin did that, he could have brought a tire repair liquid, and been mobile. I strained to see any signs of it in the distance. Damn! It was no longer tire damage Colin had to worry about.

Sometime when I wasn't looking, Dune had sneaked out of the castle and bashed it to hell.

Removing muddy shoes, I shook off the gorse and brushed off the stickers. I cooked the hare on the thick iron grill on the fireplace for dinner.

Dune stood over the fire. The flames turned Dune's features scary. His nostrils glowed. Face flushed. I threw the water we kept by the fire at his face. "Brute!"

He didn't even jump, but laughed, as water dripped off his nose.

Why did I let you abuse Miriam? Riding her to be like me, harder and harder, till the poor girl was a mess. That's not art. That's abuse. I shouldn't have taken part.

I asked, "Why are you so cruel? Stop laughing! Oh, come on, Dune. You *know* I want you to hypnotize me to remember what happened at the well house. Nothing's been right since."

I yanked the necklace off and threw it at his face, pieces of it flying everywhere. He picked up the pewter tray as a shield. The pearls clattered against it and he shielded his face, with a half grin.

I stared at my vague reflection in the soft scratchy gray and said: "Why do I look like Miriam?" I threw his hand and covered my face with my hands. I stamped my bare foot, forgetting the hardness of the stone floor. It hurt, and that made him chuckle.

He put his warm hand on my shoulder. "Yes, you look marvelous, Susan. As good as when I married you. It must be this celebration of our love that's making you young and vivacious. And our vacation healing you, making you into a whole new woman."

I smiled, pulling my lips to inspect my teeth as I bent forward to peer at the tray he held. Was it because he was putting make-up on me to make me her? I struggled to hold my lips up when I thought I saw red marks around my neck.

I lifted my fingers to my collarbone to check if the necklace had cut me when I pulled it off. No, my skin was fine. My neck looked burned with friction as I looked in the tray. My face grew more swollen and red, blue around the edges, by the second.

I screamed. I punched the tray out of Dune's strong hands, sending it, along with my hallucinations in its reflection, into the fire. I pulled the metal out, staring into the orange flames in it. I dropped it on the grayer floor and grabbed my burned hand.

It wasn't Dune going mad. It was me. Had I written the note in the alchemy room, myself? What was *wrong* with me?

I had to pull myself together and act sane.

I withdrew to our bedroom while he huffed off to his study. But I was restless. I sat in the wall seat and stared at the gilded herald. The carving and tracery, and the decorative metal work along the sides, were stunning. On it were Luke's books. I tried to read the tosh book on the giants of Atlantis, but the illogic made me clench my teeth so much I threw it against the wall.

I wandered the halls and found the small room filled with alchemical books. I wanted to light them on fire. But I had nothing against Luke.

I picked up a book from the center of the desk and threw. A photo of my twin fell out. It was taken when she was the original star of Bennu troupe, and I was her standby. It was true: I remembered little about Sylvia. "Much" meaning "anything."

I felt like two women. "Dune, take me home. I feel uneasy here."

"No."

"What do you mean, no? Aren't we here for fun? We can go any time, can't we?"

"No."

"I can walk."

"No, you can't. The only neighbors for miles won't open their doors to you, I promise. The houses near here are vacant now. There are no phone towers. No one picks up hitch hikers here.

It's either stay here with me or take your chances in the great unknown."

I thought about stealing his car. I didn't drive at all, had no idea how to, having always lived in a city where I could take public transportation or cabs. And his car was a stick shift. I had no ID or gas money. The car wasn't registered to me. I'd have to think it through. Steal cash.

"Can I borrow your car keys? I left something in the trunk."

"I keep them locked up in a safe, little Missy, and you'd never guess the combination."

"Dune! What do you take me for?"

"Someone sublet our house. If you go to the city, memory loss will be a serious problem. Here, live at the moment, and I'll take care of everything until you're yourself. Why buck the healing process?"

"I don't want cancer."

"Here, the whole of Five Eyes intelligence has your back. If you leave here now, our marriage is over. The Joint Intelligence Committee will turn against you. Why leave?"

"What do I get out of it?"

"Don't you want to see what Luke and Huld and I have devised for you?"

I had a hunger. I wanted the story. To understand occult secrets from the inside out. I'd embed inside the Nevermind, nested in the Bennu Society, nested inside something inchoate, both wondrous and vampiric. Then it would be time to go. The Club de Berne could tap me on the shoulder and say, "Love him always or we'll hunt you down," for all I cared. All the intelligence agencies in the world couldn't convince me to stay with Dune if I didn't want to. Even if I *was* the archetype of highest-level member's secret initiations.

Dune strode outside, without saying why. I followed behind him. I didn't want him hurting Colin again. The clouds sliced through the moon. The moon dappled shadow slid across Dune's body. An arrow whizzed past him! He cursed and ran back toward the doorway, seizing the arrow.

"It's one of mine," he said.

"It must be one you shot at Colin's tires."

"That lad is smarter than I expected. He figured out to make a bow. Assuming he wasn't an expert in primitive survival skills?"

"How would you expect me to know?"

"Of course."

Dune was destructible. I picked up the arrow. I weighed it in my hand, felt the smooth wood. I poked the tip into my palm. Time vibrated in both directions.

We went back inside, saying nothing.

I slept, and my dream grew more excited. I held a box shaped like an amanita. I opened the lid. I was Sylvia. A whole world was there.

As Sylvia, I laughed, my head back. I was alive. I loved trees. I cherished the bird chorus in the spring early mornings. I loved blackjack and pancakes, needlepoint with blue and purple combinations, distant lights, and watching through windows with binoculars. Each memory shook me with joy. Each memory would be distilled in the elixir. How many opened their mouths for communion and received me on their tongue, the holy spirit of the trinity, the collapsible woman, the tiny dancer, the Sylvia.

Silver Sylvia.

CHAPTER 12
THE FACE AT THE WINDOW

Dreams kept something from me.

Next morning, I splashed water from a pewter pitcher. The kitchen, on a sunken floor, with a chimney that whisked the smoke at an angle, had a modernized small window reinforced with iron bars and thick glass that opened to let out smoke in emergencies. The only window that wasn't along the top of the castle.

I prodded around to find the keys. Leaving would be noisy, even if I were strong enough to lift the portcullis. But sometimes he left it up. I was unused to requesting permission to leave. The cupboards built into stone walls had ancient, sturdy locks on them. That must have been where rare spices lived. If I found Dune's keys to get to the keys and figured out the secret way to use them. *Oh, bother.*

There, at the kitchen window, inches from my eyes, Colin's face!

Suede jacket soaked, his sandy hair darkened, flattened against his head, his smooth skin almost translucent in the clustered lightning flashes. I gasped and knocked over a goblet.

Dune called out, "Is everything all right?"

"Just being clumsy me."

"Did the thunder startle you?"

A storm was blowing over us, the wind hurling the dark clouds along, rain pelting everything, including the unfortunate man.

"Yes. Sorry, just bustling in here."

Was Colin hungry? Did his wound need tending?

Has he confused me with Miriam because of delusion from hunger? I liked the hungry look in a man, making his cheekbones angular, his abdomen concave, his waist narrow. I gawked as he mouthed something. I feigned overlooking him, pretending that the lighting created a glare on the windows. I continued moving without disrupting my stride, peripheral vision heightened. I warmed when he lay hand over heart and then opened it toward me.

Was Miriam making noises in the corridors? Was she in the room with me?

That's what he's seeing! Miriam's ghost! Haunting me! I spun. I called out her name. "Miriam, give a sign."

Meanwhile, Colin scratched on the pane.

I scurried around and put tape, gauze, and peroxide in a bag. I put in matches, too, in case he needed to start a fire for warmth, cooking, or sterilization. I threw the bag, missing some feisty shrubbery that would have obscured it from his view. Would he find it? I closed the window and moved away.

I hoped Dune wouldn't find it or realize it was missing. I'd never get the chance to help Colin again. Colin tapped against the glass, but I didn't look. It seemed he might have died from infection if he didn't have some way to treat it. But, *now what?*

I lifted my chin going about my breakfast preparations, to present to him my most fetching profile, lengthening my neck, and upturning my lips. Two men I found enticing: one inside the fortress, one outside thick stone walls. The electricity could shatter the glass into a million pieces.

I skinned a hare. I put it over the fire to cook with older gorse leaves and a side of fresh gorse salad. Not my typical breakfast. The cooking smell was better than I'd expected. Was I tormenting Colin, cooking while he watched, starving out there?

When Dune came in to eat, Colin ducked down and ran off into the darkness. I moved in front of the window. The windows had numerical symbols I recognized from Luke's books. I was code breaking.

I jumped, startled by bright light. A loud snap, followed by thunder. "That struck close!" A tree had cracked, falling, hitting other trees, parts of it breaking off. I ran to the window to see if it had landed on Colin. Couldn't tell.

I gave Dune the stink eye.

"What. Oh, come off it, Susan. Would you prefer I inform the police Colin's come back and is harassing us?"

"No, don't do that." What should he do? Or what I should do. I squirmed. The decision was an itch, a scrape, acid on my body.

"Tell me the truth. Are you and Huld framing him for murder?"

Dune said nothing.

Did he think I'd just leave it at that forever? Why didn't it affect him what I thought? Wasn't he worried I'd tell the police?

We ate in silence.

I preferred that. If he wouldn't answer those questions, I had nothing to say. Ever. Again.

I looked toward the window, as I washed dishes, at heavy rain. I didn't trust Colin, and besides, his car was ruined. Dune would catch us. Agents ordered the police around. I didn't trust the neighbors or my ability to hot wire a car or drive a stick without lessons. No visitors. There was not one person. I'd run down the road and hope someone would pick me up instead of assassinating me.

❄

I set off seeking Miriam. In one room, evidence of fire. Cooking. Fur skinned from an animal. Did Dune have an eating disorder? I could picture that, with his obsessive, controlling nature. I inspected. An ex-convict or runaway teen? I peered around for cigarette butts, porn magazines, knives. Chamber pot in the corner. A towel. Complicated charts on the walls. And bones on a plate with meat on them.

Was Dune sneaking food? He needed professional help.

I searched for Miriam's clothing. Toiletries. Notebooks she scribbled in practicing mimicking my handwriting. I smelled the air for whiffs of floral perfume.

Miriam, prettier than me, was bedding my husband. She was eating the best game, while laughing at me for thinking Dune loved only me. Wafting her aura over us when we made love, turning it into threesomes. Mean Moon Miriam. I climbed, each step with numbers inscribed. Twelve of them, to the top, a stained-glass door. An odd construction, built into a niche. I didn't understand. I tried to open, but it didn't budge. I assumed it manifested esoteric symbolism.

I considered the Egyptian stairway to paradise, with twelve steps, and a door at the top. Sirius made of mosaic. Inscribed on the door: "*13th step available on other side*."

I entered. An old-fashioned toy, clockwork movement showed an eclipse. Everything was an initiation test, a system of disorientation. Descending the stairs reminded me of the prosperous American Sarah Winchester's estate, with esoteric numerology dictating the layout of stairs going nowhere.

I felt like Miriam again, for a heady, whirling moment. As Miriam, I longed for my father's love. I longed to make a name for myself. I ached for Colin to become more than a friend.

Susan. I was Susan. *I must be getting overheated.* I went over to a pitcher of water on a table and poured some of it on my face. The shock helped me regain my Susanness. Thank God.

❄

I slipped into the cobwebby ritual room in the oratory. When I opened the burnished door, I heard rats scurrying.

Enochian sigils dominated the location. The floor painting widened in concentric circles detailed with Angels in apricot robes. Circles inside the outer band marked four diametrically opposed Watchtower positions. Inside the inner circle, stood the Moldavite Grail.

The row of cracked, darkened life-sized figures was re-arranged. Roger Bacon, John Dee, Edward Kelley, Cayce, Hermes, Bennu, Lord and Ladies of the castle and associates. Tommy, Luke, King Arthur. Dry ice fizzled from a beaker.

I sheltered behind the door in the dungeon, breathing hard. I peeked out.

He ran and snatched me.

Without thinking, I shoved him onto an alchemy cabinet. The impulse to escape brought strength to my muscles, resolve to my ligaments. Up against the wobbling wood he held my wrists. I slid out of his grasp and reached for his throat.

A phantom voice called, "No!"

Pulling back, I saw above him a heavy stone that would have rolled off the cabinet onto his head.

Had I warned myself? It wasn't a Miriam-ghost voice. I crossed her off my list of explanations.

"I'm sorry," I said. "What's wrong?"

"You can't be in here."

He pushed me against the stairwell. When he kissed me hard, I slid my hands along him: such pleasing shapes, such fierceness.

I remembered the note. Someone was looking out for him.

Though I swung my head, he turned it to face him, kissing me with those lush lips. Proud of my discipline, I shot him a scornful look and strode well in front of him.

CHAPTER 13
EQUINOX

On the tenth morning, at the dining table, we finished tough stewed hare meat and tender greens from the yard. At least we had marmite. I wanted biscuits. Dune clarified he proposed to demonstrate his adoration. Fine wine from the back of the cellar? The choicest flowers plucked from the garden? Perfume from a cask stashed away centuries?

Dune declared, "So, I promised an equinox celebration, just us two. Equinox it is."

"Not my favorite holiday."

"At this juncture, the days and nights are the same. Balanced. Overlapping. Moon and sun. Perfect equation for magick."

I involuntarily drew in my jaw. I voluntarily pushed it back out. "I'm fed up with being wed to an Agent. What got into me to consider it?"

"*I* got into you. Deep inside." He reached toward my pelvis, his animal scent strong, his viral charm full on. The fascia covering my muscles, my organs, everything, softened and opened, but then flipped, tightening, protecting me, tugging my scalp; I shrank a millimeter.

I ignored what he said. “Murders, coups, proxy wars, fake news. Nevermind territory. Not pleasant stuff.”

“Would you rather observe the fall of Western Civilization? Prefer our excellent government unravel and England be taken over by a ruthless dictatorship where no one’s even allowed to speak English? Is England that dreadful? Don’t you appreciate what our countrymen accomplished in the arts? What about literature? Why, how about Crowley’s novel, *Moonchild*, for example? Doesn’t get better than that.”

“Crowley used occult mumbo jumbo for propaganda too. I have a conscience.”

“You do.”

“And Crowley was into rituals that exhausted women sexually, so their energy could be vampirized. Drive me into town to call my lawyer.” I removed my wedding ring. I set it on the table.

“Stop saying that!”

“What do you mean? Have I asked for a divorce before?” Mad at him over Miriam?

He hissed, “Shut up. I can’t stand it when you say that.”

“Why?”

“I love you.”

“You don’t show it.”

“I’ll pretend I didn’t hear that. And, so you don’t run to your lawyer, there will be special precautions in the fortress."

Women crave being loved excessively. A desperate eternal devotion in the vast windy moorland.

He stiffened his jaw and his fists, lifted his shoulders. “My dear, the Nevermind has an occult heart. And the Bennu Society beats it, circulating blood everywhere through the veins of our government. It makes coups and proxy wars *efficient*."

"You trick people into believing nonsense."

"Persuasion using mysticism is the most harmless method to protect our countries. You don’t want to see the UK and the U.S. become anemic, do you?”

Perhaps dust swelled his face, hooded and squinty. He said, "Forget it, darling. Today in the oratory you'll quaff the best drinks you ever have. From your Moldavite Grail."

"Yummy chocolate elixir milkshakes, I suppose."

"You've had enough from the buttery."

"And the bottlery." I sure fancied that old word. It made any day better.

His voice became more bellicose as he let out the honesty held back for years. "Yes, elixirs. Moldavite is the featured ingredient, flavored with an essence of Enochian. You think what Luke does is a hobby? His alchemy is the Bennu troupe, don't you get it?"

"No. What about greatness through dance? Entertainment. Storytelling to keep the old myths alive. Culture."

"Do you suppose I care how well the audience enjoys art for art's sake? Blondie, our shows convert the audience members into true believers. The rise of Atlantis has never been closer to fulfillment. You, Miriam and Sylvia are at the core. Our strategy for energetic immortality is working."

I guffawed. "Immortality."

"Each time newspapers review our shows, more people trust Britain's ancestral right to rule because of Atlantis. Because of King Arthur. Because of British Israelism. The right of royalty to counter the agitations of Republicans wanting to drop the royal station. You expect the Agency to allow that?"

"There are a small percentage of Republicans in the country. Are they that much a threat?"

"The Nevermind does not enjoy menace against sovereignty.

I told him, "Well, whatever. I need to spend a penny first."

He countered, "No time to lose."

Yeah, yeah, we had to be in place for the proper astrological alignment or astronomical, or some such assy thing. The good of humankind before my bum's comfort, and all that rot.

I should strike you over the head with this pan. Should stick you with this carving knife. I'll prove how stupid the equinox celebration is. Maybe he'd get why he should treat me well.

When we reached the door at the end, he knocked.

I teased him. "Polite to ghosts?"

"Habit," he said. Clanking from behind the thick door. *Must be something slipping from the vibration of knocking.*

He put his arm around me and guided me ahead of him, into the oratory. I pretended I'd never seen it. "Oh, it's lovely."

Dune's laugh echoed.

I smelled unwashed skin. Heard breathing. Spied nothing.

Dune led me, steps precarious in the dimness. Next to that entrance, when my vision adjusted, I noticed the scroll spread out and lacquered onto the wall. A tiny candle underneath illuminated rich details of cursive text under the mysterious images, symbolic code.

"Who's the figure in that artwork?" I admired the man's face, artistic and delicate. When I inspected the oratory, Dune had moved the painting to a different location. Quite the redecorator.

"It's Dune's assistant, Tommy. A master of Enochian spells he incants over the elixirs. Making them is labor-intensive and complicated." Low-tech machines occupied the workshop.

The depiction of Luke was gone. Dune had carried the armor display into the center. The visor still down, a candle on the gauntlet. I suspected the armor rested on a dummy. The other gauntlet clutched something undistinguishable, a wad of papers.

Dune looked deep into me, his face near mine, his breath on my forehead. He licked his lips and moved in. No, my mouth wouldn't touch those devastatingly curvy lips again. I determined to be no longer dominated by his immense sex appeal.

We swayed, his hands feeling the sides of my body.

I flashed on how the Egyptian Pharaohs passed down their lineage: the leader died, and then his son assumed leadership, the role of Osiris. Bennu rebirthed with each new leader out of the ashes of the old.

"Was Miriam sacrificed to the Bennu cult?"

Suppressed laughter broke from nowhere. I'd lost the plot.

Dune laughed right after; echoes came in reverse order. I struggled against Dune's hands, his fingernails pinching my arms.

I wished to report him for setting up Colin, but the police answered to the Nevermind. Report him to another agency? The Five Eyes intelligence networked with the Nevermind. They'd have no problem sacrificing a random Acquisitions Editor. I wanted to squeeze myself out like a tube.

At the conclusion of the red carpet, we approached an altar. A black cloth covered mysterious objects.

Above, a shelf containing the Moldavite Grail filled with elixir.

The anvil pointed my attention to the left and the right. Right side: torture. Left side: veneration.

To my left lurked metallic implements of extreme pain. My cold thighs buckled. I envisioned fingernails and toenails being pried off. Nails driven into my arms while being squeezed by a metal machine. I was dizzy.

To my right shone a gold headdress, a gold studded wedding gown with fringe of gold, and a Moldavite necklace.

"This is an important moment for the world." Dune had gone off his head. Dissociative Identity Disorder episode. Or Bipolar Disorder.

Choice is she hero or not?

He was more off than Colin. I fretted about that deer of a man. Colin wouldn't escape the castle grounds alone. Even deluded about me, he wasn't a killer. He needs therapy to support him through Miriam's death. I'll take Colin by the hand and run like hell.

Dune peered. "You become as archetypal and revered as your most exalted role in Bennu performances. Be put on a pedestal by the entire Bennu Society and the highest echelon of the Agency. Forget bothering with the initiated masses any longer. Graduate and claim your destiny."

"Oh, come off it." I sneered. I liked being revered. But Huld and Dune were framing Colin for Miriam's death.

I heard a groan. What the hell was that?

I froze. The candle resting in the gauntlet blew out.

I wanted to ask about the voices and laughter, hallucinated footsteps. But then, Dune would realize my mind was wrong. If I escaped, how could I talk to anyone I knew? I'd be embarrassed. If I left Dune, I'd hide.

Dune held onto me more tightly while I stood in front of the anvil. My arms lost circulation.

I'd watched David Lynch's Gothic psychological suspense. I inhabited the movie *Mulholland Drive. Or Inland Empire. Shutter Island. Mr. Robot.* I was a doppelgänger fever dream, acting a play in haunted masks.

Dune pulled a cord lifting a cloth behind the altar, revealing a painting on at eye level with names under the figures: Sylvia. Susan.

The painting portrayed Sylvia, wearing the Moldavite Bennu pendant, stylized victim of the murder. In the painting, her aura overlaid mine. I breathed in, consuming her as I tranced, eyes up, as I vampirized her, killing her, and taking her place as leader of the cult. I bent to sit on a green throne.

Dune didn't stop me from bending forward, stomach in pain. This situation I'd been inhabiting involved a core offering of countless occult secret societies: life extension. Immortality through energy vampirism. An immortal aura moved from person to person with Dune's hypnotic instructions. My embarrassing dreams of being Sylvia. She lived on, coming to the fore during amanita dreams. Dune orchestrated her death.

I was glad I had finished out the season without being embedded inside Miriam.

But maybe it's meant to happen!

I gasped at Dune's hot breath on my shoulder. I noticed the shadows flicker, and I spun round. Is Miriam hiding in the castle, waiting to vampirize me? Her overwhelming presence, our auras merged. Would that explain the sounds? I looked for her, my breath coming faster. *Is Huld still in the castle, waiting to murder me while she breathes me in?*

Torn apart, I wanted to get through the ritual, my wrist stinging from his grip. There was nothing to blow my nose on. The dust stuffed my sinuses so much my face ignominiously leaked.

"Your archetypal tears enhance Luke's alchemy. Initiates into the highest level will take the elixir."

"I'm not that archetypal. Just a woman." I mean, a great actress.

"That's where you're wrong. You're much more than a woman." He lifted my hand in old-fashioned grand manner, as if for a formal dance. He directed me a few steps so to peer farther past the corner into the compartment of the Grail Bennu. The future appeared sumptuous, crimson thin cloth draped near the candle light gave it an enticing atmosphere.

Private grimoires promised secrets of existence, a waist cinch, a jewel-encrusted throne, surreal dream murals that stretched far into the shadows.

Dune said, in a matter-of-fact tone, "The Project gives the Agency clout."

Hornets stung my psyche.

"Is this what you want instead? Or to be honored?"

He gripped my shoulder blade, freezing it in place. He guided me with pressure acidic, sick doom, horror beyond everything, into utter failure.

I was pointless. The light in that corridor was gray from the dull sheet draped over the candle light. On top of a table, its surface printed on it to look like bleached-out dull poodles, were miniature pastel ceramic cherubs.

It was the restaurant I most reviled. That dull old sentimental glitter-craft vibe, ugh. Slow talk.

I felt like the floor was moving. Then, I got it. If I left Dune, I'd have less money. Divorce was impractical until I was sure my cancer healed. A divorce to die alone was ridiculous. If I ran, I might end up eating alone. The awful future wasn't poverty. It was being where no one realized I was a great actress. Not an ordinary woman eating in a restaurant with gray walls.

Gray walls in my mind crumbled. The world got sickly slippy slidey. There was nothing to hold on to. I needed to be in an institution; no, what a horrible fate. I'd do anything to hide what I was experiencing to avoid drooling from Thorazine, nurses talking as to a child, asking if I wanted to play Bingo, and if I wanted a bland cookie.

I slid into chintzy gray reality with the neon chartreuse nylon apron. This was my torture. This was my future.

I'd tried to be Sylvia. Dying my hair to have that silvery blond tone that shone a light into the darkness. I'd never been able to live up to her talent when I'd taken her place.

Sylvia, I didn't mean to kill you!

Memories overlapped my mind, being an aspiring ventriloquist as a girl. Trying to please my father by being a perfect actress. But who was my father?

It felt like one of Dune's post-hypnotic pranks: a prank I kept going even though I shouldn't. I needed to stay with Dune for continuity. Otherwise, I would fall into the abyss and lose identity, memory, decency and wake up in a grimy restaurant wearing matching beige.

I hadn't seen the wood. It was prepared with open space in the center.

"Just let me leave."

His nose reddened and moistened. "I'm not letting you go the city and tell people our secrets. No."

"I promise to keep quiet."

When he blinked, two tears rolled down his chiseled cheeks. His cheeks went slack, his jaw quivering. "It doesn't matter. You were aware what happens when you signed on to play Bennu in the show. You burn and rise from your ashes."

"I signed a contract to perform shows for an audience, as a job."

"You signed onto more than that."

"It was entertainment. Simple stuff. I didn't know it was about Nevermind."

"You read enough history to know better."

"I played a role."

"You still are. Deep down, you know you are. That's what you do. Who would care about you otherwise?"

That thought felt like dying.

He pressured me. "We have to act fast to complete this ritual. You might descend into the depths of cognitive dissonance and go into a coma. We have to act fast while you're still primed and ready to be reborn from your ashes."

I pushed against him, trying to reach the door. I yelled, "Get off me!"

He nodded. "Secret societies around the world through history try to break the code. We found the key. It's happening now. Blood in the Grail. Smoke of Bennu."

For a second, I was relieved, despite his sarcasm. I wouldn't be a nobody.

"What you do now rejuvenates top-level Bennu Society members."

I kicked him, aiming for the groin, missing when he turned. He pushed me into position centering the circle of wood. He shackled me to a pole in the center, against the image of a sun eclipsing the moon, with a fiery Bennu flaming out of it.

His icy eyes froze time.

"Let's find out how big the flames will be. Any guesses what fuels it? Hm? The fuel determines how big the fire will be. The fuel is: records of you trespassing in the oratory and Moldavite Room. Notes you hid."

Had he been in there, hiding and watching?

Movement, clanking. Something dragging coming from the other side of the room. No rats.

"Stop!" Dune yelled, and the sounds quieted. "The last moments are the most important."

I stopped.

He took down the Grail. "Here we have Moldavite, which Edward Kelley used to create gold for the emperor in Prague, with the help of the alchemical ritual people have been trying to discover since. The Enochian Angels revealed to Luke, in visions, how to emulate that ritual. You, my dear, are the key ingredient."

He bent over and rose, chanting in Enochian with each bow.

Counterpointing clanking, chains dragged near the doorway.

Crumpled notes flew from behind me, landing on the twigs. I couldn't take my eyes off the mystery. Dune counted each note. "One. Two. Three. Four." The notes didn't stop. This was the epitome of true Horror.

My plan to learn from the oratory and Moldavite Room had backfired, maybe was deadly. He took a tin of long matches off the high mantel and lit each note. I tried to turn to spot where the notes came from out of thin air, but I couldn't move from the pole.

The blaze spread through the circle of twigs and sawdust, under larger sticks. The heat was immediate, and the smoke was thick. I coughed. I wanted to hug my dress close, so it didn't catch fire, but my hands were shackled. The increasing heat turned Dune's face into a mirage.

So, he would kill me even though Miriam and I weren't merging auras in an Immortality Project? So, this was the end of the line of transference of the aura?

He cut across the vein in the crook of my right arm and held the Grail to collect the blood. He intoned an Enochian script in rhythms, his voice deepening for the performance of his life. The smoke and fire around him made his silhouette impressive.

"Your blood, your tears when it's time. With the special electrical charge, the sun and the moon of you, on this day, in this place. Far above the others, taking us to the next level of true magick."

"No!"

"Mixed with monoatomic gold, with star born Moldavite essence, the traditional betrothal gift, a stone only nobility wore. The stone of Bennu, consumed by fire, reborn from fire. Enochian Angels, please bless this mixture: may it serve your kind well. May the empire never die."

He looked over at a corner with a warning. He jumped back and raised his hands. "Would you suffer your entire life for a woman you've never met before?" he added, pointing to the instruments of torture.

Is he going into a psychotic break?

"Did you think I married you for love, Susan?"

I struggled against my shackles, breaking the skin on my hips, bruising my bones, but nothing hurt me as much as that question.

I cried. He caught my tears in a vial, sighing with satisfaction while stopping it up before the heat dried it. "Essence of Double Envy," he said. "Perfect. Now, the elixirs are nearly complete." Ah, so he said that to make me jealous. He distilled jealousy.

When he continued, I stopped paying so much attention to his every word as if the truth.

"I never cared for you the way I did for Miriam." He let himself lose control at the perfect moment. Twisted resentment. And yet, it was ritual: an emotional torment.

"Remember, nothing is ever enough. Your aura is becoming more porous from envy. Good, good. When people ingest the elixir, then their auras become more porous, too." Here's the secret: envy makes one person puncture the person she envies. She pulls from the envied one's wound, bringing the vital life force into her own body. Bringing the life she wants inside herself."

Had he been sneaking off to make love with Moon Miriam while I slept? How humiliating.

Then, he spoke to the empty room. Did we inhabit a world of ghosts?

"Now, the deed is done. Success. The essence of your Recursive Tears of envy, on this day of all days in the Grail.

He demonstrated it, gesturing in the air, nearly spilling the vial.

I imagined being drained and replaced. Nauseating.

He continued: "The emptier the audience members, void of their personalities, the more susceptible they are to the messages of the Nevermind."

As I sweated and writhed in the heat, he continued. "You taught me that. Excellent at vampirizing Sylvia. You're skilled with envy as I am with a bow."

I found it hard to stand. Dehydrated and dizzy.

"Envy made you prod your twin sister, poking her, pricking her emotions. Making her insecure. Porous. You sucked Sylvia better during rehearsals. So much so that Sylvia got distracted."

My skin hurt. I couldn't swallow with my saliva dried. My hair singed, and I swung my hair away from the flames.

"Silver Sylvia fell, more as the months progressed. She walked into things more, cut herself and forgot things. Her immune system was shot. I turned away from her. And turned to you."

Dune coughed. It reverberated; coughing came from elsewhere.

"I push transference beyond the limits ever known to man." He raised the Grail in a toast to the invisible.

He intoned over me the strangest incantation. "The egg of her ashes are in your aura. This triple alchemical love, soon to be quadruple, will change the world. Immortality is Bennu's."

Then he poured water on the small fire. The circle of sticks burned with small flames, crumbling into ashes.

He pulled me out of the fire and sat me on an ancient version of an easy chair. He patted out the burning hairs with a soothing touch. I wasn't too damaged. Singed. Coughing. In typical Stockholm Syndrome fashion, I appreciated him for letting me live. For rescuing me. So stupid.

He pulled me forward on the chair and put a pillow underneath me, so my pelvis angled up. Rest. He took off my dress and pulled off my smoking underwear and I was glad of it. A breeze against my skin instead of smoldering cloth. He gave me cool elixir to drink from the Grail.

He tied my ankles to the legs of the chairs.

"I hope you'll enjoy this part, Susan. A little sexy role playing. Have you ever fantasized making love while I wore armor? Now's your big chance."

Well, I had. A few times. Not that I would admit it after all he'd just put me through. I hoped if he raped me, he'd prevent conception.

He tied a sash over my face. I heard the clanking of him putting on the armor from the stand.

With the sash pulled off, I saw him in the armor before me. In the dim light, I made out nothing through the small vertical slits in the helmet. A dark void dressed in metal approached me. I reached out to push him away and my hand touched flesh. He was naked from the groin down. Not a good look for him. I'd never seen his legs in a less flattering presentation. He hadn't been getting enough exercise. And then he came toward me.

He squatted over me, imperious to my attempts to push him away. In an awkward position, he moved this way and that trying to line up our sex organs. I called out for him to stop, and decided I must have hyperventilated, because his shadow crouched behind him, moving at a different pace. It had to be from flickering light. But something was wrong.

I'd hoped to keep things between us civil. That had been a terrible idea. If only I'd seen through his veneer earlier and found a way to escape, even if it meant dying out there.

His legs sweated against my skin. I wasn't lubricated or dilated to allow access. I clenched up against the expected pain and then made myself relax instead, so it would hurt less if he managed the logistics well enough to penetrate.

Loud sound of chains, not sedate.

Dune stood up while turning, staring toward the corner, his legs outstretched over the chair. I saw nothing but the row of paintings. *Is he a cat, able to detect ghosts?*

His grip on me jolted loose with surprise. I twisted against his arms, gathering strength. I pushed him while he was precarious, knocking him to the stone floor.

I untied one ankle. A mirage, in the smoky dim room, he fell against his shadow painted onto air. It's the dummy, crumpling from heat.

I searched for poison solutions.

I contemplated the note commanding me not to kill him until he freed me. Trust it and let him live.

I reached to untie the other ankle. The knots were clever tight.

Dune moved in ways I couldn't fathom. Morphing, being pushed and pulled in ways he couldn't have managed by will power. He was stunned, gray rock dust covering his face, but rose, not of his own volition.

Something I couldn't see pressed against his throat. His face changed shape in the most morbid of ways, morphing from pressure into a painting by Breughel. Enochian Angels Dune were real, coming to save me?

The dummy screamed and grasped its bleeding hand.

Metal clanking again. A rebel yell came from the dragging chain, right beside Dune's head. The voice's resonance eaten by the stone of the castle echoed.

The high male voice shouted: "Do it, Dune. Free her now. She's trapped the twins inside her long enough."

The wrestling stopped. Dune held the invisible attacker at bay, his arms pressing outward, sitting up and staring. Dune sniggered. "You think you have a chance against me in a fight you've got a lot to learn. Feisty little bugger."

The voice continued. "Look, give her a rest. Let me breathe in the women from her."

There are sisters inside me? I thought only Sylvia was in there.

"Go on."

"You'd just have to do your hypnosis on me. Let her go, you monster!"

Dune cautiously let go of the attacker and leaned back on his elbow while massaging his shoulder, moving it and grimacing. Then, he raised his arm in self-defense and scooted across the floor away from the thing.

"This plays out well. You'd *do* that for me." He turned his head to speak to the armored dummy, saying, "No, leave him be."

Curiouser and curiouser.

"Keep the Immortality Project going. I'm a candidate to give the ghosts a home in my psyche. I have a history of Dissociative Identity Disorder. Cured, integrated. But my mind splits into compartments. I'll bet I could hold multiple auras."

"Fascinating." His face was alert. "Maybe that's true."

The Invisible said, "Are you willing to take that risk?"

Dune answered, "No, the real question I have is: 'Why did you take the risk of taking it in front of Susan?'"

Mr. Invisible, or Dune throwing his voice, spoke again: "Not if you go mad from guilt."

Dune, a ventriloquist with multiple personalities, one threatening to drive him mad.

But then again, had crazy rubbed off on me? I'd read that happened. Mass hallucinations during periods of group hysteria. That explained rattling and clanking. Hallucination.

The cognitive dissonance got to me. During the moments of silence, I reviewed "their" conversation. It made no sense. I was losing consciousness.

Sounds muffled. I hung from the pole, listless.

When I raised my head, and forced my eyes open, I saw my aura again. One of my favorite sensations in the world when that happened. But it wasn't the usual color I loved with such warmth of recognition. A tribe. Being oceanic. So beautiful. So always. So huge.

But this time it was a different color. Ever. My. Aura. Was someone *else's* color. Horrors!

I love you, me. Come back. Let's be friends forever. I don't want to be someone else. Me is great. It felt so comfortable. Sort of. Come back. Please!

My legs buckled under me. I curled onto the floor. Cognitive dissonance was too.

"She's going into a coma! That won't do! The ritual *mus*t complete before she does, so we can get the last ingredient. Only a few more seconds to go. If you don't leave us alone to finish this," he warned his imaginary enemy, "the alchemy won't have the power it needs. Thank Bennu, you can't reach me from over there."

So, I again hallucinated the sound of rattling chains. Typical. I faded when the voice said, "If you want to stop her from having so much cognitive dissonance, then take away the post-hypnotic suggestion of not seeing us."

"Brilliant," agreed Dune with "himself." Assuming he threw his voice. Oh, whatever.

This should be rich.

❄

Everything blurred when my eyes opened, blinking against the dust. I jerked.

I could *see* what was in the room with me! It was no Enochian angel and no prank. The painting of Tommy, at that moment, turned three dimensional! A real person emerged from the canvas, which shimmered and dissolved as the delicate assistant stepped forward.

I got it.

My mind had been trained to replace Tommy with a picture of him whenever I saw him. It was a Substitute Hallucination.

Dune's hypnotic suggestion had been brilliant. My brain had substituted a painting in the style of the old masters for the actual Tommy, standing there in the room with a chain attaching him to a hook in the floor.

When I'd hit Dune, my husband had fallen close to Tommy.

Every time I'd seen the armor, it had been a Substitute Hallucination: it was Luke, wearing the armor. Just like the pranks Dune played on actors, like when Norma saw her man as a tree. It was a common hypnotic trick, and I'd fallen for it, as everyone else does. The mind is amazing.

The source of the clanking I'd heard was Luke. Was that armor to protect Luke from Tommy? He could throw beakers filled with solvents to blind him, or he could hurl chunks of stone.

It must have been Luke who lit the fire! With the notes he saw me make when I sneaked into the oratory and the Moldavite Room. The armor display in those rooms had been him, watching me, letting Dune know I'd been disobeying his orders. Everything's coming together.

Luke swung at Tommy, taking him down. He bashed Tommy with his shield.

Was my life of any value to them, no longer being the moon eclipsed by the sun? Without that value, would I be cast off?

Tommy fell, his body striking the hammered stone, the slap reverberating in the hallways. Blood dripped from his forehead onto his pale hand, splattering in tiny droplets. Tommy growled and flung himself up at Luke, pushing him down.

"I'm too valuable to you to kill," said Tommy to them both. "And you know it."

"After your great idea," said Dune in answer. "Thanks for volunteering to be the next recipient of the sisters' ghosts."

Dune released me from the pole in the center of the fire. Tommy had fought hard to save my life.

Was Dune about to make use of the torture equipment next?

He dragged me away from it. I slumped to the floor.

He and Luke grabbed hold of Tommy and strapped him to something horrible.

"Luckily," said Dune, "the Nevermind taught me the most powerful hypnotic tricks. I can guide you to breathe in auras."

I bent over, trying not to pass out. Lost time. Cold water in my face. I came too with a shiver. Luke stood over me, with a dripping beaker in his hand.

Tommy was in a trance, staring.

"And now, the next stage begins," announced Dune.

"No, it doesn't!" I cried.

CHAPTER 14
MIRIAM

Dune spoke in a soft, droning voice to Tommy. It seemed he'd taken him through the phase of breathing in someone's aura, merging with it and overlaying it. The process already well on its way, I made out random words. When Dune asked him questions, he nodded, staring ahead as if blind. He didn't turn to look when Dune spoke.

"You," Dune said, pointing to me. He made me drink a few glasses of water, which revived me. He gave me a chocolate truffle with gold leaf on top, which helped.

"It's time for you to leave the ceremonial space before I bring Tommy to functioning consciousness. Second by second, their ghosts are being transferred from inhabiting you and going into him. Right now."

"What?" When no answer came, I was too shattered to press for an explanation about gobbledygook.

"Luke, make the preparations. Give Tommy the strongest dose possible. Tell you the truth, mate, this is the trickiest thing I've ever done. I don't like to go into important transference without years of preparation. I don't know if it works."

Luke got busy, clunking inefficiently across the floor, fumbling with a beaker with his hands covered in metallic mesh.

"Oh, for Pete's sake. You'll drop the elixir."

Luke looked over at him each time he clanged a piece. Even through his helmet, the sheepish expression underneath flashed.

Dune addressed the four Watchtowers of each cardinal direction. He called to the Enochian angels to make a doorway in the circle and to close it back after we passed, keeping Tommy static. He spoke Enochian. His gestures suggested he believed he opened a doorway in the magickal circle for me to pass through. I walked through where he led, his arm high, holding my hand as if doing an elegant Two Step.

He led me outside the doorway and closed the door. I was glad to discover my strength even when he let go of me. We passed the store room to enter the room with the cistern.

He coughed from smoke inhalation. The castle needed a better ventilation system to comfortably torture people.

He didn't stand with the usual commanding presence, hold his head as proudly, or speak with such studied tones when he led me to a stone bench along the hallway and told me to sit. I bent over, my head by my feet, dizzy and unclear about what was going on with Tommy. What had he proposed? The ritual ended for me. He'd never meant to kill me with fire, just scare me. That, I forgave. But psychopathically substituting Luke for Dune. No. Never ever.

The greatest Nevermind master hypnotist took me into a hypnotic trance. Going unconscious and forgetting one's waking life, while remembering one's dream life had been true all along.

Those were faff years you spent on priming me to carry the immortality torch, eh, Duno?

I wanted to reach out as I struggled to let go of love. Shaking, I hated myself; I hungered to kiss every inch of his face, yearning for being one with him. Taking off my wedding ring before the ritual even began had indeed been a rational decision.

Polyamory was popular in the city among the theater crowd. I was too ordinary a person, stuck in old-fashioned ideas of right and wrong. My muscles twitched, and my face twisted. My stomach burned. I was not good enough for Enochian rituals that took people beyond the realm of regular relationships, normal identities.

While I wallowed in a muddy state of mind, his hypnotic patter anti-climactically cancelled the other major, life-changing post-hypnotic suggestion, his voice tired and rough.

There was that familiar feeling of letting go as another's life force energy left my body for another body, like after a rehearsal or being on standby during one of Sylvia's shows, and the times I had gotten to fill in for her on stage.

Wait.

I let go of Sylvia's aura. Susan released. That was a stupid thought. I was Susan. No, no.

Susan had possessed. My. Mind. Shady and cold.

The last residual bits of Susan's ghostly aura left my muscles, inch by inch. What?

Sylvia sang goodbye from inside her.

Part of me had been swimming underwater in total darkness, alone, in the silence. It returned to inhabit the surface world. So strange. As I poked my head out of the water, the surface of post-hypnotic suggestion shattered. My eyes rose above the water.

I broke free.

I wasn't Susan. I was *Miriam*.

Miriam?

Miriam!

MIRIAM!

Not standing on stage this time when the hypnotic belief wore off. No audience clapping, no red velvet curtain settling on the floor in front of me after the encore.

In a castle. Covered in soot.

What the bloody *hell?*

With Dune, the most gorgeous man in the world. The man every cell of my body had ached for. The big romantic fantasy. Thinking once Susan died, he might marry me, and I'd take over her life. What I wanted more than anything. Distraction from seeing scary love right in front of me with Colin.

How did I get there and what had I been doing?

❄

It was like waking from someone else's dream and landing in yet a *different* person's dream.

I've been in limbo. Not myself. Not Susan. Dune's creation. A product of the Agent's program. But all along, still me-Miriam. Me me me.

My jaw jutted a little forward, my lips full and pooched, flattering and inviting. My posture changed to plump my breasts. The muscles along my spine popped, loosening up, as they became more animated than Susan's. I stretched and opened my rib cage.

Susan. Wait. Where's Susan? Why wasn't she able to perform? How did I get here? Why do I feel so exhausted and sore? My hair burned. My clothes scorched.

Did I kill her in my sleep? Or did Colin do it?

I was excited that I'd gotten to perform well at the last show, and so was a shoe in for being the star the next season. I didn't have to give up a life of esoteric beauty to go work in a restaurant. I'd proven I could command the stage this time with no mistakes. "Did I do all right?" I asked Dune. "Didn't mess up on stage or anything?"

"Brilliant," he said. I noticed tiny lines in his face I hadn't seen before. Had he been going without sleep? The lighting was different. Torch light. What? Why? Had we fallen into history?

"It will come back to you. It always does, right, after a little while when you're settled into being Miriam again?"

I steadied myself, trying to ignore the cognitive dissonance of my location. *Focus. Hang on.*

I sat in silence. There seemed like much more to come back this time than just doing the same choreography I'd be enacting, whether I believed I was Miriam or Susan.

Sitting, I closed my eyes and went deep, as if trying to remember a dream. Rapt audience members in the rows where the lighting made them possible to make out amid silhouettes. I executed the most difficult leaps, saying my most challenging lines with enough layers of subtext, even though they could sound like they were on-on-nose if another actress spoke them.

I shone on the night with the most press, reporters ready to make a story about "my" last night.

Other memories like hypnagogic images flashed across the theater of my vision, seeming to have no chronology or context. Swimming in a beautiful cistern. Making love under a skew whiffy painting of John Dee and the Enochian angels -- not making love with Colin, or fantasizing about Dune, but cheating on my - *um - friend* - Colin and Susan with Dune! What? How could I have? I wasn't a brazen hussy, was I? I was! How could I ever feel good about myself again? I swallowed, my throat closing in shame.

A draw bridge framed by two identical trees in front of a castle. A picture of Susan with her twin placed over an altar. I shook my head. None of it made sense. Were all Susan's memories coming through for me?

I lost my breath, remembering pain, invasive heat, flames all around me. Being inside a ring of fire. Fire and burned pieces of paper with my handwriting appeared out of the blue.

I looked down to see what I was wearing. A long, white dress. Not mine. Flecked with blood, torn, scorched, and showing skin. I lifted my hair to my nose, and my head whisked away from the smell. I said, "I want to get scissors. Where would I find them?" I wanted to cut the smell away and then a shower. Scrub off the burned-hair stink. I went to the wall looking for a light switch;

there was none. Only low shelves or something spread far apart along the wall, each with candles on top, burning out. And one to carry up the stairs.

"Would it be up there?"

As he escorted me up, with each step came new memories.

Step one.

Understanding coalesced. As a standby, I wanted to be as good as Susan. No, to *be* Susan. I could walk out on stage, spread my arms wide, and everyone would know my face from the pictures on the theater walls. Even if mine was Susan's face. I had to pull in my Miriam aura and be a nothing, whenever someone who knew about our troupe might see me. As I lifted my foot from the step, a large fuzzy spider crawled toward me along the step and I swerved so I wouldn't hurt it.

Step two.

Stone, its sharpness edge corn down like an arrowhead, smooth and scalloped. My head spun. I had to wait, to slow down; the reason would come if I started again, reviewing from the beginning.

Stumbled on Step three.

Roses at the end, for Susan. I accepted them as Susan.

Step four.

I wanted my own damn flowers.

Step five.

Living an occult fantasy adventure with Dune. I'd spread my wings wide as a goddessy type for real, not just half-performing the role of a revered archetype manifested at the core of secret societies.

Step six.

Oh. My. God. Huld had murdered Susan. My eyes stared wide open. How *bizarre* was that?

Nope. There was no way I would star in the Bennu troupe the next season. That was the end of that.

I would have to be a waitress. The rest of my life.

Papa would never love me. I knew it.

How many years before I could afford to pay back his loan? Before he'd acknowledge to his constituents that I even existed. I wanted to curl over and give in to crying in a corner.

Step seven.

Bennu Society. That was how the inner circle worked. Flurries of coups and murders. The phoenix creature I'd been playing in rehearsals, the symbol of destruction of the self in fire and rebirth from the ashes -- I'd taken that role all the way. No longer pretending to light shadows. Then, after the show, I'd normally go home to my boring house and read *The Castle of Otranto* or *Wuthering Heights* in bed under stained sheets that I needed to take to the laundromat once I cared enough to bother, until I fell asleep and dreamed of being someone else.

Step eight.

I remembered the rumor of Bennu symbolized breaking down the personality of an Agent or an asset through theatrical initiations to make him loyal.

Step nine.

A flood of memories rose. Making love with Dune, wearing a nightie, lying under John Dee and the Enochian angels, with the bed creaking music. Splashing him in the cistern, him slapping my butt and kissing me hard. Huld showing up. I was immersed in my idea of Susan. Hard to tell what I'd been projecting.

No, not making love with Dune. Being *raped* by Dune. Being abducted while under a spell and manipulated into having sex under false pretenses. How horrendous!

Step ten.

Sylvia had taken over under the influence of psychedelics.

I shook my head to clear it. I'd seen a smidgen of what was going on at the juxtaposition of the occult, intelligence agency mind control, and theatrical genius. It was terrifying.

He'd schemed to *kill* me. I didn't want to die when I'd just become myself.

Step eleven.

Since I'd been at the castle, Colin had become everything I'd needed to fall in love with him. He was wild. Intense. Animal. Not safe. Not sweet. Not predictable and business-like. Adventuresome. He knew the secrets I'd been working with for two years, consisting of Dune, auras and hypnosis. He shared the most amazing experience with me in an exotic location. He'd been my hero, proving he could take care of me, he would sacrifice for me, he wanted me. I wanted him. If I could be with him, life would be glorious.

Dune no longer turned my head: if I hadn't suffered at his hands, hadn't gotten a chance to see if it could work between us, I would have been forever infatuated and never able to fully be with anyone else.

Yet, still, would a mundane life be enough for me, day after day? Would it?

CHAPTER 15
PORTCULLIS

When we got to the top of the stairs, Dune entered the library. I followed, drawing my arms in with my feet close together, taking small steps and my chin angled down. I was free! I was me! "This isn't where the scissors are, is it?"

He raised his voice. "Do you think I'd let you have sharp implements? Waste basket is the toilet for now. Just tear up your dress into pieces for toilet paper. The water in the pitcher is dusty by now, but it will do till I come back."

Blood rushed to my face, empowered my muscles, making my heart beat fast. Tricking me into playing the role of the immortal flamingo of the Universe for the Bennu Society was not too sporty. I kicked him in the groin, elbowed him under his chin, and pulled his hair to twist his neck. "You raped me!"

"You know you wanted it."

Door knocker. Front door. Colin! I kicked Dune, so he fell into the cabinet where a row of elaborate uncut pieces of Moldavite arranged along the top fell on him. Sharp edges many times over, as if tiny trees were glass, landed on him. He yelled and pulled them off his body, each one small in his palm. He delicately placed them on the floor. Each one would have been worth at least 20,000 quid a couple years before, but with the unexpected shortage, they were worth three times that much. Some of them were broken; he searched under the cabinet for missing pieces, putting them in his pockets. I picked up one of the sharpest ones.

The creaking of the ropes. *Luke must be pulling up the spikes to let someone inside. Luke wouldn't let Colin enter.* I couldn't help hoping it was him, fearing for his safety. I ran toward the door while Dune fussed over the rocks.

The door was open, and the spikes raised. Kevin Frank! He shone as always. I'd never seen him look scared before that moment. He seemed shorter and smaller. I'd never imagined him wearing stained brown sweats.

He whispered, "Miriam? I'm sorry. Huld said he'd kill my mother if I didn't lie to everyone about waylaying Susan."

"I hope your mother's safe. Bloody hell."

"I hired a body guard."

"How did you find us?"

"I tried so many places, girl! They tried to recruit an actress here months ago. There was gossip going around about where to get psychedelic drugs and orgies with Susan and Dune."

"I'm glad she lived to tell it."

Dune called to Luke in the guardhouse, "What are you thinking, letting him in? That's the actor who 'took Susan to a convenience store for a smoke.'"

"Not a problem."

I made a move, and Dune grabbed me. I spun and sliced his eye with the sharp edge of the glassy Moldavite,which went right through the lid. He screamed and held his eye, staggering.

I ran to Kevin and grabbed his arm, saying, "Let's go!"

He resisted, planting his feet. I couldn't budge him. "No. I have something to tell them."

I didn't want to leave him there in that vipers' nest. I tried pulling again, before giving up and running out to his car, hoping it wasn't a stick shift. The last thing I wanted was stranding him, but he was stubborn.

Then, BAM. The outside portcullis fell. Then, BAM! The inside portcullis fell. We were trapped between them! Kevin held onto me. Clanking footsteps ran up from the guard house.

We looked up toward a sound above us. Luke's armored arms stuck out above us and dropped a flaming log. It hit Kevin's shoulder. He tried stamping on it but burned his shoes. Even after so many centuries, the fireplaces that heated the castle still were in locations handy for killing intruders.

More flaming logs. One after another, they filled up the small space. We dodged them, coughing. One smoking log, in red and yellow flames, rolled under me. I jumped and grabbed onto the metal grid to let the log pass by me as I hung over it, lifting up my legs. I kicked a falling log out of its trajectory, which would have trapped Kevin. The heat of metal and sharpness of the grid were too much for my hands, carrying my weight. I fell onto the burning wood.

I yelled, determined to win this battle. Whatever got me into this mess, I'd change.

One hit me on the foot. I hopped, trying to climb up the latticework, but it was too small to get my toes into even after I took off my shoes to see if my bare feet could fit. There was no place on the ground that was not on fire. My toes fit, but I couldn't recommend that to Kevin, since he had bigger feet. I climbed up higher, just as the biggest log came right beside me, one end of it knocking me, making me wobble.

It hit Kevin on the head and took him down. I lost my balance and fell on top of him, amid red flames on all sides. "Kevin! Kevin!"

I felt his pulse.

Nothing.

CHAPTER 16
THE DARK ALONE

Luke pulled me out. "You've got to learn to behave, little one. Why fight us?" He carried me to the dungeon. "That attack wasn't meant for you, but for the men harassing you." He pushed me inside, closing the door. He called through his visor and the door, "You're safe in this fortress. Let it protect you."

True, I'd asked for adventures. This wasn't what I had in mind.

I had to get back home to clear Colin's name, proving he didn't kill me. I couldn't bear to be the ruin of that dedicated man. I had to save Tommy. If Dune died before freeing Tommy from the ghosts, then Tommy would have to live with them caged inside him. That would be a damp squib.

Murder: not on my bucket list. I'd never imagined fighting a knight. I did like that sort of movie if I ate lovely dark chocolate while watching it.

I had a feeling I wasn't about to be given any delicious chocolate treats.

❄

Sitting in the cold, smelly, dank darkness for who knows how long, I wondered if this was my permanent condition. A bucket and washcloths, a loo, toothbrush and salt. A change of clothes. How long had they'd been prepared in case? It was days in there. Abyss. End. The dark itself. People went bonkers from isolation in the dark. Questions became my soundtrack.

I wish Papa would save me.

Suspecting the dungeon was nasty on purpose to keep anyone from going down there, because of something hidden, I explored the world of stench and bone. I wandered farther, shoes audibly sticking to the floor. My feet were developing callouses and blisters from wearing shoes that weren't mine.

I longed for my life. Getting goofy with Colin, working out together, dancing in his backyard in funny costumes. Beyond our friendship, I wanted him as much as I'd wanted Dune. But this made sense.

Had my heroic attempt to save the day only made everything worse? How had I had such an overheated idea as sacrificing myself for a cult? I had so much to live for. What brainwashing I fell for. Believing I didn't have value by being myself — there had to be some other way.

I gave up trying to close off my nostrils with the muscles inside them. Admitting squeezing my eyes shut did nothing to stop the smell of my vomit, I surrendered to the smell of my insides, to food that had been alive until I killed it, until I pulled it ligament from bone from muscle from organ, from lymph and vein. From sweat and fur. From feather or tooth. Life was gore. Life was death.

I can't believe it, but now, I'd rather live with Colin in a beige house in the suburbs ironing and raising crying babies, going bowling wearing stupid long skirts than advanced magick rituals and spectacular aura fireworks.

The sound of my footsteps' suction sickened my ears. My feet could barely lift the heavy mud caked to them high enough to run in that stinky goop. I twisted and fell. I put my hand down to push myself off. Squirming underneath it. I lifted it fast and brought with it maggots bending back and forth on my palm. I shooed them off.

The torchlight swayed. Everything was dark mud. The walls, the floor. My nose was trying to detect the percentage of human waste. I gasped for air. I looked around in the dark sludge corners. Yet I held onto memories of fun times with Colin. I refused to chunder. Absolutely refused.

I found a suspicious spot and held the torch there. The ceiling was dripping with black goo. I nearly fell in the muck. Grabbing onto slime to steady myself, I slid my feet along the floor, underneath the gore, feeling for a trap door I suspected was there. Something about Susan's memory. It seemed like every bone left over from every meal was thrown there. Beaks and teeth. Mangled feathers and matted fur. Whoever designed this room liked ugly. It didn't just happen to be full of death and rot. That was by design. The dungeon wasn't a place to torment people. It was a Bardo, a state between death and rebirth, according to the Tibetan Buddhists.

My foot hit something. A raised straight line. Could that be the edge of a trap door to an oubliette? I pushed the decay away from the stiff raised edge. I bent down, peered in the dim torch light, and jumped back. Human nature demands we leap away from a snake, even if it's dead. Especially if it's nailed to the floor.

I followed the snake to the tail. Another snake was nailed at right angles at the end of the tail. Four snakes of identical length made a square. And inside that square was the trap door. *How often do they have to change the snakes? Who does that job?*

I undid the clasp, took hold of the low handle and lifted. Stairs precarious with dry rot led down into the deeper darkness. Next to them was a rope.

I took the chance. Susan's memory called me down. Had she visited the castle and gone down there? I steadied myself as I walked down the slimy crumbling stairs, holding onto the floor above me with my free hand as long as I could. Then, I balanced myself only with the rope. I left the trap door open.

❄

When I let go into the oubliette, I nearly lost my balance and slipped, flailing.

The front of the step broke off, the wood spongy, saw dust spraying my nostrils. I coughed so hard I bent forward, toppling downstairs. My impact on them broke them more, and I grabbed hold of a step, only to feel something wiggling. I lifted my hand, and a bunch of worms stuck to it. I flung them off and heard a fizzling frying sound as some squirmy things died in the torch flame.

My leg twisted under me and I dropped the torch which blew out as it hit. In total darkness, I collapsed on the ground. I felt around. Yes, ground. Clean, thank goodness. Not scattered beaks and claws. Just plain dirt. I lay there, my ankle throbbing. The feel of the earth comforted me.

Something tickled my fingers. Ow! A spider-bite. I flung the little creature away and got up. I held my arms out in front of me, waving them around out to the sides, and patted the ground, taking tentative steps.

I counted my steps as I left the stairs, and didn't swerve away from a linear trajectory, so I could find my way back. The stench from above was still overwhelming but let up as I left the trapdoor. Fifteen. Sixteen. Seventeen. It seemed like space. Until my foot hit something hard, like a wall. Hoping I would not touch a living snake this time, I felt in front of me.

Smooth, cool stone. An arch along the top level with my eyes. The stone was a few inches thick. Narrow. I slid my hands along its smooth surface. There was writing on it, the words cut into the stone. Inside an indentation of a letter, my finger moved across something wet and squishy, moving. A worm.

It was a gravestone. I was in a *catacomb*.

Turning to my right, making sure my turn was an exact angle, I counted my steps in that direction. I found another grave and continued feeling my way around until I determined there were four tombstones gathered together. They faced one direction, and behind them was another, taller one, facing the opposite direction. When I continued walking beyond them in all directions, I only reached reinforcements holding the dirt walls in place. It was a small space, so I guessed it was an all-purpose crypt, but only for a small portion of the castle's family. Perhaps these were for hiding bastard children?

I felt along the largest stone's surface, from left to right. Whoever it was still lived unless this catacomb was abandoned long ago to the filth. I felt the date and was tickled I could make it out. My index finger fit into the groove. A line down, and a line across, coming off its base. An M. Making out the letters by feel was possible and grew easier as I continued the process. MARTHA PENDERGHAST. LOVING MOTHER. There were both birth and death dates carved into it; she'd died the day I came into this world. Was that Luke's wife? Dune had told me they were married a long time. He must have been devastated when she died. Unless he killed her!

Next to it was LUKE PENDERGHAST. DEVOTED FATHER.

Luke and Martha had a child? I was surprised there were no paintings of a son or daughter, at least not in the parts of the castle I'd found. Maybe there had been a falling out with the child.

His birth date was there, and the dash leading to where the death date would be no doubt carved after his death by some unfortunate engraver.

I felt the tombstone to the left of his. SUSAN THORNLEY, DAUGHTER. What? Susan -- Mrs. Dune Thornley, was Luke's *daughter?*

I couldn't believe it. She'd talked about her parents. She had come from a nice, normal family in Devonshire. I'd never asked her maiden name. She and Sylvia must have been adopted out to a family after Martha died. So, Dune was Luke's son-in-law. Well, hmm.

I felt the birth date and cried when feeling a death date. It was the date of the last performance.

I felt the next stone. SYLVIA RAINS, DAUGHTER. So, that must have been her adoptive parental name? She never married. She'd been engaged to Dune when she died, when she was still young. Her death date was correct. Two years previous.

At right angles to it, along the ground, was a flat low stone of the same width. There was no flat stone for the others other than Martha. The twins had identical birth days inscribed.

Who had carved the dates? What was I doing at the time? Sleeping, hunting, making love with Dune?

Or had Dune carved it himself?

I could picture it. The twins growing up in the castle, with no friends, a father stuck in the lore of earlier centuries, nothing to tie them to current culture, inundated with ideas about sacrificing and ruthless ritual. Their connection to the Bennu troupe made more sense. No wonder Susan had grown up to be a Moldavite thief.

I felt another tombstone. MIR . . . I drew my hand away, as if I'd felt another snake. No. No, no, no, no, *no*. I.A.M. I felt a chill. I crossed my arms, hugging myself. I didn't want to reach out again. I turned away. I'd find my way back upstairs. Retracing my steps, I stopped, turned around, went back.

MIRIAM REYNOLDS, DAUGHTER.

My stomach fell out from under me. I felt as if the hollow inside me was filling with ghosts.

So, Papa had adopted me. My birthdate. No deathdate yet.

My uncanny resemblance to the women finally made sense. I'd fantasized about Miriam when I thought I was Susan. How Gothic could I get? Incestuous family secrets were at the heart of so many of those novels.

My mother must have died in childbirth. Had that tragedy sent Luke, my father, over the edge with grief?

My world fell apart. How could it be? Papa had adopted me. The man I'd tried so hard to please wasn't even my father.

Luke must have been keeping track of where I was all along. From behind the scenes, his henchmen had encouraged me to join the troupe. I thought about the synchronicities that led strangers to suggesting I audition.

Even the way I was groomed to feel that I should be someone else -- it made sense! It was as if Papa's personality and child-rearing techniques had been hand-picked to create a daughter who would always feel she was second-best. I was groomed to envy people he loved, the famous ones, the perfect ones, the ones I had to imitate or suffer time alone. That envy molded me into a pawn of Bennu and of the Agency. Was Papa a key member of that organization? That made sense, since he was mayor.

The worst of it hit me like lead. When Luke tried to rape me, pretending to be Dune, who was pretending to be married to me. . .that was attempted incest! He didn't do it because he lusted after his own daughter, but for the sake of the Immortality. Was he the originator of the project?

I mewled in the stinking crypt of love.

There was another stone, a newer one. I traced only one name on it. Equinox.

My child was meant to be conceived on that fateful date. To be raised in the castle, no doubt, without being registered with a last name or proof of existence. To continue the Immortality Project's increasingly dense ghostly packaging of Luke's children recursively living inside each other. One more Russian doll. Equinox would have been my child and also, my sibling.

Papers crunched underfoot. I reached down, hoping not to arouse noxious spiders and stole one to read later in the light. I stuffed it in my pocket.

I turned, retracing my steps, counting them. When I got to the correct number, I reached out. No dryrotting stairwell. Nothing. I turned this way and that, so shaken that I'd become disoriented.

I covered ground, ending up against the walls, turning around. By a sense of subtle echo-location, I reached out and my finger stuck into the damp wood. People would know I'd been there when they saw the steps in worse shape. The men would bring Susan's body there surely before long. It couldn't take forever to find her body in the well and fake the forensics and get to the point of burial.

What was I thinking? They'd be bringing my body down too, soon enough. Why was I worried about being caught? Nothing mattered any more.

It was my idea to live on as a ghost possessing Tommy. To pay him back for saving my life, when he let the twin's ghosts leave me and possess him instead.

What if Dune was still there, hiding? My skin crawled.

I'd be buried earlier than they'd planned. But my sacrifice must have been the backup plan. I didn't like that. I wanted to be venerated for volunteering, at least. *Something*. Come *on*.

Luke's assistant would that night be possessed by the ghosts of all three of Luke's daughters. Susan, Sylvia, and me. The project would be a grand success.

I felt a piece of dry, strong wood. And another. Someone had been fixing the steps.

No wonder Luke had been going around in that ridiculous armor — it was so he could hide the family resemblance.

I longed for my life back again. Getting goofy with Colin, working out together, dancing in his back yard. Eating tomatoes and corn and onions. But beyond our friendship, I wanted to be his lover as much as I'd wanted Dune. This was healthier than that obsession.

It was also doomed. I was right all along that being the authentic me wasn't good enough to make someone love me. They'd run away if they saw that. Well, at least I was right about something.

Surely there's a way out.

All I found were bones.

I piled up skeletons. Clatter, clink.

I stood on bones. They moved underneath me, precarious.

I could. Reeeeeach it.

I scrambled up the top part, but as I was nearly at the top, the rope broke. As it was breaking, I raised my arms and grabbed the edge, with a gargantuan grunt.

❄

I pulled myself up the rest of the way to the sound of scraping and splinters.

I rubbed the crusted mud off the spot I was staring at. *It's a lock. Needs a code put in. I think that's the way out, if we can figure it out.* So. A series of numbers were required. I could do it. I'd been studying the castle well. All my senses turned on.

I tried every combination I could think of. The light from the torch on the dungeon wall flickered, but I was proud of how well my eyes could adjust.

I remembered the numerology of the bizarre stairway that went up to a little room within the room. It then turned around and came back down right next to itself, and then back up again to stop at: nothing at all. I applied it to the lock. It opened!

Footsteps coming close down the hall, around a bend. I recognized the gait as Dune's.

Tommy, standing right in front of me, clear-eyed, and holding a huge beaker, ready to smash me over the head.

I dodged as Tommy deflected the trajectory of the blow just in time.

"Oh. Sorry 'bout that."'

"Run."

We bolted the dungeon door back, as if nothing had gone wrong. We hid at the corner and peered around the edge to see if anyone was coming.

"Where are we going?" I asked.

"You're the one who said to run."

Maybe I need a plan.

I hankered for the wooden bathing tub covered with a canopy.

"Well. Seems like Colin and you and I could be in deep legal shite if we don't have proof of what's been going on here. I've been trying to find Luke's grimoire. Notes, letters, plans for the ritual. Some records to show a lawyer."

Tommy took my hand and we ran back into the ritual room. He grabbed things, and thrust them into my arms, picked up more stuff, and we headed out.

I ran back in to pick up a hemp bag in the corner. I hoped no one would notice it gone too soon. But then, most likely, Tommy's disappearance would be all on their minds. They'd assume I was still moping in the dungeon.

I put my papers and the few personal things Tommy picked up into the bag. I held it out for him to take the other side. The bag bounced while we ran. Tommy still got everything inside, dropping nothing, including the towel I'd been wearing. Excellent teamwork.

I guided us into a detour from who knows what destination. I ran to the wardrobe. Was my mother alive? There was the mannequin, with the wig of my mother's hair, her death mask, her clothes. I touched it. No, it wasn't a Substitute Hallucination.

Something caught my eye. An old hamper tucked away in the corner under baskets. I looked inside. I lifted out the fuzzy pastel little garments. Yes. Our baby clothes. Luke kept everything as it was when it was still his. A hot tear stung my eye.

CHAPTER 17
REVELATION

Tommy and I huddled in the oratory under a table covered with a cloth. I studied his face during an uncomfortable silence. I didn't find myself sexually attracted, but Tommy was a breathtaking man. Small chin. Narrow neck. A work of art. I whispered, "Do you have a car out there somewhere?"

Tommy's eyes widened, and he wiggled his ears. . . Of course, he didn't have a car there.

Every minute counted. Who knew where the men were and if they'd discover us? But what to do? "We can't just walk out the door, since Dune keeps that devil lock on it."

"Maybe torture him so he'll unlock it? Or torture Huld? Not so easy to hurt Luke in that armor."

Tommy set down the bag he was carrying, the cloth bloody from his hands.

Tommy was lucky being able to nab personal possessions. Coming up with an action plan seemed more important than risking getting caught in the wardrobe. I didn't want to sabotage another escape.

I took his bag, and we crept out of the ritual room and up the stairs. We stood at the top of the stairs looking to the left hall, to the right hall, and at the hallway straight ahead.

I asked, "Should we run to the woods? To a neighbor?"

I took the lead to nowhere, and as we ran, we whispered. I took ahold of his arm. "So, it must have been you who gave me the note that kept me from killing Dune. Brilliant. Susan and Sylvia would have possessed me forever if I had."

"Indeed."

I said, "You were chained. What a tosh thing to do to a human."

Tommy nodded. "It was horrendous."

Is that why Luke wore armor, so Tommy wouldn't hurt him?

While we ran, whispering, we hid in the shadows, behind furniture, in closets, our path erratic. I hoped for something better than doom.

I brought myself to ask, "Why didn't you call out to 'me' while I was here? Couldn't I, er, couldn't 'Susan,' have saved you?"

My question broke when I asked it. Dune had given me an unbreakable post-hypnotic suggestion not to see Tommy. It would have been cognitive dissonance big time if I'd heard a disembodied voice talking to me.

Tommy took the lead running, and though his gait was confident, he seemed as uncertain of where he was going as I had been. As we ran, he asked, "Would 'Susan' have even believed what I said?"

"Well, for starters, you could have said, 'Hey, you're hypnotized to have Substitute Hallucinations about me and Luke.'"

"Luke was the lucky one. If he was standing in the middle of the room, you could perceive him as free-standing armor. Me, I had to always scoot up against the wall as soon as we heard footsteps so that you'd see me as a painting. Can you imagine not moving? To be 'rats.' I almost sneezed."

"What if you had? Would that have been so bad? What if you'd told me what was going on instead of conniving with them?"

"They'd have tortured me to the limit for the rest of my life. And you too. It wouldn't have been pretty. That's what Luke told me, and I've come to believe what he says."

Tommy stopped and leaned against the wall. I stopped too, looking both ways and listening for subtle sounds, wondering what was going on. He pulled up his pants leg and showed me ragged scars along his shapely shin. Oh.

I jumped out of my self-absorption and said, "Before you get infected, we've got to treat your wounds from that crazy invisible fight. Jesus, that was a bizarre sight."

"I can imagine."

"Let's take a chance Dune's not around. Come on. I know where the supplies are. A walk-in closet off the garderobe. Not the main one the guys might be in."

"Listen to you. You know castle talk for loo."

We hovered near the little chamber with an exit to the cesspit far below. The Bennu Society liked it having the delightful old-world feel, even if it meant shitting into the wind. Next to it was the traditional ammonia and a pile of laundry. Visitors coats were not, however, hung there in the traditional way. Too much. No, those were in the great hall closet.

We listened for footsteps and then delved into the large first aid supply closet. Beside the ammonia was hydrogen peroxide and bandages.

As he sat on open pit, I tended to Tommy's multiple wounds, scraping dirt.

I observed smooth arms emerging from the continual long sleeves, shapely calves emerging from trousers. As I pushed aside his caveman hair, I noticed his slender neck and shiny hair, strawberry blonde hair roots grown halfway out. I dabbed peroxide onto his delicate face beneath the bushy beard and mustache, with extra thick sideburns.

Washing the grime and blood from his face, something was

wrong. "Oh, well, look at that," I said, pulling his beard hairs, which made an odd sound as the side of his mustache pulled up.

He stood up as I was leaning over the open toilet pit to reach the peroxide on the shelf behind him while holding scissors to cut the bandage. My towel fell off and landed in the muck far below.

I studied Tommy's reaction to a naked woman in front of him. No male reaction, but then, we *were* right next to the stinking pit. That could kill lust if anything could.

Tommy said, "Look, do you want something to put on?" Tommy slowly, stylishly removed his long over-shirt. Underneath was a gauzy white nearly transparent undershirt. I stared at his chest, and he stared back. I could made out subtle horizontal lines beneath the undershirt, as if covering bound breasts. The facial geometry with the small chin was becoming suspect. No visible Adam's apple. I could see how he'd fool men. But in that intimate moment, he no longer fooled me.

"Who are you?" I spoke to Tommy as to a woman, subtle differences in the mannerisms and tone of voice. Softening my eyes, I showed that I saw the deception, in case *she* wanted to reveal her secret and get it out in the open.

It was easy to see that she understood my nonverbal question. She exaggerated her femininity when answering, spoke in her normal feminine voice, and said, "Me."

I stopped wrapping the bandage, holding it mid-air.

"I'm Luke's assistant."

"Dressed like a man."

"Hey, it's the zeitgeist," she said, swaying her hips as if freed from a cage. "I think I can trust you not to tell anyone this. If people find out where I am, and that I screwed over the Nevermind a *third time* . . ." She shook her head, pulled off her beard, mustache, sideburns, and bushy eyebrows.

She was a gifted actress to appear as a woman to Luke and Dune living in such close quarters.

"You can trust me."

She let her face go into its natural shape. Amazing how she'd been holding it in a male fashion so realistic. The mask was down. She became female. An exquisite one.

I put on her shirt, which was so long it covered just enough so I didn't feel indecent. If I got the chance to escape, the shirt would be better than a towel. But if we would try hitchhiking, I'd still need more than clothing that, or people would think I was a slut. And Tommy needed more clothes to pass as a man.

"I don't get it. Was pretending to be a man part of the ritual? Along with being quiet?" I was struggling to understand so hard I forgot what I was doing, and I bound her fingers together for a minute.

She said, "No, just the silence part. I *despised* fooling you! Miriam, I'm so sorry."

I felt the automatic reaction to say, "That's OK," like usual. But no, that wasn't OK. Sorry. It just wasn't.

"I knew Dune had hypnotized you. I knew your post-hypnotic suggestion would make you have a Substitute Hallucination. Luke told me. What was that *like*?"

How could I answer? I breathed. Everything went in and out. I shook my head and held her gaze.

"I know. It's awful. Making the elixirs in the alchemy workshop out of your tears. I hate myself."

"I think I understand. You were enslaved. You couldn't help it." I studied her face for anything she would give me.

Running around the castle wasn't getting us anywhere. We still hadn't discovered the men's locations, gotten any clues, or formulated a plan. It was as good a hiding place as any.

I settled into conversation mode once I finished dressing her wounds. "So, spill it. Why were you pretending to be a man?"

"The Nevermind is ruthless. After I went up against them a couple times in the States, I came to England to hide out. Kind of dumb choice of a country, considering they have authority here too, but there you have it. It's what I could manage."

"How did you end up at an obscure castle of all places?"

"It's obscure to normal people, but the Bennu Society regularly meets here."

"The castle's the last place you'd want to be."

"It is. I was dressing as a man not long ago, working in an occult bookstore in the city. I don't think I fooled everyone about my gender, but the ones I didn't convince thought I was transgender, lesbian, cross-dresser, androgynous or something."

"I can see that. Trendy. An advantage, because people stick up for you. And it would keep people from prying. No one wants to stare."

"Yep. Luke came into the store a lot, asking me questions about books on Enochian magick, alchemy, monoatomic gold, and things like that. I guess he figured I was what he needed. He read me as a man, and I was glad of it, because I suspected he was mixed up with the Agents."

"Scary!"

"When he told me a couple months ago he was in the Bennu Society and tried to recruit me, I said I wasn't interested. He came a couple more times, and he seemed like he'd let it go. Didn't even ask any more esoteric questions. But in hindsight, I should have quit my job and hidden out."

"Were you tempted to join it?"

"Not at all. Bennu nauseates me. My handler created a monster to terrify me and keep me in line. He had a hook on one hand shaped like a flamingo. Bennu was part of my trauma programming. The trailer for the Bennu movie horrified me. Luke abducted me."

"Your life has been awful. Did you enjoy working on the Immortality Project at all?" I wanted to think of her happy. Enjoying her arcane work. But, not. . . not at my expense. If she'd said "yes," I would have smiled and said, "good," but not meant it.

"Of course not! Sylvia was long dead when they brought me in.

Susan had absorbed her aura at the moment she died. I guess you knew that."

"They say Dune loved her, back when she was the star of the troupe and Susan was her standby. He's been through a lot, that man." My heart went out to him. As controlling and devious as he was, he'd suffered: that has consequences.

"Well, that's one way to look at it, I guess." Her face twisted up, and she looked away.

Maybe if I hadn't been so desperate for Dune's beauty and genius, I would have been less protective of him. But Tommy's dismissive response got to me.

"Well, what about you? Look, I'm trying to show you compassion. I'm excusing you after you were part of a plot to torture, maybe even kill me. And you're dissing Dune."

"Miriam! Making excuses for abusers is *your* thing, not mine." Her voice was firm and her stare pointed. Awful.

"I'm just not a judgmental ass, thank you very much."

"I don't know how you got this way. But it's sick. It's why you haven't brought yourself to leave this god forsaken castle. I don't know if you ever will."

The closet became claustrophobic. It grew hotter with my anger pulsing my veins.

"I don't understand what you're going on about. Blame the victim much?" I raised my voice, which could have attracted attention from the guys. I didn't care.

She took my hands, and I shook her away. She said, "Slow down. Consider what I'm saying."

"What, lessons in how to be cold and inhuman?"

"Sometimes, when kids grow up with parents who manipulate them in subtle ways, they grow up being too easy to manipulate and they're easy to be taken advantage of by con artists. Let people get away with mistreating them. They think it's the best, the only 'love' they'll get; they even protect their abusers."

I had so much to say that I said nothing. It would have come out all jumbled. Animal sounds.

She spoke evenly, pausing between words. "Sometimes having parents who play mind games is worse than having parents who beat you. Some beaten kids learn to identify abuse right away and say NO. Say Absolutely Not. They leave at the first sign of mistreatment. Cut and dried. Especially after therapy."

"What are you, a psychiatrist? Or, let's see . . . a slave I freed from shackles in a dungeon."

"You mean after I risked my life to save you when I realized Luke might rape you?"

"Why, because you'd gotten bored with killing people for the Nevermind?"

"Let's go, bitch."

"Where, so you can throw me to the lions?"

"Stop it! You'll need something better to wear if we'll escape. To your wardrobe. You lead."

We didn't run this time. We walked, with decisive footsteps, on opposite sides of the hall from each other, not speaking. I admit, I stomped a bit.

When we got to my boudoir and went into the wardrobe, we were close enough to whisper. I wasn't sure I cared what she had to say.

"I was forced into being an Agent assassin. I didn't even know I was one. Well, part of me did, but my handler was in control of that part. My handler gave me Dissociative Identity Disorder, by traumatizing me so much when I was little. Made my mind split into pieces."

"The old MKULTRA trick. Oh. I'm sorry, Tommy." My throat had trouble opening wide enough to get that out.

"The initiations create loyalty, too, you know. They break you down and you rise out of the ashes into being an Agent above and beyond anything else-- Bennu bird style."

"Like mine on the equinox?"

She said, "You got off easy. Huld must have gone through an initiation just as bad as mine."

"That's right. That's the point of the cults and secret societies the Agents at the top are part of."

I changed into clothes and put on a second set on top, so I'd be ready if we made it out of there.

"So, tell me, what did you do that bothers the Agents?"

"You know who the American guy, Brandon, is, right?"

"The underground video journalist who goes on about conspiracies. The person the Nevermind hates most."

"I exposed elements of crimes by the Nevermind. I collaborated with Brandon. A lot of whistleblowers collaborated with him. He's been doing his thing for years. Sources give him information behind the scenes, sometimes even going on his indie video show online."

"Are you N--? How are you alive?"

"I went underground. Please call me Tommy. Never let N-- slip. Or 'she.'"

Silence.

I waited for more, but I could see her focusing on making it through the pain, so I was merciful with my questions. We were our own doppelgangers screeching through time and space, torn between two people not only inside of us.

This had to change. All of it. I could do it.

CHAPTER 18
GASLIGHTING

"As long as we're stuck here, can we team up against Dune? Persuade him to destroy the elixir?" I asked.

"Maybe. He went into the kitchen with the lock. Maybe we can find it and figure out how it works."

"It's our only hope. The windows are too thick to break. I've tried them. The modernized one was too small to squeeze through."

I ran past the larder and peered around the cupboard, checking that Dune wasn't sneaking up on us. I tried to figure out how to help her at the same time as swooning over Colin. Feral Colin, my intrepid savior. How many of us have loved two people at once? Most, I'd wager.

If she answered, I didn't hear it.

Food had passed through the kitchen. Someone had come to the castle with supplies. Why couldn't we have gotten food deliveries all along? I would have loved fresh meat pie.

The sink and drainage, which once must have been functional, made me cringe: slippery moss and rust and a continual worthless drip. Hardly able to take that sound, I worried about whether

Tommy and I would be punished. Opening the door, I peeked into the dining hall. I tripped over the laver at its entrance. The stone basin for washing stank. I was glad to share the castle experience with a friend, someone to release tension with, to play with. To escape with.

We poked around everywhere, underneath cabinets, on top of the high ones, hidden in cups turned upside down.

"Let's gaslight Dune," I suggested, narrowing my eyes. "I know a way to drive him looney."

"Ooooh, you do?"

I whispered to Tommy. "You know Enochian. Can you teach me Enochian angels calls?"

"What, right now? Saying what?"

"What kinds of things do they say? How's the weather?" I asked.

"No, more like, 'Hey, wouldn't this be a great storm for an Apocalypse, buddy? More or less. No way you could learn Enochian fast. Sorry."

"Is Enochian the lost language of Atlantis like they say?" I asked.

"Oh, palease."

"Tell you what," I said. "I'll throw my voice."

Tommy said, "Now you're talking."

I explained, "My father got me ventriloquism lessons when I was a young."

"Lucky kid."

"After a while, it was total immersion like when you go to a foreign country and don't speak English. Some days I wasn't allowed to say anything much unless throwing my voice."

She laid her hand on my arm. Just *like* an American. Always touchy when they meet you.

"Later, Papa took me to 'channeling' lessons. So, I could pretend to bring through someone else's voice. Faking someone dead was better than me talking about the school dance. He left that theatrical stuff behind when he got on the political track."

I remembered the letter in my pocket when a corner of it poked my arm. I took it out and glanced at it. Stationery I'd used when I was in Jr. High. "My handwriting!"

"What?"

"In the oubliette, I found a letter I wrote to Mama."

"What was that doing there? Were you close to her?"

That made no sense. I didn't remember my first few years. We had no family photos from then. "Mama was around until I was seven. She wanted Papa to get over his theatrical interests, so she left the room when I was doing mime routines."

"Why?"

"She pictured a political career for him. He gave up his theatrical pursuits to study law and public service. But he didn't progress enough for her. She took off with a wealthy official of some sort. I never heard from her again."

"She didn't even call or write to you?"

"Well, three letters, spread over five years. I answered them, but she mentioned nothing I wrote, like she hadn't bothered to read them." Had they been hijacked? Agents grooming me for the Immortality Project?

As Tommy and I huddled behind an ancient room divider, wondering where Luke and Dune were and if they'd come looking, Tommy spoke in a bizarre inhuman voice. She made Enochian sounds that made us both laugh, covering our mouths and shaking.

"Right blinding, that." I mimicked her wacky Enochian angel sounds with a high pitch, without moving my mouth. I had to prepare for whatever circumstances lay before me.

"How do you do that?" she asked.

"Easy peasy. To make your mouth impossible to see move, lift your tongue to the roof of your mouth. Smiling is the position to keep, if you can, with your jaw a little forward."

She said, through the teeth of a cartoon smile, "Could get eerie if Dune's saying something horrible. If the angels are on about the end of the world and we're standing there with a constant fake smile: not good."

"Glory be. Hallelujah and pass the Apocalypse!"

"This is just too good." She rubbed her hands together and wiggled her eyebrows.

"Press it against your teeth to make consonants instead of pressing your lips together."

When she tried, she sounded a goof and a half.

"Maybe you should practice more."

And so, she did. Cuddled together, we made quick use of our time. Coaching her in secrets, I had her practice to get it right. That was even harder when whispering. To keep from laughing, I pinched myself when we imagined a variety of scenarios to make them crazy.

A faint sound in the distance. Dune walking toward us, down the hall. His footsteps had a distinctive long, proud gait. I pulled Tommy with me into a storage closet and hunkered down in the darkness surrounded by. A tarp was handy to cover us with so Dune wouldn't see us if he looked in.

Dune's footsteps gave away where he was in the hallway. There was no door between us other than the closet. Not having to hide mouth movements made ventriloquism so easy it wasn't even ventriloquism any more. Using the sounds of Dune's footsteps, as I estimated which painting he was walking past, I mimicked how I imagined each historical figure would have talked.

Tommy and I slid together sweaty, our voices hoarse as we grew low on air.

I wasn't sure what painting he was beside because his were footsteps were so far away, so I started with a generic male voice. "Greetings to thee, oh Dune. The veil is rent these nights. We speak. We speak to you."

"What!"

"The question is, doth thou listen well."

"Jesus fucking Christ!"

His footsteps stopped and stumbled. It sounded like he was turned around.

I didn't pretend to be the voices of the figures in the paintings far down the hall. That would have been too far for the vocal direction to be convincing. But the ones near the kitchen, yes. The odd sound created from being in a closet made it sound like the subjects of the paintings were speaking from the distant past. This was too good.

"Ah, wilt thou walk past me, Dune? Tis I, John Dee, whom thou have consulted all these years, while I remained silent. Yes, I heard thee, even when thou didst not speak aloud."

"Dee! I. I love you. I revere you. What can you tell me?"

"I'm proud of thee. Thou hast put in much work. Thou and Luke have learned alchemy well."

"Thank you! Your words mean the world."

"But thou must reconsider. All is not as thou thinketh. What thou art doing is not wise."

Luke exclaimed, "But you were the one who started that trend to begin with long ago. Amalgamating different country's myths and religions. Making it look like legends were real, so you could mess with cultures' prophecies and take them over by getting them to come."

"Thou art correct. King Arthur and the Grail and all that rot." I made myself laugh in Old English male. Best guess. "That's why I now cometh to thee to stop the trend. Make no more elixir. Tis the work of the devil. I came to see the error of my ways. Yes, the queen, Walsingham and I created a great empire. But at what cost? Now go, and sin no more."

The footsteps stopped. Tommy and I covered our mouths to squelch giggles. Turning the tables was gratifying after being cooped up with fear. Being in fear for our lives made our humor even more desperately uproarious. Yet, silence was key.

He approached again down the hallway.

I cleared my throat quietly as I could, lowered my voice even more and took on the voice of spymaster Walsingham as Dune was, I hoped, under the painting. "My friend Dee is correct. The Agents of the Nevermind must put a stop to this deception we started long ago in London. The American president brought back into the public eye the lies we began, but which, in Heaven, we'd hoped would stop. Thou can imagine how they make us cringe. King *Arthur?* Come now."

I whispered into her ear, "Can you be the Enochian Angels? In Enochian, say, 'Hey, Dune. We were just kidding, silly.'" And she did. Apparently.

Dune cried out, "Oh my God. What? Angels, you teased me all this time? Bloody hell!"

Dune's footsteps hesitated when he walked into the kitchen. He was looking for us, but I could tell he was first going for the scrummy candied ginger Huld had brought us. Recognizing the sound of the little box, and the crinkly paper, I could tell from how he tore into it and dropped it his hands were shaking. I hoped the candy would soothe his soul just a little.

Is this a horrible idea? Dune was coming over to the closet. *He might only notice the tarp and not look under it. But he might.* The soles of my feet were so wet and slimy my shoes felt like they could fall off. The closet door opened. Were we doomed?

Tommy jumped out with such a rush that Dune must have jumped back from the ruckus and missed me under the tarp which I pulled back over myself. She leaned against the closet door as she exited, shutting me once again in the safe darkness.

She said, "I changed my mind, Dune. I'll not hide from you anymore. Do with me what you will. I'm not afraid of you. I have Sylvia and Susan inside me. You won't kill me. You can't."

"What were you thinking? Hiding in here. I should have thrown you into the dungeon with Miriam."

"Oh, God, no. Sorry, Dune. I had to save her life. She's a

person, too. But between you and me, she's such a bitch that I couldn't stand being stuck in the same room with her like that."

My breath came so loud to my ears that I covered my face with my arm. "What if I'd been wrong to trust her? What if she'd turn me in so she could consume my aura and remain an asset to them?"

Blanche. Had to trust her.

Tommy spoke as the Enochian angels. I didn't understand what the words meant. Was she good enough at ventriloquism yet to fool Dune? Or would our plan fall apart? If she could convince him, he'd never question what he heard in the hallway. Maybe my Old English deceit would lead to Dune steering the Agency to becoming, well, less deceitful. Ahem.

Dune answered the angels in Enochian too, his voice cracking.

Once the Enochian conversations quit, he said to Tommy, "I can't believe the angels said I have to open the castle door to let the energies flow. This would be a special night. Everyone's expecting the big show. You know what that means, don't you? I must put you back on the chain until the party. It won't be long. Guards will be posted there, so you can't get out. And you're the woman of the evening. Such as it is."

"My pleasure. I'm looking forward to showing that bitch what it takes to be the Grail Bennu."

Had I misread Tommy? I'd told her my secrets. I'd put my life in her hands as soon as escaping from them. She'd been toiling underneath me all this time while chanting Enochian calls over elixirs, letting them set me up for trauma, for rape, for burning maybe to death, maybe not. How much of their plans did they let her in on?

He and Tommy left. As they walked through the castle, I heard the rattling of the chains, and then the front door. Then, I heard Dune ranting in Enochian, a distracted, broken man.

It was my chance. He was too bewildered to notice me leaving. His world had just fallen apart.

Creeping out of the closet and peering both ways just in case, I walked to the door. I ran from one shadow to the next, crouching.

Voices. Our party was starting.

CHAPTER 19
PASSION

My shoes sank into the wet ground imprinted with other footprints that were larger than mine. When I got far enough from the castle, I called Colin's name while leaping from rock to rock to throw the men off my tracks.

Surprisingly, I heard nothing. I wandered farther, the land endless, beyond the trees and rock walls before me. No one. *Is he audacious enough to hide in the trees where Dune saw him?* He'd have to trust Dune would leave him alive. I felt for him, the right and left sides of my collar bone tightening the muscles around them as I imagined being him out there all that time.

In the vast distances I glimpsed through the trees as I approached the open moor spreading downward rolling hills, slanted white rock erupting in gnarled angles, their edges dirtied like fingernails of a man who gardens for his life.

I couldn't get lost with the castle looming in the distance. I'd been warned not to walk places because of animal traps. As I leaped over a stream to the shadows on the other side, I hoped I remembered where they were.

I lay over the edge of the stream, washing my face and looking in my reflection. Little circular waves faded into stillness. That experience turned me into part of the world again, seamless and undisturbed. I hadn't seen it since I'd been abducted to the castle other than in the pitted dullness of the hand pounded pewter. Dune had done up my hair very much like Susan's for the Equinox ritual. I hadn't taken it down and it was turning into a wilderness.

"Colin, I've come to my senses!" I called breathlessly as I got far enough away from the castle to risk it. The land was so vast that he could have been lying far away. I didn't want to leave the forest and expose myself to the men in the moor below. The forest gave up nothing. When I left it, I crawled, sliding along the ground, hoping to look like a rock.

I explored the landscape for hours. The day was young when I'd started out seeking Colin, but it was growing dark and cool. I was thirsty. My voice was hoarse. Far from the castle, beyond the forest, down the rolling moors, my hair blew over my face, whipping against my eyes. Crawling and raising one hand to free my hair, with low shrubs scratching me, I decided I was free of the Agents in the castle.

My heart pounded, and I soared into liberation to be me, as I had always been, in the world outside the castle. My world. Green and achingly beautiful hills, clumps of trees, golds and umbers, rusts and yellow splashes. I could do without the Nevermind and Bennu, thank you very much. No more troupe, no more being mesmerized by Dune. Living simple again.

I ran, my breath coming bright and my legs moving of their own accord. I headed along the ground toward the road to catch a ride. If I escaped, then I'd return for Colin and Tommy later.

I spied Colin among the cliffs. Wonderful man! He ran toward me, then hesitated, until I spread my arms out wide. He bounded, and I thought he would pick me up spinning.

But he didn't even hug me.

"I know," I said, looking downward, the heather spreading out before me, with their tiny leaves hardy, the shadows of each one sharp and deep against the others, lit ruddy by the sun. I shaded my eyes when I looked at him, a silhouette against the poem of a landscape.

We're inside a story, I thought. *The edges of our story are like moss, the little viney spots in the yard by the terraces and the spaces between the fence posts and the rocky hill, inhabited by glowing imagination since I was a child giddy with breathing into other worlds.*

"Miriam! Are you OK?"

"*You?*"

"Never been better."

My body couldn't help but inform me that living feral suited him: the freckly suntan, the jacket torn to reveal his lean arms that made me want to kiss them and press myself against him everywhere; his hair longer than I'd seen it and fallen over his eyes like I liked it; smart beard, a band of mud across his face, the intensely longing look of a lost boy like my favorite actors. The brown of his eyes contrasting with sparkling corneas whiter. His movements more expressive, larger, his face animated and glowing. I needed to touch him so hard I pressed all the way through him to the other side.

He said, "We might hitch a ride out of here."

"There's not much of anyone driving out here, not for a long way."

We walked on anyway. Words were stupid. We walked in the silence made of the magnetics flowing between us.

When we stopped to drink at an old well by an empty barn, I queried, "How did you know I was here?" I pushed relentlessly until I turned the crank, and the chain rose toward me, the water glistening in the bucket. I rinsed the tin cup attached to the well by a mossy chain and filled it. I raised it to his lips as we gazed in each other's eyes.

He answered, "I asked around to everyone I could get a hold of. I assumed, like the director announced at the show, she'd taken off with her husband someplace secret. Kevin wouldn't speak. Imagine Kevin not saying anything, right? He seemed spooked."

"How?"

"Just the way he was looking around, I guess. Huld was nowhere. I asked Norma if she knew where you were. What a sweetheart. And, so, I headed out here because I thought Susan might have answers."

“How did Norma know Susan -- er, I was at the Penderghast castle?”

“She didn’t. When we were hanging out, she said an actress had snuck into a party at the castle. The girl was kicked out, but she got ahold of out-of-this-world drugs. Made her see visions that answered her questions about reality. Or some such.”

“No doubt.”

“So, when actors were asking about the best place to get drugs, the actress said this was the spot.”

“That make you think I’d be here?”

“Norma said she heard Susan and her husband went to the parties at the castle on the hush-hush, so, I might find them here for a party. There was always a bash a few days after the equinox. She was planning to crash it, so, she gave me the address. Well, I guess the party is tonight.”

“I'm glad you came early for the party.” I started to hug him, but he pulled back and tightened his jaw.

“I almost didn’t.” His fierce eyes glinted when he glanced at me sideways. His hackles raised, his shoulders up and his hands in fists. “Can you imagine how I felt when you skipped out on me? Come on, girl! What were you thinking?”

“It’s not what it seems. It's never been what it seems.”

“What it seems is complete insanity.”

“Did you report me as a Missing Person when you couldn’t find me at first?”

“I tried. The police laughed.”

"If I disappeared, you would have been charged with my murder and spent the rest of your life in prison."

"I had time to think about things going wrong while I was hunting, gathering and making merry with the stickers stuck to my boots. I'll be ever curious to find out if any of the unsavory futures are real."

"I'm so sorry. I didn't think I'd see you again after the police took you away. How did you get back? Did you rent a car?"

"No, you show them your ID to register a car; that would have been unwise since I skipped out on bail. Paid the last driver I got a ride with to bring me close to the castle. He'd heard people died cause of being attacked by ghosts in the entryway. He dropped me off in front of a neighbor's house. That was as close as he'd get, and that made him shake. He got this weird look."

He lifted his upper lip and rolled it outward so it looked like a caveman. He raised it on one side and lifted his eyebrows, jutting his chin forward and widening his lips apart to show me his teeth like a chimpanzee.

I grabbed his shoulder when I laughed, bending over and holding my stomach. I pretended to be a cavewoman too, with a bow and arrow, creeping curled over, hunting him, stepping onto the balls of my feet first, the silently leaping on him.

He laughed too, a sound that made me tingle. That voice! How did Dune's mesmerism deafen me to its charms for so long? How I'd missed playing with Colin! It was everything!

I asked "Did the neighbor bring you? Maybe we could get a ride with him to his house and go from there?"

"I wandered around for a crazy long time making it to a couple neighbors' houses to see if they'd bring me the rest of the way. No one answered when I knocked. Smoke was coming out of the chimney in one. In another one, the lights were on and I saw the curtain moving. They turned off the lights. Guess they're a suspicious lot around here. I walked the whole way. For you."

I lifted his hand to my mouth and kissed it. I barely licked his thumb before I let go and I watched his face, glad to see the twinge in his lips, a dimple form on his left cheek. His dimples were addictive. More, please.

I said, “We might have to go to the interstate before we can thumb a ride.”

He caressed my cheek, saying, “The police would snatch us."

"If they catch us thumbing there."

"It’s worth the risk," he asserted, taking hold of my wrist and squeezing it, staring into my eyes. We had to get away to civilization.

I hesitated. “But is it legal for you to be here? If they catch you, wouldn’t you be in trouble?”

“I skipped out. But it won’t matter with you standing by my side, alive and everything. We can prove you’re you instead of Susan. So, I'm not a killer. Easy, right?”

“I don’t know; they've got an in with forensics.”

"Who does? Who's framing me? The owner of the castle?"

"That's one. Plus Dune. And Huld." And the whole damn interlocked intelligence network, a living spider web. A web skilled at making its victims think what it wants them to.

"You've got to be kidding me." He shook his head and laughed, bent to pick up a couple chalky red rocks.

As we walked on, he gracefully flung them as if skipping them, though there was no water. While our calves swished against the stiff plant life, he let his hand slide down the side of my body. I felt electricity beneath my skin, my muscles, and bones, my most intimate areas opening, tingling with adventure, with memory of how intense joy can be, pure happiness, instead of doomed longing or deluded fantasy enactments.

The heat between our arms felt sparks igniting me. I furrowed my brow and thighs. I wanted Colin inside me, as me, as one being, made of friction.

I wasn’t going to spoil the peak experience of my life. I was falling in love with Colin. In real love at last. I was loose in my body, and swaying my hips felt like freedom. Life was blinding. The brightness of discovery, the companionship something I would never grow tired of.

“I don’t understand what happened, Miriam. Did you run away with Dune?" He gently placed fingers under my chin. I could feel his breath. He raised my chin. He wouldn't let me look away from his eyes. "Why?”

My eyes stung, and I started to lift my elbow to dry them. But before I did that, I wanted to go somewhere to hide, blow my nose and wash my face. I would try going into among people, retreating, trying again until I could speak without sounding like I was underwater. I restrained myself from wiping my tears and I let him see. I'd never done that. I was out of my head.

“I waited a long time after the show. Was it wrong to give you the flowers?”

“No, leaving wasn’t about you.”

"Did we miss each other after the show? Did you take off when I went looking around on the grounds for Susan and Kevin? I thought you knew we were supposed to be looking for Susan inside the theater, and they told me to check out back. Did you think I rudely went home without you?”

“I’m sorry. There was so much I couldn’t tell you. I wanted to open up to you why our troupe was so strangely successful. It's psychology. Because of Dune hypnotizing us. And training us to work with auras, too. We all signed non-disclosure forms.”

“I don’t understand.”

“Thank you for not giving up. What a hero.”

His hands pressed against my body with power I didn’t know he had. His tongue sought the inner reaches of my mouth, and when he pulled the hair at the center nape of my neck, arching my neck back, my knees buckled with submissive pleasure. I was so woman.

He’d become the wild animal I’d wished for. He’d thrown off the cloak of respectable domesticity. And since he was learning the intensity of my life I'd keep secret, I could let out my Gothic and storm wild with him. He pressed against me.

I pulled his energy through me and cycled it over my head, curving down his body.

The wind blew up my skirt. He reached to touch. We pulled off our clothes and threw them down, restraints in a zoo.

He ran a circle around me. He picked me up and ran. Zigzagging through bushes, leaping over rocks and rivulets, swinging around trees, we crossed each other's paths.

Screeching and hooting, we made bestial sounds: none domestic, no pets, nothing caged, nothing waiting to be eaten. Wild, wild, *wild*erness creatures. Not small ones, either, nothing mousy. *Big.*

We found a small clearing amid trees that would hide us. The spot.

He held his arms up over his head, pretending to have antlers.

I found solid sticks and beat rhythms on a rock.

He drew on his body with hands full of dirt.

He drew on mine.

We made wreaths out of leaves. We put them on each other's heads. I stuck flowers in mine. He put branches in his.

He sang a spontaneous primal melody.

I joined in, improvising high and low all around, our voices wailing louder, rising together. If only we also had fire.

We became our own fire.

Birds sang. He pushed me up against a tree.

He made love as I had never experienced. Full of life force that flows unimpeded through rushing rivers and flying eagles.

I pulled his energy into my womb and up my body, out my heart into his, as I'd learned from Dune and from Luke's grimoire. It was more powerful than drawing in Susan's energy, and more empowering than sending my aura wafting out into the audience when doing a show. To circulate it with someone I loved, who saw and loved me for who I was and wanted the best for me felt more enlivening than it had when circulating it with Dune, who was using me.

My pleasure had plenty of land to fly over, with no neighbors to hear, the castle too far away. Joy grew.

When we were spent, I cycled my energy back into my body and instructed him to focus on his own energy, and only his, being centered in his belly. I'd learned. Magickal hygiene was nothing to sneeze at.

I wouldn't have to give up the call to adventure if I settled with Colin: it was part of us.

I'd trained for two years to become a mythological being, a Holy Grail, a paranormal set of Russian dolls. Would I be good enough company just playing me? Doing dishes and taking out the trash in an ordinary house with electricity, running water and mobile phones.

Would this moment of glorious wildness with Colin be enough to sustain us for the rest of our lives? We couldn't let it slip into sad nostalgia as we grew ordinary and hunkered over dusty desks full of numbers in the back of a cobwebby basement.

We promised we'd regularly head to the woods, strip and run, bring drums, bring matches for a bonfire, and make him antlers he could attach to his head. Roll and grunt, leap, pretend to fly, make up our own damn songs. Be us. Free animals in our hearts.

We dressed, mimicking and interrupting each other with the physical humor that came to us naturally when together. We couldn't talk fast enough. Regular speech could never be enough.

"Could we steal Dune's or Luke's or Huld's tires and put them on your car? It's still in the same spot."

"The tires are bigger. They wouldn't fit on the rims. Can we steal one of their cars?" He elbowed me, a mischievous boy.

"They keep the keys in a special lock box. I don't know how to hot-wire, do you?"

"Never thought about learning that trick. Guess I should become devious minded."

"Do you want to sneak into your car to get anything?"

"No, too big a chance. Let's head straight to the road."

"There's open space between." What I meant was that they could kill us and this could be our last chance to be together, minute by minute. Each moment becomes precious when each one might be a major portion of your future.

He held me close, and after we kissed long and hard, we walked on, going outside the forest onto the windy moors.

He asked, "What's the story with that one bloke, anyway?" Colin strode along with arms and legs straight, making me laugh. "Why does he go around in armor? Is he a nutter?"

"I guess growing up in this castle would make anyone wacko. Luke wants everything to be like it was in the past. I think he wears it to protect himself from his assistant, even though most of the time I've been here, she's been chained."

"Bizarre. Tell me more."

"It's a lovely castle." I was choking up and stopped myself by gazing at the gorgeous building and counting the stone teeth along the top. A drafty, cold hub for the intersection of the occult and propaganda. And the setting for the romance of the century.

"No, really. What's Luke thinking? That armor has got to be uncomfortable." He gestured as if wearing it, lifting one shoulder and grimacing.

I quipped, "It's a cold castle. He's going around in a self-generating heater."

"OK, well. Maybe Luke wears armor to hide that he resembles me. And how he looks an older, male version of Susan. And her twin. Our sister, Sylvia."

"Now your mind is taking you to new places, I'll say. Does he look like a dapper woman?"

"I don't know. I've never seen his face. Colin. Luke's our father."

"That's incredible." His pupils dilated.

When we walked away from the castle again, I offered, "In the worst-case-scenario, Luke, and maybe other Bennu Society people, must have chosen Papa as the best person to adopt me. To mold my personality to become a revered member of the Bennu Society, like Susan was."

"No! I don't believe it. That's a cruel thing to think of your father. Do you think he's that Draconian?"

"I don't know. He's got some weird tattoo, I don't know what it means. . ."

"Just because he's the mayor now doesn't mean he was in on the scheme. Do you have any evidence?"

"Why else would he and Mama want to adopt me? They didn't seem to love me much."

He spoke as he walked with a looser, more confident stride. I hadn't noticed how tall he was. The way he bent backward, going down the hill, the way his muscles moved, he was mesmerizing. Alive. His eyes twinkling. "I think a lot of us feel that way about our parents. It's often not how the parents see it."

"Dune, you know, the man --"

"I know. The police called him by name. Not a moment I'm about to forget soon. What's the deal with him?"

"He was married to Susan."

"Guess he's got a type."

"I know, right? But his game's a lot bigger than pheromones."

"Since the director announced Susan would disappear with her husband on a vacation, I asked around after the show and the actors said Kevin had driven her to the convenience store to get cigarettes before the show and she . . . What?" I was shaking my head no. "Wait, is she here?"

"No, she isn't, though her body will be soon. She's dead. Huld killed her before the show. They set up Kevin and Susan with post-hypnotic suggestions triggered by those little paper fortunes. They got them to smoke cigarettes out in the well house."

"Weird. So, those fortunes were more than random fun. Pretty macabre decorations I've got at home."

"I think maybe Huld knocked Kevin out and killed her, weighed her down and threw her in the well. I was breathing in her aura at the time, so . . ." He blinked. "Oh, never mind. The thing is, the director said Susan and Dune were going on vacation, so, no one got suspicious when they didn't notice them around the city."

Colin held his head. "What a good cover."

"He abducted me while I believed I was Susan."

He exclaimed in a series of sounds that weren't words.

"And the worst of it, Huld's an Agent of the Nevermind, right? So, he set it up with an Agent who is a forensics expert."

"Why?"

"To substitute the findings about the body to look like Susan's body is mine. Like I was killed after the show. Around the time you were looking around the grounds for Susan."

"Since you're sisters. Same DNA, same appearance, that would be a perfect cover for a murder. Amazing."

I held his hand as we walked. "As soon as Susan's body is found, the report is ready to go. They spread rumors that that we were a couple, and you abused me."

"Your friends think that?"

"She's in the water somewhere. That's why Dune got you to check the well house. They got witnesses."

"Son of a bitch! When I was there, someone snapped a photo. I thought it was because it was a romantic old structure."

"Well, that seals it for me. Her body must be at the bottom of the well."

"And we can tell them about Susan's body and how the blokes murdered her, covered it up and abducted you."

"No. Remember, they're Agents. That's what they're paid to do."

"But why? How does that serve England? It makes no sense."

"You know there's a huge overlap between occult practices and intelligence agencies, always has been throughout history. Just look at John Dee and Edward Kelley. Just look at Madam Blavatsky and Theosophy."

"And Crowley and Huxley. And the Greek Oracles. The Isis cult."

"Right. They're getting Agents riled up about this thing called the Immortality Project. I guess it keeps them enthused. It gives the Bennu Society clout. And the Bennu Society's embedded in the Agency. The troupe is more connected than I realized."

"Immortality? What does that have to do with you? Because you played Bennu?"

"See, here's the thing. Weird, I know. I breathed in Susan's aura while she was dying. She breathed in her sister's aura while she was dying."

"I guess I can see that. But what I don't understand is this. Why did you go along with living with Dune and pretending to be Susan?"

"He hypnotized the standbys to believe we were the stars when we'd take their places, until the final curtain landed. He whisked me away before that moment. I thought I was his wife."

"Hm."

"No, really."

"Hmm." He looked at the ground, and his hand went tense. He dropped my hand. "I don't think hypnosis is that powerful. I've read you can't commit a crime unless it's what you want. Did part of you want to be Dune's wife? He's a stunner. Brilliant and well-off. I've been out here all this time and I'll bet you could have figured out some way to leave with your good friend Colin once you figured out you were Miriam. Did you make love with him? Is that what this is all about?"

I said nothing. I couldn't lie. But saying, "Yes" in that moment of vulnerability with Colin was harsh. I tried to answer his questions. We walked in silence, with space between us widening the farther we walked.

I wasn't acting out Susan's personality in full, because I got it wrong. Sure, I was influenced by her and maybe took on bits and bobs memories, or maybe tuned into them through the collective unconscious, the oneness of auric substance. I was probably mostly acting out my *idea* of her, though.

If I'd been abducted by someone other than Dune, would the post-hypnotic suggestion have had such a strong hold on me? How much did I cooperate with my capture?

In the brief moments before I had the full induction, I'd considered that her disappearance could have been my fault. I pondered the possibility that I'd incapacitated Susan by breathing in too much of her aura. Or that maybe Colin had done something, so she couldn't perform that night. I'd opened my mind to the possibility that Kevin had stolen her away for unknown reasons.

It gave me the chance to become her, not just that night but for years to come, for my career to shine, to continue working with Dune, to provide solace for the man I most admired once his wife was dead. Gave me the chance to not worry about leaving the role of the immortal Bennu bird, revered Grail of esoteric seekers and secret society members, and thus the dubious Agents.

I'd tried not to think what those powerful people did behind the scenes; I'd focused on Dune's occult vision of thrilling sensuality and fervent costumed spectacle that took me beyond mundane existence I'd shared with friends like Colin.

Not that I had many friends. Probably no one else had even noticed I wasn't around anymore. I mattered to him, even though I was ordinary. But the last show! I was glad I'd gotten the chance to prove myself, to be great. Would I have missed that chance if given the choice?

"I'm sorry, Colin. I'm an awful person."

"Maybe you are." We stopped. He looked away as if in pain. He'd risked his life for me and I wasn't worth it.

"I got caught up in trying to be Susan."

"It wasn't enough for you to be regular-person Miriam, discovering intriguing interest in ordinary-person Colin. It never will be."

I said, "Dune learned hypnosis from the Nevermind. The masters of persuasion."

"Oh, that's your excuse, is it?"

I stammered. "I thought of you. Even when I thought you were a stranger. Even though you were a crazed murderous tramp trying to abduct me."

"So, if you're with one man, you think of another, then? Not sure that's the woman I'd want."

"Isn't there a right answer? Stop it! You've waited for me all this time. Did you think I was a virgin?"

"I don't like to bet against the odds. I like my life to make sense."

"So, why are you here?"

"I wanted to save you. I thought if you disappeared without telling me goodbye, there must be a problem. Because you were a nice person, I *thought*. Thank you for the reward and I hope you have a nice life with Dune. I'll be on my way, now."

Had my obsession with being Susan ruined me? No! This couldn't be happening!

I figured on explaining the Substitute Hallucination. I couldn't be blamed. I'd even been fooled about Luke and Tommy being in the castle the whole time. I needed redemption.

Just then, a whizzing arrow missed Colin's chest.

Another arrow came fast; he ducked, and it hit my arm. Bleeding from the puncture along the side. I opened and closed my hand, painful as it was. The arrow didn't keep me from moving my muscles. Pain swelled my eyes, burning with tears. The pain seemed larger than my arm. It hurt out into my aura. It burned everything forever.

Colin nodded to get approval to pull. He hesitated. He grimaced and did the deed.

I covered my yell, pressing my mouth into my shoulder. I bit my sleeve. As I yelled harder, I bit my elbow, muffling my yell, and I rocked back and forth to distract the pain.

I tried moving my arm. I wasn't sure it would work.

It did. I could move fingers though my thumb was iffy.

My stomach was embers.

Colin's eyes were so bright, his mouth so curvaceous. I stared at his face, trying to keep him real, second by second. With me. My love. Not torn away. The muscles in my body clenched with the desire to hold onto that moment, to kill the future coming toward us.

From behind a tree in the distance appeared Luke, who rose from behind a bush running as he came into a crouch and ran upon us fast, his armor flashing. He must have crept up to keep clanking. He pulled me away from Colin. Brown passionate wild animal Colin.

I screamed and reached toward him, but he ran into the forest shadows and down the rough cliffs.

CHAPTER 20
THE PARTY

Luke grunted, "Sorry." He crooked his leg in front of mine and kicked back at an angle. My leg sabotaged me.

I fell on the ground. My throbbing, bleeding arm cocked up my landing, and I slipped sideways.

Luke grabbed me and flung me on top of his metallic back. I scrambled to balance myself on his shoulders, holding onto his helmet. I flailed, until I sat on his shoulders, my legs on his chest, his hands holding onto me, the cold metallic mesh digging in.

"How could you?"

He didn't answer other than "Sorry." He ambled underneath my pounding thighs, his stride faltering, as he veered from side to side.

I tried prying off his helmet, but it wouldn't budge.

I banged on the armor on Luke's back. It seemed to inflame his dedication to take me back to the castle, my prison, his footsteps clanking.

I cursed at him, twisting his head. I set up an undulation with my body moving like a sine wave. Our dance teacher had taught us that move.

He sang something tuneless in a thready voice.

I have to change.

My tears streamed down his cold metal shoulder, bumping my cheek, bruising my cheekbone. I recognized the sound of a tear drop hitting his armor. That was the sound I'd heard in the hall when he was standing there before I could see him. He was crying.

We slogged through the wet landscape. We passed expensive cars parked in the driveway.

"Father?"

His voice grew hollow. He took a deep breath. He choked and gulped. "You wouldn't want to miss the party, would you? Our guests are arriving. And we're the only hosts."

That's it? I find out he's my father and that's *it*?

Wait, I was hosting a party? I should have at least dusted. My eyes darted, and images ran through my head about silverware and punch bowls. *I haven't made a seating chart. How hard it is to keep people from being miserable at dinner. Is there even a dinner? How about tea? Will they have to meet people they don't know?* "Where's Dune? Did he send you?"

"Dune's gone off his head. He's blathering away about how Dee and the Angels told him everything he'd done was a mistake. Everything. The whole walk down the hall when he took Tommy to the oratory, paintings chatted him up. Takes his work too seriously if you ask me."

"Oh, really?"

"Don't ask me. He's going on about how he wants us to let you go free. He's hiding out from the party, doesn't want to show his face. You know, the party we had to prepare for while you were living it up in the abyss. The party celebrating the Project culmination. The culmination didn't go the way the guests expected."

They wanted me to be pregnant with a Moonchild named Equinox.

❄

I didn't want to spend my future visiting Colin in prison. Not that he would want to see me. He deserved a lovely life in a house, with nice hot meals, and walks in the park. He deserved to meet some nice woman someday. I'd give up on love, myself. Obviously, I wasn't made for it. Not that I had anything to give up. Colin was over me. He'd found out who I was.

When Luke crossed the threshold into the castle, I smelled the familiar scent wafting. Herbs and incense. I kept looking toward the door to the castle, but every time big men posted guard next to it.

I wondered if I should scream the truth. But the Agents would cheer.

He carried me to the closet by the loo and peroxided and wrapped my arm. I loved him when he took off his metal glove and gave me heavy pain medication and a natural antibiotic.

I wanted to escape the guards posted at the doorway. To hide under someone's car and see if I could survive hanging under it on the long drive back to somewhere.

But when Huld came in, Luke said, "Yep, this little one escaped the dungeon. Dune will be pissed."

"No, he won't even care at this point. He's given up."

"Well, don't let her get away. I'm shattered. I doubt she'll bother fighting too hard in a den of Agents, but just in case, here, take this extra helmet so she doesn't stick her nail into your eyes or ears or try to strangle you." He plucked it from a wall decoration and threw the roses resting inside it. The helmet covered the neck, so I couldn't strangle him. Damn.

Huld reached out to take me from Luke. Luke bent forward with a sigh, and I slid off. Huld picked me up and hoisted me onto his shoulders.

"Nice helmet. Cute."

He asked, "So you want to wear the Moldavite Tiara of the Grail Bennu for the party, do you?"

Well, yeah. The sparking tiara *would* validate my existence. I'd be the best. The one consulted about decisions I cared about in the Agency. I could tell Papa. If it weren't top secret government business. "No! I don't. What are you on about?"

"You want to sit on the throne in the Reverence Room. You want everyone to recognize that you have blinding truths to offer. Don't you?"

"No!"

"Yes, you do."

Yes. "No."

"I know that trait. Little recognition hog?"

The torches were lit. I hadn't gone into the great hall. The shields and banners displaying the coat of arms across the white-washed walls dusted. Members of the Nevermind apparently met that day in the great hall, their voices echoing, reverberating off the loft ceiling in the inner ward. A juggler dressed in a jester outfit wove through the crowd, nearly burning himself in the fire flicking out of the chimney. All the while, the wind blew down and out, whooshing through it.

The Agents would approve of my horrors. Did they gossip over tea?

I rode on Huld's shoulders in a medicated throbbing daze as he walked among the wooden benches and trestle tables through the crowd. One Agent got off with a fit bird. Two others bent over the Enochian chess set in the corner.

Agents bowed when Huld and I walked past, some with compassion in their eyes, some shaking their heads, others ignoring me as if I didn't matter as a human. They talked among themselves, some in dramatic tones, setting off the narrative tapestries. The most important sat in high-straight backed chairs with stuffed arms and seats. The chests along the walls were covered with linens and fancy treats that someone had brought. Everything was exciting. Everything was a breakthrough in consciousness. The Agents were becoming breathless discussing the Immortality Project.

There were two or three nubile recruits to the Bennu Society. Made my stomach turn. If they said no, would they be killed so they didn't reveal secrets?

When we passed by one, I shook my head and mouthed to her: don't do it.

A fat Agent chatted up a fit bird who kept stepping back from him, as they leaned on the stepped buffets, wooden planks with shelves covered in drapes topped with silver platters. Whenever we wandered near them, I could make out a few words. "The one true King of the Briton's prophecy . . ."

"Stonehenge druids and Camelot . . . the Roman emperors. . ."

"The right to the Welsh throne too. . ."

"You see, the search for the Holy Grail, which we believe was Moldavite, fallen from the Heavens . . ."

"Those kings were bloody spin doctors," I yelled to Huld into his helmet near his ear, and the fat Agent glared over at me across a few heads. "Acting like King Arthur was real. And their faux Arthurian heritage gave them whatever rights they wanted." I pulled Huld's shirt, the mane on a horse, to get him to go in the chatty Agent's direction. He laughed, neighed and complied.

The Agent dabbed his forehead and wheezed. "King Arthur conquered several territories for England that Geofry of Monmouth didn't even record. And don't you agree they should still belong to England? But mean people stole them away."

"They did?"

I bent, pressing my ribs into Huld's shoulder, to whisper to the pretty recruit, saying, "Mythological excuses are still excuses. Don't believe a word these spin doctors say."

The wainscoting lining the walls had been polished, the floor strewn with rushes, mimicking the glory days. Who had done this? Was Tommy let off her chain at night when I was sleeping next to Dune, and set to work like an elf?

A posh twit instructed a recruit about competing ancestries. "Magicians in Atlantis were good and the ones in Shambhala were bad, you see."

"Oh? I read it was the other way round."

"You can't always believe what you read. That's why joining the Bennu Society is so useful. You learn more secrets about the world with each initiation."

"I do like learning truth."

"Then, you'll love this Society. And, believe me, they'll love you." The man flicked his fingers along the crack of her buttocks, and below the curve, flicking back and forth. I watched, mesmerized.

Overlooking the great hall, in the minstrels' gallery, musicians played, seated on a narrow balcony with a balustrade with the wood gone shiny from musicians grabbing hold to keep from falling off, I supposed.

I looked around, trying to find someone I could confide in, if I could get away from Huld, someone who could slip me out with him, maybe in costume, so the guys guarding the doorway wouldn't stop me. Kicking, screaming and raising a ruckus would get me nowhere with the Nevermind crowd. They didn't care I was mud and blood. Me against everyone. But maybe someone had a heart.

I asked Huld, "What happened to Kevin Frank? The post hypnotic suggestion got him to obey the fortune and go out to the well house to smoke. Susan's fortune did the same thing to her?"

"They had a little chat and were getting ready to come back in when I chloroformed him and put him in his car. His parking spot is close to the well house, and it's in shadow. I gave him a heavy dose, so he slept for a couple hours. Must have had an awful headache and sore throat when he came out of that one. By that time, you and Dune were getting in the car."

"He chased us down the road."

"And I told him what was what. He came with me and I let him know he had to play the game or else. He was supposed to say he took Susan to buy ciggies at the store."

On either side of us, an orgy was happening. And it was only 9:30. Someone had an orgasm, but instead of shouting, "Oh, God," she was shouting something about bacon. *Gross.* Then, I realized she was referring to the thirteenth century Franciscan Friars, Roger. Or was it Francis, from centuries later? Pretty much just as weird.

An Agent standing next to us leered at them, then leaned over said in a Connecticut accent, "I've heard Luke got Bacon's giant mirrors from a museum."

"Oh?"

"Shame you didn't follow through on the plan to become the next Grail Bennu. You're sexier than the alternate. This Tommy person? I'm having trouble catching up."

"Shhh," I said, "He's right behind us. I think he heard you."

"Mushrooms?" the Agent said, holding the red psychedelics out toward me.

"What? Oh, no thank you."

"Have you ever done them?"

"It's how I first believed in auras. I saw colors around people. And I saw Huld poke a hole in someone's aura and draw the energy out through the hole. I told myself later it was just a hallucination."

"Why?"

"Well, I'm a rational person," I said, not convincing myself.

"Now, your tears are an elixir, from what I hear." He held out his finger, waiting for permission to touch my tear duct. I nodded acceptance. He breathed in.

I guided his finger tip to the corner of my eye. "Yes, Recursive Tears."

"Has a ring to it." I could see layers in him. The psychedelic must have been enhanced. It was working fast. I wanted to keep peeling them back. He said, "It's sad people taking the elixir will believe they're being liberated from the cycle of reincarnation."

"They'll feel fantastic. Like they're getting everything they ever wanted. Superhuman. With a past life as a giant in Atlantis."

"They'll pay out the nose for the workshops, audio books, videos for Living as a Giantkin."

I said, "They'll realize they're an incarnation of Isis. They'll promote the message of the Nevermind. The royal right to rule."

I recognized two of the Agents talking to each other. Where had I seen them? Oh, yes, one was in the Moldavite protest on TV! Bizarre. Ones I recognized from our audience.

At that moment, Tommy burst open her shirt, buttons flying everywhere. She unwrapped the binding to expose her breasts. She crowed.

What was *in* that snort?

When she spoke, I got it. Sylvia had emerged inside of her. And the ghostly woman (or repressed part of Tommy) coming to the fore was an exhibitionist.

The gobsmacked crowd ooooooohed. The silence inspired a change in music. Someone took up a guitar and strummed fast, accompanied by someone playing a bass. Plugged in, even, Gothic and dark, intense, throbbing.

The people in front of her rushed toward her to get the first feels. Their eyes widened, making their overdone clownish make-up crinkle.

One person laughed, staccato as a goat, while bowing up and down to Tommy. "Of course. That explains so much," the person said.

Their shoulders, covered in soft fur, brushed up against mine.

Tommy flitted past me, wearing the tiara. So, she was queen of the universe, now, was she? She was the Grail Bennu. Could have been me. I'd carried Susan and Sylvia all that time. And Tommy was getting the credit because she was doing it now. I was invisible. Nothing. A nobody. Second best.

Some Bennu Society twit blew powder up my nose through a straw. Sudden pain, an ice-cream headache mixed with a nose bleed. I sniffed.

I turned to see who it was, but the man had disappeared behind the oversized Bennu effigy in front of me, the feathers obscuring vision.

Tommy was being worshipped. Tommy was passed over the heads of the crowd on a stiff magic carpet, the fringe around it dangling against the Agents' faces, making two of them sneeze, and drop her.

I grabbed the tiara off her head and put it on mine. Sure, it was crooked. I didn't care. She was the new Grail Bennu. But I had the goods.

As Huld bounced up and down, I let my arms ride the air. It was being on a bull slow motion.

As best as I could tell, it was Sylvia, who, taking charge of Tommy's body, picked up a decorative sword and swung it around while she talked, her voice silky. Everyone backed away, bumping into each other, laughing.

Identity was a fluid we drank of, sloshed out of the goblet, and passed on until it was our turn again to try the new go-round. The scariest thing I'd ever experienced. Nothing was solid any more. It was a hallucination from the golden liquid in the goblets. And the liquid was an elixir made of my tears.

I couldn't let poor Tommy ruin her own life by housing Susan and Sylvia. Yes, Tommy was brave and graceful in her role. She held her head high and her neck taut, angled her shoulders with attitude. Trained in the Nevermind policy, she was a good sport. I had to admire her. All the more reason to keep her from taking the fall for me.

Sylvia laughed. Even in Tommy's androgynous little body. Sylvia's tinkly voice came through Tommy's vocal chords as if someone had turned them into wind chimes. The voice that made you remember how incredible life could be. The voice that made you wish you'd lived your life to the fullest moment by moment. That made you want to live forever. Done more face exercises than you did. Hadn't cocked up and eaten those pies. Had listened only to music by pale men who trembled, never fat men past their prime.

I hated Dune. *He loves Sylvia. And Susan. And he'll love Tommy, too. So what if he "loves" me? It's means bugger all. I was just his orgy. Three women in one body.*

The muscles in my chest tightened with hatred. I'd wanted him with my body electric, thinking I'd be always on the outside, never able to let my body press against his lightning. And then, while tricked into thinking I was his wife, I got to do that. And it was fantastic. He was a monster.

I closed my eyes tight. I couldn't take how awful everyone was treating me. A castle full of people, none of whom would protect me. Rather, all wanted to use me for their own purposes. Including my father. I wanted to escape so, I couldn't stand it. There was no way I could injure the guards and run away with no one seeing me. Trapped.

When Huld neared Luke, I grabbed and poured a pot of scalding hot coffee into the slits in his helmet and ran away. He yelled, flailed, and his fingers worked fast with the fiddly things along his breastplate. He was able to remove it, which then allowed him to lift off his helmet and throw it too. Everyone was watching. Everyone was quiet. And then, people sniggered. He looked nothing like a noble knight.

His blue eyes, which I'd glimpsed behind his visor, looked like mine and my sisters', though his head was narrow, much of it covered in a squiggly pattern. Chunky, ratty tufts of sweaty blond hair stuck out in random places amid rough bald spots. Poor Luke. I felt awful for him.

He looked at no one, slowly took off the rest of his armor. He wore sweaty short sleeves and shorts. His hands and arms were scarred, his legs were scarred with intense burns from long ago covering his body.

He walked, barely making a sound, down the hallway. Everyone was silent. He closed the door. And that was that.

❄

A scuffle at the door. It was Colin! He hadn't left me forever. Did he forgive me? Surely not. But he was a gentleman, so he cared about saving my life. Colin brought men heftier than he was. Neighbors, apparently.

He must have talked to one. Maybe found him driving by. And that neighbor rounded up the others.

"Get out!" yelled Luke at the intruders. "All the neighbors were warned not to set foot on these grounds. You know the curse."

Luke stood tall, his arms open wide to hold onto each side of his ancestral doorway protectively. Poor guy, being tasked with keeping his heritage alive in a fortress meant to keep enemies scared and at a distance. No wonder he had issues.

Huld ducked and disappeared into the crowd.

The tallest neighbor wearing a sheepskin vest said, "This man says you got a woman, and a man held against their will."

Most of the Agents turned the other direction or covered their faces.

Luke hesitated. He retorted, "Sure, have a look. If you see anyone held hostage, you let me know, mates."

A guard grabbed Colin and was starting out the door with him when Dune smirked and said, "Ah, more lovely guests."

The guards hesitated, and Luke looked at Dune quizzically. Then, he grinned and nodded.

If the neighbors freed Tommy, what would happen? No chance of Dune removing Susan and Sylvia from her psyche. She'd be possessed forever. Maybe that wasn't a good thing.

I looked over at her to intuit her take on it, but she was acting out of character for Tommy. She'd switched to Sylvia mode. Sylvia was all for the Immortality Project continuing. She headed toward the door. She scratched the neighbor down his face.

He backed up, aghast. He looked up and down the topless "man" with breasts. "You have no right to take me!" said Sylvia. "I'll kill you before you do."

"Grab her!" I yelled at the neighbors. "She's not in her right mind. She's being held against her will." She's . . . "Possessed" would not sound rational. "Drugged?" "Hypnotized?" "A nice psychic vampire with a ghost inside of a ghost inside her?" "Speaking as a dead but willing participant in an Immortality Project that she doesn't want you to mess with?" Yea*h, that should do it. Anyone would believe that.*

"So, that's the woman, is it?"

"No. That's the lad. *That's* the woman," Colin said, pointing to me.

A neighbor with a weathered face and huge gray eyebrows sticking out shadowing his eyes said, "I'm Randall. What's the problem, Miss? Are *you* here under duress? Or is this bloke speaking out his ass?"

"I was abducted! I was locked up in solitary and left to die in a dung heap full of skeletons. I was nearly set afire. And she was chained." I pointed to Tommy. "Please, please take us away from this awful place!"

Most Agents were heading for the shadows, leaving the room, but one daring Agent grabbed me, and we wrestled. I poked him in at the base of the throat and he gagged, backing away.

At that point, Tommy's eyes glinted, and from inside her body, the ghost of Sylvia grabbed me around the waist and pulled me back into the crowd. I doubled over, my feet sliding across the floor, as revelers knocked us around.

She grabbed my hair and pulled me toward her, so my forehead pressed up against hers. Her eyes penetrated mine.

Our noses pushed up, and I know mine hurt like hell. We breathed in and out of our mucusy nostrils louder by the breath. We sounded like the awful stupid neighbor kid in a kid's cartoon. The whole menacing effect was lost. We wrestled on the floor.

This isn't happening. Any moment, I'll wake up back in Colin's room and drink weak tea and eat bland scones with no jam, and they'll stick to the inside of my mouth, and I'll dab at them with a colorless napkin.

Sylvia bit me with Tommy's teeth. We had it out, there on the castle floor, amid the intelligence agents wearing their most occult outfits for a special evening worshiping Tommy and me.

Being isolated in a castle wasn't turning out to be isolated.

She arched feline and glistened her eyes at me as if they were diamonds. She hissed. I hissed back.

Someone called out, "Catfight!"

If they didn't want to mess with a feisty woman, they shouldn't have picked me. My blood was hot, and I was hopping.

My adrenalin flowed, but I gathered my wits. I pulled back. I let her hit me, and I stood there, doing nothing.

I couldn't battle it out to the bitter end with Sylvia. Her auric residue was inside Susan, and I loved Susan. And Susan's auric residue was inside Tommy; I couldn't hurt Tommy any more. Tommy had saved my life. Tommy had done terrible things in her life, but it was only because the Nevermind had mind-controlled her. Once she'd escaped, she'd become a hero: a whistle-blower.

With her at the helm of the Bennu Society, the Nevermind had hope of a more ethical direction.

I wondered at first why the guards were standing there, grinning, instead of kicking out the neighbors. And then, I got it. Tommy and I were making fools of ourselves. No way the neighbors would want to rescue crazy scrappers.

I took a deep breath, pushed her onto the floor, and just walked away and got lost in the crowd. I wanted to call out to the men, "I'm Miriam. Colin didn't kill me." But in that din, that wouldn't have registered if they didn't know the back story.

Instead, it would probably backfire, making them wonder if he was a murderer. If they looked into the matter, they'd find out he'd skipped bail, and they could turn him in. The police wouldn't give Colin a chance. He was an enemy of the Nevermind.

I pushed closer to the neighbors.

One neighbor said, "This is the strangest thing I've ever seen in my entire life. I'm glad we came."

Another said, "I'm not taking a chance on that half bloke half bird. But blondie's a beauty. I like'em feisty like that."

Another said to Colin, "You've got quite the taste in women, mate."

One of the neighbors said, "We can drive in closer to town and call the bobbies."

Colin looked at him, shocked. He must have told him not to go to the police, considering he'd broken the conditions of his bail. His face blanched, losing its sexy new tan, other than the red blotches peeling on his nose and cheeks.

The neighbor said, "I'll get the police. You can't get away with this."

I heard something loud dislodge above me, and a screech begin slowly, growing louder as it moved above my head toward me. There was a SSSHHHH sound, and my vision went cloudy. I couldn't turn to see it the way Sylvia was holding me. Everything happened at once.

I tried to ignore whatever was going on that scared the men. I yelled as loud as I could, "The police won't do anything. This is a den of Agents, and they protect them with their lives, no matter what." My voice was garbled from her grip around me when I called out to Randall as he ran away from ghosts flying toward him. I wasn't sure they could hear me over the increasing noise, with my voice coming from so low to the floor. He was out the door, so I put my volume into calling out: "If you want to get help, round up a Shambhala posse. Try the Free Tibet club at uni."

The Agents hiding from being recognized, a huddled bulk in the hallway, turned toward me en masse, glaring, a terrifying sight.

Sylvia came up from behind, pulled my shoulder, turning me around to face her, grabbed a lamp, and knocked me out cold.

❄

Soft ticklies against my nostrils. I sneezed. I awoke to pain in my head. I tried to raise my hand to the bump, but discovered a silky white rope bound me to a chair. A cheerful Little Person in a top hat was sitting sideways across on my lap, his legs slung over me, swinging. He was chatting to an older woman beside him wearing flamingo feathers in her tall green hat, her hair brushing across my eyelids, making me flutter my eyes.

"Ooooo," said the Little Person, when he saw that, as if I were being flirtatious. "Speak of the devil."

"Where's Colin?" I asked and wished I'd said nothing, as any movement made my headache overwhelming.

"Chicken Little must have run away when they mentioned the police. The rest of them ran away when Luke played the 'cursed castle' card."

I searched through the mist that was my mind.

The woman with the tall green hat, which clashed with her squarish coral dress, stuck her index finger up and bounced it up and down. The tip of her finger was mesmerizing. Then, I realized I was meant to look up.

In the makeshift rafters was a pulley with a very thin wire, with a gaggle of ghosts attached. Cleverly made ones, not the usual teenage prank with sheets. The ghosts had nozzles attached to them and were in the last fizzling stages of spewing out mist. No wonder the neighbors had fled, with mist-breathing ghosts flying at them top speed over a giant and a dwarf, a man with breasts, and cavorting people in stages of undress and obvious psychedelic intoxication.

So, *that* was why they didn't shoo neighbors. It was their big chance to scare them at once and prove the reality of the curse. They'd never be back after that after seeing what a wild bunch we were. I wondered what they'd do if they ever figured out they'd been tricked.

I hankered for bowling with Colin and his elderly aunt.

"Luke's unveiling the new elixir. Something you're on intimate terms with, I understand."

"It's made of my tears *under duress*, if that's what you mean."

"Recursive Tears. With Susan inside you, and Sylvia inside her." She kissed her fingers like an Italian chef and on opening them outward, said, "Primo!"

"You'll be on the tongues of the best men in the country. Aren't you proud?"

"This many people take that shite seriously? Oh, I get it. Are they pretending to go along with it? Isn't it the placebo effect?"

The woman stood. "I don't know what you're on about. You of all people!"

She reached out her hand to the Little Person, who grabbed ahold. She pulled him off me like a naughty child and set him down. He waddled away with her, dignified in his black formal suit, turned back toward me, tipped his top hat, and jiggled his butt at me when he turned back.

I strained against my ropes. I needed to lie down and sleep off the pain in my arm. I needed analgesics.

I needed to stop being star struck, to outgrow the lie they were better than me. This wasn't sparkling charm and sexy good times, wasn't cutting-edge consciousness technology, wasn't necessary machinations by intelligence agents to keep the UK and U.S. running smoothly in sync. Well, sure, it was those things. You know.

If Papa finds out the elixir is my tears, maybe he won't make me pay back the loan right away. Maybe he'll see it as doing something worthwhile with my life.

Agents stood in front of me discussing opium trades with the Golden Dawn and some Canadian millionaire. Behind them, other Agents discussed the Tavistock Institute's latest finding on reviving Dissociative Identity Disorder.

One Agent gave me the stink eye. One drunk Agent toasted me and made me the devil horns with her fingers. Another launched into me, yelling, bending over me, his hands against my legs, until a sexy woman walked by and he put on a suave expression and followed her.

Randall returned, walking through the door which was open to party goers going in and out. The guards went over to him and grabbed him as he stared up at the sheets on the pulleys. "Hey, sheets! What the hell? A hoax! What a bunch of horseshit!" The guards shoved him out the door and yelled at him not to return if he knew what was best for him.

Had he come back because he cared about me being held hostage? I mattered to someone, not just because I was playing some metaphysical role? I mattered to Colin, too. And I mattered to Kevin. I couldn't believe it. Not having to work desperately, impossibly, against all odds, to prove my value.

I saw violet. Vivid, deep, velvety violet around me.

My heart skipped a beat. I was seeing my aura!

I fell in love with myself. My aura was so beautiful. I was someone worthwhile to take care of. Not to subject to taking on someone else's mannerism and handwriting and vocal tone.

I spread out my astral arms. I wanted to be *me*. To live my future. I wanted to dance inside that violet, to celebrate it, to make it strong and impermeable. To help it live a long time, enjoying bird songs and trees and trying to persuade Colin to love me. Dancing and acting if I could get something that paid well enough, but if not, waitressing.

But had I realized that too late?

CHAPTER 21
BUSTED

Tommy held her arms over her naked chest. She looked distractedly through the crowd. She didn't act like Sylvia any more. That feisty she-ghost must have retreated into Tommy's subconscious. Unless the aura-ghost thing was a psychological product of hypnotic suggestion. Embarrassing.

Tommy lunged, reaching for her shirt draped over a chair.

At that moment, an Agent balanced a bowl of green ice cream against his hip as he dug into it with the other hand. He waved his spoon around, flinging the ice cream off the spoon onto her right breast. "Oh, sorry, sorry." He reached out to wipe it off her skin with his fingers. What he couldn't wipe off, he smeared into the tiny breast, jiggling it. His conscientious focus turned into a puzzled frown.

Then, he raised his eyebrows, knocking the frown off his face. "Hey, I know that breast." Keeping his finger on a constellation of little moles, he stared at her face, eyes open wide.

He turned to yell to the room. "Listen! Grail Bennu is a traitor! She betrayed the American Nevermind big time and then disappeared. This is N--." Of course, he said her full name. It's only me keeping her identity from you, dear reader, to save her life.

Since no one was paying attention to what he said, he called out with wider gestures over the din.

She threw on her shirt.

"This 'Tommy' has *zero* respect for the petrodollar agreement Kissinger made with Saudi Arabia. She thinks it's fine to let any country go off the petrodollar any time they want to without the Agents helling'em down. Anti-American slag."

The ginger man behind him turned around, his mouth open. Then, he, too stared at Tommy's pert little breasts, and said, "Maybe she's trying to redeem herself by doing good work for the Agency now? Workin' for me."

Tommy said, "What I need to redeem myself for is murdering people for the Agency."

The ginger Agent looked confused. "What's your problem with assassinating enemies who are destroying the world? It's how governments have worked since the beginning of time. Get a grip."

The woman with her arm around the ginger man exclaimed, "You're N--? I remember hearing what you did to protect countries trying to nationalize their banking. I don't understand. You prefer total chaos? What about people counting on their savings maintaining value? You think they have no rights to retirement?"

At that moment, I saw huge hands appear between people in the crowd, grabbing Tommy, and pulling her off to the side. Huld bent toward her, fiercely whispering something and shushing her. He threatened the three people who realized who she was, and they dispersed into the crowd.

Tommy said to Huld, "Hey, you knew Sylvia was an exhibitionist. It's not my fault she couldn't contain herself."

Huld hissed at her. "Why did you go and blow our cover? And now, Dune will find out you're N--. At least, he'll know you've been tricking him into thinking you were a man. Do you have any idea how he'll punish me for 'not figuring out who you are?' He and Luke will be embarrassed that they never even caught on you were a woman . . ."

"Sylvia comes to the front of my subconscious when the shrooms are around! But she's gone now." She crossed her arms across her tiny breasts.

Huld said, "Let's face it. You'll have to step down from Grail Bennu now you been recognized by Agents. Who knows who they might could tell? The nemesis of the Nevermind, here, at the Nevermind party, being worshipped. Scandalous."

"I know what that entails," she said, with a slicing motion across her throat.

"This work I did grooming the sisters ain't going to go to waste, little Missy. Respect our investment."

"Am I done for?"

"No. All isn't lost just yet. The rules are dramatic, but flexible. You still have Susan and Sylvia inside you: you're still our Grail Bennu. Our Madonna of Eternal Renewal. Our Bennu of all Bennus."

"Your traitor of all traitors." Tommy raised her chin at him.

Huld agreed. "Yes, but you have a skill set no one else has. Enochian language. Poison. Multiple personality tendencies programmed. Spying proficiency. Yes, I know N--'s story well. Maybe you can add something extra to convince the board to let you live."

Tommy's mouth looked tenuous. It could flitter away at any moment.

Better for the world if Tommy took on the Immortality Project. I didn't want to see her ruining her life connected to the agency she'd exposed and escaped. She'd be vulnerable to blackmail, always afraid of her identity revealed.

Huld said, "And look at this crowd. The most elite in the business. Who are they going to give contracts to if we lose their business because of you, huh?"

"I'm sorry."

"The three Agents who know could even be convinced you're not N-- if we play our cards right. If there's good enough reason. Something better than you having Sylvia and Susan inside you."

She trembled. "That would be good."

Huld made a proposal. "So, how about I kill Miriam while you breathe in her aura."

"What!"

He ignored me and continued. "That would make up for inconvenience tonight. Or, if you don't cooperate like that, well, I throw you up on stage right now and announce I've cleverly discovered you've the traitor behind the revelations on Brandon's videos."

"They'd have a hard time worshipping her after her little hissy fit," remarked an Agent.

My mind raced for options to propose. The pain in my arm made it harder to think fast. I pushed past the brain fog as hard as I could. Hmm. I could jump on stage and out Tommy to the whole crowd. There'd be no going back. Surely, she couldn't redeem herself after that by taking my ghost inside her. But I didn't want to sacrifice her life for mine. Vicious.

Tommy said, "Lots of women have given information to Brandon. I could get lost in the mix."

Huld continued: "Come on. Bennu members and Agents would tear you apart like Osiris." Huld smiled. "Would be the entertainment to make tonight legendary."

"Tommy could influence the international Agency to change everything. Gut the Tavistock Institute's mind control agenda. Slow down the opium trade in the cult network. Stop American false flags altogether. She's a wild card."

Huld patted her on the head. "Settle down little Missy. You're our Bennu Grail: just vampirize Miriam and keep her ghost inside you along with her sisters. And I'm sure your little secret won't matter anymore. The Immortality Project would be as spectacular as we imagined."

This whole thing seemed so bloody unhinged. I asked, "What, you think this Immortality Project will go on forever?"

Huld answered, "Things aren't going according to plan. You aren't holding the fourth sibling inside you: Equinox. So, no, not unless Tommy can house three spirits inside, making her into a Four. Then, the foundation is solid. The house will not fall. Ghosts never leave a building built by masons using the proper proportions."

I felt a chill. I hated to see Tommy caught up in a scheme that was never meant for her, but for me, instead. Still, if she went along with the crazy scheme, it would keep her from being killed by the Nevermind. My death was the *only thing* that would keep her alive.

My neck was getting a crick looking back and forth between these two. Huld said to Tommy, "If you absorb her while she's dying tonight, that will give the Agents the rush they came for." He did the throat slicing gesture.

I wasn't sure how I felt.

Huld said, "If you do that, we can keep the revelation about who you are quiet. Otherwise, we'll crown the next Grail before the night is over. Some random woman from the great hall." He made a sweeping gesture.

I couldn't believe I felt jealous. I could be replaced by some bimbo. Hm.

Tommy said, "With my sacrifice as the warm-up."

"Obviously."

I was going nuts trying to find some logical way out of a bizarre situation. The more insane a reality we have to adjust to, the crazier places our minds have to go. I'd gotten comfortable having my sisters inside me. It's not like it hurt. It would only be fair.

I stepped forward and bowed low in front of Huld. "Take my

life. Kill me while Tommy breathes in my aura. I'll take the chance I'll . . . sort of . . . live on inside of her."

"You are offering yourself in good faith? You're ready to step up and take their place? Not just remain a standby in the Immortality Project?"

"I am, sir."

"So be it." Huld made a slight, crisp bow. He held out his hand, crossing fingers over the others. I mimicked the gesture. He smiled. "I'll talk to the people who found out." He moved into the crowd.

I was giving up my life, so Tommy didn't die for me. But who was I kidding? I was doing it to make Papa proud. My biological father too. I could be the daughter someone wanted me to be. No matter what it took. I had to admit. That's who I was. I was learning to love the pathetic reality of who I was.

I had embraced my shadow. Not run.

It's better to die in glory than be a damn waitress.

❄

As my death approached, my chest opened the floodgates, flowing love into the world. Gratitude for living. Music and birds and trees rushy in the wind.

It was so hard to say goodbye to being a body. But if there was anything to the Immortality Project, my aura might continue.

I wished I could say goodbye to Colin.

In the next nights, would he come creeping in the shadows to see me through the windows? Would I be able to come to the fore in Tommy's psyche and watch for him? Go to him at the window? Write a message and hold it up to the glass for him to read?

I pushed against people in the ballroom to get into the hall. I was being watched by guards so I didn't stray. They were like those paintings with the eyes that follow you everywhere. I had to let my imagination go. I hugged myself.

I'd come out at night into the fore of Tommy's subconscious and sleepwalk. I would write my memoir about being abducted to the castle to be part of the Immortality Project. Or a novel about it, safer. I'd get it to Colin so Be Yourself Publishing Company could have dibs on a book I knew they would love to publish. A book that exposed the inner workings of the Nevermind and the mythologies at its core. People needed to know how our countries were run.

It was romantic. If he stayed around the castle grounds, when I was possessing Tommy, I'd write him a note and hold it up to the window. "I'm not Tommy right now. I'm Miriam, possessing Tommy. Come." Colin would live on, outside, eating roots and berries, day after day, month after month, because he loved me like wildfire. His hair would curve over his eyes. He'd be sexy. I'd feel the effects running through Tommy's body.

Possessing Tommy, I'd go to him. We'd stand there, with the glass between us, our arms up, our hands pressed together, our bodies against the surface, both of us topless. My breasts squashed against his smooth chest, the cold surface making my nipples harden, with a lock of hair falling against my nipples. I moved back and forth, reproductive life force stirring in my loins. I'd breathe hard and see his chest rising and falling fast and hard, and we'd sync up our breaths. I'd push my pelvis against his.

I'd write the novel, call Tommy "N-- " so I wouldn't get her in trouble. I'd call it *Encore*. It would be honest. It would be horrible. It would be fiction. What honest autobiography isn't? For Be Yourself Publishing to release. Colin would make a cut.

I'd go to the window whenever Colin showed up in a storm, his face against the dripping pane, like Cathy in *Wuthering Heights*. We'd tear off our clothes and press toward each other's bodies. Move in rhythms that became our world. Touch ourselves. Be free of the castle while becoming one with it. It would be impossible to tire of each other. We'd grow feral. Climax with no need for touch. When we orgasmed together, lightning would crash the sky. Thunder would extend our spasms. It would be horrible. It would be romantic. It would be everything.

Checking out Norma from across the room, I sure hoped she didn't get sucked into the Society. Yet, I didn't want her to be driven away.

I had to half-admit I knew my fantasy of Colin sticking around and making out through the window with Tommy's body was off the deep end. Colin didn't even respect me anymore. I was being romantic. But I still wanted to write the book while I possessed Tommy. *When Norma comes back to the castle again, she'll take my manuscript to him.* Would he find someone else by the time the book was done?

Besides, I didn't even believe in possession. It was only the auric residue that continued in a person. I would die, pure and simple.

❄

Huld found me, not letting me think for many minutes on my own. He pulled me into the hallway, and I cooled down. I'd been panting in the heat. Breathing super-fast thinking about finding the only way I could think of to be lovers with Colin, even if it meant being in Tommy's body.

Were we alone? Could we talk frankly? "Where's the Dune-geonmonster?" I asked.

"Moon Miriam, I enforce the rules, now, not Dune. He's done been knocked out of the picture. That man lost all hope for the Immortality Project. He don't even care what you're doing. Last I saw him, he was in the solar, miserable."

Well, that's two down. Easier for me to leave this castle. Luke was out of it, too.

I couldn't help my fierce. I moved close to him. Just as Tommy had told me I should hate my captors, not love them for the bones they threw me. I raised my voice. "You killed Susan. You were part of a ritual where I could have been raped by my father."

"You wasn't supposed to know it was Luke. Dune wore the armor, right?"

"That makes it better?"

"Wouldn't it have? You know you can't get enough of that pretty boy."

"Agents are bloody mass murderers."

"No."

"No?"

"I work for an intelligence agency. I'm doing my duty I was raised to do."

"How nice for you."

"It's how I get paid. For the good of the country. Every big country uses occult stuff."

"The Nevermind Agency makes propaganda to convince people that absurd mythology is real. They use the Bennu Society to do it. So that our governments can manhandle whoever they want with impunity."

"And there you have it, doll. If you say so."

"The whole Atlantis VS Shambhala crap."

"You can always stay here. Go through with being sacrificed." He stuck out his tongue and held his face over a candle, making the garish shadows. "Possess the hell out of Tommy. I never liked that wanker, anyway. She was part of the Agency too. I guess it's the thing people like us do. Let her breathe you in while I kill you. You'll be in a little nest with Susan and Sylvia."

"All the sisters in one little ghost cemetery in their father's castle."

"What more do you most want?"

I put my hand on my chest and was quiet. "Papa would be proud if he found out I was the Grail Bennu. The most prestigious thing to be in the world. That might be enough for him." He'd love me. Papa would love me. I moved my hands, preparing to hug myself before I caught the pathetic gesture. That was embarrassing.

"Oh, I know you, birdie." He grinned. "Your papa got a nice face. Strange how his hair's brown, and yours is blonde. But you got kind of dud for a brain under that hair. You never thought about that?"

I had. I thought Mama had an affair with a blond man. But I didn't care. Papa was Papa. It wasn't his fault.

"Is that why the Agency found a man impossible to please to adopt me? So, he'd raise me with no self-esteem? If that's not monstrous, what *is*?" I kneed him in the leg for emphasis. It didn't even wobble.

"You want monstrous? I'll give you monstrous: my parents taking Human Growth Hormone in the Giant Jack cult, starting in 1990, when they was thirteen. And you know why?"

"So, they'd turn into giants."

"You know why that was a big ass deal? If they was giants, that proved they was worthy to important supergiant ghosts from Atlantis. You know, that story countries use to win its wars. In the world wars, they was all doing it."

"Some won the legend; others lost it."

"Right. Shambhalaheads didn't come out on top."

"Right, not after the Theosophical Society switched from the Russians to the British alliance."

"My parents was giants, so the soul of the Atlantis bloke could make them pregnant with me. They taught me to believe I was the reincarnation of a giant. And he was like, doop doop doop. I ain't had a body to incarnate into since the glory days. I'll just take this one."

No wonder he was such a natural for the role he played on stage.

"While my folks sexed it up when I was conceived, bunch of people put their hands under their bodies. They all together raised them up to super-giant souls to get their attention. So they could fight it out among themselves who wanted to inhabit my body. 'Hey, come on in, supergiants; you'll be glad you did. You can make the New Atlantis happen in England. Just like you always wanted.'"

I did my best to look elegant to the Agents walking around in the Great Hall. I had to play the role right. Put myself into it.

Huld reached out to my face and turned it to look at him in the eyes. We said nothing. He said, "You act like you're the only one put through the initiation. My parents gave birth in a ceremony to pull in souls of Atlanteans. Then they gave me HGH once I reached puberty, so my body would be worthy of the superhuman race." He held up his arms like a body builder. "That's some messed up shit right there."

I put my hand up to touch his shoulder. "That's awful, Huld. I'm so sorry that happened to you. That must have screwed up your head."

He bent over, putting his eyes right in front of mine. "Oh, I almost forgot." He reached into his pocket and brought out a large block of chocolate. "Here."

"Well. Thank you." I took it and held it awkwardly as we talked. Dark chocolate treat. He wasn't so bad.

I blushed. I knew everyone was susceptible to the Stockholm Syndrome when their captors did anything that helped them. It was a survival tactic people had always had, throughout history. A bank could be robbed and every hostage came to love the robbers if they were held long enough and given small favors. The crazier the situation to adapt to, the crazier the victims had to become to avoid cognitive dissonance. They excused their captors because they depended on them. They appreciated small favors, like not being killed.

He stood straight again. "Whatever. The horror is Susan's personality taking you over all this time ain't been much about her aura. It ain't about hypnosis."

"What do you mean?"

"You projected whatever you imagined Susan was like. Obviously, you did a terrible job of letting her ghost come through. This project is just grasping. That was biggo success."

"Do you think their ghosts were inside me? I mean, I knew sketchy things."

"How do I know?"

"I guess I could have been getting it from Morphogenetic Fields. You tune into things only other people could know."

"Maybe some of it."

"I let myself be deluded?"

"Admit it. You knew what you were doing coming out to the castle. You can't say you didn't fantasize being married to Dune. I saw you kiss the fake wedding ring you wore, ready to take over every night. You think people didn't notice?"

I stood there, unable to even move a muscle.

He cocked his head when he said, "You know what they say about hypnosis. Can't make anyone do sompin' they don't want."

❄

I pushed through the crowd, not caring if I bumped into people as I strode. Bodies moving to the left and right of me. I wanted to take a breath of air not so used by nasty people. I pushed my way to the hallway, near enough to the guards that there was free space. No revelers wanted to be under their solemn, watchful eye. Surveillance is never fun.

Norma came to me. She'd seen me signaling to her earlier. I'd been watching her make her way through the crowd.

"Miriam! I can't believe you're here, too," she said.

I gave her a tiny nervous signal to follow me, and I turned away as if I hadn't seen her. We went to the private part of the room. Agents standing around us were tall enough to shield us from anyone who might realize I knew her.

She asked, "Are they recruiting you to the Bennu Society, too? What's up? Wait, are you OK? You're covered in dirt and stuff."

When she reached out to wipe a smudge off my face, I sniffled.

I *wanted* to ask her to let me go home with her. But the guards would stop me at the door. I wanted to ask her to tell the police to come save me. But they wouldn't jeopardize the plans of the precious Nevermind. I couldn't think of *any* way to make it out alive. I had to make what was happening positive. Or I'd just explode.

So, I did it. "Say, I have to ask you a favor fast."

"Er, yeah?"

"There's a good-looking guy, just a few years older than me, named Colin, out there roaming around the castle grounds. Sandy hair. You might have met him at an after-party, not sure. Suede jacket. He's hiding, so it might hard to talk to him, but if you call out you're my friend, he might answer. If you can find him and tell him Miriam said you were his ride home, he'll come to you. He needs to get away because his car doesn't work. Just try not to let other people hear you calling him if you can. Norma, I know, it's a tall order."

"It is. You want me to wander around in the dark trying to find someone whose hiding? Why, is there danger? Who is he?"

"My friend."

"Um, OK?"

He'd be able to buy a working car, back home. Get back to work. Live indoors, eat normal food, go to the doctor. My *Wuthering Heights* style fantasy of kissing his lips pressed against cold glass, while he languished in the shadows of the castle, wasn't as good as knowing I'd save him from myself.

I gave her a kiss on the cheek. I tried to act normal. "So. How's your engagement going?"

"I'm so excited! I fancy Reedsy so much. I couldn't be happier. If you'll be around in two months, come to the wedding."

I said, "I don't think I'll be able to make it. But thank you for asking. And, congratulations. I don't know what will happen with me. But this is what I'm aiming for. Someone will be writing a manuscript. I want you to come back exactly three months from now, exact date and time. Can you do that?"

"Well, I guess so."

"If all goes according to my plan, the manuscript will be rolled up and disguised. And sticking out through the bottom of that window." I pointed to the only window on the ground level. "Tell no one here."

"I promise. I guess. Kinda weird, Miriam."

"Grab the manuscript. It will be called *Encore*. Give it to Colin when you get back to the city. He's acquisitions editor for Be Yourself Publishing. He'll know what to do. Maybe I'm optimistic, but the book will bring in good cash for him. And, hey, tell him to give you a commission."

"Oh. Well, thank you. I guess?" She looked at her feet and scratched her head.

"You'll feel great if you do it, I promise."

"What kind of book is it?"

"It will be Gothic. So, the usual liminal state of consciousness that's neither dead nor alive. Abduction. Immortality. Incest."

"This is exciting."

"The adventure of a lifetime."

"Or deathtime."

I asked, "And in the meantime, do you have anything to write with in your purse?"

I wrote a note on the back of the envelope she gave me. *Colin didn't kill me. I'm still alive. I'm being held against my will. I can't say by whom. Colin tried to save me. Miriam.*

I kept trying to write on the note that our own government was keeping me hostage. But then, my case would get thrown out and covered up. The paper would be destroyed. No, only *Encore* could explain it.

And if I was dead, having it published wouldn't hurt me. Sure, he'd need to go underground if anyone was likely to find out he was the acquisitions editor. But the cause was worth it. I signed it, dated it, and licked it.

"Give this note to Colin. Handwriting analysts can prove it's my writing. They might call you to testify that you saw me."

"What!"

"I can't talk now. The book will explain everything. Can you put this envelope in a baggie or tissue? A pocket in your purse? OK, look, I'm touching inside the envelope. There won't be other fingerprints there but mine. That should do it. I licked it, if they need DNA. If you can't find Colin, can you give it to the police?"

She read the note. "The police think he killed you? What the hell, Miriam? Why don't you tell them yourself?"

I leaned in close. "Please walk away after this and act like you don't even notice I'm here. I'd rather no one know we've talked. I walk away, don't take it personally."

"What's going on?"

"To answer your question, I would tell Colin myself, but I'm being held hostage. If I tried to walk out that door, the guards would stop me. In fact, everyone in this whole castle the recruits, would. And if the recruits saw too much, they'd be in danger. So would you if they find out."

She gasped. I nodded.

I looked over at Norma. I don't know why I couldn't tell her the truth at that moment about the people we'd worked together with in the troupe. But it felt so impolite. Besides, they'd have to kill her.

I'd said so much I was worried someone had found us together.

An Agent winked at me. It was sickening. I couldn't take it anymore. I pushed him away. He ricocheted off the wall and crashed into Norma. I turned and ran into the crowd. I held my breath to slide through them, pushing their bodies this way and that.

❄

A scuffle broke out on the other side of the large room. I made my way, checking to see if the guards might be distracted enough I could instead sneak out and hide under someone's car. I'd risk riding to the city holding on with my might, hoping the road didn't rise to meet me.

An Agent shouting at Tommy snarled, and grabbed her, knocking her crown off her head. "You think you can hide your identity you got another thing coming. You think a critic of the Agency can take charge of the society at its inner core you're insane. Totally insane."

"And who do you think made me this?"

The Agent started to hit her but relaxed his fist. "I'll tell everyone. No one is listening now because they're thinking boobs. This'll get their attention for my announcement." He lowered her trousers, to reveal her lush unshaven, strawberry-blonde bush and pale, toned thighs.

I wanted to do something. They'd tear her apart once they realized her identity as the woman who twice brought media attention to the problems in the Agency. If she stayed under cover, she could do good. It couldn't last long though. It was too good to be true.

Too flimsy. She'd be outed, and my sacrifice for her would be for nothing. Was it worth giving up my life for her? How crazy was I? I barely knew her. It was her fight, not mine.

She tried to pull away from the Agent. He threw her to the floor, pulling her pants off. The other Agent who'd noticed who Tommy was pulled off her men's boots.

Agents nearby who still saw Tommy as their new Grail punched *those* Agents, and hell broke loose.

Guards left the door to tend to the fight. A melee was my big chance to escape! Abandoning her made my stomach burn so much I wondered if I was getting ulcers.

I needed to get out with my life. I could return and save the others.

An Agent led Norma toward the exit.

I didn't see the other young women they were trying to recruit. They must have left. So, Norma was the only person I could leave with. The rest of them were part of the conspiracy.

I fought my way toward Norma. She was pulling her fingers through her thin hair, and detangling it, strands of hair falling out onto her shoulders.

The crowd had thinned, but those left moved toward the fight, and I was going against the flow, bumped this way and that. I reached Norma, grabbed her frumpy marigold-pattern dress, and pulled her away from the Agent escorting her out.

I whispered to Norma, "Take me with you. I've got to get out of here! Let's run to your car. Please!"

She took my hand, and we dashed toward the door.

The band on the stage behind the fight sang about peace, trying to calm everyone.

At that moment, I saw a man putting on his coat. He was facing away from me, and his coat covered his body shape, but I could tell who it was. Papa! And there he was, leaving.

No, don't go, Papa! Our only contact for years had been formal letters about the loan. I wanted to run up to him and show him I was important. I was someone he could approve. My lungs seized up. Papa! Do I still matter to you so little?

I would matter to him if I were crowned Grail Bennu. That was my big chance for Papa to love me and I turned it down.

Now Tommy would be it. The thing I'd yearned for, crying in my bed night after night, year after year, when I was young. I'd lain in bed saying the phrase over and over, "I want to die. He doesn't love me. I want to die."

If I'll die, it might as well be to make Papa love me.

I'd hardly been able to get out of bed in the mornings after awful nightmares of him walking away from me, not even acknowledging me. This was my nightmare come true. There was nothing that would make him care, nothing but for me to be the grand Bennu bird, the jewel at the top of the Society crowning the intelligence agency spanning two continents. And if that didn't work, what was the point of being alive?

I impulsively let go of Norma's hand. I ran, jamming into people, to the table nearby, where I'd dropped the crown. It was still there. I put it on. I wasn't the Grail Bennu anymore, but "I" would be living inside of the Grail Bennu. Same thing. Wasn't it? To him, anyway, it would be.

And even if Papa didn't care, my real father would. Luke would be thrilled. Two fathers who loved me. Redemption. Crazy. Damaged. But redeemed. For just being nothing but stupid little me for so long.

I pushed my way to the stage and climbed up onto it, scraping my knee. I had to get his attention before he left, not as little ol' nothing second best me, but as a *Someone*.

I gave the signal for the band to stop playing. I took the microphone and said, "Never mind a silly fight. I can give you a much better show right now. Demand Tommy come up and join me, to be the vessel. The vessel holding not only Susan and Sylvia, but me too. To hold Luke's daughters. Demand Huld to join us on stage, to be my executioner. Demand Dune to join us on stage to be the hypnotist."

"Dune?" asked Huld.

"Bring him here. The time has come for grand sacrifice. If you take the elixir, you'll be able to merge with me while it happens. You'll be able to journey with me beyond life, and then you can return."

If Papa took the elixir, he could understand me.

Huld left the room.

The Agents struggling against Tommy stopped, blood lust on their faces. Agents cheered. One growled. Others had pained or stricken looks.

I nodded to Norma, who was standing by the door waiting for me, her thin mouth open, dropping first on one side then the other.

I indicated for her to go ahead with the original plan, mouthing the words over the din. This made for a great book to bring up questions about the Agency and vindicate Colin.

Sure, it would put Colin in danger if the wrong people figured out which acquisitions agent was responsible for the book. But it would be better than being imprisoned right away for murder. The plan endangered Tommy, but that was nothing new for her. It was a lifestyle choice she'd made a long time ago. She could fade into the shadows again and take Colin with her.

Norma screamed, her voice ragged. "No!"

Both guards headed toward her. She watched them approaching until they tackled her. One hit her over the head. The thud was sickening. She continued moving, pushing against him. The second guard held her while the guard with the weapon bashed in her head again and again.

I screamed for them to stop, but what did they care?

Blood flew everywhere. Her skull broke open, and brains fell on someone's shoulder.

Someone laughed.

It was my fault she was dead

Poor, sweet doomed Norma! How horrendous.

The Agents wouldn't allow a sacrifice to occur in front of someone who hadn't made the choice to join the Bennu Society and been sworn to secrecy. Initiates got broken through traumatic rituals to create loyalty. Someone like Norma had no reason to keep quiet about what she saw. She had to be eliminated. I never felt so guilty in my life. I held my stomach and pressed my mouth.

I could only tell myself that she was crashing the party,

looking for drugs. So unless they recruited her they might have not let her leave with her life.

My visceral response to seeing Papa had thrown out reason. I was a child. I thought about getting a proud smile from him, him holding me over his head when I was little, when he told me to be someone great one day. Even if it was Marcel.

And I wasn't even his biological daughter; yet the people who raise us hold so much power over us. Every lesson they teach, from infancy onward. I scanned the crowd and couldn't find him. Had he left before my moment of glory?

I cried on stage. People's eyes were turning back toward me. I couldn't find Papa anywhere. And then, I saw. When he turned his head and looked up out of the shadows, I saw.

It wasn't even him!

I threw the Grail Bennu tiara at the floor by Tommy.

I crouched to climb off the dais. The deal was over. Killing Norma, that was it. How hideous.

And without her finding Colin, or taking the manuscript to him as planned, it wasn't the same. I'd have to write the book myself, while alive, like a normal person does. And Papa. Papa wasn't there to see me being honored by a sacrifice. I didn't want to become immortal because some random man who looked something like Papa was waiting to see my head get chopped off.

I sobbed on the edge of the stage, trying to climb down, but Agents grabbed my feet and pushed me backwards, sliding on my buttocks.

"Sacrifice! Sacrifice!" yelled one, and others soon joined the chant.

Dune and Huld entered the room, neither looking happy with the other. In fact, Huld seemed to be holding a knife to Dune's back. So, Dune wanted to abandon the project but Huld wouldn't let him! Damn that giant!

"But first," boomed Dune's voice, as if he was trying hard to convince himself as much as everyone else. Everyone got quiet. "The elixir for all!"

"Yay!"

"The Moldavite has been charged according to the most secret mystical traditions."

"How much should we take?"

"One drop, you'll experience the high of spiritual oneness with the person you touch and tune into."

"Two drops?"

"You'll feel empathy and understanding for her."

"Thee drops?"

"Her memories."

"Four?"

"She'll feel yours too."

"Five?"

"Hold onto Miriam and you'll bond so much you can travel with her on her journey on the Ark of the Heavens. You'll know what it's like to die. To be a ghost. And then you come back."

"Six?"

"The legends say, it makes the Bennu rise again from the ashes. Want to be someone else? Be Miriam now!" He turned around and meekly handed a vial to Huld and kept one himself from the collection. Huld, with a menacing expression, pointed with the knife in toward the stage, and Dune got up on it and slumped.

Huld, with a benevolent expression, his knife stuck in his belt, wandered among the crowd of open mouths like baby birds. He placed drops of the Recursive Tears elixir on one tongue after another. Neither Dune nor Huld took it. Dune watched, curled over dejectedly, from a corner on stage.

Huld called out, "It will make your aura permeable for a while. It will make her aura permeable too. *Very* permeable."

He came my way. No, that didn't sound good. That didn't

sound good: energy taken from me; their nasty energy gunking me up; raped by auras.

Huld reached up and grasped me, and with his giant hand, squeezed my jaw until my mouth opened. He dropped in clear fluid.

I figured homeopathy just had a placebo effect. And monoatomic elixirs came with such grandiose claims I figured that was hype, too.

I wasn't too worried. I could still see my good ol' violet aura. My friend, my companion, my true self.

Hands. Hands reached toward me, touching my feet as I sat on the stage. They pulled off my shoes. Their fingers tickled the soles my feet. I jerked my feet up and couldn't help laughing horribly. More fingers tickling, caressing, flicking, pressing into me with their fingernails.

I struggled to get up, but Huld held me, with a paradoxical gentleness, and pushed me even closer to the edge. Hands touched my face, at once, covering every inch, thick fingers, calloused palms, greasy fingertips, a finger that smelled like poo, fingers that had picked noses sticking into my nostrils. Hands responsible for deaths in coups. Children burned with chemicals, screaming.

Hands responsible for proxy wars. Rapid fire gunshot. Loud. Screams. Shattering glass. Faking humanitarian aid for the news cameras, carrying children away as if saving them, then shooting them in the head. Hands gouging out the children's livers and kidneys to put on ice to be taken to the transplant ship docked off shore. The sound of the chest slamming, the wheels carrying it screeching.

Hands that had blackmailed. The trusting face of friendship, the warm eyes, the gentle smile, the bullet through the teeth.

When I was given a dose of the elixir made from my tears from the ritual, on stage, the skin surrounding my aura was broken. I went beyond. That was the meaning of the painting.

This was beyond the pin pricks of envy from the past. This was dissolution.

Their auras flooded into mine without filter. And with them, because of the influence of the elixir, came the Agents' memories, the thought forms vibrating imprinted by extreme emotion, ghosts in the auras. They would not lose their memories. But they'd know I knew them. Our lives became transparent to each other.

I saw back-room deals over opium, saw child prostitutes being drugged. Organs being harvested. A leader being sodomized with a knife. Saw, heard, smelled from their point of view. Each one of them touching me, as their auras wafted into mine, filling my purple with brown feces, black evil, bubblegum pink pretense.

My violet, my true self, which I'd only so recently come to see and love. My most precious possession, myself, me, not someone else, not pretending to be someone else, not wishing I could die and be reborn someone different. Me! The one and only me! Being sucked into the Agents so they could experience the novelty of someone else from the inside out, to experience empathy. The purple strands of color surrounded their bodies, to be owned by them, to be theirs, to be no longer only mine.

Being able to experience another's life was better than a movie. It was their reward for their service to the country, killing, blackmailing, bribing, everything they had to do to keep the balance of power as the government wanted it to be.

I writhed around, thrashing but couldn't stand any longer having my stomach uncovered. I held it with both arms, feeling as if I were vomiting straight from my stomach, as if everything I'd eaten that had created my cells, my structure, my brain, was being withdrawn, tickling my stomach on the way out.

I tried to remember what was going on, what led up to that, but I felt the answer to each question leaving my brain. I was too drained to think, too overwhelmed with their memories and personality traits and emotional patterns to identify with what it was to only have my own.

I tried to hold onto only my true memories: the ochre color of my favorite scarf wrapping in the wind around my eyes at the waterfront; a goat butting me wanting to be fed outside a barn; the way the right angle of light on my eyes from the bathroom window lit up my brown eyes enough I could see the green.

I could see farther back in them when they were lit up green. It was a world in my eyeballs when I'd get up close to the mirror and gaze into them: luminous and incredible, the reverse of everything if you go far enough back. Not comparing my reflection in the mirror compared with whatever women Dune had looked at last.

One man put his forehead up against mine, then rolled his head so his left eye was in front of mine. I couldn't move my head. Huld had it in a vice, pulling my eyelid up.

The Agent stared into my eyes, holding my eyelids open, his pupil tiny and cold lined up with mine, sucking my aura from one overly permeable aura to another. Elixir surprise.

He *blinked.* Horror of horrors, his eyelashes scraping my eyeball.

And back up, even more sharp!

Huld let go, and I wrenched around.

The comforting smell of bubbling oatmeal every morning: I focused on that. Each thing I remembered from my life I could then have trouble finding again with so many memories flooding into my mind. Memories were pulled from my eyes, from my ears, my mouth, my nose.

An Agent held out his hands and cried, lowered his head, then looked up again, his eyes wide. "I'm Aaron. I'm asking for forgiveness. Please." I looked into his deep brown eyes, seeing his father beating him over and over. Seeing him going to Confession and being buggered in the booth.

He and other Agents moved away, hesitantly, after they

touched me. They got thoughtful. They cried. One put his face in his hands and knelt. I was helping them reconsider their lives.

I yelled, my voice feeling as if it were being sucked into the Agents' ears. "All it takes is one of you to stand up against this. This is beyond being turned to a ghost. I mean, everyone dies. But this is torment beyond belief!"

Before I could finish a request, an Agent's mouth pressed to mine, his tongue holding my lips open as I panted, and he sucked the words of the sentence out of my mouth. The air pulled through, my membranes dry, my tongue dry from the vacuum.

I squirmed and bit his tongue. He jerked away.

I yelled again. "Write the story of what happened. Do it anonymously. I don't know." But why would they care? Knowing my life and how I was mistreated by them wouldn't give most of them enough reason to care and change that to want to detail the Agency's abuses.

My beloved familiar core violet was leaving my body. There wasn't enough time to replenish it from the universal flow. There wasn't enough. I was dying. After a life of trying as hard as I could not to be me, I'd learned to value being myself. It was what it took. My light purple selfhood glow of life! To be metabolized by the Agents of the Nevermind.

I called out, as bravely as I could, barely able to even hold onto who I was: "You'll have me inside you, now. Let me change you."

My body felt heavy. Moving my limbs at all seemed too much work. Only their sickening tickles made me move involuntarily, trying to curl forward to protect my stomach, but being held with it open to their fingers fluttering and poking.

I said to the ones who could hear me, "Tell the truth about the Bennu Society. Be me all the way. Go so full on, you can remember everything about my life. Come on, blokes, make the experiment work. If the elixir doesn't make you do that it failed. Work that elixir. Work it."

I felt something like a reverse bowel movement. The hugest, stinkiest turd pushing up inside my body, made of mundane ugliness of day-to-day lives of cruel men, their bellies bloated, their hair greased back, their belching breath a fright.

At first a mush of their memories, their thoughts, their subconscious goals. But second by second, the memories separated out, became clear, haunting me. Becoming the new awful me.

I'd displaced their gunk with my aura. And it had to go somewhere. My body had been drained of my aura. So, theirs flowed into mine: nature abhors a vacuum.

It was Shiatsu, when pushing on a point on the body to get the congested, dirty blood flow to stop, then pulling the fingers away to let cleaner blood flow.

I'd never realized how precious I was. Had been. One of a kind, lovable, with insights no one else had, memories of butterflies and dandelions, goodness of heart, making so many people smile.

We know what happens when old people ingest young blood. They get more youthful. But what happens when young people ingest old blood?

I thought of how people given organ transplants remember things from the lives of the donors. If the donors liked radishes, the transplantee stopped hating radishes, and loved them. Even though they didn't know the donors until they found out later.

I was becoming a dark Agent. My porous psyche had no willpower to stop the process.

Hands everywhere, bodies pressing against me, as they siphoned off everything. And replaced it with the auric gunk created by their need for secrecy and conspiracy, for the necessity of murder and blackmail, to protect the power of the UK and network with the U.S. Deep State.

I loved them.

The elixir made me accept them for their flaws. I saw their

wounds, their sad childhoods, their parents who didn't love them. I saw how they thought they were doing the right thing for their country. How they wanted transcendent experiences through rituals. How they'd been blackmailed, were driven by addictions, had been abused as children.

Could I take their darkness, take all into me, leaving them none, making them better people, making better decisions for our countries, replacing their selfish cruelty unleashed upon the world with my integrity, my honesty? Could I change the Agents forever? Be a martyr for the good? Would they stop creating coups and proxy wars against innocent countries and refuse to do so when commanded?

Could I give them more of me, more, and more, and more, so much that one or all of them would change, become a good person, and write the book of the memories they shared with me? Memories I could, sickeningly, feel dampened too much, diluted too much, by the Agents' gunk. I might not write *Encore* when Tommy sleepwalked if I was incapacitated. But maybe an Agent could. Could life be that miraculous?

Dune had trained me well to suck in Susan's aura to the precise amount required, not too much, not too little. I had the skills to suck in as much as I wanted. And I decided to want. I sucked, a vampire for goodness, drew out their dark into me, transform them, cleanse them. Purify their awful.

I remembered little else but their deeds, their wives, mistresses and girls they fancied, their mansions, their cats and their favorite shows. I was ready to die with that inside me, and maybe, the memories but maybe no longer the emotional effects of those deeds inside them. I sucked, I pulled with my might, pulled out the emotional effects of the traumas they experienced since birth that made them who they were.

Since they'd taken the elixir, they'd remember my memories. It would change them. Could they become more me than themselves? Could they see the error of their ways? This was the first time the Recursive Tears elixir was used. It could go any direction, have any effect. This was a monumental test.

If they pooled their memories, they could form a club and write the book together. They'd *want* to give it to Colin for Be Yourself to publish before he went underground to keep from being offed for exposing them.

It would be *Encore*. "Call the book *Encore*," I shouted. "*Encore*! *Encore*! *Encore*!" It would sell as long as the readers were smart enough to understand the subtle nature of the aura. If it reached the readers open to something that could remind them to love themselves, I would be a hero of our age. Or was I being optimistic and naïve? Yes, yes, I was.

N-- would have to go underground too, but that was her modus operandi. The Agents would willingly go down. They'd accept imprisonment as proper punishment.

My body itched everywhere. I broke out in a toxic red rash. I scratched the hives, big raised inflamed skin patches getting ever redder and more pronounced. Could organs itch? They could! Even my memories itched like crazy.

Life itched. Only death did not. I could see its nothingness in front of me. I longed for it to come. I would die and take their darkness with me and their shady business deals and backdoor viruses would dissolve into dirt. My body would be buried in the grave below us. Not as Luke, Dune, Huld, and Kevin had expected when developing the project, their crowning achievement, but as the person who ended the Immortality Project.

Hands, hands on me, grabbing my chest and pushing the ribs out of place. Fuzzy faces nuzzling up against mine, tickling my nostrils, stinky breath blown into my nose, fingers reaching inside my bra, grabbing my nipples, pulling my breasts out over the top of my dress, mouths fighting for them, my hairs pulled out, pulling my head down. I could see nothing over the crowd.

I vampirized them, sucking them dry, as Dune had taught me to do with Susan, but more aggressively, faster. They fell around me, gasping. One went into convulsions. Another grabbed his heart and yelled, falling over dead. Another fainted straight away.

I was seeing into the soul of the Nevermind.

They wanted to be me. To be someone other than themselves. They wanted it so, they licked the floor like dogs. They wanted the elixir to turn them into supermen.

I understood. I had been like that too.

Those desires were destroying the Agents before me. I'd destroy me too if I didn't change.

I felt the old version of myself dying, a new one reborn. I would never be the same.

Cold metal against my hand. Something subtle about it was warm despite the temperature, was gentle instead of insistent like the rest. It was Luke! But no, that wasn't right. What was going on? I reviewed reality. Luke had removed his armor, and I hadn't seen him since he slunk off into the shadows without it. This aura belonged someone else inside the armor. Who could it be?

His energy moved into mine and pulled mine away from me.

It felt different: Love. Not the twisted love of Luke for his daughters, whom he wanted to keep "alive" as long as possible. A familiar love.

I saw one of the man's memories infused in his aura as it entered the vacuum created in my body from my aura being sucked out. It was Colin inside the armor! How lovely the elixir could be for lovers, their energies moving into each other so they understood each other from the inside out, from the one one's perspective.

I saw the memory of the two of us climbing a tree, sitting on its wide branches, bouncing up and down on them in the fog, singing in harmony, the one time we tried opium. Opium being the scourge of the British empire, we refused to do it again, but that one time was timeless, dreamy, the bouncing repeating on multiple tiers of delight, and desire for each other we consummated when we climbed down, and he pressed me against the tree trunk.

The three Agents who played the role of Moldavite protestors came together to touch me. The one with his hands on my right arm was smirking. As he drew in my aura I watched him trying to keep his expression intact, the muscles of his mouth quivering and tightening, jerking down on one side.

Who made that shadow following Luke along the hallway? Had he knocked him out or something and taken his armor?

Not only that, he'd taken his box of the Recursive Tears elixir! He held it in his metal covered hand, knocking his other hand against his chest armor, making a loud clang and got their attention.

He turned again, and touched me with his free hand, as he held it there. It took no time for my world to twist and face in the opposite direction.

He wore armor.

Me. The value of me. I loved myself, loved Colin, wanted to make love with him in a tree. I'd learned how to reverse the flow of energy when I stopped needing to be on call for Susan. When I had taken over for her, and the curtain landed the last time.

I didn't have to succumb. I could flip it back, impossible as that sounded. And impossible. To reverse the energy I'd taken in, to stop them from pulling any more of mine, to retrieve me from them, despite being nothing, weak, and forgetful of myself.

I was chelating their auras. Detoxing them through me, returning them pristine.

It took everything within me, the most gargantuan effort, drawing deep inside, a burst of adrenaline that left me shaky enough I could barely stand. But I did it. I yelled, and Agents' eyes widened, and some even clamped their hands over their ears. I didn't stop yelling.

Raising my arms out in front of me, flattening my hands, I yelled, "Stop." I opened my eyes as wide as they went, took the biggest breath possible, asserted the value of being myself, not someone else, more strongly than ever.

I breathed myself back in and kicked out what wasn't me. I didn't give their darkness back to them, but let it dissipate into the air. The Agents could be forever lightened and brightened. I could only hope.

I didn't know what they felt any more. I knew what I felt. Me, Miriam, Colin's beloved, who loved him more than I ever could before when I felt second best, nothing, shame, like I should die trying to be someone else.

I was precious! I was the little girl who had rescued a robin and put it back in its nest. I was the teen who had danced more gracefully than anyone else.

No, no, no. That comparison didn't matter. It was tainted, it was dark, it meant someone else was second best. I had danced. That's what mattered. That was me. I'd loved dancing, despite my fear of doing it not as well as someone famous, as not being that famous person, and Papa hating me. I loved dancing for its own sake, for joy, for love, for the moment in this wonderful awful world.

That was when it came clear. I was just like them. We all wanted to be someone else.

They were rabid, foaming at the mouth for the chance to drink the Recursive Tears Elixir, to be someone else for a while.

To be me, who was someone else when the tears were taken.

The Agents idolized Tommy because she was Susan and Sylvia. *Once she becomes me, too, these guys will thrill to her.*

More people to distract from being just them. Just ordinary people.

They tried so hard to do what they thought they were supposed to. To put on the act of being heroic secret agents, never scared. Being tough guys. Being them once they got into bed and checked how much hair they had left and watched a movie and ate ice cream and snuggled under the blankets and dreamed they lived another life. Not so adventurous. Playing with a collie dog on the beach.

I loved those Agents, trying hard to do what they felt was right for Globalism, to bring home a pay check so they could support their kids they didn't even want, but their wives or husbands did, so they did it to make them happy.

I used my might, willed my aura to rebuild its protective skin, to keep me in, and them out.

I then experienced the most intense feeling, overwhelmingly loud in the world of imagination, beyond anything I'd imagined, even moments before when the Agents pulled my life from me and gave me their gunk.

Victory. I was again me. And that was perfect. I could see my purple aura again, my me, my always-friend, my precious self. I was enraptured with the chance to exist, to live my life. *My* life. To be just me. I loved me so very, very much.

Tommy stood on top of the stage, leaning against the corner, watching everything. Her sensual mouth kept its softness when she looked up at me. It was a lightbulb moment. I knew what to do to save us.

I smiled slightly, my teeth the perfect distance apart, my lips open just the right amount, from the ventriloquism practice in my youth. I'd practiced the voices when I was far enough away from Dune. It was time for my big performance to free Tommy, and free Susan and Sylvia's auras back into the Everything.

I threw my voice, ventriloquism above the crowd, as convincingly as I could under the circumstances. Without moving my lips, I spoke using the voice I'd used, while hiding in the closet, to represent John Dee. "Dune, I command thee."

I pointed at the picture, moving my mouth, saying, "Look!"

Without moving my face again, I spoke for Dee while continuing to stare at his picture wide-eyed. "Thou must now release Susan and Sylvia from your 'Tommy.' It is time for the Immortality Project to end. I shall despise you until you do my wishes.

Once you do, you shall be in my highest favor once again." My face didn't move a smidgeon.

I said, "John Dee speaking from his portrait!" diversion being the secret to throwing one's voice.

Dune stood, stunned.

I continued throwing my voice, speaking as the Elizabethan alchemist: "The time to release Susan and Sylvia's ghosts from your noble assistant, who deserves great reward. You must obey me or risk the wrath of the Enochian angels forever."

Dune blanched. He seemed to start to say, "No," to the ancient master of the angels, but muffled himself and bowed. His forehead tightened and reddened, while his hands turned to fists, his lips losing remaining color.

Tommy had been practicing too. She looked him in the eye, then threw her voice to the ethers, without moving her lips. She used a wacky smile, as she raised her eyes up and made the inhuman sounds of Enochian angels. I don't know what she said to him in that Elizabethan spy language, but he stood tall, resolute, and set his jaw.

He turned to her. She looked innocent.

Dune motioned for Huld to bring him a chair to the stage. Huld looked taken aback, his cynicism dissolving, becoming a true believer in the Angels finally at the moment they were announcing they were worthless.

I watched, doubling my vision, looking with my peripheral vision at the surrounding space. I saw blobs of different colors, making her aura clown-like.

Dune pulled the flamingo feather from her hair. He went straight into the hypnotic induction. With graceful movements of his arms as he touched her with a finger, asking her to tell him which finger it was, as he spun her, with her eyes closed. He asked her to tell him how many fingers he was touching, which he said an incorrect number. While he overloaded her senses, he masterfully inducted her into a trance state.

He set her in the chair.

He then broke the hold of the original post-hypnotic suggestion, which could only be broken by him.

The colors of her aura flashed away as Susan and Sylvia's auras dissipated, leaving only one color, a solid teal. Tommy leaned her head back and smiled while holding up her arms as if she were under a waterfall on a warm sunny day. Her gemlike aura color brightened and expanded. I'd saved the day, with her help. I couldn't have been more chuffed.

She was no longer Grail Bennu material but was respected for having played that role. An Agent bowed to her, and others followed.

Dune miserable. Huld horrified.

Dune held up the set of elixirs in glass tubes with burnished caps, stuck through the holes in little latticework shelves. "Take a look at the batch we made. You're looking at the culmination of twenty-six years of work, right here in these vials. There will be no more." He set it on the altar.

"What the hell?" yelled a couple men.

"Bollocks!"

"We may not have the Grail Bennu anymore, but we have the elixir that arose from it. From the ashes! Luke, it's your choice who you have the privilege to kill, of those who have offered themselves to the possibility by their choices."

Dune pointed at Tommy, and then at me. Tommy looked around, her eyes wild, but what could she do in a room full of Agents? I didn't make a move toward the dais, so Huld grabbed hold of my shoulder, pinching it, and lifted me onto the platform before he climbed onto it.

Colin, his Luke-disguise still working for him, picked up the box of elixirs from the table and raised it above the crowd of Agents. He knocked his other hand against his chest armor, making a loud clang, and got their attention.

He raised the box of Recursive Tears and dashed it to the floor, with a crash that echoed against his armor.

Gasps made a symphony, pleasing to my ears. Perfect distraction!

Agents stopped moving for a second, and then one after another, bent to the stone floor, with dirt of centuries ground into it, and licked the liquid interspersed with broken glass vials. Blood from their tongues spread, making the liquid red. When each Agent came up for air, his lips were a mess.

The guards by the door looked around, one holding onto the door but stretching his body toward the crowd, as if a dog watching people eat meat around a table. They looked at each other and ran toward the elixir, joining in licking it up off the floor.

Tommy leaped off the table when no one willing to stop her was watching.

Everyone crowded the widening pool of clear elixir mixed with glass and dirt from their shoes. Grown men stuck their fingertips into the liquid and then sucked on them, jostling against each other, crawling, bending, shoving.

I stood and watched Tommy huddle beside the thick fuzzy coat the fattest man had worn, which had dropped off the coat rack onto the floor beside the wall. I threw something against the opposite wall to cause a distraction.

Tommy curled up inside it, pulling over her small frame. There was no way for the guards to know. Then, she moved toward the door at a snail's pace. She reached up and grabbed a mask off a table as she passed by it. The guards were so immersed in the elixir experience that Tommy made it out the door with no one seeing her but me.

CHAPTER 22
WOODLAND

Colin grabbed me. He threw off his helmet. We ran to the door. Liberation!

I shook dizzily and stumbled, but he pulled me along with him.

As soon as we got outside and closed it, he stopped me. We looked around: no one standing there, no cars close. I watched his face staring at the door, listening with senses keened like an animal's. No one approached.

He put his hands on my shoulders, then stepped back and slowly lifted his visor, showing me soulful hazel deep-set eyes with long sandy lashes, set in freckled tan skin. He removed his helmet, shaking out his hair, spiky over his ears. A warm wave washed over me. My team mate in escape.

He bent, with a conspiratorial laugh, gleeful glint in his eye, as he poked me with his elbow. "I'll take off my armor if you take off yours."

We ran faster. Where are we going? Colin held up a set of keys and pulled me toward a red car parked in the distance. He must have taken it from someone's jacket in an entry closet. As we ran to the parking lot, Colin tore off one piece of armor after another, throwing them on the ground. We jumped into the car and raced down the long, winding drive.

"Where's Tommy?" I asked.

"Who's Tommy?"

"The topless woman dressed like a man. Was wearing the flamingo feather. She was the Grail Bennu." I wasn't sure how long he'd been wandering through the party in disguise; he had learned something about the value of the elixir while working the party.

"You run in weird circles, girl."

I said, "I don't know if it's safe for us to go home. What if they send Agent enforcers after us? Maybe we should find a motel?" Staying some place so commercial and mundane was too foreign. Repugnant. I wanted to howl and hunt and roll in the mud and be my wild animal on the windswept landscape, alive, alive, alive! My feral feelings for Colin couldn't be trapped within four quiet walls. No chatty room service, no ice dispensers, no TV sets, no vacuum cleaners down the hall.

"No, they'd ask for registration. Same reason I didn't get a rental car. We have to stay hidden."

"Besides, we should stay out in the wilderness tonight nearby, so we can keep looking for Tommy. Take a turn as soon as you see any place in the forest to drive through the trees."

"They're thick."

"Not everywhere. There are patches."

We wove along the narrow, empty road raised up over ditches on each side, that we were veering off toward, as we sped away from anyone following us. Colin turned to see if we'd passed any handy openings. It was dizzying. I wished to hold onto him without making us wreck.

A narrow opening caught our attention as we passed it driving fast too fast for a gentle turn. In the past days Colin had gone feral too. I grasped the seat belt and braced myself. My neck swerved into the head rest.

We bumped and bounced as we dipped into the ditch to the left, and toward the forest, over briars, vines and bushes, bounding over rocks, and going straight for a big tree. I breathed in so fast my lungs hurt.

I covered my face and yelled as we drove toward the tree, and I ducked from the commotion to our left, from crackling and crunching, scraping, and the shattering of glass when a branch flung itself through the driver's side open window, knocking Colin's head against the steering wheel.

With his forehead pressed against the wheel while the branch in slow motion moved forward scraping his scalp and hit the windshield, breaking it, and slid out as we continued to drive forward, scraping my face, and slicing Colin's jacket so his skin shone through, slender, his ribs showing, burned with a stripe of red.

He cursed, angling forward with an intensity I'd never seen in him before, a determination to take the chance of death or escape, counting on his acumen to drive between close-knit trees until he slammed on the brakes.

My seat belt dug into my gut. I grasped the seat belt and braced myself. My neck swerved into the head rest when Colin turned the wheel. We bumped and bounced as we dipped into the ditch to the left, and down toward the forest, over briars, vines and bushes, bounding over rocks, and going straight for a big tree. I breathed in so fast my lungs hurt.

We drove through the crackling and crunching, scraping. A branch flung itself across the driver's side window and slid out as we continued to drive forward.

He grasped the steering wheel hard, his knuckles drawing my attention to their slender, animal utility, his veins heightened as his muscles kept us going off the narrow opening between the trees.

He put his head back against the rest, and so did I, closing my eyes, breathing. We were not dead. We were together.

Life spread out before me. Before us.

I couldn't wait to be a waitress.

❄

We got out and covered the car with branches we'd knocked, and leaves. I hoped against hope we'd find Tommy before dawn.

But first, I had to recuperate. Lying on the ground, the personalities of the Agents palpable around me. I imagined the auric residue being pulled into the ground, releasing from me. Removing invisible gunk required salt baths, sage, scraping it off with crystals, I'd read in the grimoire. The throbbing sensation of them pressing against me subsided.

I had sparse aura left. Their gunk had left me. My natural life force was inside the Agents.

So, I drew long breaths, pulling universal revitalization toward me, charging the ubiquitous substance of the atmosphere violet with my signature vibration. Drawing sustenance from the center of the earth, from the sky, I sat and meditated, closing my eyelids, turning my eyes upward. I imagined my consciousness rising out of the top of my head into the high levels of my aura, seeing gold above me, and drawing from it into me, packing the electrical nutrients around my body.

I imagined cutting cords between myself and them so they stopped drawing from through them or push their own gunk through the cords into me. It wasn't perfect, yet.

He took his torch from the glove compartment and we tromped off toward the castle through the underbrush. At least, I hoped we were getting the direction right. Not time yet to call for her.

"I noticed Huld in there. From the troupe, right? What's he doing out here?"

"Complicated." I panted, leaping over a fox hole, my ankle

going weak out to the side, but I recovered. The twinge of pain was tolerable. Colin's temple had swelled on the site of impact. He looked at me, and lifted his eyebrows at me, to show I should continue.

I continued. "Huld's an Agent and part of the Bennu Society." When he looked away, furrowing his forehead, I explained, "Secret societies have always intertwined with intelligence agencies. Gather information, pass secrets, manipulate beliefs, tear down the Agent's ego through the Osiris Slain/Osiris Risen ritual so that they're reborn loyal members. That's who's at the castle tonight. That's a nest of 'em in there. It's complicated."

"Yeah, I noticed. After I sneaked in and put on Luke's armor, I talked to Agents, asking questions."

"So that's how you came up with your elixir scheme. Brilliant."

We kissed, seeking ears and necks, collar bones, souls.

The circle of desire below expanded, ready to accommodate the entry of his selfhood into mine, the physical oneness, a shared experience after such intense loneliness, the coming together of the two of us, after such longing, in the moonlit woods, by the red smashed car, the song on the radio echoing in my head, the singer's voice reminding me how sexy life was.

The moonlight on his skin. I reached out and pulled his jacket apart more, and the shirt underneath.

He breathed hard and his head fell back.

I kissed his taut skin, away from the redness. I breathed on him, and touched his skin just with a finger, barely touching, sliding.

He bucked against me and I swayed with him, as if we were ocean waves. Our audible breath excited me. The wonders of his body again after so long apart, so long living overlapping nightmares. Distant yet connected, even when I didn't know him.

Even then when he was a crazed stranger waiting to abduct me if I set foot alone outside the fortress there was electricity between us. His body steeped in the wind and sun, gorse and the hunt. How fortunate I was to have him. To be me. To have a normal life.

He'd do well with the publishing company, assuming he hadn't been fired for being gone so long. I leaned in and whispered, "If you're still acquisitions editor, I'll write a book for you. Called *Encore*. If you take it on at Be Yourself, it will change your life if you're ready to go all the way. With whom I am, no secrets. And how the world works."

He caressed my cheek, searching my eyes, the corners of his lips turned up with a child's, the shadows under his cheeks art in the moonlight, his hair covering one eye, the sensuous curves of his face mysterious in its shade. Bones and lashes.

"I can feel you from the inside," he whispered back, panting, "when I touch you. As if my awareness is moving through you. What it is to be you."

"Did you take any elixir?"

He pressed his palm against my pleasure mound. "A drop."

I turned to fire. I moaned.

He whispered, "Can we mix ourselves without boundary?"

"All of me can go into all of you. And circle it."

The idea would have worried me earlier. He gave without hooks. But I had the sense it wasn't a strong enough storm to rage through me full force. His love would have gotten stuck against obstacles in my body, memories from childhood, clenched muscles, hesitance.

I had been a lie. A pretense of being someone else. The lifelong hope to *one day* be someone else well enough to be loved.

Instead, at the castle, I had become my true self. Violet frequency of universal bliss. An aura I saw around me as far as my vision took me. Grand. Proud. Nothing insignificant.

The mist made diamonds of moisture in his hair. Moonlight glinted off the diamonds.

He picked up a piece of wood, and beat it against a stump, a drum. Boomboom. Boomboom.

I danced around the stump, low to the ground, and leaping. Boomboom. Boomboom.

Colin reached out to my breasts jutting over my dress. He slapped the left one then the right, flicked one nipple, then the other. Not too hard. Perfect. I leaned back against a knotted trunk, raising a leg to wrap around him and draw him close, his pelvis against me with my ankle. I pushed my hips away from the tree and toward his, then us both to the tree, clenching him with my ankle over his round butt, setting off a rhythm as if it shot up through the trunk and branches and leaves.

"Imagine our energy rising above us together through the tree," I said. "Turn your eyes upward to direct the flow. Don't let it leave here." I pressed with my ankle against his hardness pulsing against me. "Just extend upward. So, we're light together all the way up into the highest levels of our auras."

He took hold of both my wrists and lifted them above my head, pinning them to the gray bark with one hand that encompassed both wrists at once. Our hard breaths went in sync.

He thrust against me and with his quick flick upwards, his aura flowing through the core of my body, glowing to my inner vision. My eyes closed as I swooned.

When he put his hands against my breasts, the light grew there. He leaned forward and kissed me in between them. His chest against mine, moving his head to my right, nuzzling his cheek against mine. We breathed in sync, alternated, he breathing out when I breathed in.

The energy he'd sent up my body rested in my heart and then flowed over to him: pure love, communication, outpouring of esoteric liquid fire.

I'd sent the energy to trees before, reaching out to touch them, and speak to them with heart vibration, warming them with gratitude. I knew they resonated.

Love flowed from my heart to his, and I pushed it down his body, pushing the flow with tiny muscular movements, directing it with my eyes as I scanned the center line of his body. When energy reached his crotch, he thrust, and sent the life force up through me to my heart. We cycled it.

He said, "We're light circling through our bodies."

"I am you."

"I am you."

We didn't make love. We didn't need to.

Moving our bodies sent exquisite energy between us, divine, powerful light. We cycled it fast and faster, moving it with our undulations. As we did, we pressed our bodies against each other with delicate thrusts until the motion became precise, tiny, ecstatic. Behind closed eyelids, it burst, fireworks of passion-deities present in every molecule.

When we stopped cycling and pressed our bodies against each other in silent stillness, the energy whipped up through me so intensely, it threw my hips forward toward him and my head back and I yelled, and he yelled, his body in sync with mine.

We stood there, hands on each other's hips holding each other up while we leaned back and yelled into the forest far from the loud castle. We were *it*. The eternal itness of things. The universal life force that had no end, but was the trees, rocks, stars, rivers.

❄

Then, we pulled ourselves back into our own individual bodies.

"I am me. Just me is brilliant." Me.

"I am me. Just me is brilliant." Him.

When I opened my eyes, and breathed on his eyelids, making his lashes flutter and open, I got to experience Heaven. For a second.

I couldn't believe it when he looked away, silent. "As fantastic as that was, I don't know, Miriam. We made good friends. Are we doing the correct thing now?"

"Why wouldn't we be?"

"I can think of a few reasons." "A few" sounded like a euphemism for "a million." Or was it one? Dune.

As we walked, drinking water from a tiny stream, searching up in trees and in holes in the ground, we remained silent. I tried to tell myself the endless terrain inspired quietude. It was also four in the morning. We punctuated our conversation with shouting for Tommy.

"What was the point of ghosts flying through the castle?"

"*Crazy*, right?"

"And there you were, telling Randall to go to the Free Tibet group, while they ran away from the sheets. Sick timing, if you ask me."

I laughed.

"No, really. You want innocent people involved? Get them killed."

"Horrible!" My heart hurt. The worst thought ever. I deflected with, "I wish we could let the neighbors know the ghosts were just smoke and mirrors."

"It was hard to get the neighbors to show up. It was hard to get the first bloke to open the door when I knocked. Wicked fast guard dogs around here." He shook his head. "Clever ghost trick, though, Luke's treating the neighbors like children. They'd be mad to find out they'd been tricked."

I said, "They have the right to realize the place isn't haunted. And so should their children. They shouldn't have to grow up afraid of the place for the wrong reasons. But they should know what awful things go on there, right?"

"Slow down." His lips were so beautiful, I stared at them and caught my breath.

"'The curse' protected the castle. I guess it protects the Nevermind and Bennu Society stuff that goes on there. So, they can get away with abducting innocent women." I gave him time for the "innocent" remark to sink in to his subconscious. It wasn't my fault.

"Mmhmm." He wasn't giving in on that one. His eyes appraised me, glancing up and down, not hiding his distrust.

"It keeps anyone from robbing the place."

"Got to be worth a fortune."

"Sort of. The main thing is, they have most of the Moldavite in the entire world stashed there."

""Hoo *hoo!*" He skipped.

"The prices already were high, right, because it's the rarest gem ever."

"And people buy because of the Shambhala legends about spiritual properties."

"The price has gone astronomical since the Agents bought everything up." I lowered my voice so if he didn't hear me that's OK. "And stole some." I cleared my throat and pointed to something in the distance.

Even though it was my sister and Dune who stole it, I still felt guilty. I couldn't bring myself to tell him yet.

"No doubt the Agents have fanned the flames about the spiritual properties to make it worth even more."

"That's right! I discovered that secret in the castle."

"But the shows your troupe puts on compete against the Shambhala-heads. I don't understand." He reached out to touch my arm, and I felt sizzle.

"Ugh. I know. I didn't realize until I came here. Now, I'm the expert."

"From the inside out."

That stung. "Bennu members get access to the Moldavite stash in the castle. They do mystical rituals to charge it with spiritual energy, to fit the legends about immortality and special powers."

"That's disgusting."

"Yeah. . . sort of incredible, too."

"You can't be serious."

"In an artistic way."

"A load of steaming crap is what it is."

"They worshipped me."

"Oh, well, how *lovely* for you!" He rubbed his wounded arm through a hole in his mud-caked jacket and he spit.

"Can't keep looking for Tommy any longer. I'm beat."

"Let's risk going in closer to the castle in the morning."

"If we do that, though, we can't shout out for her."

"Well, we agree."

We lay a few feet from each other, shivering on the cool ground in the densest clump of trees, nestled inside bushes. Before long, his breathing changed: asleep. I reached out and pushed his hair out of his face and caressed his cheek.

CHAPTER 23
CLASH

The way Colin glared at me when he opened his eyes, I wondered if he'd dreamed me doing something awful. As if real life wasn't enough. Gave me a stomach ache.

As dawn was breaking, we set off to look for Tommy. My legs were stiff and wet with gorse stuck to them. The wind was biting, picking up, giving me goosebumps.

Did he dream of me in Dune's arms? In a castle by a fire in a soft bed while he was outside scraping twigs and hitting arrow heads? Me wearing a tiara and prancing, the proud mascot of a perverse secret society? Him trying to save me and getting punched?

If he'd taken more of the elixir than just a drop, he'd have been more empathetic. He would have understood what was in my heart.

My memories. My dreams. Oh, God, no. That was the last thing I needed. Tommy had advised me to give my all to winning him over.

He said, "Tommy's probably found her way to the road by now. Maybe traveled in the dark through the open spaces. Either picked off or picked up. Do you think we should return to the car?"

"She wouldn't head for the road, with all the Agents leaving the party. Let's go on in closer. She might be hiding. She might be waiting."

"What's that?" Crunching leaves made us duck and scoot, huddling behind a low bush.

"There's a bunch of them!" he whispered.

The sunrise showed landscape details. I poked my head over the bush just in time to see an Agent approaching, and another walking parallel to him. And another parallel to him. An organized search.

"Hey!" shouted a gray-haired woman.

We jumped up and ran. The only way open, without Agents, was toward the castle.

The Agent who had shouted called as softly, "Miriam! Shhh. Quiet. Slow down. I won't hurt you, promise. Drank elixir. So, how could I?"

He ran up to us and pushed us on the ground, glancing toward Agents, who hadn't noticed us. He hugged me and then hugged a very surprised Colin. Aaron: the man whose eyes had implored my forgiveness after ingesting the elixir.

"Are . . . Are all the Agents sweethearts now?"

"Don't know. Most of them went home. There were a mad bunch of hyenas when you didn't get sacrificed. Thanks to you." He poked Colin, whose face looked like he'd eaten something gone off. "You know how to kill a party, you know that?"

"My specialty."

"And it didn't go over too well when the Enochian Angels killed the Immortality Project. Freeing the sisters from Tommy, man."

"I hope they've gone into the light."

"Oh, jibber jabber."

Hah. "Yeah, or whatever."

"Come on. Maybe I can get you to my car without the Agents seeing you."

"How? They're everywhere."

He got up and jerked his head. We got up too, and he put his arms encircling us, huddling conspiratorially. He pulled us to stand on either side of him, his cloak covering us so from behind a fat person with three heads. "Duck." So, we became a fat man with six legs. But who was counting?

This was great. My sending of loving forgiveness to Aaron had paid off. We ran at different rates, being such different heights, over loose rocks and sharp plants, jiggle jaggling, our arms sliding off each other, our breaths loud inside the coat. The cars remaining were spread out in the parking lot, his being on the near side to the castle. Going into the belly of the beast required trust.

I noticed cars and trucks pulled off along the driveway into the castle. The Agents had parked in the lot. So, who were they?

We heard shouting behind us.

"What's happening?"

"Look! Aaron's found them!" If only the sun wasn't making the morning so bright we might have had a chance.

"Leave us alone," Aaron yelled, and we separated and ran zig zag. There was no good option looming, no good place to run. I slid on a rock and turned just in time to see an arrow whizz past my ear. If I hadn't slipped, I could have died.

Agents on either side of us, more than I'd realized, fanned out across the landscape. Some stood, fumbling, walking this way and that. Others set chase, corralling us closer and closer to the castle. Two held bows and arrows aimed at us. My heart leapt up into my throat.

We were goners.

An Agent called, "Hey, you! Are you the thief who stole my car?"

Wind whipped up. Trees bent, their leaves shaking. It was

hard to tell what I heard. Sounds of gravel coming toward the castle, a bevy of cars. Were the Agents who left the party returning? Us against them all?

The motley crew of cars steering along the driveway didn't look like the right kind for Agents.

It took a minute to put it together, as I zig zagged across sharp stickers and thorns, when the cars parked, and people got out. I recognized folks from the evening news protest about Moldavite. Others from the protest outside the theater, and the hecklers. Of course. I'd asked the neighbor, Randall to round them up.

The Agents with bows and arrows approached us, but they stopped and stared at the protestors getting out of their cars. They lowered their bows. A pot-bellied man dropped the arrows to the ground and stood there looking innocent. The other hid the bow behind his back.

I wondered who was inside the castle. The door was open and the portcullis up, no doubt for Agents going in and out as they searched. Surely, they hadn't left the castle unattended, but why was no one closing up the fortress?

Randall waved at me. I did my best to wave while scrunching my body up to be as small a target as possible. Then, he pointed across the driveway. More cars, of a dustier, clunkier kind than the city hipsters, young Mongolians, and New Agers had driven in. Most of them women, most of the others slender young men, and a frizzy-chinned, floppy person I couldn't identify as either gender.

The protestors got out and pulled out cardboard signs. Oh, dear. Cardboard wasn't the best weapon at a castle. The protestors organized into cluster, huddled, and then marched, chanting, toward the castle.

They held dog-eared signs such as "Stop, Don't Look, Don't Listen," and chanted, "Hey Hey, Ho ho, Now, it's time to let them go!"

Sweethearts! Incredible.

Sure, they believed in silly legends about a land that didn't exist. But who was I to judge? People everywhere believe in their religions or that their governments are looking out for them or that their neighbor is channeling Mother Mary. I wanted to hug them. But more than that, I wanted to get them to leave. I didn't want to see anyone hurt.

I realized whoever was inside the castle must leave the door open still to lure the outsiders in, and then trap them between the portcullises. Surely, they wouldn't throw logs on them, but they'd have people contained and scared.

I stopped in my tracks, mouth open. An eerie sound came from below the steep hill. I glanced at Colin. Were there Enochian Angels after all? I strained to stand on my tip toes to see what approached us. Bobbing white things coming up the hill into view. What in the world? They had eyes, but unlike any I'd seen.

A row of people wearing sheets. Dressed as ghosts. Their eye holes and mouth slits at disconcerting wonky angles. The sheets blew, whipping their bodies, making the scene even more surreal, especially with twigs and even a thin tree branch flying in front. They made eerie Oooooooo noises, louder and louder, and raised their arms, walking in sync toward the castle. Two on the ends wielded axes, swaying them back and forth in unison.

The neighbor who returned and noticed the sheets and pulleys used to scare them earlier must have rounded up the others and told them they'd been fooled. That explained the row of muddy trucks parked off the driveway. They'd gathered in the hill below before their grand entrance. It was quite the performance. Made a statement to the hoaxers loud and clear.

Protestors grabbed each other and shrieked. "Ghosts!" Others held their hands over their hearts or hunkered down. They disengaged from each other as the neighbors got closer, their blue jeans sticking out below the billowing sheets, boots clunky with mud.

Ironic that the neighbors and protestors gathered to rescue Tommy and me from our captive state in the castle, and we weren't even in there.

The Agents chasing Colin and me wouldn't dare kill us with them watching. We had enough allies to outnumber the Agents.

I had to keep newcomers safe. Otherwise: a shit show.

"Don't go into the castle!" I called to the protestors when I realized they were headed straight for the door. "It's not safe. And I'm here." So? Oh yeah. "I'm a hostage."

"Thank you for coming!" reassured Colin. "I appreciate you caring. You might not want to get involved, though. Hello?"

I wasn't sure any of them heard us over their chanting. Maybe the tallest protestor did. He stopped walking, the others piling up behind him.

I didn't want to ask the protestors to fan out and look for Tommy and get picked off by Agents. Would the Agents be that bold? It wouldn't be easy to excuse too many random deaths with so many witnesses. I called over the din, "The other woman . . ."

No one paid attention. The protestors walked straight into a death trap.

I ran toward them, but an Agent grabbed me from behind. He swung me around, his stubble scratching my cheek. His breath smelled strong, which was to be expected, I supposed, as he'd stayed at the castle overnight after a wild party to find us and take us down. I started to shout but he put his hand over my mouth.

The protestors, oblivious to what happened, never turned their heads from their goal of the castle, chanting too loudly to hear my cries. I kicked backward, aiming for the groin, and the Agent leaned back. I screamed louder and disengaged from his grasp.

I ran to the front of the line, hoping no one sent arrows through the arrow slits or any of the other myriad options of attack against the kind-hearted rescuers.

Grabbing an arm of a person at the front, a short Mongolian

man with a round head and a bowl haircut, I twirled him and pulling him, shouted, “Stop walking! The portcullis will trap you!”

He punched me on the jaw. "Hey hey, ho ho, no one tells Nate where to go!" The others kept walking.

I pushed them backwards, shouting, “No, I’m on your side!” I walked backwards in front of the line of protestors heading toward the doom of the entryway under the horrors of the gatehouse, getting closer and closer to where the spikes could close on us. I would *not* let these innocent people die.

My nightmare come true: someone pushed me beneath the portcullis. I scrambled sideways, scooting from where the spikes could skewer me. Above me I saw the familiar doom, with murder holes where at any moment hot sand, rocks, scalding water, or burning logs could come flying toward me. A sound. A rumble in the ground. Shouts around me and someone pointing up.

Nothing.

A second chance at life. This time, I’d make it count double.

Colin joined me, and we pushed the protestors away from the doorway with all our might, crawling against their forward motion. Someone large stepped on me. We grabbed the ones who entered the entryway and pushed them backward. They fell against the others, who stopped to pick them up and console them.

“Leave her alone,” said Colin, his arms outstretched. They pushed past him as if he wasn’t there.

“I’m Miriam! I’m the one you came here to save!”

One protestor stopped, stared at me for a second, and yelled, "Stop. This is Miriam. Save Miriam!" They circled around me, hugging me, stepping on my toes. They Ommed in my ears. They had no idea the danger they were in so near the castle. Anyone could drop something off the top, off the top of the gatehouse on us. But at least no more portcullis danger. “Move away from the castle,” I commanded. “It’s not safe.”

One of people wearing a Free Tibet button said, “Wait a

minute. You're Susan, aren't you?" Ah, that familiar voice. A heckler from the show.

"You play Bennu. In shows all about Atlantis, with nothing about Shambhala at all. Like Shambhala just doesn't even exist."

"Yeah, like it doesn't even matter."

"The director gave you a whole Grail made of Moldavite. I was there. I saw it."

"Moldavite belongs to Shambhala devotees."

"There's not enough left to go around. Give us the Grail."

"Give it back! Give it back! Give it back!"

"I'm not Susan."

"Shut up. Yes, you are."

"No, she isn't," said Colin, bitterness in his voice.

Telling them I played her standby wouldn't be any better, so I let it go. I didn't even have the Grail, myself anymore, but if I did, I'd damn well hang onto it.

A branch flew by in the wind. I ducked, grabbed onto Colin, and screamed. *Would I ever recover from being traumatized by those burning logs flung at me?*

The Agents stood back, many of them among the trees, remaining anonymous. But one shouted, his arm waving from behind a boulder: "This woman hates Shambhala."

"What? No." *I mean, not any more than Atlantis. It's stupid manipulation.*

"Bitch, what have you got against the only perfect place on Earth?"

The protestors stepped back and talked among themselves.

Meanwhile, the neighbors in ghost costumes advanced, with synchronized axes. Had they practiced at home?

The protestors, looking nervous, glanced at the neighbors and shuffled closer to the castle. Looking up at the potential dangers above, they shuffled back toward the ghosts.

As they edged toward their cars, I pleaded, "Are you going to take us with you or not? Please, please get me out of this place. I don't know where Tommy is." I turned toward the forest and called out Tommy's name.

"Tommy the crazy scrapper? Yeah, we don't want to take him/her, anyway."

"Oh, come on."

"No, you don't want to take her," said the trouble-making Agent. "Tommy charged Moldavite with special spells. Anti-Shambhala spells, I might add." That was going too far.

Another Agents said, "And this woman," pointing at me, his arm outstretched, the only body part visible as he hid behind a tree. He faltered and stopped.

Female protestors looked elsewhere paying him no attention. They'd shifted their demeanors. Their chins down, they patted their hair, opened their eyes wide, stuck out their butts, held in their tummies, stood with one leg in front and bent.

The Agent followed their gaze. I did too.

Dune the Magnificent shown resplendent before us.

"Hello, ladies."

Tittering. The few men in the group postured. The women pushed past them toward the front of the line, dropping their signs.

Whenever Dune's eyes landed on them, they raised their eyebrows and pushed out their lips.

The two protestors, the leaders in the front, were a romantic couple, but Dune bent and kissed the hand of the woman, holding her hand, lowering and raising his long black eyelashes one miraculous time. The other women glared at her and stepped away. Her man looked horrified as he stared at her hand in Dune's. He lengthened his body, the muscles in his neck pressing his veins outward. When he spoke, he seemed to struggle to make his voice low and husky. "Hello."

"Oh, I hadn't noticed you were a lady," said Dune to him.

The man's fist tightened. The veins popped even more.

His woman looked at him as if reassessing and nodding in agreement that he was a lady. Compared to Dune.

Her man pulled her aside, and they began a whispered argument, with jagged movements, staying out of the game.

Another protester held out her hand for a kiss, and Dune bent to it. "Pleased to meet you. I'm Dune." The other women perked up and moved forward, jostling her out of the way, and raising their hands daintily. One kept giggling, her hand over her mouth. "And this is my wife, Susan."

The women gave me the stink eye.

Dune bowed suavely and offered, “What can I help you with today?"

"We came for that woman," said a man, his voice wavering.

"You wanted to speak to my darling?" He pulled me to him. The women looked like they'd prefer to get me out of the way of their flirtation.

"We were told she was held hostage, along with another woman."

Dune grandly gestured toward the open door, an oh so reasonable, magnanimous gentleman. "If anyone is in there, she's welcome to join you."

“Yes, please take me home with you," I said. The women weren't willing to chauffeur a Shambhala-hating rival for Dune's affections. Much less Moldavite-Tommy.

"This man," Dune said, nodding toward Colin and then at the approaching ghosties, "is a suspect for the murder of his girlfriend, Miriam. Has he been going on about her being missing?"

The ghosties stopped in their tracks. "We can't believe a word you say," said a reasonable bloke. "You tried to make fools of us.”

"Yeah, how stupid do you think we are? Those ghosts in the castle; they weren't real."

"We'll show you real." A neighbor with an axe stepped forward.

A protestor, arms crossed tight against her chest, looked at the neighbors as if disgusted. One protestor stood in front of Dune, her arms out wide, as if to protect his extraordinary handsomeness with her life from anyone rude enough to question his godlike perfection. Dune put a hand on her waist, and she bent her head back in obvious ecstasy.

Newscasters would convolute ever-changing ways of explaining this clash. They couldn't dox Agents or question that level of secret governmental decisions. I hoped the protestors and neighbors accepted bribes and take any threats seriously about revealing information to the public. I didn't want to see anyone get hurt.

One of the protestor men shouted, "I recognize you" at an Agent who had poked his head out from behind a tree. "Hey, everybody, it's Ernst. Our organizer! No wonder he missed our meeting today."

"Impostor!"

"Infiltrator!" That explained so much.

"Get him!" The men in the group ran toward Ernst, no doubt emboldened to appear macho. The Agent pulled his bow from behind his back and shot an arrow at the one in front. It hit him in the thigh and he went down fast.

Two other men grabbed him and carried him toward the cars. The others scattered, other than one, who leaped on him and wrestled him to the ground. The two men wrestled, rolling around.

One woman took out a cell phone and seemed to record video.

An Agent ran to her and grabbed it.

Others took out their phones in solidarity and the rest of the Agents descended on them, wresting their devices away. "No pictures. No video. No word of this to anyone. You'll 'live' to regret it if you break those rules. We're protected by law. You're trespassing against your own government."

I ran off to the side of the crowd, waving my arms, warning

people not to take out their phones. I didn't want to see them lose their devices. The ones near me backed away from my whooshing.

A loud crack! Intense pain so many places at once.

A rock had landed on the sloping front of the castle, breaking just as falling rocks were intended historically, against that brilliant fortress design. When it cracked against the slope, it had shattered into high velocity shrapnel. Several shards lodged into my body.

I tried to pull one out and identified it as volcanic glass. Moldavite. I was the only one hit.

Who stood up there? Huld? Luke? One of the other Agents? None of them would throw away a 60,000-dollar piece of rock the size of a small potato that didn't belong to them.

One of the protestor men bent toward me and looked at the shrapnel.

"Moldavite! She's part Moldavite. Have you ever seen anything like it?"

"It came from nowhere."

"The great knight Parzival's Grail is the stone that fell from Heaven."

"The alchemist's Philosopher's Stone."

"It's a miracle."

"She's sacred."

A wail from above.

A protestor man declared, "She's our savior. The King of the World has spoken."

"She's from Shambhala!"

"She's part of the Great White Brotherhood!"

"An ambassador from Sirius gave us Moldavite. She's part Sirian."

"No, Orion, not Sirius." A scuffle broke out.

I hated myself. I half wanted to be sacred. I half wanted to be their savior. Wanted to be a myth come true. The Grail.

And Colin knew. One look at my ambivalent expression. He turned around and walked away. I started toward him, my feet sliding on the mud.

Protestors ganged up on me before I got far. "Shambhala! Shambhala!" They touched me with worship in their eyes. I stung, bleeding around the Moldavite.

"Tibetan monks have written that the King of the World will gather an army of people devoted to Shambhala. We'll destroy evil. The Moldavite proves it!"

Luke called out my name. I looked up to see him towering above us, dark against the sky, his old burn scars, red bubbles covering every visible part of his skin. The wind pushed him closer to the edge and people gasped.

"I loved your mother so much." Everyone grew silent. "Your sisters were only three years old when she died giving birth to you." He choked up. He wiped away tears.

I felt that monster with my heart. In my heart.

"I'd never seen such adorable creatures as you and your sisters. I was raising you fine."

This man had cuddled me. He'd tucked me in. He'd fed me.

Colin stopped walking away and turned. *Please wait for me, Colin. I don't want to be something I'm not. I promise.*

I tore in two.

"You would have had a great life here. You would have never left. Why not?" The blustery wind pushed him forward again.

"But the adoption agency took you. After Martha died, women tried to snag me, left and right. One or two of the women were total nutters. Social Services thought I turned into a playboy with unstable mother substitutes for you, so they took you away. First Martha gone, then you girls too. Too much. Too much to stand. Why do you think I'm covered in scars?"

"Why?" yelled a neighbor.

"I paid someone to do it to me. He poured boiling water on me through the murder hole. My life would be dedicated to my family. You were all the family I had left. I wanted to die I missed you so much. I was in a coma for a month."

I felt horrible I'd scalded him with the coffee. And then he had to show his embarrassing scars to the whole room.

My real father loved me. He'd wanted to keep me and my sisters around forever. Even if that meant turning us into ghosts. Ghosts to keep "alive," one inside the other, in the castle, never leaving him again. Not letting them die of natural causes and escape. No, they had to live with him in the castle as a ghost slumber party.

And he'd wanted the unthinkable. To keep our ghosts inside his living young daughter or son. Named Equinox.

I wanted to love my father. But during the equinox ritual, I'd promised never to forgive without reason.

"Stay with me here? I'd protect you. You'd be immune to the law. We could do green ceremonies together. Don't leave me again."

I didn't know what to say. We looked into each other's eyes. He waited, pulled a rope off his neck with the vajra, "thunderbolt" wand made of Moldavite. He held the wand up in the air: the tallest thing on that part of the castle, holding an antenna. He swayed in the wind, nearly stumbling off, but he smiled and regained his footing.

Dry lightning struck the thunderbolt wand. Smell of seared flesh. Luke landed with a sickening thud next to me. The angle of his head was wrong. His brown and pale wrinkled scalding scars had fried to black.

Dune cried out. I bent to touch his warm neck gingerly. No pulse. Loss had twisted my father. He died unable to release.

I hung my head, curled over his corpse. I reached out to hug him, pulled my arm back, reached again, and hesitated, my fingers curving shadows on his back.

❄

"Luke is your father? You're a . . . princess or something?"

"No, I'm not. And I'm not from Shambhala, either. I'm just *regular*."

Colin smiled widely, his teeth so white.

He returned and stood over me. Would we be together after my stupidity? He came and put his hand on my shoulder. "You're not 'just' anything." He kissed the top of my head.

The protestors stared at Dune.

"And I'm not his wife. Look. Susan." I tightened my lips, pulled in my chest, sucked in my cheeks, and acted out her mannerisms: the poised expressions on her face, and her cracklier voice, walking, muttering something. I acted out moves from the show -- careful to choose some that had nothing to do with Atlantis. I did the most potent impression.

I remembered. Carrying a ghost. "She" was the substance auras were molded out of, imprinted by my idea of Susan. "She" was an egregore, growing its substance from my constant sculpting, and from the audience's focus on her.

A protestor twirling a sign that said, "Free Women" and on the back, "King of the World Free the Moldavite!" stepped up and narrowed his eyes at me. I tightened my muscles, making my legs taut and the bands stand out in the most pleasing ways.

He said, "Yes, that's how Susan acted in the Bennu show."

I told them, "Susan is dead."

They talked among themselves, and neighbor ghosties stepped forward.

"The guys who killed her have an in with forensics. They pretended her body is mine. They're blaming the murder on Colin."

Could my risk win Colin over?

Dune, unblinking, standing just as tall and straight as ever, smiled like an invincible movie star. "Those are quite some claims, my lady."

The protestors looked back and forth at us.

If I said Dune covered up his wife's death, they'd hate me.

They preened again now he was available. Not married to me. One of them unbuttoned her jacket despite the cold wind picking up. Another one took off her glasses. One unpinned her hair, and it ruthlessly blew in her eyes.

One of the protestor men looked at me resolutely. He stepped forward, and I stayed strong to prepare for him hitting me. He leaned forward, reaching out his arm and put his hand to my ear. He whispered, "You can ride with me. I can take you. I'm Nate."

"And Colin, too?" The last thing he needed was to drive a stolen car home, and not just any car, an Agent's car.

"No problem."

Yes!

After talking to everyone one by one, Colin lifted up his hand in victory, something shiny in it. Colin bounded over holding out a pair of tweezers. Guess someone worried about ticks? He dug out bits of shrapnel. I put my sleeve in my mouth to bite.

An Agent reiterated to the crowd, "Remember, if *any* of you breathe a *word* about any of this, you're dead meat."

The protestors looked shocked all over again.

The neighbor ghosts stood stalwart. Making their point didn't require much else.

The boyfriend walked back to the crowd without his girlfriend, who stayed back a yard away and ogled Dune. Boyfriend said, "If the piece of Moldavite didn't come from Heaven, where did it?"

The rock would have fit into my hand. I raised my hand against the sky as if holding the stone inside my open fist. Teetering on the edge of the world. Then I threw straight down that invisible stone with all my might. I imagined a sound-track.

I said, "Luke dropped it to shatter against the slope. It's an old-fashioned weapon. You should try it."

"No one would drop a big Moldavite. That's big bucks. That's insane."

"You're trying to tell me that bloke was not insane? You got to be joking."

"He had plenty to spare," I said, regretting it. Do *not* go there. Do *not*.

"Yeah, he's rich, dimwit." One protestor, I couldn't tell if it was a red-faced male or female, made that observation while stomping boots against the cold.

I was glad no one caught on about my real father having a stash of the green stone. If they knew the stone bought up from the market, and even stolen from the museum, was on the other side of that wall: crazy-time.

At that moment, Huld loomed in the doorway.

"Mr. Atlantis," said a neighbor ghostie holding an ax.

"Mr. Axe Murderer," said Huld.

"More for effect, really."

This was the strangest day. How could I choose which day was the strangest during the last weeks?

When would there ever be another chance to storm the castle?

Not that the rocks belonged to those protestors. The museum deserved its supply. The rest were legitimately bought. I'd seen the receipts. Encouraging theft wouldn't help anyone.

The situation made my ears want to explode. Local people most adamant in their love for the Stone from Heaven. The majority of gems in the world, with no more available at stores or online anywhere any more. . . Untold riches on the other side of the wall.

I wondered how much of Luke's money had gone into the purchases of the meteoric glass. The Agents had used his obsession with getting his daughters back in the only way he knew how. A desire doomed from the beginning.

Luke was dead. So, I said, "You could say, he was a collector."

He collected things that meant most to him. Daughters.

I didn't mention Dune and Susan's museum heist. Or how the hoarding project of the Bennu Society intersected an intelligence agency. An agency that sponsored airtime for legends featuring Moldavite's purported mystical properties. A project to drive up the price of Moldavite not only by artificial scarcity but by riling up people to clamor for the gem because of their traditional Shambhala legends.

And the intelligence agency, using the Bennu Society to do their occult work, prompted protestors to fight people into Atlantis ancestry. That got lots of press, even more people wanting Moldavite. With Huld playing the role of the giant from Atlantis in our troupe to sold out audiences, the subject always raw.

"Free the Moldavite! Free the Moldavite!"

What if I go in? Just me?

Huld still dominated the doorway. But he could be taken. *And* Dune could be held. A whole crowd of people there could overwhelm the Agents. *I could take Moldavite and distribute it to these fine folks. If I give it to the protestors, I should give it to the neighbors. Riot time big time. Riot riot riot. Everyone getting burned.*

Still, I moved toward the door. I peered inside around Huld. I saw no one. Empty?

Huld bent and breathed, "Are you a traitor? Turning against your own country? We do our patriotic duty. We put time and effort into funding secret ops. If these losers steal our collateral, how do you think the government will get Psy-ops money? You think they'll raise money in nicer ways? No, they will not. I guarantee you they will not."

Huld was right. I'd have to think about that.

And Tommy and I had closed their Immortality Project. I'd ratted them out for framing Colin for Susan's murder. How many reasons should the Agency have for hating me?

One Agent, standing behind a tree still, beckoned me.

A trap? He could kidnap me, kill me, blackmail me. But his eyes. They looked so warm brown. His pupils must have enlarged with love. Because I took the chance. I went to him. Aaron.

"In there," he said, jerking his head toward the castle. "When you took my dark away. When you showed me the light." He grabbed my back and pulled me to him. We hugged a long time. When he pulled away, tears streamed down his cheeks. "I'm sorry."

I walked back to the crowd of lost people. I was unsure what future I wanted to make happen.

An Agent behind the closest tree beckoned me to him, too. I remembered him from the elixir party. I trusted him. He hugged me too. "Beautiful," he said, holding my hand as I walked back to stand with Colin.

The neighbor ghosts looked to be getting antsy. Two of them wandered off toward the cars along the driveway. *No, don't go!* But why? What did I want to happen? Epic battle? How could that go well for them? But so perfect. So perfect for something.

What did I need? To escape with Colin. Tommy wasn't around. If the crowd kept dangerous Agents at bay long enough to give them a head start, we could get back to civilization. Stay somewhere unexpected. Maybe check in with lots of people so we wouldn't be so easily extinguished. To laugh again with Colin, having good times. Different gym, most likely. Not have our lives hijacked. Free of distractions to loving each other.

I needed to get the rest of the shrapnel removed by a doctor. I bled. Whenever I moved, the sharp edges of the glass could cut into me and slice a nerve.

"Ernest, you rat fink!" yelled a protestor. "How can you be an Atlantis-lover? The Brotherhood of the Shadow? How can you be with them when you've led us? The Brotherhood of the Light?"

"Yeah! You showed us Shambhala stories in the books. What the hell, bro?"

"Myth fight!" called Colin, an elementary school kid, making me giggle. God, I loved that guy.

Huld asked, "What's not to admire about Atlanteans, considering they descended from Poseidon? You *know* Beaumont said the British Isles are Atlantis, right?"

"Bull."

"And they were giants. In fact, I am a super being returned." He looked upset his role was questioned.

Oh, what a crock. He was raised to believe that. I mean, Beaumont did write that in his book. But Huld knew better. The remains of giants were inconclusive of any such history.

"No, you're not," said Aaron. "Stop lording it over everybody. Get a grip, man. It's propaganda and you know it."

The whites of Huld's eyes reddened. He wheezed.

Poor giant. Like me. Raised expected to be something more than himself. Raised to pretend to be spectacular. And worse, that was his patriotic duty, how he survived, how our country survived. To insiders, he admitted he was just a bloke, and the UK was just a plot of land. But admit it to the rest of the world without breaking in two?

Dune said to Huld, "The Enochian angels told me Kelley never made gold in front of the King in Prague using Moldavite."

"What are you talking about?" asked Dune, breathless.

"Angels said to tell the world the truth about our lies."

Huld blanched.

"That Geoffrey of Monmouth just made shit up. For the sake of imperialism."

"Cheers to imperialism."

"Dee has renounced imperialism in the afterlife."

"Keep the faith."

"No, Huld."

"Dune's right, you know," said the Agent who had hugged me behind the tree.

Huld grabbed his chest, his eyes widening in their sockets.

Dune caught him, making the hypnotist stumble backward.

An Agent came up behind him for added strength and together they lay Huld toward the ground, not far from Luke. "Is there a doctor here?" called Dune.

A protestor came forward, saying, "I'm a nurse." He bent to examine him, and to give him mouth to mouth, pressing on his chest. "He's gone."

Young as he was, he'd kept his heart going much longer than most with gigantism. Those years acting out the royal giant from Atlantis on stage had kept him in good shape.

Dune brushed Huld's hair back off his face and closed his eyes.

❄

Dune walked a few yards from me and entered the castle, leaving the door open. That genius must have felt so alone. Two close friends both dead within the hour. Both cracking because of me, Tommy and our friends the imaginary angels.

As horrible as the men were, I felt for them. They were who they were. We are made of what formed us.

Protestors looked up from my father's corpse and glanced around with eyebrows raised. Time to storm the castle? Blood lust reddened. I suspected they'd loot and smash if they did.

I stood in front of the doorway ready to close it if need be.

Because looting wouldn't dent the role of intelligence agencies and secret societies working together to create propaganda for endless war. If we'd make a difference, I'd lead the charge.

Now, to get across they'd been duped. . .

The sheeted neighbor chumps still hanging around leaned against trees in the distance, posture drooping, axes leaning against a stump. Two rubbed their necks in sync. A man with a hat dangling precariously smoked a cigarette through a sideways mouth hole. The smallest paced. He approached my direction then back again to rejoin the rest.

"How much are you considering the historical reasons for the Shambhala VS Atlantis battle going on here? We're people trying to get along. Why are you getting so upset with your friends about which ancestry is best? It's divide and conquer. You're being played! We need to unify instead."

"Come off it, lady."

I implored, "Consider Madam Blavatsky. She was trying to unify Russia and Central Asia. India, Mongolia, China, and Tibet. She did that to be strong and oppose British colonialism. For better or for worse."

"Free Tibet!"

The smallest neighbor in a sheet approached then rejoined the others, pacing again.

I followed through on my plea for logic and reason. "Madam Blavatsky wasn't just randomly reporting on the legend about the King of the World coming from Shambhala to liberate Buddhist Asia because she stumbled across it and it was neato."

"Blavatsky rules!"

I added, "She promoted communism to combat Britain's power over India. She distorted the legend for a political agenda. Now, whether that agenda was good is beside the point. I don't care. My point is that she changed the legend. It's not necessarily true about the King of the World using Moldavite to beam transformation."

"Free the Moldavite!"

"Of course, British intelligence agents weren't down with Asia ganging up on them. How could they be? They countered it with brilliant ways to prove they had the right to rule, like King Arthur and Atlantis."

"Down with Atlantis!"

"When Annie Besant and Leadbeater took over the Theosophical Society, they changed everything. The allegiance wasn't to Russia anymore. It was to Britain. And it worked out for England, didn't it? The myth of Atlantis won. Shambhala lost."

"To hell with Atlantis and the evil Brotherhood of the Shadows! We want pure. It. Ee! We want pure it ee! Pure it ee now!"

A few of them were getting thoughtful, and the surrounding ones didn't seem to like that. People were shoving each other. Spats broke out.

Colin said, "Listen to the lady, will you? Calm down a minute and think this through. It's not about whether Shambhala or Atlantis is the good place. The myths were tweaked to make people take sides against each other. Don't you see? That's happening again, right this instant. Take a step back from polarization and hysteria. Take a deep breath."

What a smart teammate, that Colin. I wanted to write *Encore*. To hand the manuscript to him. I wanted him beside me always.

More of the protesters went silent. Two or three grinned. The others fidgeted.

"That makes sense," said a neighbor trying to pull off his sheet without untying the rope around his neck. Laughter broke out here and there.

A neighbor wearing red plaid said, "I never believed in Shambhala or Atlantis anyhow. I mean, who in their right mind?"

That did it. Fist fights in the back. Someone got a bloody nose. Neighbors and protestors went at it. Some protestors took sides with neighbors.

I saw a shadow coming up over me. I ducked down just in time to miss someone's boot. The Agent swung it around, the sharp hard heel coming back around in my direction. I ducked again.

He stopped when Enochian Angel language wafted over the charged landscape. Wait, what? Was I wrong all along about them being only a political subterfuge, a hoax made for spies and their prey?

The Agent wandered in a daze toward the source of the sound, which had a strangely soft timbre.

The smallest of the neighbors in sheets pointed behind her

and said, "Did you see that flash of light? Something's talking from over there, there, where it flashed."

"I saw it too," said Colin, with a tone to his voice I wasn't used to hearing. Puzzling. A few others joined in, saying they too must have seen it. Why yes, they did. It was a miracle!

Dune emerged from the castle, a set of envelopes in his hand. He stood still and answered the nonsense syllables. "You want me to tell them --."

The Enochian angel's command: it was Tommy! I glanced to the side, didn't want to give away her location. She sure was a master of the male tenor voice. And she'd picked up my misdirection lesson well. Pointing behind her, brilliant. Dressed in a sheet. The perfect disguise.

A hand on my shoulder. I spun, crouching, dodging a potential boot, and started a punch or a block, whatever it turned out to be as I turned. I hoped the Enochian angel would save me again.

Dune, smiling behind me, his high cheekbones too gorgeous to bruise. He held the set of envelopes waiting until I noticed. He sorted through them and wind blew his hair over his eyes. I looked for patterns in the words as he shuffled, holding onto them. Each envelope displayed a condition. One was, "*In case of Miriam's death and Dune's.*" His fingers hid the rest of the statement. Another had the words, *case of Dune's Divorce*.

He looked up from underneath its shadow. He looked through some others, to make a show for my sake, and handed me an envelope and with both hands, folded it into my palm against the wind. "Here. You earned it."

The whoosh of the wind, my shimmering blonde hair blowing against his tanned face.

The fight gained drama as one threw punches harder than before. Someone fell into me. I caught myself with my hands on the ground before I fell hard against a hip. I rubbed my wrist, and the envelope flew away.

I chased the envelope which landed on someone's face, then

slid off onto someone's shoulder. I grabbed. It soared free from the crowd and I chased it into the trees. An Agent, sitting with his feet bent up underneath him, leaning against the tree, grabbed at the envelope.

I opened the envelope: Luke's will. Signed, dated, and notarized with a stamp of approval.

He'd left me two million dollars.

As soon as his lawyer learned of his death, the money would be deposited in a bank account to access with a special untraceable code. Good thing I never had to go to the bank, because otherwise, the Agents set a trap to nab me.

I sat on the ground.

And he left me two tons of Moldavite to do with what I wished: in a month in a container at the address given, to be accessed with the code in the document.

I could access it under whichever legal name I preferred. Susan or Miriam. His Nevermind lawyer handled such things in the legal and financial worlds.

I'd ship some to the museum in the Czech Republic. Maybe that was the trap. I'd be cautious. But how tempting to consider. No, it didn't matter. I would not go underground. A life as a fugitive might work for Tommy but not for me. Not for Colin. So, we'd just walk right up to that container.

But I'd send an anonymous truck with some stone. Not all of it though. Not by a long shot. Other people could use that dull green rock. I was fond, myself.

But there was more. I read the section below it where he left something to Dune. Dune didn't look surprised by it.

Ah. His castle. "If Dune remains my son-in-law and is currently married at the time of the pronouncement of my death to one of my daughters who resides in the castle, dead or alive. If Equinox has been conceived, and lives, Dune also gets the castle."

CHAPTER 24
CONNIVING

The crowd thinned. I needed to persuade Nate to head out soon and give us our ride. First, I needed to get a good myth fight going. Fists flying would distract Dune from even noticing we were gone until it was too late. Colin and I would leave. Together. Unless Tommy had made other escape plans, she'd join us. The world was my oyster.

I went up to Nate and caught Tommy's eye. I pointed to our driver, gesturing for her to join us. She shook her head and pointed to one of the sheeted neighbors. She pretended to drive, turning an invisible steering wheel. So, good. She had a solid ride to protect her identity better than going with us. I nodded, and she spoke to the man.

They walked away toward the muddy trucks, such a minor event no one paid any attention.

She turned around before she was out of sight and waved.

I threw her a sweet kiss, designed to go unnoticed by anyone else.

I would miss that plucky woman.

Hail Tommy. Hail N--. A brave hero for our times.

❄

I schemed. Once we got into the city, I could squeal on my sister. Since Susan was dead, what would it hurt to tell the press she was the thief? Well, one thief. There was Dune, too. The museum could get their ton of specimens back. But, going up against him and the entire Nevermind would be a disaster. They needed the profits when they sold the rocks at the peak of the Shambhala VS Atlantis frenzy when it was worth the most money.

If I ratted out Dune and Susan, the Agents working with the judicial system would insist I was Susan. Behind closed doors, they'd put me away for robbing the museum. No public court case, no visitors. No nothing.

Dune sneaked up behind me in the woods, taking my hand. I was sure I'd seen the last of him.

"Dune, if I'm incarcerated for the robbery of the museum, because of the Agents' pretense I'm Susan, I'll never let you rest. If I'm forced to be Susan, I'll get a divorce in prison. There's nothing to do about it. You'd have to give up the Penderghast castle."

He darkened. "Wouldn't you like a castle? No pesky Huld or Luke around to bother you anymore. You'd never need work again."

"I'll prove I'm a free woman." Free to marry. What delicious thoughts were arising in my mind around that sentence I didn't dare say out loud.

"You think anyone cares about a random standby going on about birth certificates and ID cards? No one will see them other than Agents handling the case. You'll disappear from the public eye. They'd say you forged the identity documents. You resemble your sister; your dental records have replaced hers in the databank. Your fingerprints, your DNA records, and the DNA makes sense for her the proper heritage. It's set up. Luke's naughty

Immortality Project is over now, my love. Just a good old-fashioned love story in a castle." He bowed and kissed my hand.

"Colin?"

"Your crusty ol' friend will never come bothering us again. The evidence he was the murderer . . ."

"Stop it! I can't believe you think you still have power over me. Isn't it obvious I've fallen in love with him? It's not the olden days when a woman was arrested if she left her husband."

He narrowed his eyes with a threat. "If you noticed, my wife can lie dead in the castle and I still receive my inheritance from my father-in-law."

"Well, you've got no problem there, do you? Susan is dead. I saw her tomb in the dungeon. Just admit she's your wife, and you're good to go."

He lifted an eyebrow and stuttered. "Did you see a fresh grave?"

"No, I didn't."

"An Agent came to the castle today. Her body was found yesterday in the well, bloated beyond recognition, other than the signature golden hair," he said, lifting mine. "It's going through the due forensics process, though the lab is *managed*. So, no one is in her grave. The timing is off for me to receive the castle if you leave. You know who screwed up the timing?"

I said, "I did." So, this was his plan. It wasn't only lust for a type of woman at made him capture me, for having an etheric orgy, for creating the mystical elixir, for doing Crowley's magickal Moonchild Working to help Luke's twisted need for family, to give the Bennu Society clout, to raise money for the Agency's psychological operations. It was to inherit the castle. What a bastard.

"That corpse is Miriam. So, the body will go to a graveyard, next to the mayor's pre-paid plot."

"You can't mean it."

"If you will not play along and be Susan alive, then you need to be Susan dead. The Agents who left will have reported Luke's death by now. The coroner will be here soon; Luke's lawyer filed the papers with him long ago. Once Luke dies, the coroner is to check the grave-site to make sure which conditions are fulfilled to decide the contingencies of the will."

"Nasty job, that one."

"Going there wasn't too filthy for such as one as you."

He continued to pull me toward the castle.

I asked, "Don't you care about being a good person?"

"Have you ever seen such a beautiful person as me?"

What kind of narcissistic question was that? No, I hadn't. Honestly. On the outside. But the inside. . .

I proposed, "Let Tommy, Colin, and me leave. Tell the Nevermind you don't know what happened to us. Forget this 'Susan' business. I'll give you my entire inheritance. That should be enough for you without needing a remote castle, too. Wouldn't you be happier living in the city?"

"And meanwhile, you make a stink trying to clear Colin's name? Not hardly."

I'd give up my chance of freedom for Colin. He had told me before Dune captured me that I needed to accept myself. Who was I? I could have grabbed the neighbor's axe sitting there nearby and gone at Dune. But I was no murderer. And I had no love for prison. I was a corpse-to-be?

I shouted out to the crowd, "He's threatening my life!" No one seemed to hear me over the din, so I took a big breath for a louder shout, only to have it interrupted by Dune's palm over my mouth.

He picked me up, a bride on the wedding night, and carried me over the threshold. Protestors cheered. Others shouted. Colin called out my name, running toward us, but Dune shut the door and locked it with that awful special key.

❄

He carried me up the spiral stairway into the high room where Huld had visited. I had set it in motion when I waved to Colin out that open window. Dune threw me on the table. I jumped up, feline, scratching him and running to the window, calling out to no one, though jumping from it meant death. He threw me again. "Must I tie you down?"

"No." I sat there on the wood, fierce fury burning my eyes. I didn't want to kill him. I wanted to live and clear Colin's name. Otherwise, my love would go to prison for my murder.

I heard someone shout below the window. "I thought I saw Susan up there. Come around here!"

"You mean Miriam, stupid!"

"No, she's crazy. She's Susan."

"No, you're crazy if you believe her."

I had to admit calling for help did nothing. There was no way to enter the castle.

I felt the strength rising in my muscles. I wanted a chance to live free once I loved who I was. No longer trapped by Papa's expectations. No longer pretending I was something I was not. Being my violet one of a kind self. Telling the recurring story of mystical propaganda agencies through the ages. I was still young. I was in love.

I leaped up, grabbed Dune and wrestled with him, reaching into his pocket to take the key to the front door without him noticing it. I slipped it into my pocket and let him throw me back down. I wished it were a longer and sharper regular key. I could stick it in his ear, his eye, or his throat.

He clenched me around my neck. He held on so long, the reasons to live faded away. I wanted to breathe. But then I gave up that hope. He would never give up.

Why bother hoping anymore? I was in intense pain, could die and the horror would stop. So shaky I hardly cared anymore. I'd tried everything. My life was slipping away, and the pain was leaving me. I felt a peace come over me. It wasn't a terrible ending. I'd experienced love. Colors were fading away, everything going gray. Dying wasn't as bad as I'd thought. My muscles relaxed into a smile. No more struggle required.

"Have you rethought things? Do you want to live?" he asked.

I nodded weakly. I wasn't sure without oxygen.

He let go slightly. "Live here with me. Don't tell anyone what happened."

I tightened my muscles to hold myself together, breathed as deeply as I could to gain one more ounce of strength. I couldn't let the castle's secrets die. The public deserved to know how intelligence agencies have always worked with secret societies to fool people with mythology. If Colin didn't agree to publishing the book, I would keep him safe and hold *Encore* inside, a baby never born. But if Colin could handle the repercussions, I'd risk everything to write the truth.

I glanced at Edward Kelley's portrait. I cleared my throat and got in the mindset of an Elizabethan con man. Good thing Papa had trained me to imitate famous men since childhood.

I muttered to see if my hoarse voice worked for ventriloquism.

In my best guess at the Enochian scryer's voice, I said, with still lips, "Dune, my son, thou art ready to become an angel. This is your finest moment."

Dune flipped around, looking behind him. When he turned around, I was staring at the portrait of the alchemist, eyes open wide.

"My son, walk to the window. Do you see the Enochian angels waving to you from the sky? Some would say they are invisible. You, brave man. I know you can see their light."

He walked to the window and looked toward the setting sun.

The people gathered below could catch him if he fell and prevent his death. But he would be incapacitated enough I could escape.

"Stand upon the ledge." He did so. "Prepare to fly." He

crouched, holding on, looking down, wavering. He waved, to the sound of more shouting.

"Don't jump!" called someone below.

"We'll catch you! Frank, move the shit slop over here from under the loo. That'll soften the blow." I was glad someone would save his life. I didn't want to kill him.

If he realized I was throwing my voice, he'd rescind his offer of letting me live. The people below saw him standing there in the window of his own volition. A victim of mystical lies made up centuries past by an intelligence agency working with a secret society. I didn't believe in karma one bit, but still, karma.

"Are you ready to sacrifice your riches for serving the lord on another plane? You will turn into glorious light."

"No. I don't want to sacrifice myself." Dune turned and stared at Kelley's picture.

Kelley's voice insisted, "It is now time to trade your ordinary life for the good of the country. For transcendence. Your chance will be over soon. Act now."

"No."

He backed away from the window, shaking.

He came toward me, his arms out toward me, ready to finish the job. I ran toward the doorway, but he grabbed me before I got there. "Did you hear what Kelley said?"

In my voice, I said, "He's overestimating you."

I had to reframe it. Self-sacrifice wasn't his gig, then. Too bad, because he was set up to be caught when he jumped. I heard the voices below saying, "Good, he's not going to jump. You can draw the box of softness back."

Frank whooped in relief.

"I've got to clean up, mates. This is bollocks. Drinks on me at my house?"

And the other voices clamored in hardy agreement. They seemed to be walking away.

Kelley said, "Dune. If you fly now, you'll become the *head angel ruling over the Enochians.* They'll do what you tell them to do." Dune glanced at me, smug. "You'll love it. It's your reward for your hard work. There are riches on that realm more luxurious than you imagine."

Dune turned and flung himself out the window, calling out the language of the imaginary angels, first with joy, but as he lowered toward the ground, the words becoming garbled sounds of dread.

I pulled myself to drape my body over the window. The neighbors below, in various states of costume, spun around to see him fall. But by then, there was nothing anyone could do to save his life.

CHAPTER 25
PROMISES

I ran out of the castle into the fray. No one seemed to notice other than Colin, who ran up and lifted me into the air.

He called out some inflammatory sentences about Shambhala and Atlantis, which got everyone throwing punches and insults at each other. He tapped our homeward driver on the shoulder. "Ready to go? We'd appreciate it if you are."

Off we walked down the hill toward the driveway with no one missing a punch.

"Would you mind driving, mate?" asked the protestor. "I'm Nate. Kind of banged up at the moment."

"No worries." Colin took the wheel, and we left up the driveway, the car rocking a little in the wind.

Nate said, "Oops, forgot to filler up. Out of petrol, mates."

"What?"

"Just joshin' ya. We got plenty."

When I turned around after we made it down the road a ways, it seemed like a car had followed us. That wasn't good. Or maybe it was just a neighbor or a protestor. Could have been anyone driving on that road, but how often did that happen?

"I'm Miriam Reynolds," I said to Nate.

"Oh, Reynolds. Any relation to the mayor? No, just kidding."

"I'm his daughter. Not that that means much. He never mentions me, so it's not like the constituents think about me."

"You two aren't close?"

"Not hardly."

"Guess I can't get you to introduce me, then. The mayor is a hero of mine."

"Really? Well, I mean, maybe. We haven't talked for a long time."

"That's OK."

"I need to call him and tell him I can pay back his loan with interest."

Colin asked, "Do you think he'd be any help to keep us out of a mess? He must have pull with the Nevermind, right?"

"I assume he's been in with them all along. He adopted me to teach me not to love myself. Set me up psychologically for all of this wacko stuff."

"Maybe."

"I don't know, lady. He was nice to my friend. He helped when the police were trying to pin something on him."

"I think you should give it a shot," said Colin.

"OK, when we get reception, I'll call him on your phone, Nate. And I'll introduce you."

He said, "Agents took my phone. I was trying to take a picture. Guess that's a crime these days?"

"Only when you're endangering national security."

We were getting close to the reception zone.

"I've got my phone," said Colin. He took his eyes off the road, loosened his seat belt, and pulled it out of his pocket and threw it on the seat next to me. "I've kept it turned off, batteries still charged. Waterproof case, too."

I liked how he thought of everything. Did things that made sense. And after our adventure in the castle, he'd have a wildness in his soul forever. Enough to make him perfect. Perfect for me.

A big bump, and the car lurched forward. The car behind us was pushing us. I could make out an Agent driving, and another one sitting next to him. Colin pushed the pedal fast and said, "Nate, I'm sorry. Is this OK? I mean, this might . . ."

"Go for it, mate. I'm down. Give it all you got."

We sped around the cars, dipped down in the ditch, turned on a dime, everything a small car could do that a big one couldn't do. But before too long, they caught up.

Good thing they'd overnighted at the party where they weren't allowed to have any modern weapons, just bows and arrows. We couldn't be blamed in a public legal system for anything that had happened to anyone. We were innocent. But still, I felt like I was about to be caught and chastised for the deaths I'd left in my wake, and maybe killed for it. What worried me most was poor innocent Nate, a high school boy caught up in a car chase.

Colin's driving remained more or less legal; no one could cite him for reckless driving and put him away. He didn't risk commuters' lives. But he weaved in creative ways I'd never imagined he could do. He was not still in the friend zone.

He went through a light with moments to spare.

Behind us the Agent's car screeched, slid sideways, went up over the curb. It veered into something. I couldn't see what was going on behind us in traffic. All I could make out was the car exploding into flames. I saw no one exit the doors. No one else was hurt as far as I could tell. It sat on the curb blazing as we drove away. A fire truck siren started up not far behind it. I saw no one else coming for us.

"Holy!" yelled Nate.

It was no one's fault but theirs. We hadn't caused a wreck; we'd just been driving. I looked back to see people stopped around the car, taking photos, proper witnesses to the fact we weren't even part of the wreck. We could continue driving on.

I had a feeling the Agents who had turned when taking the elixir, whether from the placebo effect or not, would prevent other Agents from coming after us. Even though they'd heard me talk about turning it into a book.

After a long respectful silence, Nate's voice faltered when he said, "No pressure, but. Had great reception for a while, now. You want to introduce me to the mayor?"

I called him. And I was surprised by the warmth in his voice. "Miriam, you sound different."

"I am. Different."

"Good for you, my girl. It's about time."

Good for me to be different from who I was. Because who I was wasn't OK. But still, it was a compliment. I lost it. I sobbed into the phone. Nate offered me a bloody tissue.

"I've gotten into some trouble. But I want you to know, first: I can pay back the loan. With interest."

"Excellent. I was right to believe in you, then."

How embarrassing. For a second, I almost wanted to lie. I glanced at Colin, who was watching me between looks toward the road.

"No."

"Oh. Is someone else helping you out?" He faded. Thought I'd managed financial success doing what I wanted to do, however obscure, however ambitious, despite the odds.

"I had an adventure. That's the trouble. I think I earned the money."

"You sure earned it," yelled Colin, angling his voice toward the phone.

"I'll second that," said Nate. "Or is it third it?"

"Still . . . Papa, are you proud of me enough to tell the world I'm your daughter, on TV? It would help me out of a jam."

"How did you get the money? Rob a bank or something?"

"No, but that's just it. The Agents of the Nevermind will say I did. And they'll say I'm someone else. That I'm Susan Penderghast."

"She's the actress you said you were trying to imitate, but you never got it down."

"Yeah, I was trying to be her from the inside out, but I didn't understand who she was. I didn't get her essence right. She's the thief who stole the Moldavite from the Czech museum. But, you know who she is."

"The most popular performance artist in England these days among the dance crowd."

"No, Papa, listen. What's something about her that's more meaningful to you. To our family. You don't know she's my sister?"

His sound of surprise was so honest at that moment I suspected he wasn't in with the Agents.

"I had no clue. No wonder you look so much like her, then. Now it makes sense."

"Can you tell me about my adoption? You know who my father is, right?"

"Ah, you found out. I wondered if that might happen someday. No, I wasn't allowed to know who adopted you. That's how these things work. I thought you knew the process. Guess you weren't paying attention to how laws work? Legality not your strong point?" His voice was losing volume and interest. But he seemed disappointed in my memory, not worried that I'd found out the secrets of his connection with the Agency. *So, sometimes mayors aren't in on conspiracies. Hmm.*

That changes everything.

That meant he and Mama adopted me because they wanted to. Not because they were in on the Agents' plan to mold my personality. No doubt the Agents chose them to warp me. By being their flawed selves.

"Papa, please help me. I need to prove to the country I'm not Susan. If you say I'm Miriam, in front of people on a TV appearance, that could save my life. And my . . . my boyfriend's too."

Was he too embarrassed by me to get me up there for no reason, just to say, "Hey, look at my loser daughter. She lost her job. Looks like hell. Started boinking some guy in the last few weeks and is now calling him her boyfriend. Boyfriend! What's he going to amount to, anyway? I'll still have to keep supporting her. Pretending she'll pay me back. Well, guess what, everybody? Miriam was just given money, so she can pay me back! Yay! Goodie."

"Well, I don't know. . ."

I sang a song he'd taught me.

"I'm on my way now to a park dedication. Breaking a champagne bottle and gold plate specials, everyone donating big bucks. Press. Meet me in half an hour at our special park you played in when you were young. Where you practiced Henry the VIII."

"Oh, Papa, thank you so much." I couldn't say how much it meant.

I didn't want to show up, and some Agent show up with guns blasting. But I could tell from the scenes on the news that Papa had plenty of top notch Security at events like that, so they were prepared in case I was being tailed.

Colin got quiet. I tried asking him questions from time to time and it seemed he didn't even hear me. Was he rethinking the recent strange events? Deciding he didn't want to be involved with an irreverent wench eager for drama?

He pulled the car over, down a road a way, pulling into a driveway by a rose bush along a fence.

"This isn't the ideal place to do this, I know," he said.

"I know. You're wearing clothes we've had on for a long time," I said.

"You can borrow my suit that's in the back in the dry cleaner bag," said Nate.

"Thank you. That wasn't what I meant, though."

"You guys going to be on TV? Did I hear right? Maybe there's a restroom there you can wash up in. Touch up a little of the blood."

"Oh, so sorry, Nate! I forgot to introduce you to Papa on the phone."

"That's OK, I guess."

"Come meet him at the park launch. If you don't mind driving us there."

"That's cool. That's *very* cool."

"What I meant," said Colin, "was, can you get out of the car for a minute, Miriam? Give us a moment, Nate. See . . . see ya in a minute." He crossed his fingers and cute Nate enthusiastically crossed his, too. He didn't look like he had any idea why. But his youthful, encouraging expression and quick little nod forward was adorable. It made me ready for whatever would happen to be wonderful.

I liked it when Colin crossed his fingers.

He bent down on one knee.

Oooooooooo!

He looked down, shook his wild hair, knocking a leaf from it, and turned his face up to me with those deep brown eyes, his hair wild, emanating lit-up feral beauty. He opened out his palm, showing something wrapped in a red leaf. He ceremoniously, unwrapped the leaf.

Inside it was a ring woven from gorse. In the place of a stone was a tiny baby wild rose.

"I'll get a real ring if you say yes."

I couldn't complain. There wasn't a jewelry store on the castle grounds. But I liked the gorse and rose ring better than anything made of stones mined in dubious ways. No, I wanted him to weave me a new ring when that one fell apart. Then, one day, another. I would weave them for him.

"Miriam, would you do me the spectacular honor of being my wife?"

Life flew up from the ground at me, covering me in waves. Brightness, wonderfulness, "Yes."

Nate jumped out of the car, turned his head to the sky and

hollered. It was a melodious holler, but animal, too. It was perfect. And the sky was such a deep cobalt blue.

❄

Papa handed me a glass of champagne when I walked up to him at the park, blocking me. I'd been going in for a hug. He gave me his own glass, with a regretful look into its pale shimmer. It must have been good for him to savor it so much. I looked around for a place to set it, then took a chance by balancing it on the grass.

"Saw you on TV."

"Oh. Was there a Missing Persons bulletin or something?"

"You've been lost?"

"Yep, the Agents could have gotten away with murdering me, with no one even noticing I was gone if Colin hadn't taken up with me."

"I missed you, too." His voice dripped sarcasm. "No mistaking that was you taking over for Susan at the theater. You did a bang-up job of mimicking her. You going to replace her next season?"

"I didn't know you were at the show."

"I saw the clips, and they called you by her name."

"You've been watching local culture news about Avant-Garde theater extravaganzas?"

"No, this was national news because of the protest about regulating sales. First it would be Moldavite. Then it would be all gems, all minerals. Who knows what next? And everyone's alignment with Shambhala or Atlantis would be in a database. Not a good precedent."

"I totally agree. Susan and her husband are a big part of the reason Moldavite has gotten so much more expensive. And my biological father is too."

He nodded. He was treating me like my opinion mattered. Or like he cared what it was. Like now I was an adult . . . Or maybe now I had been someone else spectacular. . . Or did my body language tell him I cared no more? I held out my hand and stared at it. I wasn't trembling. My eyelids weren't lifted too high, my smile too angelic. I could talk with him and stay calm, just be myself. I didn't want to plead with him or yell at him and stamp my foot.

Was it *me* having trouble accepting *him*?

"You're who you are, Papa. I don't expect you to be something different."

Papa took a noisy sudden breath. Was that hiccups? Or a burp. He held on. His chest rose and fell. "I never thought I'd hear you say that," he said, pulling back, tears in his eyes.

I took a step back and gave him a warning look, to suggest: don't make me feel bad about myself again; I won't accept it any more.

"I'm sorry, girl."

"I love you, Papa." I embraced him. I'd never felt so close to him in my life.

I didn't mention Colin for a while. I didn't want to diminish my new bond with Papa. I checked in with Colin and he was smiling benevolently. His combed hair was behaving itself ,and Nate's suit fit him well. His new short beard suited him. I could see his skin, glowing, with no Medieval soil on it at all.

Nate stood with him, his round face, under his round bowl cut, looking super perky, his nose red on the end from a bruise. Like a good sport, he held his elbow in the other arm like a sling.

This was not an ordinary moment in which everyone had awakened to alarm clocks, showered and put on folded clothes from a drawer dusted that morning and eaten a plate of bacon and eggs.

When it was time, I filled Papa in on the core story of my abduction and Colin and Tommy, Nate and the neighboring farmers and the nice Agents helping me out. I told him how I'd learned insider's knowledge I could pass along to him. And, if he was in the mood for a piece of Moldavite to stick on the mantle, I could swing it.

He toasted me. "Cheers to that. Well done."

I called Colin over and introduced him. Papa was in a rare mood, such as I'd never seen him. I'd found the right thing to say to him. What he'd needed to hear. I'd been judging him so long.

"We have something to announce."

"Oh my." My father took a sip of champagne and lifted one eyebrow, pressing his lips together toward the center into a mischievous wrinkled mush. He'd probably practiced that trick; the corners of his dark eyebrows had gel in them, making them curve up to a point on the ends. It suited him.

After seeing Luke's face, scorched as it was, I couldn't imagine how I'd convinced myself I looked like Papa. We can believe anything if we have to.

"We're engaged," I said. "I'd like your blessing."

"Welcome to the family, son. I see things are going to get interesting around here."

When the camera woman brought her equipment up to him, turning the lens on him, he said, jolly, with one side of his mouth up high, "I'd like to announce that my daughter, Miriam Reynolds, is engaged to Colin Markus. He rescued her from some dangerous men, and for that, I'm eternally grateful. I will see to it personally that these two are supplied everything they could need to remain safe from anyone who might think of harming them. My staff will be tasked with watching over them."

Body guards walked up behind him and stood, square-jawed, big arms flexed, hands over their guns. This would be a great shot for the newspapers. Any Agents seeing that would think twice before bothering us.

He'd never introduced me since he'd become mayor. Rambunctious cheering broke out among the crowd.

After all the celebrating by the guests died down, he moved on to the next announcement. "And this nice young man, Nate

Korman, has been instrumental in the couple making it home. Thank you, sir."

Nate lifted the right side of his thin lips in a crooked smile. He raised a warped, frayed sign: Free the Moldavite.

I'd hand him a chunk of rock when my inheritance came through. The crowd chatted, shaking hands, pouring drinks, making deals. My violet aura rolled out like rounded, heavy, gray cumulous storm clouds around me. And I loved it always.

IF YOU ENJOYED THIS BOOK, REVIEWING IT ON AMAZON AND GOODREADS WOULD BE WONDERFUL!

CHAPTER 26
ABOUT

Tantra Bensko teaches fiction writing with UCLA Extension Writing Program, Writers.com and Tantra Bensko's Online Writing Academy. She also edits manuscripts with Book Butchers. She has an MFA from the Iowa Writers Workshop and has had hundreds of stories in magazines and anthologies. She lives in Berkeley, California.

Encore is Book III in The Agents of the Nevermind series of standalone novels about the heroism of exposing social engineering. The first book in the series, *Glossolalia*, won a gold medal from the Readers Favorite awards. Nancy, here referred to as N-, inhabits Book I and Book II.

Being a Gothic novel, *Encore* is naturally Psychological Suspense and also Romantic Suspense, as both of these descended from the original genre. *https://flameflower.wixsite.com/encore* is the website for this novel. If you enjoyed the romance in this book, check out *Floating in Secrets*, another Seductive Psychological Suspense. *https://www.floatingonsecrets.com/*

Tantra loves to hear from readers, so please contact her any time at flameflower@runbox.com.

If you loved this book, nothing would make more difference to its success than your review on Amazon and Goodreads!

Made in the USA
Middletown, DE
15 November 2021

52518794R00220